Only in London

Only in London

HANAN AL-SHAYKH

Translated from the Arabic
by Catherine Cobham

Pantheon Books, New York

All rights reserved under International and Pan-American Copyright
Conventions. Published in the United States by Pantheon Books,
a division of Random House, Inc., New York, and in Canada by Random
House of Canada Limited, Toronto. Originally published in Arabic as *Innah
London Ya Azizi* by Daral-Arab, Beirut, Lebanon, in 2000. Copyright ©
2000 by Hanan al-Shaykh. This translation originally published in
Great Britain by Bloomsbury Publishing PLC, London.

Pantheon Books and colophon are registered trademarks
of Random House, Inc.

*Grateful acknowledgment is made to the following for permission
to reprint previously published material:* GOLDEN BELL SONGS: Excerpts
from "How Much Is That Doggie in the Window?" by Bob Merrill.
Copyright © 1953, 1982 by Golden Bell Songs. Reprinted by permission
of Golden Bell Songs, administered by Music & Media International Inc.

Library of Congress Cataloging-in-Publication Data
Shaykh, Hanan.
[Innaha Landan ya'azizi. English]
Only in London / Hanan al-Shaykh ; translated from the Arabic
by Catherine Cobham.
p. cm.
ISBN 0-375-42133-5
I. Cobham, Catherine. II. Title
PJ7862.H356 I4613 2001   892.7'36—dc21   2001021574

www.pantheonbooks.com
Printed in the United States of America
First American Edition
2 4 6 8 9 7 5 3 1

Acknowledgements

My gratitude to Marsha Rowe for her help
and to Eve Arnold and Carmen Callil
for their invaluable support.

My thanks to Leighton House, The British Library—
particularly the Oriental and India Office Collections for
letting me handle rare manuscripts—and to
British Telecom for taking me up the BT tower.

TO TAREK AND JAMAN MALOUF

AND

TO LONDON

Only in London

Prologue

Amira's shriek, 'Woe is me, woe is me, woe is me', drowned out the chorus of 'God is most great, God is most great' from the other passengers as the aircraft hurled itself up and down like a yo-yo. Her relentless lament, together with the turbulence, completely unsettled Lamis, the woman sitting next to her. My son, Lamis thought. How could I have left him? And then: My bag, my passport, while the aircraft straightened up and she tried to gather the fragments of herself together.

A young Englishman stood to help an air hostess to her feet, but Amira's racket made it impossible for the passengers to regain their composure and their senses continued to work overtime, picking up on any slight tremor, especially now that they had been made aware of what was so familiar that they usually forgot about it: they were roaming through the great unknown in a tin box with wings.

Amira wailed and flapped her wrists at anyone who came to reassure her. Her fingers looked like little fishes with sparkling rings around their necks and brightly coloured tails, and her broad face resembled the bumper of an antique Oldsmobile, with its heavy make-up and big gold-rimmed spectacles, and her light brown, shoulder-length hair, teased to make it look fuller. Several times she stood up as if she were trying to escape, and her bottom stuck out like a small table, big enough to take an ashtray or a glass.

Amira screamed and cried and ignored the soothing words, whether they came from Lamis or the Gulf man accompanied by his nephew, whom she had chatted up at Dubai Airport, and who was turning round from his seat near the front to tell her that God

1

had heaven and earth in his hands, or the Englishman from across the aisle, or even the Captain, who had left his cockpit and was walking among the passengers reassuring them, like a nurseryman inspecting his trees.

'Don't cry,' Nicholas was saying, hoping that Amira would open her eyes and respond. 'Everything's fine. The turbulence is over. It won't happen again.'

'Woe is me! Woe is me! God preserve me!' Amira wailed, thinking to herself: I repent, oh God, I repent. Please don't punish me.

As soon as the plane had taken off she had begun counting pounds and putting them into envelopes in wads of five hundred.

'It's just a bit of turbulence, that's all,' Nicholas said.

This only rekindled Amira's hysteria, and her sobbing gathered momentum as she saw herself plummeting through the air once more.

Nicholas looked at Lamis, who appeared so composed, and he raised his eyebrows and pressed his lips together as if to acknowledge that he could do no more for Amira.

Inwardly Lamis herself was shaking with terror. Her precious British passport: the flight attendant had already announced its loss several times.

A few moments later Nicholas found it on the floor under the seat in front of him and handed it back to her. Lamis thanked him – the Englishman had given her back her life – and as she did so he looked back at her for longer than he meant to, thinking of the naked Devedasis he'd seen two days before in the stillness of the temple at Khajuraho, with their seductive bodies, full breasts, bracelets on their arms and ankles, rings in their ears, girdles around their waists and ties that hung down at the back – whether they were sitting, standing, looking straight ahead or to one side, with their hair flowing or their faces raised, they evoked desire.

A flamboyantly dressed man clutching a wicker basket came wandering down the aisle, confident that he would find what he needed in Business Class. He leaned across and jogged Lamis's arm. 'Excuse me, Mamselle. Please, have you got a sedative? My nerves . . .'

Lamis reached into the zip pocket of her bag for her packet of sedatives, wondering how this man with the basket had guessed that she took them.

'*Merci, merci*. Heaven sent you to my rescue, Mamselle.'

Amira, whose weeping fit had subsided, stopped reciting the Muslim creed to prove to God that she'd repented, and looked at them.

Lamis offered Amira a sedative, but Amira shook the little fishes at her. 'No, no. God forbid! I wouldn't want to be half asleep if something happened.'

'Mamselle, Mamselle. I want to tell you a secret. Please swear you'll keep it to yourself. Swear you won't tell on me . . . I've got a little monkey in this basket.'

Lamis looked at the wickerwork receptacle that the man was holding against his chest. It was so tiny. How could it hold a monkey? She didn't want to get involved. What if he were arrested? Nevertheless, she forced herself to ask, 'What's wrong? Has it escaped?'

'How could it? Its feet and hands are tied, and I keep the basket stuck to me like a leech. But I need to give the monkey a pill to make it sleep or it will chew its way out.'

'I gave you one.'

'I know. You gave me two. I'm not crazy even though I might look it, but the monkey won't swallow the pill unless it's hidden inside something else, like grapes or chocolate.'

'No, sorry. I haven't got anything. Ask the stewardess.'

'How can I ask her? Everybody's so busy! She won't answer me.'

When Lamis showed no interest in saving him he turned to Amira. 'Please, Madame, make a fuss like before, and ask them for food. A piece of cheese or chocolate.' He leaned down until his face was almost touching hers. 'There's a monkey in this basket.

3

I've got to send it to sleep before it disgraces me and they put me in jail. I have to give it a tablet inside some food it likes.'

Amira needed no encouragement, and she began to wail again, and flap her wrists. 'God preserve me! God preserve me! My blood pressure's going down. I feel dizzy. Please bring me a piece of bread, a bit of chocolate . . .'

The stewardess brought both and Amira felt uneasy because she'd promised herself that she would become an honest woman. Yet wasn't helping people a good deed? She gave the food to the man with the basket as soon as the stewardess disappeared. He thanked her and tried to kiss her hand before he vanished.

'Praise God for our safety,' the Arab passengers repeated to one another when the Captain announced that the descent to Heathrow would begin in fifteen minutes. For once the overworked phrase really meant something. The Gulf man stretched round from his seat and called back to Amira, 'Praise God. You should always trust in Him.'

When she heard the word 'Heathrow' Lamis thought of Edward Heath and Hampstead Heath, of grassy slopes, wooden benches and street lights, of Jill Rowe, her son's old nursery-school teacher, and of her son asking if he were learning 'Row, row, row your boat' because the rhyme contained his teacher's name.

Everything was green. Even the streams and rivers were a shade of green. The Arab passengers craned their necks and exclaimed in wonder, and Nicholas too caught his breath. He'd forgotten how much he missed the presence of green, and how it made him feel at one with the world. The doctors in the Gulf had actually been known to prescribe a summer in England for their patients. In Oman every patch of green was looked on as a miracle and the media would present pictures of blossoming plants as if they were announcing new oil wells. Nicholas reached out a finger, like Adam, towards London, the finger of God, and Oman receded and became a distant planet – it was as if he'd never been drawn to its terraced mountainsides.

4

The man with the basket re-entered the cabin and, ignoring the objections of the air hostess, went up to Lamis and Amira.

'I'm going to die,' he told them dramatically.

Lamis felt pity for the man.

'Would you like another sedative?'

'No, no. The monkey's sound asleep. I'm the problem now. I'm dying of fright. They'll find the monkey and arrest me. Shall I drown the monkey in the toilet, or tell the stewardess I've found a stray?'

'Don't be afraid, I'm here, and there's no X-ray,' said Amira. 'Let the plane land first. Go back to your place now, and trust me. Trust the Lord, I mean.'

'Just tell me something, Madame. Do you know a restaurant called Tabbouleh?'

'In Edgware Road? Yes, a stone's throw from where I live.'

As she'd promised, Amira stayed with the man after they left the aircraft. She hurried him along until they both caught up with Lamis, obliging Lamis to walk beside her and the man with the basket – whose name was Samir – while he pushed the trolley carrying both the women's cases and the monkey's basket.

To distract Samir further, Amira said, 'Look! Everyone's admiring your clothes!'

Samir looked down at the Versace shirt he was wearing under a big heavy overcoat, and at his long brightly coloured scarf and his cowboy boots, and grinned.

Amira looked at Samir whose long face, long nose and long sideburns were haloed by frizzy hair that he had obviously tried to straighten. 'Are you sure you're not Klinger in *Mash*?' she teased.

Samir laughed. 'That actor does look like me. You're right, Madame. His ancestors were Lebanese.'

The cab driver was waiting, carrying a board on which her name was scrawled, 'Amira Fayiz', but as soon as Amira saw the parked minibus she wanted to shout at him for bringing such an unattractive vehicle. Instead she looked around for the Gulf man and his nephew. When she couldn't see them anywhere she thought that God must be helping her to repent, and offered Lamis and Samir a lift. Lamis felt cushioned and relieved: she'd been dreading travelling into London alone. Then Amira spotted the young Englishman who, with all his heart and soul, had tried to calm her down in the plane, and called him over.

Chapter One

I

Lamis turned the key in the lock and the sound made her jump and look round fearfully, but she was alone with her case labelled LHR. She stepped over the threshold and the place had that neglected smell. When she saw that the cases and boxes, which were supposed to have been shipped to her in Dubai after she settled in, were piled up in the hall just as she had left them, she burst into tears and felt trapped.

'Never mind. Have a good cry. It'll do you good,' she said to herself.

So she cried a little more and then stopped suddenly, as if she'd fulfilled some obligation. She collapsed on the floor, intending to kiss it as she'd thought of doing when she landed at Heathrow, like an exile returning home, but she was overcome by a fit of coughing. The moquette was tickling her nose and the dust getting into her throat. She stood up and walked round the flat.

She had imagined herself storming into her son's school, calling his name, Khalid, looking in every classroom until she found him, then hugging him, asking him to forgive her, but the urge to do so subsided for the moment. When her son was little – she started crying again at the thought of him – his cars stuck on the carpet, and he'd had to play with them in the kitchen.

She went into the kitchen and then into the bedroom where she lay down and stretched out, feeling her ribs, like a cautious peasant checking for abrasions on a cow he wanted to buy, overlooking the flaws under its skin. She was angry with herself for lying down, disappointed she didn't feel the surge of energy she'd anticipated when she set foot on English soil. Why was it that when you longed for something and got it, you wanted something different?

A month before, straight after her divorce, she had left London for Dubai, where her parents and her married sister lived. Encouraged by her sister, she planned to set up her own business there, making artificial trees to decorate homes and offices. She had bought vast amounts of dried flowers, branches and all the necessary equipment from the New Covent Garden flower market in Vauxhall and shipped it ahead to Dubai, but she was only there two days when she found herself wishing she were back in London. Her life had turned into a kind of nightmare in which she was pushed in different directions and that tangled her up like the threads of lace in the fingers of an unskilled seamstress.

Dubai customs were suspicious of her clearly labelled packages; they opened them and found five dried poppies, including opium poppies, with seeds. For the sake of those dried poppy pods, like pomegranates, only smaller and prettier and plumper, her British passport was confiscated and her case referred to the Dubai criminal investigation department.

For days she trailed after her brother-in-law like a sheep following the shepherd in search of pasture even when she felt he was leading her towards a mirage. She was led out of one office into a bare room where she was photographed holding a tray spread with the five stalks of dried poppies. From there they sought out wealthy, well-connected people who might be able to help them, and followed up leads, through corridors and waiting rooms in government ministries, constantly being reassured by officials saying, 'We used to boil poppies to make a sleeping draught to give babies, you know, but that was before the change in the law' – all to no avail. Lamis watched Dubai change in front of her eyes, from the place where the official stamped her passport as casually as if it were a restaurant bill – which, as an Iraqi refugee, was something she'd never experienced before – to a place where she was being rolled around from official to official like a ball on a snooker table for a whole month, until someone, on a whim, finally dropped the case. That decision gave her back her freedom but left her petrified. The country's legal system was a nest of spiders weaving a web among its dog-eared papers. She discovered later that those in charge of her case were only puppets and time-wasters who received people in their offices and sent them away with lying promises, and not one of the legal representatives they met had bothered to take up her case with a department superior or any relevant authority.

She considered calling Khalid at his boarding school and making a cup of tea. She thought fleetingly of her friend Belquis, but decided to wait until eleven before contacting her – then she'd ask Belquis to help her go back to her husband and son. She had decided this in the minibus when she saw the houses and semi-deserted hotels with their depressing net curtains, like stage flats with nothing behind them, and she had felt suddenly terrified of being back in London alone.

Her eyes focused on the BT tower through the bedroom window. The familiarity of the flat was preventing her from facing reality. She shouldn't have stayed here, even though her ex-husband insisted she could use the flat for as long as she wanted, adding that he would pay all the bills as usual. 'It's just because he wants you to come back to him,' her sister said. 'He won't lose hope while you don't have anyone else.'

Lamis had lived with her husband in this furnished flat during the early years of their marriage. When they moved out into their new one, her husband kept the flat as an investment. From then on it remained empty, except when they used it as an overflow for guests visiting London. In the beginning Lamis only returned once a month to let in the cleaning woman; later she had started to visit the flat from time to time in order to be alone, to read or listen to music in total freedom, without feeling guilty.

The familiar objects aroused feelings of loss and regret. It should be a Beverley Sister who feels this way, not me, thought Lamis.

She looked around at the slippery pistachio divan, at the stain left by the singer's head on the pistachio-coloured bedstead and at the couch covered in rose-patterned damask where the singer must have sat with her two sisters practising the horse song, the Queen Mother's favourite; in the adjoining bathroom she must have belted out, 'How much is that doggy in the window?'

Lamis's mother-in-law had been so proud of the fact that one of the Beverley Sisters had been the previous tenant, even though the group was unknown in the Arab world.

The way the singer had her cupboards built to accommodate the various lengths of her clothes and the different heights of her hats had impressed Lamis. She felt a secret admiration for this woman who imposed her will on things. Lamis did not dare even to think about what she wanted, still less how it might be expressed. She always let her husband decide for her, and her mother-in-law decided for him. When they first moved into the flat, her mother-in-law had the cupboards redivided, and her husband took the lion's share while Lamis portioned her clothes out among several cupboards in another room and the little passage leading to the guests' bathroom. At the time Lamis thought she was in the lap of luxury: in Beirut before she married she'd only had space for the couple of dresses she owned. She found herself humming:

> *How much is that doggy in the window?*
> *Woof woof*
> *The one with the waggly tail*
> *Woof woof.*

Lamis started crying again. When she'd agreed to give up custody of Khalid – as the one walking away from the marriage – she did it on condition that she would be able to see him whenever she wanted to. She couldn't have imagined how painful it was going to be. It was like a hand being betrayed by the beauty of a rose, unaware of the thorns that surround it. She'd learned that song with her son. She thought again of calling him at school. She could just picture his room, and yearned for her old home. Was it possible that she was never going to see the other flat again, although she'd spent a year furnishing it? She longed to roam around it, look into its cupboards, delight in its colours, gaze out at the park and at the lake where the birds ducked and dived in the morning mist, and sometimes in the sunshine, instead of gazing at the BT tower with its girdle of frying pans and casseroles.

She hurried to the telephone and dialled Belquis's number, but stopped before she reached the end. Was Belquis still her friend? Didn't friends of newly divorced couples become like footballs, not knowing which team's net they were going to land in? She should contact her ex-husband directly and tell him she wanted to go back to him. She dialled his mobile, but stopped before she pressed the final digit.

What was she thinking of? That was the world she'd run away from. She reminded herself she'd hated life in her marital home so much that she'd begun to see it as a figment of someone else's imagination, like the Addams Family living their Frankensteinish life in the heart of an ordinary town in America. She reminded herself of her mother-in-law's hard face with its scolding expression telling Lamis: Slow down, don't go out too much, and her crude references to her marital duties.

Go to Soho this afternoon, she encouraged herself. You can be there in ten minutes. No guilty conscience, no feeling that you're letting people down any more. You're free, free.

She made herself think of the London she once saw, and how she had wanted to live in it unattached when she'd walked one day on her own to take a Venetian candelabra to a shop called Stitch for repair, and felt so carefree, envious of the people of her own age she saw sitting in a café, and of a young man arranging flowers in a shop window. Her mother-in-law had tried to stop her going, saying no one had heard of Stitch, it wasn't well known, and Lamis's husband joined in, volunteering that the streets of Soho were full of sexual deviants, the place was synonymous with drugs and alcohol. But Lamis went, and she'd not been in any hurry to go home. She'd had an orange juice in a pub, and gone downstairs to the Ladies where an English song over the speakers made her heart beat more quickly. But now the possibility of being able to live like that was as distant as the sun from the earth.

After her divorce came through she did not run barefoot through the park shouting 'I'm free', as she'd promised herself. It was the night before she left for Dubai and she had sat in the hotel room, chin in hand, confronting a bottle of champagne in a bucket and watching the ice melt. She'd thought of a friend of her father's who'd been arrested at Athens Airport for possessing a piece of hashish. When they let him go after a few months he immediately missed the prison routine. He'd liked sitting with his fellow prisoners under a fig tree playing chess.

The empty flat was managing to defeat her. She lay down on her stomach, thinking that perhaps she ought to expose the backs of her knees to the light; she'd read in a magazine that this was good for jet lag.

'You've ruined yourself and us, just like your father did,' her mother wailed over the telephone from Dubai on learning that Lamis was asking for a divorce. 'What about your son? Have you no heart? Did you forget you gave birth to Khalid? If you wanted a divorce you should have made his life hell so that he'd have been the one to ask for it, not you!' she screamed in a deranged voice. 'Or . . . or . . . made him fall in love with another woman, even if you had to find her for him. Why don't you learn to play these tricks? By asking him for a divorce, you idiot, you aren't even entitled to a loaf of bread, let alone your child. Oh God. Every-thing will be lost – two buildings in Beirut, two flats in London – all that wealth will be down the drain. But now, listen, you have a British passport, you can sue him and get half of everything . . . even more. You can get custody of your son. Just listen to me.' Before this, her mother had been floating on air, revelling in the gossip going around London and even in her home city of Najaf, saying that Lamis was living like a princess, in the same building as a lord whom the Queen once visited: Her Majesty had gone up in the lift Lamis used and had dinner in the room directly below her sitting room.

All these memories made Lamis tremble like a feather. She stood up, opened the window, leaned out and screamed, but everything beyond the flat looked still and lifeless. She lay on the bed again, embarrassed at what she'd done. As the seconds passed and she heard no sound at the door of the flat – no call from the porter asking her what had happened, no police car or ambulance screeching to a halt, sirens wailing – she became convinced she was suffering from the same loneliness as Eleanor Rigby in the Beatles song. She'd been fourteen years old when she first heard that song drifting out of the Officers' Club in Damascus, her family's first stop after leaving Iraq. She'd looked in and seen the soldiers dancing the tango. At the chorus, 'All the lonely people, where do they all come from?', the men switched to an Arab dance, and shook their hips to the beat. She always thought that 'Eleanor Rigby' was a cheerful, funny song until she heard it again in London.

Now Lamis's head was pounding, her insides churning. She wondered whom she could call. The only people she knew well were her in-laws and their friends. Other than that there were acquaintances: her son's Arabic teacher, who thought Lamis was superficial – a lady who lunches – or Fifi, the Arab employee at Selfridges, who'd asked Lamis over the telephone if she were Arab, like her, because she ordered lots of olive oil. Her gaze fastened on a nail the singer had knocked into the wall to hold a picture: the ghost of a Beverley Sister, was that the only person she could think of?

How is it that I don't know a single English person to invite for a cup of tea, or a beer? They're out of bounds to me, just like the city. The only people that I've had direct contact with are the Beverley Sisters, a few doctors, and of course the General.

She used to see the General with a nurse, who would force him to walk, pulling him by the hand like a big dog, and he would resist and complain, and occasionally shout, but nobody listened to him under the towering trees around the square, where the houses resembled army barracks. The General had fought in the Second World War, in the Libyan Desert at El Alamein, and he had been with his regiment on leave when it put in at Beirut, Port Said, Haifa and Cyprus, before returning to the front. The General had been different from the London taxi drivers who talked to Lamis about their exploits with the services in Aden or at Suez.

One day the General heard Lamis calling her son. 'Khalid, Khalid. Come along, darling.'

Her son was playing with a small powerboat on the pond in the square, changing its direction with a remote, when the nurse approached. Lamis was sure that the woman was going to tell her off for shouting at her son to keep away from the fountain, which had already drenched Khalid's hair and clothes. That's what they were like, the English, poking their noses in to criticise. 'Look, bicycles are forbidden,' a stranger had said to her, pointing to a notice by the entrance to the square, before going up to a woman who was walking a small dog, and saying, 'Read the notice. It's forbidden to let it off the lead.'

'Excuse me. The General wants to know if you're an Arab, and, if so, from what country?'

But the General did not let the nurse finish her polite smile. He tried to explain to Lamis, speaking with difficulty because his mouth was partly paralysed, that he'd been in Palestine during the Second World War, and it was the most wonderful period of his life. While he was there he'd met a Lebanese woman called Nadia Haddad whose husband worked in a bank. They'd corresponded for many years, even after she'd returned to Lebanon. But then he'd lost touch with her at the start of the war in Lebanon.

He signalled to the nurse to give Lamis his card.

'But I don't carry them about with me, General. In any case, your card would be of no use to the lady.'

The General mustered all his strength to speak, but his

sentences were disjointed and mostly incomprehensible, except for one: 'Please, I wonder if you could find Mrs Haddad for me?'

The nurse spoke to him rationally, as if she were talking to a normal person. 'But this lady isn't Lebanese. She says she is Iraqi and she lived in Beirut for a while, that's all.'

The nurse tried to get through to the General, who seized Lamis's hand and bent to kiss it, murmuring, 'Ava Gardner.'

The next time Lamis saw her, the nurse was on her own. 'At last we've found you!' the nurse sighed with relief. 'I was beginning to be afraid you weren't coming to the square any more!'

'My son wasn't well.'

'Oh dear. Is he feeling better?'

'Yes, much, thank you.'

The nurse handed Lamis four envelopes containing letters dictated by the General and addressed to Nadia Haddad.

'But I don't know Nadia Haddad.'

'It doesn't matter. The main thing is the General's doing something he enjoys. He's full of optimism now. He doesn't give me trouble when it's time for our walk. He's eager to see you and it seems remembering Nadia Haddad has done him a lot of good. I'm pleased for him.'

'What shall I do with these?'

'Nothing. But I promised the General I'd give them to you. It will please him to know you've got them.'

Lamis was struck by the care the nurse took to carry out her patient's wishes, and decided that this was a particularly English kind of sincerity.

The General's telephone number was still in Lamis's little address book. There were only a few names there, and next to them, phone numbers, although she knew, even as she wrote them down, that she'd never call these people. All the same, in her mind she was afraid to lose their names: the actress she met when Khalid trod on her dog's tail, the stallholder in Kensington Market who asked her to bring him amber rice from Iraq before the Gulf

15

War, the American woman in Harvey Nichols, and the mother of a child who'd been at nursery with her son.

'Is the General there?'

'Who's speaking?' another voice interrupted. 'The General's been dead five years. Can I help?'

'No thank you.'

She replaced the receiver. 'He's died and left me.' Instead of laughing at her own absurdity, she felt a momentary shock. She redialled the General's number.

'Hello. I called a few seconds ago about the General. I've got some letters that he wrote to Nadia Haddad, but because of the war in Lebanon . . .'

The voice intervened. 'I'm sorry. I don't understand. What do you want me to do?'

'I wondered if you'd like to have these letters?'

'What do I want with letters written by an imbecile at the end of his life?'

Lamis remembered the nurse showing her a photo. 'That's the General. See how handsome he was!'

'Oh, and that must be Nadia Haddad. He's right. She does look like Ava Gardner. Who do you think that is? Her husband?' Lamis had turned the photo over and read, 'King David Hotel, Palestine 1946'.

It would only take one invitation from an English person for her to have a way in: one ant leads the whole column to a grain of sugar. She heard many stories about men Arab women fell in love with simply because they were English: a butcher brimming with virility as he cut the meat with an air of skilful deliberation, a house painter who read philosophy in his coffee break, a bursar at the children's school, a male nurse in the emergency room, a newsreader who appeared every evening, inaccessible behind the television screen.

When they were applying for British nationality, Lamis said to her husband, 'Who shall we ask? Is it possible that the only English people we know are doctors?' In the end their papers were signed by her son's riding instructor and an Iraqi who'd acquired British nationality after he had emigrated following the 1958 revolution.

Should she contact Mr Collins?

Mr Collins was the gynaecologist. He was the one who knew she'd remained a virgin after her husband's early attempts at making love, and he knew when she lost her virginity, and when she became pregnant. He witnessed her stomach swelling month by month, and he learned where she came from and who her family were, and he guided another Arab out of her; an English hand plunging inside her, acting as a mediator between her, her offspring and her husband. He was very gentle and sensitive. 'I'm heating up the instrument so that it's nice and warm.'

He let her know the results of her smear test on a formal card, white with decorative print like an invitation to a party. 'We are extremely happy to inform you that . . .'

A special relationship grew up between Arab women and their doctors, the only British who came into contact with their bodies.

Lamis knew of one Arab woman who found some comfort in going to see Mr Collins week after week to ask for a pill to make her want to have sex with her husband, or at least to be able to bear it.

'There's no such pill! How about a glass of wine?'

'No, no. I don't drink.'

'Tell your husband you don't feel like it.'

'No. No, I can't. Poor man, I don't want to hurt his feelings.'

'There's no such pill. Trust me.'

'And trust me, I don't feel like it any more.'

'Have you thought about divorce?'

'I love him. We've been married ten years. But I can't stand sleeping with him.'

'I can't help you. Sorry.'

'You're the only person who can.'

'OK. Get up on the bed and I'll have a look at you.'

'No thank you. Bye, doctor, bye.'

Lamis picked up the phone and dialled the gynaecologist's number. The secretary answered. 'Would you like an appointment?' she asked.

'Yes, yes,' said Lamis hurriedly.

'The first one's in three weeks' time. Mr Collins is extremely busy.'

Lamis remembered the man at the opera who'd asked her if she liked *Aida*. Where was he? He'd seemed to be on the point of inviting her to go with him to *Aida*. It was during a performance of *Carmen*, but Belquis was there and she'd listened disapprovingly to every word he said.

The man sighed from time to time and Lamis questioned him raptly about the plot.

'Why did Carmen do that? I don't understand. Even though she loves him?'

'They should have a translation. The thing is Carmen no longer loves José!'

'But what did he do to make her stop loving him?'

'Nothing. She's bohemian. She likes having a lot of different lovers,' the man whispered.

Lamis listened avidly. 'Carmen warned him from the beginning that, for her, falling in love was like a bird alighting for a moment then flying off. She tells José quite clearly that she's gone off him.'

Lamis was feeling guilty about sitting in the opera house all dressed up while her husband and son waited at home. She was as restless as a lizard's severed tail until suddenly it seemed that Carmen herself had rejoined her to herself, body and mind. By the end of the performance she was so relaxed that she could hardly stand up, and when she returned home she wished that she could make herself invisible and collapse into bed alone.

Reverberations from other worlds used to linger with her after she went to the opera, the cinema, the theatre, the ICA, where she saw how people viewed life differently, and at home she would take comfort even from a ticket stub buried in her jacket pocket. These activities used to give her the strength to survive the constant presence of her mother-in-law, and the smoke-filled mornings and evenings when her husband's friends ate, discussed politics and played cards.

Lamis opened her case and smelled Dubai, the mingled scents of air-conditioning, dust, spices and government offices. She felt afraid and slammed the case shut again and sat down on the bed. She was not going to put off sorting out her new life. Procrastination was the thief of time. She thought of calling Amira and apologising for not being able to join her with the Englishman and Samir for dinner, especially after having assured the Englishman that she would when he'd asked in the minibus. She put some music on to cheer herself up but stopped it again after the first few bars. She didn't want the music to lull her into a false sense of well-being. She took a notebook and pen out of her bag and wrote:

This is going to become my country. I've stopped living a temporary life.

1) I've just arrived in London and this is a hotel.
2) Look for a flat to rent.

She crossed out the second line and wrote:

2) Learn English properly.
3) Look for a job, any job. Start to save money. Take the tube or the bus. No taxis, unless it's an emergency.
4) Make friends with some English people.
5) Find somewhere else to live as soon as possible.
6) Stop eating Arab food – not because the garlic and coriander make my breath smell, but because this kind of food makes me feel safe and secure and reminds me of childhood and home.

She reached out to put the phone on the bed, and happened to glance in the mirror. Hurriedly she added point number seven:

7) Stop wearing black kohl on my eyes.

She stood up and began to wipe the kohl away with cotton wool and cleanser. Without kohl her eyes were naked. She was reminded of a snake shedding its skin, discarding it among the cacti. Once as a child she saw a snakeskin, dried and crackling in the wasteland on the outskirts of Najaf, looking like a plastic bag patterned with shapes of light and dark brown. She didn't dare touch it, and her father explained that the snake had taken off its dress to change into a more elegant one for a wedding. 'The snake took off her dress out of doors,' Lamis exclaimed. 'Wasn't she afraid of going to hell?'

Lamis looked at her eyes in the bedroom mirror. They showed her someone who would never cheat, or be devious.

For the eye is the door into the soul.

In Beirut her mother had decided that Lamis should marry the Iraqi who owned the modern building whose basement they sheltered in with other local people. Her mother was impressed by his grand apartment and its marble bathroom, which he let Lamis and her mother use once during a lull in the fighting, and she saw the way the Iraqi looked admiringly at Lamis when most of the people in the shelter had eyes only for the food that the women of the neighbourhood vied with one another to prepare. When the Iraqi declared his interest, Lamis told her mother she wouldn't marry him. Back at their tiny flat her mother pleaded with her to accept that rich suitor, sent from heaven to pull them out of poverty and give them back their dignity, and after Lamis refused, she turned her gaze to some distant spot, as if saying to her husband, 'Leave her to me.' He tried to suggest, not too obviously, that she should go easy on the girl, but she snapped her eyes shut threateningly. Then, several days later, when Lamis finally agreed to the marriage, her mother lowered her gaze almost humbly to express her delight.

Should Lamis blame her eyes for the course her life had taken? They say that the eyes are more precious than the costliest jewel. Or should she blame the mirror?

When Lamis was a child the other members of the household,

even the birds in their cages, were so wrapped up in themselves that only the sight of her own reflection seemed to confirm her existence. She used to look at her face reflected in water, a pair of scissors, the cap of her fountain pen, a bowl of soup, an empty cup, in the toilet bowl, between her legs, superimposed on the reflection of her bottom.

The mirror took her into another world of vivid colours and imagination, where she had her mother's blessing, since her mother was always talking about beauty.

Would she have taken an interest in me if she hadn't thought I was beautiful? Lamis often wondered to herself.

Her maternal grandmother used to shout at Lamis to stop staring into the mirror or it would snatch her away inside it. When her father told the old lady to stop her nonsense, her grandmother recounted many tales about mirrors: once a man consulted a soothsayer because he doubted his wife's fidelity and the soothsayer gave the man a small mirror telling him it would reveal whether or not his wife was unfaithful – if she were, it would whisk her away inside it. Lamis always remembered this story and asked her husband for a mirror when he wanted to give her a present, but the mirror never took her away from him.

In the renowned holy city, Najaf, Lamis's mother made friends with the wives of the theology students who came from Cairo, Beirut, Damascus, to study, so she'd be able to borrow the women's magazines they brought with them on their visits to their husbands, and she asked them to buy her fancy modern necklaces and lipstick with the money she was always trying to save.

She took Lamis with her when she went to the dressmaker. The moment they arrived, the dressmaker used to send her own mother out of the room, telling her it was time to make dinner. As soon as she left, the dressmaker would push the table up against the door – she didn't want her mother to come back into the room and see the fashions Lamis's mother chose; the way they revealed

21

the wrists and ankles, and the bright colours of the materials never seen in the city before, not even in its flowers.

In times of danger Lamis would stare at her own reflection to calm her down. She saw herself reflected in the circular pieces of metal that hung from between the blue beads of the necklace they put round the neck of the mule that travelled with them when they fled Iraq across the mountains and valleys of Kurdistan.

As well as their two suitcases, her father carried his lute and her mother a plastic bag holding a pleated skirt. Lamis's father urged her to put it in one of the suitcases, promising that if it were ruined she could buy another, but her mother wouldn't listen. 'It's pure silk. I'm going to put it on as soon as we get to Damascus.'

They were all frightened of hyenas. Her mother was also frightened of rain and wind in case her skirt blew away, and she held the plastic bag close to her when it was her turn to sit on the back of the mule. Lamis's father was so concerned about his lute that the other members of the group they were travelling with became convinced that he had money stashed away inside it.

When her mother tried to dissuade Lamis from asking for a divorce she said, 'If God hadn't wanted you to marry, he'd have fed you to the hyenas when we were escaping from Iraq! We should take every opportunity to thank God the hyenas didn't eat us.'

Lamis opened the bedroom window and called out to the London air, 'I thank God the hyenas didn't eat me!'

A pigeon flew off, startled by her shout.

If I was still married, she thought, I wouldn't have dared do that.

This realisation gave her some satisfaction and she found herself smiling. She spun around like a whirlwind, and prepared to go out and buy beans or lentils. Her grandmother used to say to the sick, the sad, the lover, the widow, the divorcee, 'Fortify your stomach with pulses, and God will give you courage.'

22

She thought she would fortify her stomach before contacting her son, but in the end she dared not leave the flat: her ex-husband and his mother had closed the door to London in her face.

II

Although Samir was barely able to take his eyes off Nicholas in the minibus from the airport, he noticed they no longer seemed to be driving through London. The green parks and grand buildings had disappeared. Signs on a restaurant, a chemist, a dentist, a letting agency, a shop, made him think they could have been back in Mazraa Street in Beirut: 'Come in and you'll find what you're looking for. We speak Arabic', 'Unwanted hair removed by the most modern methods', the Moonlight Café, Maroush, Ranoush Juice, Beirut Express, the Elegant Clothes Store, and there were Arabs in long white robes, black abayas, and contemporary fashions.

'My goodness!' he exclaimed involuntarily. 'It's incredible! Mazraa Street has moved to London! I remember when my father, God rest his soul, used to take us to the Salwa Cinema in Mazraa Street, and buy us sesame buns, and I always wanted to sit in the front row so I could try to touch the actors in the film.'

The driver of the minibus stopped outside the Lebanese fast-food restaurant, the Tabbouleh. Samir said goodbye to Amira and Nicholas and glanced around at the street before he pushed open the restaurant door. A blast of shawarma and chicken kebab hit him in the face. His entrance caused a stir among the youths frying falafel and squeezing orange juice behind the counter, and they winked at one another, and the young man at the cash desk started to hum a tune.

Samir caught sight of himself in the mirror that stretched the length of the wall behind them. 'Mama, you're right to laugh at me.' He smoothed down his hair. 'I've just come from the plane, as God's my witness.'

The youths roared with laughter because he referred to himself in the feminine and talked like a woman. To their astonishment Samir joined in.

A customer stood up from the table where he had been sitting with a blonde woman and walked over.

'Does anyone know a guy called Faruq?' Samir asked the youths behind the counter.

The man came up to Samir and pointed at himself.

Samir put his bag on the floor and held out the basket, finding it hard to believe that the stout, unattractive man in front of him could be the brother of the beautiful youth who'd persuaded him to smuggle the monkey to London. 'Are you dumb? Why don't you speak?' Samir asked.

The man nodded his head to indicate that yes, he was Faruq, and he was mute.

'What a fool I am! I'm sorry. Your brother didn't tell me. Anyway, he'll be here tomorrow,' he said.

The man patted Samir on the shoulder, then opened the lid of the basket, deftly moved the newspaper, empty biscuit wrappers and jumper aside, and saw the comatose monkey. He rested his head on his hand and covered his eyes, to ask Samir if the monkey was asleep.

'The bastard's got addicted to the pills,' Samir said.

Faruq carried the basket out, followed by the foreign woman. Samir dropped back to say in confidential tones to the youths behind the counter, 'The dumb man's sister's in hospital here. She's dying and I smuggled the monkey out of Dubai so she could say goodbye to it. She raised the monkey like her own child. Fed it from one tit while she fed her son from the other. Give me a falafel sandwich for the monkey.'

His words ricocheted like a firecracker along the line of waiters.

'Ask the monkey if he wants tartare sauce with the sandwich,' said one sarcastically.

24

The man drove for less than five minutes and parked his car in a narrow street lined with white houses that looked like hospitals, shabby and decrepit. Samir followed the couple to the front door of one of them and noticed the rubbish and dirt piled at the ground-floor windows, and the peeling paint. Was it possible that there were places like this in London? And buildings with no lifts? Faruq and the woman started to climb the stairs and when the woman found out that the flat was on the top floor, she sighed loudly and crossly. So even the English said 'Oh God'! She was both pretty and ugly. Samir was surprised she never once smiled at him. This didn't happen often. Women were generally cheerful in his company, even when he didn't open his mouth. Perhaps she had a period, or was sensitive because her boyfriend was dumb and fat, and had little black hairs sticking out of his ears. Samir was suddenly afraid that the couple might slam the door in his face. He'd been wrong to hand over the monkey to the man like that. He hurried after them and pushed between them on the stairs, determined that the exchange should take place: the monkey in return for a thousand pounds.

The flat was dirty, unbelievably neglected, its contents scattered chaotically about, the blue carpet stained with patches of brown. Only the chandelier hanging from the high ceiling of the main room testified to the building's venerable past. The man held the basket out to Samir and Samir heard him say, 'Get it out, so we can see it.'

'What a world we live in! I swear he spoke! It's a miracle! So you were pretending to be dumb. What for? So you didn't have to ask what my trip was like? For twenty-four hours, even before I got on the plane, I didn't know if I was coming or going, and my heart was beating like a drum. I only became human again in the minibus. Don't I get any thanks? Your brother knelt and kissed my feet when he was trying to persuade me to be a courier for him. I risked my life and future and five kids out of pity for your sister, and now you're ordering me about as if you're God Almighty.'

'What's wrong with him?' interrupted the woman.

25

'He wants me to get on my knees and thank him.'

'He's right. You should.' She turned to Samir. 'Thanks.'

'OK. Thanks, brother. Now make it wake up.'

Samir bent over the basket to take out the monkey. It opened its eyes for a moment, then closed them again.

'It's still drowsy. The sedatives haven't worn off yet. Come on, where's the money?'

'They told me to give you eight hundred pounds.'

'You're lying. A thousand pounds cash down.'

'The other two hundred's for your board and lodging, until you leave.'

'A thousand pounds and I'm happy to go without eating or sleeping.'

'You won't find a hotel here for less than a hundred pounds.'

'Don't worry about that. You give me a thousand pounds. I'm ready to sleep standing up if I need to.'

'When it wakes up I'll pay you. For all I know, it's dead.'

Samir hurried over to the monkey and pulled it out of the basket. He placed the animal on a piece of furniture that had once been a sofa.

The woman gasped. 'Oh, it's tiny. Only as big as a chicken.'

Samir kneeled and rested his ear against the monkey's stomach. 'Look! See how my head's rising and falling. That means it's breathing.'

He put a hand to the monkey's mouth. 'See, its breath's burning hot.'

'I forgot to ask you. Has it been to the toilet?'

'Yes, of course. In the plane it asked to go three times, and washed its hands afterwards. It's very well behaved!'

'What?' shouted the man. 'Didn't they tell you that it . . . ?' Then he checked himself and forced a smile.

'Your brother told me it mustn't get out of the basket even if it had a shit. Leave the shit in the basket, he said, otherwise we'll get into trouble. They're afraid of diseases in England. They don't let you bring in animals or shit or food.'

The Englishwoman took a book out of her bag and sprawled on the other sofa, reading. Faruq sat in a chair, looking impatient. Samir squashed himself up beside the monkey and fell asleep.

The monkey stirred before Samir. It leaped up and urinated into its hand, watched by the startled Englishwoman, then rubbed its hand dry on its fur. She shouted, but it was too late – the monkey made a leap for the chain supporting the chandelier.

'You wanted it to wake up. It just has,' remarked Samir.

Samir and the man tried to entice the monkey down. The more violently the light swung, the more delighted the monkey became. It sensed the woman's fear and leaned down towards her, baring its teeth and shrieking loudly. Samir laughed. Each time the woman tried to make a run for it the monkey hung down off the light, blocking her path.

'Tell it to stop. It'll bring the ceiling down on top of us.'

'Stop that! Do you hear me? Stop it! See. It doesn't listen. It could be up there for twenty-four hours.'

'Is it going to act like this all the time?'

'Unless you give it a sedative! Come on, pay me the thousand pounds. Let's get this over with.'

'As long as you don't leave me with the monkey.'

'OK, don't worry, I'll take it to the patient.'

'The patient?'

'Your sister. Have you forgotten about her? I smuggled it from Dubai to London for her sake.'

The monkey gave a series of short, piercing yells and turned its beseeching eyes towards the woman. She began screaming too, and the monkey went silent and gazed at her with interest.

'Come on. We'll take it to your sister, then go our separate ways,' said Samir.

'Tomorrow. Let it rest now, and you must want to rest too.'

'I've got things to do. I need to be on my way. I've got friends waiting for me to phone.'

'If you set foot outside that door, you're getting nothing.'

'How can I be sure you're going to give me the money if I stay?'

27

The man reached into his pocket and handed Samir a bundle of pound notes. Samir took it and, as he counted the money, the monkey landed on him and clung on. Samir put the pounds in his pocket, out of harm's way, and found himself hugging the monkey, which put its finger in its mouth and rested its head on Samir's chest. Before Samir knew what was happening, the monkey had snatched the bundle of notes from his pocket. By the time Samir had gathered up all the scattered bills he felt completely exhausted, but the man would not let him out of the flat and kept urging him to do something to make the monkey defecate.

Only the sight of the building opposite and the trees in the street outside made Samir feel that he was actually in London, unlike this semi-derelict flat. He toured around inquisitively like the monkey, and stopped asking when the man's handsome brother was going to arrive. He'd imagined him wearing a silk robe, a cravat and leather slippers, standing at the door of a room with logs burning in the grate, and he would have led him into a bedroom full of erotic paintings with blue films playing on a huge video screen. But Samir no longer cared since the reality was turning out to be so much at odds with the fantasy, and he was sitting in this ugly place with a man and a woman whose eyes and hearts were fixed on the monkey's backside.

'Maybe it's going to do a shit. Look, it's got its legs apart.'

When the monkey bounded off again and sat swinging on top of the door, the man yelled, 'Shit, for God's sake, and let's be done with it.'

'Perhaps if you did it in front of the monkey, it'd imitate you.'

'Are you sure? Or are you having me on?'

'Try. What have you got to lose?'

'But how can I do it in front of you?'

'Why in front of me? In front of the monkey.'

'I don't want to go the bathroom and be by myself with it. It's crazy.'

The monkey leaped up on to the wooden curtain rail and hung

upside down by its tail, which, taut and curled like a ring, bore the monkey's full weight. After a few moments, the monkey righted itself and clung on to the curtain. It jumped off, and the curtain and rail came crashing down. The monkey clapped its hands, shrieking with excitement, and jumped on to Samir's shoulder. Samir whispered in its ear and the monkey bent close, imitating Samir's movements.

'What? What's it saying?'

'It wants something to eat. Let me go and buy it something to eat. It's hungry, poor thing.'

'I'll go. Tell me what it wants.'

'Pistachios, peanuts – but in their shells – eggs, bananas, bread and biscuits, flowers, little shrimps – and if you can find a dozen flies. I'm not kidding. It adores flies.'

'I'll only be a minute. Keep your eye on it.'

The man slammed the door behind him. Samir went forward on the tips of his toes, taking long steps. He stopped, remembering his bag, and went back for it. The door opened suddenly and the man came back in.

'Seeing that I'm responsible for the monkey, it ought to be locked in the bathroom while I'm gone in case it escapes,' said the man.

'Don't worry. There's no chance.'

'It would set my mind at rest.'

Samir put the monkey in the bathroom, tore off some toilet paper for it to play with and left it there. The man locked the bathroom door, put the key in his pocket, then made for the stairs.

'Back in a second,' he called as he double-locked the flat's front door from the outside.

'Go then, and I hope you don't come back,' muttered Samir.

Samir raced over to the phone and took Amira's card from his pocket.

'Madame Amira. It's Samir. Samir with the monkey . . . I can't. I've been kidnapped . . . Yes, the man's locked me and the monkey in. He's waiting for the monkey to go to the toilet. When it's been, I'm free. Everything depends on the monkey's shit, pardon my language. I swear to God, it's the truth, Madame Amira . . . Yes, yes . . . Yes, he's given me the thousand pounds but not before he squeezed me like you squeeze a lemon. That monkey's shouting its head off.'

The monkey was beating on the door, pelting it with objects, letting out loud angry shrieks. Then there was silence. Water began to flood out under the bathroom door into the passage. The monkey shrieked again and Samir was afraid the whole flat would soon be under water.

He called to the woman, 'Get up. Are you going to go on reading while there's a flood?'

He rushed to put his bag on the table and checked that his passport and the thousand pounds were still in his pocket. He found his coat and put it on top of the bag. Perhaps the monkey's activities were going to give him his best chance of escape, if the neighbours came running, or the fire brigade showed up like he'd seen in foreign films. But only Faruq arrived, cursing and swearing as he gave the bathroom key to Samir, afraid that the monkey would take its revenge on him.

The floor was under water; a cake of soap, a bottle of shampoo and the toilet brush floated on the surface. The bathroom curtain was chewed and torn, the plastic rail lay on the floor and the curtain rings drifted in the bowl. Foam obscured the mirror and a grubby towel had come to rest on the monkey's shoulders. The man followed Samir and began searching round in the water, as if he had lost something precious. Bent almost double, he tiptoed around the edges of the bathroom rug, which had curled up into a boat shape, and only stopped when the monkey bared its teeth, laughing and gesticulating towards him.

> *Give me back my freedom,*
> *Let my hands be unchained,*
> *To you I gave everything,*
> *Of me, nothing remains*

sang Samir, flinging his head back and wringing his hands with emotion, in imitation of Umm Kulthum.

The man laughed in spite of himself. 'Has anyone ever told you you should go on the stage?'

'All the monkeys I've ever met! What do you want with me, man? Let me go.'

'You'd leave me to deal with the monkey?'

'I'll do you a favour. I'll clean up the bathroom, then I'm off.' He began rolling back his sleeves and turning up his trouser legs.

'I'll give you fifty pounds extra if you help me think how to make it shit, then you can go.'

'The zoo! Get the zoo's number for me.'

The man dialled directory enquiries, then the number of London Zoo, and handed the receiver to Samir, who adopted the accent he had learned from watching American cowboy films. 'I have a monkey that won't go to the bathroom. I mean the toilet. I don't mean to have a bath, I mean to go to the toilet. What should I do?'

The receiver was put down at the other end.

'What fluent English!' said the man malevolently.

'Why don't you speak to them, then, or your lady friend? What's she doing? Is she planning on reading three whole books today?'

'I'm afraid they'll come and take the monkey away,' said the man.

'Right, what do you think of this idea? I've got an English friend.'

'Are you mad? An Englishman? That'd be asking for trouble.'

'This one's different. He shared a taxi with us, and knew the type of monkey it was – a name like cappuccino coffee. He recognised it from its white beard and tail! What do you think? Shall I talk to him?'

'Watch he doesn't find out where you're speaking from.'

'I don't know myself.'

'All right.'

Samir leaped up to the phone and called Amira.

'Madame Amira. Please, do you have Nicholas's telephone number?'

'Listen, don't waste your time. He likes girls.'

'I know, I know. But it's the monkey.'

He dialled Nicholas's number. As soon as he heard Nicholas's hello, he shouted, 'Oh Mr Nicholas, God loves me – I found you! I am Samir, remember me? With the monkey? He, the monkey, is not going to the bathroom, I mean to the toilet, do you understand? He cannot shit! Can you help me make him shit? OK. OK. Sir, I'll give him dried prunes . . . OK . . . OK. Lots and lots . . .'

But Samir was not allowed out of the door until the following day, after the monkey had passed the pellets with the diamonds that it had been fed in Dubai stuffed inside grapes. As the man bent down collecting them with a spoon in one hand and a bag in the other, Samir thought of stealing one but was distracted by anger. 'Criminals!' he shouted. 'I'll report you to the police. You've kept me prisoner here.'

The monkey was faster than the man at picking up the stones but as soon as the man brought it a bag of pistachios, it dropped them. The man counted the diamonds and gave Samir an extra two hundred pounds. They left the flat and, as the couple went down the long flight of stairs, Samir threw the monkey at them. 'There you are,' he said sarcastically. 'You'd better hurry. Your sister must be waiting for it.'

As if for the first time, Samir inhaled the London air and looked up at the sky. 'I'm free!' he cried. 'It feels so good!'

He suddenly found himself wrapped in the monkey's embrace. He turned around in a panic, but the couple had disappeared.

'In the name of God the Compassionate, the Merciful!' he shouted.

Then he saw them in a black cab. The man stuck his head out of the window and said, 'You're right. Freedom does feel good!'

Amira went into the building known as the Birds' Nests off the Edgware Road. She shook Nicholas's hand. 'Bye. See you later,' and gave the minibus driver who had carried her case into the lobby ten pounds, instructing him to drop the Englishman off.

The porter looked stunned. A ten-pound tip? And what was she doing with a smartly dressed, blond man – a real Englishman?

Amira was appalled by the sight of herself in the lift mirror. The dark freckles had spread over her forehead and cheeks. Were they that bad in Dubai? Or was it simply that anything not perfect showed up in London? Still, the English liked a tan. It gave the impression you'd paid a lot to sunbathe or ski.

White suggested ice and snow in these Western countries, not purity and beauty like at home.

She quickly unpacked her case, taking out the cushions she had stolen from her cabin in the client's yacht in Dubai, not because she liked them, but to satisfy her desire for revenge. She was gratified, as well, by the sight of the bottles of perfume and jars of cream she had helped herself to from the British girls' cabin after they had all gone ashore and left her alone on the yacht.

She looked at her watch. The Gulf man and his nephew from the plane wouldn't be ready to receive a phone call from her just yet. She dialled Nahid's number but couldn't get through. Her friend had probably still not paid her last phone bill, which had come to over a thousand pounds.

In the kitchen Amira could find no trace of the two beer cans that she had left on the table before she went away, to test whether the porter ever entered her flat and snooped about during her absence. Never mind, he'd soon be running errands for her, whether he wanted to or not. Unlike his predecessors, who'd done odd jobs for her in exchange for free sexual services, the new porter didn't seem to fancy Amira. He'd even gone so far as to report her to the police, claiming to be afraid for his family, especially for his daughter who'd soon be ten years old. But the policeman he'd spoken to, a friend of Amira's, told the porter that if he wasn't comfortable with the job he should ask for a transfer. Nobody could say for sure that Amira was breaking the law, as long as she was working in her flat and not in the street. 'And anyway we're talking about an Arab with other Arabs, so why should we interfere?'

Amira cleansed her face with rosewater. She soaked a cotton-wool pad in olive oil and passed it over the dark patches on her skin. Then she sat on her bed and dialled the Gulf man's number. The nephew answered. 'My uncle's at the hotel.'

'But isn't that his house?'

'Yes, that's right. But we've got several floors here and he's afraid of tripping on the stairs because his eyes are so bad. He's having the operation the day after tomorrow.'

'Can you give me the hotel's phone number and the number of his room?'

She wrote the numbers down on her hand and felt as pleased as if she had been handed a ticket guaranteeing her work for the rest of her life. She experienced an unfamiliar rush of energy and hurriedly removed everything from her face. She applied a pink cream, then a white, and put on the gold bracelets she had bought in Dubai. She bundled Nahid's present into a bag, and rushed off to Nahid's place. Nahid was out, and she searched fruitlessly in her bag for a pen and a piece of paper. She finally found a piece of chewing gum, which she unwrapped and put in her mouth. She stuck the wrapper through the door, hoping that Nahid would discover the signal later, and then headed in the direction of Bahia's flat, which overlooked Hyde Park, anticipating that she'd find Nahid there. Before she turned towards Bayswater Road, she couldn't help but stop to admire the flowers and fountains and the curve of Marble Arch. I ought to live here, she thought. This is the real London. Not 'little Arabia' as the English call Edgware Road these days.

Bahia welcomed Amira coldly, disguising it so well that only

Amira saw through her manner, but as soon as Nahid caught sight of her she shrieked in delight, 'London without you isn't worth an onion skin.'

'I've missed you all like mad. It was a lousy trip,' said Amira, switching her Moroccan accent to an Egyptian one. Ever since she'd watched Egyptian films as a child, with their crafty and coy and glamorous film stars, she'd felt that life with an Egyptian accent would be infinitely more fun.

'God! What happened?' asked Nahid.

'Nothing.' Amira was staring at another woman in the room, whose head was covered with a scarf. 'I know your face.'

'Don't you recognise Katkouta?' Bahia trilled maliciously, proud that the star ex-dancer, Katkouta, was visiting her.

'I was wondering where I'd seen that beautiful face before.'

'Thank you,' said the woman in the headscarf.

'Right, so tell us what happened, Amira. They say Dubai's paradise. Couldn't you take the heat and mess, or are we English now?'

Amira ignored Nahid's question and addressed Katkouta.

'How are you, Madame Katkouta? We're honoured to have you in London. I used to love seeing you dance . . . especially in the films, with Abaza.'

'Thank you. Thank you very much. But are you telling us Dubai doesn't live up to its reputation?'

'The Natashas! They're everywhere, like grains of desert sand or a plague of locusts. A reserve army of blonde ants foraging for food, sent by the communists to cream off the Arabs' wealth and give us diseases. And to think my poor nephew spent his youth in one of our prisons because he believed in their red flag! Those Russian floozies have taken over – they're everywhere, the hotels, the shops, piling up their trolleys with cellphones, irons, hair-dryers, anything electrical, and clothes, perfume. I suppose I could just about have accepted all that . . . But for a Russian to stand there singing Farid al-Atrash's "Rose in my Heart", that was too much.'

'Who cares?' Nahid said. 'Why do you always hold the ladder horizontally, Amira? Live and let live.' She turned to Bahia. 'Come on, aren't you going to tell Amira about your latest gadget?'

'It's not a gadget,' Bahia protested. 'It's a cooling system I've had installed in one of the small rooms. It's for keeping furs in all year round; it protects them from moths and they stay as fresh as a daisy. You're all very welcome to use it. One hundred and fifty pounds a year. And,' she added, 'if you've got any dried *molokhiya*, bring it with you and store it with your fur, because ordinary fridges spoil its taste.'

'I gave my fur coat away to your mother,' Amira reminded Bahia. 'Don't you remember, Bahia, when you made your mother close her eyes and feel in the bag. "Guess what it is," I said, and the poor woman shouted, "How lovely! We're going to make *molokhiya* with rabbit!"'

'You always like to humiliate me, Amira,' Bahia said angrily. 'My mother was joking. Besides, the coat was all moth-eaten and you looked like a gorilla in it!'

Amira interrupted their laughter crossly. 'I was joking too. You take everything so seriously.'

Nahid tried to smooth things over. 'You know, Amira, you can go into this cooler and stay there for five minutes and it tightens your skin, as if you've stretched your face with clothes pegs – here,' she demonstrated, 'and here. How many times a week did the specialist say, Bahia?'

'Once a week,' Bahia replied. 'If there's something like a party, for instance, then twice, but that's strictly for special occasions. Don't kid yourself, though. It won't make you lose weight.'

'Who wants to lose weight?' Amira knew full well that Bahia was referring to her.

'For one, the woman who went to the dentist to have her jaws wired together,' Bahia answered without looking in Amira's direction, 'who started processing her food and shovelling it in between her teeth. And the woman who convinced herself that Jesus was watching every time she opened the fridge door or reached for a piece of cake. She made herself stop because she didn't want to upset him – "He's suffered enough already." '

Nahid tried to keep the peace. 'My sister's husband wanted a divorce after she put on too much weight. And then he married his secretary, and my sister couldn't get any money out of him – even the judge blamed her for being overweight in the first place!'

'Can you believe it? Egyptian TV warned its female announcers that they'd be dismissed if they didn't slim,' put in Katkouta.

'It's an international conspiracy. Arab men are rejecting their Arab past, and following the West – broad hips used to be a sign of beauty.' Amira was defensive. Her recent client from the Emirates and his friends in Dubai had made her doubt her female charms. The excess of flesh covering her body had taken life all of its own accord, established a foothold without being invited.

'Come on, Nahid,' said Amira, tiring of the subject. 'I want to buy some material. Let's go to Speedy Gazelle's!' She turned to Bahia. 'Tell the truth. You've had a nose job.'

'Me? God forbid!' replied Bahia. 'I've lost five kilos, and all of me's got thinner.'

Nahid and Amira went out together. As soon as they were on the pavement, Amira reproached Nahid for her small-mindedness and told her she'd become just like the others.

'You're all friendly with Bahia because she lives in an expensive block of flats and makes herself out to be something special. The day the wife of that wretched old Saudi man of hers decides to visit London, he'll throw Bahia out and pretend he doesn't know her. And that fridge thing is only there to stop her rotten money stinking. As for her old man with his limp, he was after me, I swear. I agreed to go with him once. I felt disgusted and I told him I didn't want a penny. He pays girls to massage his crippled leg. He says that's what geishas do. A geisha would never touch a crippled leg! Afterwards he wanted me to sit downstairs by the fountain with him. It's so cold there it makes your teeth chatter, and the lute player was pathetic. Not only that, but the old man had invited half a dozen Swiss and British bank managers, and they never took their eyes off the floor. I felt so embarrassed for them. And what about that virtuous lady Katkouta, Egypt's leading dancer? If she's repented and become a born-again Muslim, what's she doing spending time with Bahia? She must want to lead us back on to the straight and narrow. Or doesn't she know how to enjoy herself except with people like us?

Nahid shrugged non-committally. She sensed that there was something bothering her friend and asked gently, 'Now tell me, Amira. Tell me. What happened in Dubai?'

'Do you remember Muhammad from the Emirates?'

'Spare Tyres? Of course. How could anyone forget him? What's happened to him? Did he die and forget to put you in his will?'

'Be serious, Nahid. He treated me like a dog. From the moment he saw me in Dubai, he put the knife in. He tried to destroy my dignity, my beauty. He said he regretted asking me to go out there with the other girls. He played tricks on me and went off. Imagine! Twice I accompanied the whole lot of them on board the yacht, but he only took the English and the Russian girls ashore with him. He left me behind as if I was a piece of garbage . . . trash!'

Amira found herself remembering the day Spare Tyres first saw her undressed. 'Eve driven naked from the Garden of Eden,' he'd breathed, because he'd never seen a woman without her clothes before. 'Hold me up. I feel I'm going to faint. Your body is as slender as a ben tree. Your breasts are like two ostrich eggs, your stomach a field of daisies, your bottom two sand dunes.'

Later Muhammad had told Amira that when he'd returned to the Gulf he'd tried to persuade his wife to sleep naked with him, threatening to divorce her if she refused, and bribing her with gifts of expensive jewellery, until one night she gave in on condition that the room was pitch dark.

All the same, as soon as his wife entered, he turned his face away. 'Oh no.' He'd seen the way her soft breasts hung down like the udders of a half-starved goat, and her fleshy stomach, like a pile of spare tyres, rested in heavy folds, one on top of the other.

'But that wasn't because he liked the blondes, Amira. He was just looking after all the money he'd spent getting them there in the first place. He was making sure of his investment. And remember, he's desperate to prove his virility, that he can still perform.'

'He told me I'd put on too much weight. He even left instructions that the hotel clerk should ask me for a deposit if I decided to stay for a few extra days. To put it bluntly, he abused me and paid me peanuts.'

'Then what happened?'

'I left the hotel and went straight to the airport, but not before I wrote him a note: "Dear Muhammad, I now realise why you like to make love in the jacuzzi – it's so no one'll know you are impotent." '

'Good girl, Amira. But come to think of it, why didn't you pretend to be pregnant, like before?'

'Not only pregant, but expecting twins,' Amira laughed ruefully. 'But the trick backfired. He started to give me advice and tell me off, saying what I was doing was wrong, I was bad. He turned into a preacher all of a sudden.'

'I don't believe it! How bizarre! I told Stanley the other day that he'd turned into a preacher!'

'Did you say Stanley?'

'Yes, Stanley in flesh and blood. I bumped into him in Edgware Road and he started lecturing me about my future!'

'How funny. Though I don't blame old Stanley. I'm thinking of my future, Nahid. And yours, too. I'm thirty-eight years old. I've become used to silk and jewellery and good food. I can't stop doing what I do and try to live the decent life now.'

'And don't leave out the hot running water, and taking taxis everywhere, and Harley Street doctors.'

Amira and Nahid reached Oxford Street and turned down Duke Street but instead of entering the famous fabric shop esteemed by Indian and Arab women, they chose to sit in a café and eat pastries. Amira gave Nahid the present she had bought for her in Dubai, a pair of gold earrings each in the shape of a birdcage containing a miniature bird. The birds made them smile. If Nahid had been with her in Dubai, thought Amira, everything would have been much lighter, and all the serious stuff would have become farcical. What they did and where they went together united them, brought them closer. It made their friendship stronger. They were like two batteries charging each other up.

They joked and gossiped just like in the old days, when they had been at the peak of their vitality and youthful desirability, not needing to try so hard to make sure their customers wanted them. They laughed about when they'd taken the tissues they'd used for wiping up punters' sperm and burned them, imagining that the smoke made a magical incense to entice the men back again. And each assured the other she looked beautiful and sexy and, of course, far prettier than Bahia, and they agreed to meet the next day, when they'd have a serious discussion about their future.

IV

Nicholas opened his case and scattered his clothes about desperately as if he were a diabetic seeking his insulin fix. He saw the towel and his features relaxed as he unwrapped from it the gold and silver Omani dagger he'd had his eye on for months, picturing it on the wall beside his desk, complementing the wooden chest from India and the straw fezzes from Sri Lanka.

'Fantastic!' He stood back, congratulating himself on his purchase – now his flat was complete.

He went around the flat welcoming himself home. Everything was just as he had left it. He watered the plants, although there was no need to since Julia, the cleaner, watered them diligently once a week. He hated the unfamiliarity and loneliness that confronted him every time he returned to London or went away to Oman. Did he want the couch to open its arms and hug him, or the cushions to clap their hands in greeting? He went into the kitchen and filled the kettle. Instead of walking away as usual, he stood and waited for the water to boil. He sat on the couch with his mug of coffee and noticed the stain where he'd rubbed the upholstery to remove some chocolate. Then remembering the dates he'd brought back from Oman he tipped them into a bowl and ate five, then took the stones into the kitchen and fetched his mail. There was a letter from Anita and, at the sight of her pretty sloping script, he was prompted to be ruthless; he sorted through the rest of the post and threw out everything that looked uninteresting before he read her letter.

Anita wanted to know if he'd lend her his Indian wall hanging – she wanted to use it in a photo. Was this one of her schemes or a genuine request? He glanced at the Rajasthani cotton hanging embroidered with gazelles, snakes, lions, flowers, and huntsmen on horseback blowing horns. Anita had passionately wanted to make love on it.

'But it's lasted for two centuries. I have to take great care of it,' he had protested.

That only made her want it more and she had finally persuaded him to take it down off the wall.

The last time he saw Anita he told her as gently as he could that, if they continued to share a bed, it would have to be as friends only. She didn't seem upset or embarrassed, and didn't try to make him change his mind. She smiled her wide-eyed smile and said, 'OK, sister and brother.' But then she looked at him fearfully. 'My brother,' she said softly, 'we must breathe fast so the spaceman thinks we're plants. The plants in space breathe out loud, you know. Look! See him? He's coming towards us.'

Her playful fantasy aroused him and distracted him from his resolution that he wouldn't take his trousers off again for a woman unless he was in love with her. Sex was becoming boring, routine.

He was lying on his back, the covers drawn up to his chin, and he reached out for Anita and she pulled him on top of her. Her panting breath entered his mouth and snaked along his backbone and Anita was no longer pretending. 'Promise me, brother, pro-mise me, that you won't desert your sister who lives in eternal darkness. Do you know how awful it is to be blind?'

He dialled her number. He missed her friendship and the company of a woman who offered more than small talk and social niceties, which were all he'd exchanged with any woman during the last six weeks in Oman. But there was only her answering machine. 'Anita. It's Nicholas, I've just got back.' He repeated this a couple of times, knowing that Anita sometimes put on an answerphone voice.

A letter from his father asked if he'd delivered the copy of the Bible translated into Arabic to Sayf in Oman. (It lay with its three thousand pages on the table in front of him.)

> Your mother hardly moves these days. When she went to see the specialist the other day, a nurse took her down to be weighed on the scales in the hospital kitchen, just as if she was a sack of potatoes! She says it's my fault, and if I'd had a different occupation she'd have kept her figure. You know how generous people are round here. They bring homemade cakes and biscuits every time they visit, and she says she can't refuse them but, between you and me, she likes making cakes herself too!

Nicholas laughed at the final paragraph of his father's letter:

> Anyway, she'll find that if we visit you in Oman eating dates isn't quite as simple as eating cake, I'm afraid. There are all those obstacles – the stones and sometimes the skins. The doctor's told her three dates equals on average a small spoon of sugar. Never mind! Never mind!
>
> Hampshire's so damp, Nicholas. I do hope your mother will agree to come to Oman with me, especially as it is a treat from our favourite son. I've told her we deserve the break, and she should think of it as a holiday. No more, no less. She wouldn't

have to put up with the appalling conditions we found in Palma de Mallorca two years ago, when we stayed in that place belonging to a friend of a friend, with no kitchen. All those thousands of German tourists, literally baking themselves in the sun. She's so vexed about the fact that we can't really afford a holiday, and she doesn't want to complain, but she can't stop herself. I've told her it seems a suitable place for travelling to in the winter months. It wouldn't be that difficult and, in any case, a visit to Oman would have its advantages. As well as getting us away from the daily frustration that we personally, and the Church as a whole, suffer, of trying to drum up funds, it'll give the local youth a different view of us – show that even the Vicar and his wife can enjoy adventure and travel to far-flung places.

There was a letter from Liz, too. Her handwriting was etched on his memory. Nicholas was reluctant to open it but went ahead out of loyalty. She'd sent him a newspaper cutting about a Byzantine exhibition at the Metropolitan Museum in New York and a postcard on which she'd written that she welcomed him back to London and hoped to see him soon. A wave of displeasure hit him, occasioned not only by the message but by the card: an unflattering picture that made the Sultan Mahmut's throne in the Topkapi in Istanbul look rather like a frog.

Over the last few months, ever since Nicholas had started to work in Oman on his secondment from Sotheby's, Liz had hounded him with stories relating to the Arab world: an article about Saddam Hussein, another about Arab belly dancers hiring bodyguards because they feared Islamic fundamentalists, news of Hafez al-Asad's illness, an item about Egyptian boys who were paid a few pounds for lizards that sold in the West for a hundred dollars apiece.

He was still in the process of escaping from Liz's famous 'eye', the very thing that attracted him when they first met at Sotheby's five years ago. He had been astonished by the discernment of Liz's 'eye'. It was like some independent entity, a magician finding

43

solutions to riddles, interpreting the movement of a feather, a faded colour, an equation, a tale from history. Its retina was a website of information stored in different languages; its iris focused unlike any other, distinctive and individual as a fingerprint. Nicholas became enslaved by this eye, which was so superior to his in its knowledge of art and its passionate intensity. He listened and the eye revealed all, and it favoured him with a look that was never bestowed on the other employees of Sotheby's or its clients or even the works of art themselves.

Nicholas lost his head when he realised that this eye, admired by so many, was at his service, sleeping, smiling, moaning in pleasure, smitten with jealousy, and he fell passionately in love with Liz. Her eye drew him in, made him feel that he belonged, that he was at the centre of things; it schooled him in London: through Liz he learned its streets and lanes, its neighbourhoods, went to its clubs and restaurants and parties. But then she wanted to marry, and he didn't, and she left him.

After a period of confusion and a few fleeting relationships, however, she came back to him, making no mention of marriage. His happiness at her return was indescribable; he felt at the time that London was not big enough, and to celebrate, they went together to Florence, but instead of reconciliation, Nicholas found he wanted to end their relationship. As they climbed the walled road in Fiesole, he remarked that it must feel like this on the Great Wall of China, the hard stone underfoot, the fields spreading below, and Liz immediately retorted that his comparison was misplaced. 'I was only talking about the feeling, Liz,' he protested.

They wandered through the gloom of the tiny church at Fiesole and the monastery's dark wood-panelled rooms. They both loved the Fra Angelico painting and frescos. After a while Nicholas was drawn to the bright courtyard outside, leaving Liz with her guidebooks and art papers. He stood by an arch and looked out on to the yard, where a monk was moving among the humble plants and flowers with a watering can, murmuring softly. There were birds in a cage built against the near wall: eating, splashing in a water bowl, swinging in a little basket in the centre, and twittering at the entrances to their houses. Nicholas watched the flow of their constant movement and the jumping, changing colours; the occasional bright feather fell as one bird groomed another. Liz came over to him and asked what he was doing there.

'This little courtyard is really lovely. Let's sit out here for a bit.'

'Come back inside. I want to show you something in these frescos.'

'I want to show you this courtyard.'

'It's pretty.' She hadn't looked at it. 'But come with me.'

After a few days Nicholas felt completely alone.

As soon as they returned to London, he left Liz to her own devices. He felt he'd escaped from her clutches; that he no longer had to take refuge from the coldness of her eyes while she tried out all her intellectual, sexual and psychological remedies for their failing relationship. However, she didn't finally leave him alone until he said to her that he was no longer interested in a relationship with anyone.

He found himself throwing her card in the bin. He went to fetch more coffee and dates, then took out his diary and a few sheets of paper and sat down to make calls. He pounced on the telephone as if he had only just discovered its existence. He noted down the dates of public auctions; he rang the Royal Academy, Leighton House, and a few galleries. The enthusiastic responses to his calls restored his sense of well-being – this was ideal, a life shared between the two places: London and Oman. He rang Sotheby's. 'Nicholas here. I came back this morning.'

The more calls he made, the more he felt he'd not left London at all. As life streamed back into his flat he became increasingly pleased with the Omani dagger, but he was tired from the journey and decided to catch a couple of hours' sleep before doing any serious work. As soon as he put his head on the pillow he had a vision of Lamis and the way she'd accepted her passport, as if he'd been handing her something rare and precious. He recalled the pleasant intimacy of the journey from Heathrow in the minibus with the other three Arab passengers. He sat up, checked the time, and called his secretary in Oman. When he answered, he asked what the name 'Lamis' meant, and held the line, waiting, until the secretary came back to him and said, 'Lamis – it means "soft to the touch".'

When, in the minibus, he'd asked how to pronounce her name, she'd stressed the 'm' and the 's', showing even white teeth. She had beautiful, delicate hands and, like most Arab women, her hair was coal black, a long river held in at the nape of her neck.

He had noticed that when she replied to the stinging questioning of the Moroccan woman, she spoke softly, with a hesitant manner, and he remembered that he'd thought she could have stepped down from the temple walls in Khajuraho. Her dark wide eyes looked newborn, as if she were staring around trying to comprehend everything for the first time, and they betrayed her. It was erotic. So was her big smile, her long hair. As she took her sweater off he couldn't help but notice her firm breasts. She seemed vulnerable, uneasy, not composed as he'd first thought. He wondered if she were ill, although she looked healthy enough. He couldn't bring himself to ask her if anything was wrong. Even though most of the Arab women living in London insisted they were modern and didn't conform to the Oriental stereotype, he felt that an invisible barrier separated him from them once he began to work at Sotheby's. There he met Arab women who wore smart, expensive clothes and had elaborately styled hair. Did they set themselves apart, or feel superior? He never looked at them for too long or too directly. Whether they were art students or prospective buyers, he never dared do more than glance in their direction, even though he was often in the more powerful position as he explained the details of this or that antique.

He was also confused by the way their entire personalities seemed to change, chameleon-like, so swiftly. Despite their well-groomed appearance, their mild way of talking, the Arab women who arrived at Sotheby's showed sudden bursts of ferocity and equivocated as they tried to pump him for information about the prices he expected certain articles to reach at auction or what sums the other Arabs might bid. When he discovered that these women were fasting during Ramadan he was completely lost. He tried to enquire, without giving offence, how it was that they were fasting and yet didn't wear the veil, only to become more perplexed by their response: 'How are the two things connected?' But Lamis had seemed somehow different. With a small stab of excitement, he remembered that he'd overheard her mention that she was divorced.

The phone rang. It was David, an ex-colleague from Sotheby's, asking whether the Omanis were interested in the gazelle. A tenth-century gazelle that had stood in a pool for hundreds of years in the gardens of the Umayyad Madinat al-Zahra near Córdoba – a palace with about five hundred rooms for men, two hundred for women, and fifty servants who fed leftovers to the peacocks, scattered seed for the birds and tore up twelve hundred loaves of bread a day to feed the fish in the palace ponds – before ending up in an Austrian castle. Had Nicholas returned to London to bid for it? The gazelle was a rare piece. It would fetch one of the highest prices paid up until now in an auction of Islamic artefacts.

'Can I ring you back, David . . . later this evening, or tomorrow morning? I have to dash.'

Nicholas left his flat and went down a side street to his car which he had left in residents' parking just off Eccleston Square. A neighbour opened the window to tell him that he'd chased away some youngsters the other day. 'They probably assumed the car was abandoned, you know. Next time you go away, perhaps you could get somebody to drive it for you from time to time. That would help.'

Nicholas thanked him, feeling both a little annoyed and grateful. London was less anonymous than he'd assumed. But perhaps he should sell his car, or give it to his parents.

He drove along Park Lane up to Marble Arch then towards

Edgware Road where Amira lived. He parked around a corner and walked, observing the familiarity of the surroundings. The word 'halal' appeared on all the restaurants and supermarkets. The Arabs used it for women and for meat – why? Perhaps if he understood more of their language, he would be able to solve the enigma of their personalities, their customs and culture. A man accompanied by his wife was looking at every woman who passed; the wife meanwhile was muffled from head to toe, her face masked. A Filipina maid was with them, dragging a child along with one hand; the wife held on to the other, and both women carried shopping bags full of bananas and melons. He suddenly wondered whether Lamis shopped here for Arab food. Two men were discussing some important topic, each touching his prick in turn, as if pressing a button to make his voice come out of his stomach, and they wore boots festooned with silver circles and buckles which struck the street's surface as they walked.

The smell of un-English food wafting from the entrance of Amira's block transported him back to Oman with its private houses and permanently drawn curtains, heavy and inert, as if made of concrete. Amira stood at the door dressed to kill: ludicrous lipstick, not helped by the smudge of it on her teeth, green eye-shadow to match the buttons of her suit, which threatened to burst apart each time she talked, and shiny bouffant hair.

'Have I come too early?'

'No. Not at all.'

She was wearing perfume that enveloped her like a garment.

Nicholas blinked. The room was decorated with prints in gold frames depicting scenes from romance and legend: a girl was carving her lover's name on a tree trunk and wiping away her tears; a naked woman was lying face down with an eagle perched on her bottom, spreading its wings. 'A real find in Bayswater one Sunday,' proclaimed Amira, when she saw where Nicholas was looking.

She went behind a small bar that occupied one corner of the room, and asked him what he'd like to drink.

'Do you have wine? Red or white. I don't mind which.'

There were flowered curtains and fake gilded Louis XVI sofas; a couple had broken backs, revealing the plaster under the gilt. A glass tabletop rested on a giant metal scorpion, or was it a spider? Two black birds with gold eyes, beaks and claws, were fighting for possession of a large egg, like the ball in a lavatory cistern, mounted on a gold stand.

'Is it coriander or cumin that I can smell?'

'You must be hungry. Shall I order some food from the Lebanese restaurant now?'

'I'm not hungry, just curious.' Nicholas asked, 'Did we arrange to meet at eight?'

'I've forgotten. Eight or nine, it doesn't matter. Oh, Samir called and said he was still waiting for the monkey to go to the toilet! He won't be able to get here.'

'Oh, he rang me . . .'

'I gave him your number.'

'He was making me laugh. Then he hung up. I think it was turning out well enough. And Lamis, have you heard from her?'

'Lamis hasn't called. I don't know her number. Do you?'

'No.'

'She's sure to come. We Arabs are always late.'

The telephone rang and Nicholas's heart jumped. It was bound to be Lamis giving her apologies.

Amira spent ages looking for the phone, and Nicholas became annoyed, disappointed. It was over before it began. Lamis had vanished from his life. But he knew where she lived. He felt encouraged. He would write her a note. What would he say?

The phone was still ringing and Nicholas was tempted to join Amira's search. 'Hello,' she finally answered in a subdued tone and a slightly different accent. 'One moment, please, one moment.'

She winked at Nicholas. He jumped to his feet to talk to Lamis. Amira continued to talk into the phone.

'Hello. Yes, this is Amira. It's lovely to hear from you. It doesn't matter!'

49

'Is it Lamis? Get her number!'

'Tomorrow's fine. Sleep well!'

Amira hung up and burst out laughing. 'Lamis must have bewitched you! No, it wasn't Lamis.'

Nicholas laughed, wishing he could suggest that they go and fetch Lamis. He sat on a sofa that jutted out into the room.

Amira poured a glass of whisky, added ice and offered it to Nicholas.

'Thanks.' Nicholas accepted the drink that he hadn't asked for. 'What do you think it's best to do?' he asked.

'We'll wait half an hour then order dinner here in case she comes late.'

'Do you suppose something's happened to her? She was rather subdued on the drive into London.'

'Light-headed. She probably hadn't eaten anything because she wanted to be a size zero. I'll order some food. What do you think?'

'Shall we wait? I'm not really hungry, are you? So, do you live alone? Do you work?'

'My husband's in Dubai and I work in precious stones. More whisky?'

But Amira wasn't like the Arab women that Nicholas met in Oman at cocktail parties, who didn't listen or concentrate on what was being said. Their eyes roamed over their surroundings, seeing nothing; they were scared of their husbands; sometimes they crouched, silent and catlike, afraid even to make their necklaces stir. Nor was she like the Arab women he'd seen on the beach, who lay under the palms in their smart bathing costumes, their varnished toenails like painted lips on the sand, indifferent to their surroundings and especially to foreign visitors. Was it their lack of curiosity or, as he'd wondered in a moment of vanity, did they consider him intrinsically uninteresting as a blond man with a hairless chest?

They wore earphones, listened to Walkmans; Western pop singers caressed their eardrums, and Hollywood movie stars their eyes, creatures like the constellations in the sky, of different clay from ordinary mortals.

Amira stood up. Nicholas heard the ice clinking in her glass as she put it down somewhere behind the sofa. Suddenly he felt her take hold of his shoulders. It was warm in the flat and he had removed his jacket. Her nails dug into him, scraped over his shirt. Surely she was not trying to seduce him? She was pressing her chest against the back of his neck and he felt the heat of her breath. She slipped her hand down his shirt and he bent forward away from her, although he was reluctant to hurt her feelings.

'I'm sorry, Amira,' he said. 'You gave me a shock. You're an Arab woman, and I don't know what . . .'

'However hard they try, they can't imprison my body. I can be myself with you. I knew that even if I threw myself at you you wouldn't judge me too harshly.'

He was tongue-tied, conscience-stricken.

'I'm sorry I . . .'

'I know. I know. A man isn't an umbrella. Press the button and up it goes.'

Although he was utterly embarrassed, Nicholas had to laugh at Amira's way of expressing herself. This defused the situation and, as Nicholas left, she leaned forward and kissed him on his right cheek, then his left, then his right again. 'Three times, that's how we do it,' she pronounced.

On the way back to his car, Nicholas noticed an Arab man negotiating a price with an Arab prostitute, in English, and Edgware Road seemed suddenly very much part of London after all.

Chapter Two

I

It was a cat that met Lamis when she pressed the buzzer at the arranged time and the entrance door opened. She followed the cat up the stairs to the attic, where the English teacher was drinking coffee and looking out over Primrose Hill.

'Do come in, Lamis. Have I pronounced your name correctly? I hope you don't mind me not coming downstairs. Please. Sit down. Tea? Coffee?'

'Nothing, thank you.'

The cat circled Lamis, rubbing against her dress, her shoes, her bag.

'She wants to get to know you. Is she bothering you?'

'Not at all.'

'So you want to perfect your English?'

'Yes.'

'May I ask why?'

'I want to live in London.'

'Where are you living now?'

'In London.'

'When did you arrive?'

'Thirteen years ago. But I don't feel as if I've been living here. I've stayed within a completely Arab environment.'

'Of course. You needed your Arab community, especially if you had to leave because of a war . . . the Gulf War?'

'I left before that.'

'Yes, of course. The Gulf War already seems so distant.'

The teacher sat in an armchair, and asked Lamis to sit too.

'I'd like to ask you a few questions, if you don't mind,' she continued. 'This is important because, if you take lessons with me, it's not only your way of speaking that will change. The movements of your tongue, everything related to your voice and larynx will have to change their habits radically. But it's not just your pronunciation – it goes deeper than that. Arabic is your mother tongue – altering the way you speak affects your personality inside.'

'I understand.'

'I'd like to know why, after living here for thirteen years, you've decided you want to acquire an English accent. And why did you choose to come here, to England, rather than some other country in Europe?'

'I came to London because I was going to marry an Iraqi, and he was already living here. But we're divorced now. I have a son here, who's still at school, and I've realised I want to assimilate. I need to look for work. I think having an English accent could be the key.'

'In other words, you've taken England as your second home.'

'No, as my first home. I left Iraq when I was twelve years old. I don't think I'll ever live there again.'

'So, you're pretty determined. That's good. Right.'

The teacher talked so much that Lamis began to feel sleepy. That's the English, she thought, always dissecting everything and looking on the black side. Surely it's not impossible to learn to speak English like the English, without all these dire warnings.

The teacher scolded the cat for knocking a pen and a sheet of paper to the floor, and trying to do the same to a big dictionary. She apologised to Lamis for the interruption – there was nothing the cat liked better than to see things fall. 'I'm sometimes afraid she'd enjoy watching herself falling from the attic window.'

Fifty minutes later Lamis left holding an exercise sheet with instructions to practise the top two lines. The teacher's final words of advice rang in her head like a bell: 'Turn on the television. Go to the theatre or the cinema every night if you can, and talk to your English friends. Keep away from anything Arab, even in your mind. You should stop eating Arab dishes, because subconsciously you'll be saying their names.'

'All right. I'll try.'

Lamis congratulated herself on having ventured out to see the English teacher. Earlier that morning she'd been on the point of ringing up to cancel; she'd stood paralysed in front of her bedroom window, having woken up with her heart palpitating, dreaming she was still in Dubai. She opened the curtains – curtains made all cities the same, hiding the outside from view and leaving you alone with your fears – and gazed out at the BT tower in the distance. She looked down at the yard on the other side of the street, dotted with tubs of flowers, and at a woman changing a child's nappy in the flat opposite. Turning round, she could see the cardboard boxes and suitcases heaped up in the hall. She left the room and stood over them for a moment, like a fox watching its prey, uncertain whether to strike. She went to call her son's school, but put the receiver down as soon as someone answered – what could she say to him? That although he was her son and she was his mother they were going to live apart and just meet from time to time? She looked surreptitiously through the window again. There were the office workers already crouched over their desks in the opposite block, and the comical-looking pipes resembling metallic plants that belched out smoke from the office roof.

In the morning the BT tower changed from a Disneyland creation studded with coloured lights to a dismal grey watch-tower. From the bedroom window she could also see expanses of cement with grass breaking through the surface, a church dome in a beautiful verdigris green that seemed out of place, and a single tree trying its best to survive in the midst of all the bricks and mortar.

In Najaf, the holy city of Iraq where Lamis was born and raised, she had had to steal looks through closed window shutters; the tiny bathroom window was deliberately designed to be too high for anyone to see out of or into. The furtive, youthful exchange of glances reached its peak during the religious celebrations of Ashoura, when the young women peeped out from under their black veils, and the young men peered through the blood running down their cheeks while they struck their heads with swords, and called out the names of the martyrs, dead for over a thousand years: 'Haydar, Haydar, Haydar, Abbas, Abbas, Abbas.'

That woman who was arranging her child's clothes in the flat opposite would have no idea a city like Najaf even existed.

Lamis saw her neighbour close the curtain, move it aside a fraction. She had her son in her arms. Did she think Lamis was spying on her?

After she had left the English teacher, Lamis had continued to walk, confident that she would not run into her mother-in-law or her husband in the streets of Primrose Hill, and hopeful that the speech lessons would enable her to discover the other London – or Londons – that the native Londoners knew and lived in. She thought of Elissa, the Phoenician princess who founded Carthage in spite of her brother's opposition. Like her, she wanted to stretch the boundaries. When Elissa's brother grudgingly granted Elissa a piece of land no bigger than an oxhide, Elissa asked her followers to stretch the fibres of the skin lengthways and widthways, width-ways and lengthways, until she'd finally outwitted her brother: her kingdom reached right to the seashore.

Lamis moved between cafés and streets. Looking around her, she studied the little front gardens planted with flowers and shrubs: she glanced into the front windows of houses and flats where the occupants had placed a bouquet in a vase or a rocking horse to gladden the eyes of the passers-by. Previously Lamis assumed that anyone who lived in these places must be happy. With an unpleasant twinge of misery and irritation, she remembered the curtains and the bunch of flowers on the table in her own flat, the one she'd shared with her husband and Khalid; right now her husband would be clutching his mobile phone, his mother would be sipping coffee and, at half-term, playing with her grandson, the television blaring on and on.

Further along Lamis noticed two pieces of tinfoil stuck on a branch: each had a black circle in the middle like an eye – they *were* eyes. They were attached to some bushes growing together, clipped into the shape of some kind of animal with a tail.

It was the first time she had laughed since returning to London from Dubai, apart from being amused by the Lebanese man with the monkey. I should apologise to the Moroccan woman for not going to dinner that evening we arrived back, she thought suddenly.

Whoever transformed those shrubs into the form of an animal must be creative, with a sense of humour; perhaps it was someone like her father. On a visit to London a few years before, her father had shown no interest in the exhibits at the Boat Show at Earls Court; instead he'd wanted to know about the unfamiliar flowers planted around the displays.

She glanced over the hedge into the front room of the house. She could see a packet of China tea on the kitchen table. Was it a woman who'd pruned the bushes this way? She walked on, then a sound made her stop, turn round. A short man carrying a shopping bag – an orange protruded from the top – was opening the gate.

'Excuse me,' Lamis said.

He looked at her without speaking. He was middle-aged, nice-looking.

'Is that yours?' she asked, pointing at the topiary. 'Is it a dragon?'

'Well, yes, it's part of the garden. Actually, it's a dinosaur.'

He turned away and went up the front path. He seemed to be in a hurry. Perhaps he didn't want to talk to a woman who couldn't tell a dinosaur from a dragon.

The infrequency of taxis in the street troubled Lamis. But why? What was the hurry? she asked herself. She could walk from here to her flat, even though it would take an hour. Why was she worried about finding a taxi? She could take a bus or go on the Underground. A taxi was not a security blanket, or a buoy to hitch up to in the city. She wouldn't get lost. She had eyes and ears. She could read the names of the streets and understand directions. She could wander about, stop and eat somewhere. But she arrived at a main road and stood, feeling guilty, impatient, waiting to flag a taxi, just as she had in the past, when she'd imagined everyone anxiously waiting for her at home, and she only relaxed when she saw a taxi for hire and was safely inside it.

She entered her flat with a pang of regret; no one with whom to go over the events of her day: the English lesson, the walk that stretched the boundaries of the oxhide, the few hours that were taking on the gloss of happiness.

The phone rang and she went to pick it up immediately. Belquis was on the line, reproaching her for not being in touch. 'Oh Lamis. I just rang your parents in Dubai, and they told me what happened. I didn't know you'd come back, and it never crossed my mind that there'd be all that fuss about the poppies. I was really worried for you.'

Lamis tried to act naturally. She thought of explaining to Belquis that she'd taken a decision not to see anyone from her past, that her friendship with Belquis was mainly due to her marriage. But she couldn't bring herself to say anything and, with a tearful sense of defeat, she agreed when Belquis suggested they meet at Leighton House where there was a performance and exhibition to celebrate Lord Leighton's centenary. As soon as Lamis put the receiver down, however, the winds of normality blew over her, and she decided to ring her son's school once more. The secretary told her to try again in two hours. Lamis hesitated then, on an impulse, left her name with a message for Khalid: 'This is his mother. I've just arrived back, and I miss him very much.'

It's the truth, she told herself as she hung up. I'm his mother even if I have divorced his father. I'll always be his mother and nobody can take that away from me.

With a burst of enthusiasm, she circled the boxes in the hall, and opened one of them and took out a package. As she began to undo the wrapping a pair of feet belonging to a small ivory statuette of a

Japanese woman emerged. She had the feeling that those feet were going to trample on her fingers and she rewrapped the figurine and replaced it in the box. She had packed other items that she liked better, which her mother-in-law had criticised because they did not broadcast their price or because it was not immediately obvious where they had been bought. Her mother-in-law once told Lamis that the wife of an acquaintance had half a million pounds sterling on her back at a charity ball.

'How do you know?' Lamis had asked in annoyance.

'I added up the cost of her clothes and jewellery on a calculator, because I knew the price of everything she had on.'

At the thought of this, Lamis nearly went off the idea of going to meet Belquis. She wandered into the kitchen and switched on the kettle to make a cup of coffee. The smell of the coffee instilled a spirit of adventure in her and she hurried to dress, thinking sentimentally of the Nescafé advertisement with the girl by the sea who wipes away her tears, tastes the coffee, and the sun comes out and the music plays:

I can see clearly now the rain has gone . . .
It's gonna be a bright, bright, bright, sunshiny day.

She decided to dress differently. She wanted Belquis to see her as someone who was happy to be divorced, free: neither repressed nor reckless, but balanced and composed. She chose a see-through shirt with bold designs over a white camisole and wide trousers. Instead of their uniform of high heels, she wore flat shoes with long tips, like a pair of Aladdin slippers. She fastened her hair loosely at the back; it looked as if it might come undone at any moment.

'Leighton House, please. Holland Park.'

'What?'

'Leighton House. Lord Leighton's house in Holland Park.'

'Oh.'

The taxi stopped in front of the house. The depression that had returned to Lamis during the journey lifted as she smelled a sweet fragrance and caught sight of the tall trees, but then she made out Belquis's hairdo and her spirits sank again. Belquis stood looking at her watch; she patted her hair and adjusted her shirt collar.

It took Lamis back to the past, to the cult of the single brand: the Chanel bag, the Chanel buttons: the intertwined 'c's, like a pair of forceps, signalling that their wearer was entitled to be part of the circle. It reminded Lamis of the numerous charitable functions where the women vied with each other over their clothes and social status. Women who took classes at Sotheby's and Christie's and elsewhere, in table decoration, the English tea ceremony, geology – with special reference to precious stones – the history of chocolate, bridge, flower arranging. Afterwards they met in a restaurant, feeling that they'd earned it, confident that they could say they hadn't wasted their time in this country. Belquis was like them, and at the first suggestion that Lamis would divorce, she'd been like a hen pecking insistently at the ground and wailing, 'You mustn't divorce, you can't.'

'But I get nausea and feel faint, sick. I'm not happy.'

'Perhaps you've got an inner-ear infection or a tapeworm, or you've been eating too much chocolate.'

Belquis had advised Lamis to try Feng Shui to gain peace of mind, and although Lamis did not really believe in it she had gone so far as to change the iron bedstead and the cloudy mirror and put flowers by the bed. The flowers made her throat tickle, and her husband complained constantly of a headache and woke her up every night to ask her to get him an aspirin.

Lamis drew back. She had to get away. She couldn't face Belquis. She edged back out of the entrance; she stayed close to the wall and scanned the cars on the road, praying she'd see a taxi with its light on.

How is it that Belquis doesn't mind waiting for me for three-quarters of an hour? she wondered. She's loyal and generous, that's all, and I ought to be ashamed of the way I'm behaving. I should go up and hug her, and instead I'm running away. I'm afraid that when I look at Belquis it'll be her husband's face I see. He'll be hiding behind her hair, telling her off for still talking to me.

Many of the women she knew during her marriage had the strange habit of metamorphosing into their husbands on certain occasions, especially at charity balls, and taking on not only their names but their physical appearance. Lamis used to find that she was talking to an ambitious building contractor, instead of his serene wife, or realise that Nirmin and her necklace studded with precious stones had disappeared, and in her place was her diplomat husband nervously straightening his tie. Even Evelyn, the foreigner who made candles, had been transformed into her husband in public, a broker stowing files away in a briefcase. She supposed that they probably saw Lamis herself in the guise of her ex-husband, smoking a fat cigar and receiving people, holding forth on his political views: 'I've tried everything. I've made my fortune. I'm in my fifties, I've achieved what I set out to, and now I want to go into politics.'

Down the street Lamis saw a taxi with its light on and put her hand out, but ahead of her she saw Belquis rush out of the garden and beat her to it. Lamis walked back and re-entered the garden, unflustered, as if she had just arrived. She looked at her watch, expecting to hear Belquis's voice calling, 'Lamis, Lamis.'

As if on automatic, she paid for a ticket and joined a group of five people who were sipping champagne. To the others' surprise, since a glass of champagne was included in the price of the ticket, Lamis refused a glass. A guide led the group towards the museum door, through which could be heard English voices, interspersed with the rattle of dishes and cutlery and the ring of crystal: 'Of course, your excellency, would you like more cognac?'

'Are you going to play Brahms?'

The guide was slender, elegant. She gestured to indicate that the group should follow her. They went into a dining room where a waiter was eyeing a table on which could be seen the remains of a meal: crusts of bread, dishes of grapes and cheese, and lilies and candles. He began collecting up the dessert plates, including a

60

plate that had not been touched. The voices came again: 'The sauce was splendid. My compliments to the chef.'

'Thank you, your excellency.'

An actor entered who looked like a young painter. Although Lamis did not understand their conversation, she listened carefully and eventually worked out that he was an up-and-coming artist who had criticised Leighton's art: he had accused Leighton of being tied to privilege, of being unable to escape his aristocratic birth, and now he wanted to apologise. Could the waiter arrange an appointment? Lamis could not take her eyes off the actor; she stared at the veins standing out on his temple. Lamis imagined herself stealing glances at a man like that from a place at the head of the table in the tableau. He would show her his paintings and she'd listen to him, then she'd rise from her seat trailing her long dress behind her like a peacock's tail, disregarding the silver cutlery, the crystal, the vase of flowers, the carafe of wine, a half-empty glass and even his paintings, and approach the end of the table, where she'd stop and offer him her mouth.

Lamis caught a phrase in the actor's speech: 'a lotus in Holland Park', and gazed past him, at the purple walls and the Persian rugs. The rest of the group began to move on. The guide looked at Lamis sharply and asked her to hurry. An actor cloaked from head to toe in a white abaya was waiting in front of closed doors. He delivered a welcome peppered with Arabic, 'Greetings, Hajj Abdullah, Glory be to God', before he flung open the doors to a vista from *One Thousand and One Nights*, and the brink of the abyss.

Turquoise domes overhead, brilliant tiles depicting birds drinking from fountains, borders of white and black and grey mosaics, Victorian columns holding aloft Qur'anic verses painted in blue.

Lamis did not share the wonder expressed by the rest of the group. She gazed around at the various shades of turquoise, the domes of the mosques, with a feeling of familiarity. Behind saffron tiles, mausoleum walls and wooden lattices, she could envisage women who were desperate to become pregnant, to see their husbands return, or to be cured of illness; women whose features were blurred behind the circles and squares of the carved screens. She tried to remain unmoved, and yet the sound of the muezzin affected her: when she was a child her father had taken the call of the muezzin as an opportunity to hide in the basement and play his lute undetected. Incense drifted through the room. Its fragrance distracted her; it infiltrated the dusty weave of the Persian rugs and the crevices between the floorboards, drowning out the perfume from the Smarties-coloured orchids dotted here and there. A member of the group whispered, 'It's like being in church.'

'It's incense,' his companion replied. 'Frankincense.'

'Frankincense comes from the Arab world.'

'Of course. The Three Kings and all that.'

The group moved on. They viewed Lord Leighton's studio, a crucible of ideas, colours, dreams of faraway countries, all together in the convolutions of a single brain; traces of anyone who had ever sat in the room, lain down, wept, laughed. The atmosphere of the past hung on in this little portion of space, nestling in the high corners, out of reach.

Lamis was irritated by the actress in the studio. She knew she could have played the part better. She doesn't know how to lie on the sofa, she thought, or to look out through the wooden lattices. They frame images engraved on our collective memory, not theirs. I know what those silent artefacts would like to say. I know their history and what they've seen. If only I could lie there while Lord Leighton mixes his colours and silence envelops the house and the wind rustles in the trees.

Lamis opened her bag, looking for a piece of chewing gum. She wished something would happen, but what?

She wanted to be part of a larger group that night, with a focus, a purpose. Perhaps this was what she should do in the evenings from now on. Explore the lives of others. From Lord Leighton to where? Why should everyone have to be atomised, discrete, a separate individual? What if the eye that watches over existence was exhausted, and wanted to sleep?

Every time anyone in the group exhaled, there was a whiff of wine or champagne. They walked on. Suddenly Lamis was in darkness again. There were candles flickering here and there, on the staircase, and at doorways, giving an air of solitude to the house.

Somebody brushed against her shoulder. She saw the gleam of spectacles and white teeth. There was the sound of breathing. A woman's voice said, 'Sorry.'

The warmth of the passing intimacy receded and Lamis was aware of being on her own again. The room seemed empty. One of these people must be feeling as she was now, but not making a move. Wasn't this, too, how the English were?

The people in the group dragged themselves along as if mesmerised by the sound of their own footsteps on the wooden floors and the Persian rugs. They looked at one another only briefly, by way of greeting, when they came face to face with some other member of the group in the dim light. Then they were at the end of the route: the room where Lord Leighton had coughed his last.

She couldn't believe that this had been his bedroom. It was a hermit's cell: a simple bed against a bare wall. At night Lord Leighton had withdrawn into himself, away from beauty's lure.

Lamis came out light-heartedly, her guilty conscience about Belquis gone completely. She could never return to her previous life, not even for a moment, and she was glad she was divorced. She wandered into the bookshop thinking that if Belquis had been sincerely interested in the exhibition, she would have gone in on her own as well. Belquis only wanted to find out exactly what had happened to Lamis in Dubai and, in exchange, Belquis would have told Lamis exactly what people were saying about her, and the latest gossip about her former mother-in-law. Then of course Belquis would also have been able to let the others know that she had been to the exhibition and to report how amazing it was, and feel superior.

Lamis decided to buy a book about Lord Leighton. She was in the process of making her choice when she abandoned the idea, put the book down, and hurried out to buy another ticket for the tour. She had seen the Englishman, Nicholas, the one who found her passport and who insisted on helping her carry her suitcase to the entrance hall when they dropped her off from the minibus.

He was talking to a woman in her forties.

Lamis went up to them. 'Nicholas, do you remember me? I shared a taxi with you.'

'Oh! Lamis. How wonderful. How are you? Sorry, Pamela . . . Lamis.' He introduced them, adding, 'We waited for you that night.'

'It's nice to meet you,' Lamis said. 'Are you taking the tour?'

'Not me,' Pamela snapped.

'Pamela's one of the creators of the show,' Nicholas said, 'and well, yes, I'd love to take the tour. Twenty minutes in the nineteenth century. Not a bad idea at all.'

'Let me get both of you tickets, then,' Pamela said.

'I already have one.'

'Then I'll get one for you, Nicholas. Oh, I just remembered. We still owe you for the incense, don't we. For this time, and the last.'

'It's good that I stopped off in Dubai. I completely forgot about the incense when I flew to India.'

This time Lamis had no intention of letting the darkness impose itself on her. She knew the walls of the tour of Leighton House, and the steps and doors, like a blind man who has found out by repetition and practice how to avoid the pitfalls. And as a blind man finds his way to where he wants to be.

She pretended to be impressed by the performance although she was seeing it for the second time. Only when she smelled the incense and heard the call to prayer did she respond to the surroundings again.

'Like in church,' she whispered, imitating the Englishwoman she had heard.

'The incense is getting up my nose,' he whispered to her. 'I'm trembling. I want to confess.'

'Confess?'

He took hold of a strand of her hair and squeezed her hand. A sound came from him, of pain or pleasure. She did not understand until he touched her face, tracing his finger over her features as if he were drawing them. He did it again and she touched his finger, and then he kissed her very gently on the lips. She could smell the orchids and the white lilies that perfumed the place. She felt her heart flutter and then pound in embarrassment as Nicholas brushed her lips again as if they were alone. They were alone; the group had moved on to the next room. His mouth was like a bee that had discovered nectar. Then he pulled her along to rejoin the group as if nothing had happened, and she was not expecting it when he returned to her lips as if he'd come to pick up something he'd left behind. Strange things happen after a Badedas bath, and after a divorce, for she'd received her first proper kiss from a man.

Her grandmother used to say, 'Live and learn,' and now she was doing both.

On leaving Leighton House they strolled down Holland Park, past the lit and darkened houses. Lamis could not concentrate on what either of them said. His kiss was still breathing inside her. She did not know in which direction Nicholas was leading her as they walked, but realised that they'd made their way back to Leighton House, where Nicholas had parked his car. She was hoping that he wouldn't ask about her car. For the first time in her life, she was embarrassed at the thought of confessing that she couldn't drive. She was also hoping that he wouldn't ask about her occupation, but he hesitated, and then said, 'Are you going home? Shall I give you a lift?'

'Yes, thank you.'

Did he think that she wanted to leave? She'd been withdrawn during their walk. Maybe he thought she was regretting their kiss.

While Nicholas drove, Lamis regarded herself dispassionately, amazed at how, in the space of a few moments, she'd been stripped of her confusion and loneliness.

Everything seemed far away and unimportant: the divorce, the boxes and suitcases piled in the empty flat, learning to talk with an

English accent, the search for a job – as if all she desired was a man who would kiss her exactly as Nicholas had done, in the London night.

II

'Come on, let's take the bus, Amira. It's getting cold. When my make-up gets cold, it fades . . . believe me. Besides, the bus stop isn't near the Dorchester. Nobody will see us getting off.'

'But what about the tree guarding the hotel, with all its lights like hundreds of Rudolph-the-Reindeer noses?'

Amira and Nahid waited until they found a taxi. Amira told the driver to drop them at the Dorchester. At the hotel's entrance she tipped the porter five pounds, and the two women, pretending to be composed and sure of themselves, were ushered to a table in the lobby that was converted into a tearoom every afternoon, where they sat down, confident in the knowledge that the beauty of the surroundings, the melody from the piano, the dinner lights, the fragrance from the huge bouquet of flowers, created the essential European atmosphere that would summon two Arab punters in no time.

The arrival of an Arab entourage interrupted the hotel's usual routine: several attendants followed one woman, whose footsteps made no sound as they crossed the thick carpet and the mirror-bright marble floor. The black abayas worn by the women stood out against the starched, ice-white hotel tablecloths. Whispers rose above the sound of the piano, 'S . . . s . . . princess . . . princess . . .' and surged into the head waiter, pumping him with vitality and self-importance at serving someone as imposing as an Arabian princess.

The Princess was seated at a table. One of her entourage, an Englishman, spoke to a waiter; another, an Arab, turned his attention to the Princess's three women companions, then both men left the four women at the table.

'She must be a very important princess,' said Nahid. 'One day,' she joked, turning back to Amira, 'you'll be a princess.'

'But did you notice her hand? I think she has some sort of disease. It looked as if she was wearing a spotted glove.'

The two women sat mesmerised, still as statues, watching the Princess. Other people, Arabs and Westerners, were staring discreetly at the Princess's table, and the piano player started to show off.

'When I was a child the teacher asked me to return her teacup to the staff room.' Nahid spoke at last. 'I was so proud I put my own lips to the mark left by her lipstick before I put the cup down.'

Amira was not listening. She continued to keep her eyes fixed on the Princess's table. Another woman entered. Immediately the head waiter was beside her, a master of protocol, guiding her over to the Princess. The newcomer kissed the Princess on both cheeks, and then kissed her three companions, and one gave up her seat so the visitor could sit next to the Princess. Yet as soon as the woman sat down, her beauty, her expensive handbag, her magnificent jewellery, were eclipsed, even though the Princess had left her face plain, with no make-up other than the fading lipstick on her mouth. Her clothes were expensive but modest. She wore a diamond-studded watch on her wrist, and one ring. Her shining jet-black hair was her most attractive attribute. Her neck was fat; her arms, clothed in the fine wool of her jacket, were fat. Amira suddenly came to life.

'Please, Nahid, tell me the truth. Swear on the life of your mother. Am I as fat as the Princess?'

'God forbid, no. It's all in your mind. It's all because of Spare Tyres Muhammad. Just take a look at her enormous feet, will you. While your legs and feet . . .'

'OK. I'm not going to ask you again. You're not being honest with me. How can you see her legs, when her skirt reaches down to the floor?'

67

'Look at her ankles. Just look at them. They're like two garlic pounders.'

'OK, OK.'

So what if the Princess's feet were like two garlic pounders, thought Amira. Although her own legs and feet were very attractive, having nice feet and legs never made her secure or gave her assurance. Her feet never stepped on hotel floors and rested, one leg crossed over the other, one foot firmly rooted to the ground, safe in the knowledge that no one could ever chase them away. They never convinced her she would find a good punter.

The Princess was sitting at the table like a guru; her place in the world was secure from the moment of her birth, everyone in the palace waiting for her first cry. When Amira uttered her first cry, it was echoed by the disappointment and regrets of the women who attended her mother during her birth, who wished that this baby girl could return to the womb, and stay there while they prayed to God to change her sex.

Amira could imagine the Princess playing in the palace garden, while she sat with her brothers and younger sister around the radio in Morocco, listening to an Egyptian play. One of her brothers came in, screwed up his nose. What was that stink? Approaching Amira, he knew. His face showed his disgust. Amira's underpants. She had to queue for the toilet, and couldn't wait. Afterwards, there were no clean pants for her to wear. When Amira was ill in bed with a fever, only the cat noticed. Amira's teacher gave up on her parents and it was she who taught Amira how to clean her teeth, and to gargle with salt water. Amira started to steal money from anyone; she stole sanitary towels from shops to replace the rags that never absorbed the blood, and left her clothes stained. She stole hairpins and soap – she wanted to be clean and fresh, to meet the man of her dreams. One day she did, though his teeth were rotten; he told her he was going to get a university degree, and a job, and then he would be able to fix his teeth.

Amira's mother reneged on her promise to the family of Amira's fiancé to give Amira a trousseau of a lounge suite, refusing to sell her gold bracelets to pay for it. When Amira threatened to take her own life if her mother didn't fulfil her promise, her mother screamed and threw the pail of water at her that she'd been using to clean the house. Amira fled to the rocks by the sea but once there she changed her mind and decided to approach her aunt's husband and ask for help: he'd lived in London, he'd worked in a hotel kitchen. However, when she told him that she'd been going to kill herself he didn't ask why, he only shouted in an accusing tone, 'What's happened? You're not trying to tell me that one of my children has drowned?'

'Nahid, the Princess looks Moroccan too, don't you think?'

'And Egyptian,' Nahid responded. 'We're alike. Aren't we all Arabs?'

'I wish, I wish.'

Amira let Nahid take the first punter. She didn't want to work that night. She waited until the Princess decided to leave, then walked out behind the retinue, and observed that one of the companions was handing out money from a fistful of fifty-pound notes: to the piano player, to each waiter, the doorman, and one, two, three, four, five, six notes to the head waiter.

A driver with a Rolls-Royce was waiting for the Princess and her retinue. Watching their heads as the car drove off, Amira concluded that the Princess would never be left all alone whatever happened.

Amira walked down the steps of the Dorchester Hotel and gave the porter who opened the taxi door a ten-pound tip, promising herself that next time it would be fifty. She'd made a decision: she would never stretch out her hand for five hundred pounds again. She didn't want to remind herself that she used to accept three hundred.

She entered the taxi in a manner as unruffled and impassive as a Cleopatra carried by her countrymen. She spoke in a low, soft voice to the driver when she gave him her destination. Many dreams, cheerful ones, made her smile until she realised the taxi was passing Wasim's hair salon, and she tapped on the glass and shouted to the driver to stop immediately.

Wasim was working in the back room of the salon, the one reserved for veiled women, although, in fact, it was used by women who smoked, and by sex-starved women who enjoyed Wasim's touch. The voice of Warda al-Jazairiya came from the speakers and there were dishes of Lebanese food stacked on a tray in the corner of the room.

Amira waited while Wasim finished doing the hair of a woman in her fifties. He played with her hair, brushed the woman's cheek as he pulled her hair forward. The woman scolded him contentedly. If only I could pass myself off as a male hairdresser, thought Amira. I could manipulate these women as easily as chewing gum, and flirt with them even more outrageously than Wasim – they'd give me bigger tips than they do him.

'Wasim, I want you to tint my hair black, and straighten it like silk. I want it cut just below my chin, and no spray, no teasing, just shining like an eggplant.'

'I don't think that's a good idea. It will make you look hard. Believe me, Madame Amira, the older a woman gets, the lighter her hair should be. Now if you were fair-skinned, I'd be the one to suggest it; I'd be pleading with you to tint your hair blue-black, or tulip black.'

'Wasim, I know what I'm doing. Can you start now?'

'No way . . . tomorrow . . . any time tomorrow. By the way, do you want to see the wigs Bahia ordered?'

'Yes please.'

He looked into the mirror and gestured at an apprentice hairdresser. The young man opened a cabinet and brought over a bag of wigs, which Wasim handed to Amira. She picked out one after another, and finally chose a blonde wig. 'I'll try it on at home,' she said to Wasim, 'and decide whether it suits me. Either way, I'll bring it back tomorrow.'

She left and walked along Upper Berkeley Street. Noticing the back of the Cumberland Hotel, she remembered the Gulf man from the aeroplane – she was not only putting on weight, she was getting thick in the head as well! How could she have forgotten to tell Nahid about the Gulf man? But wasn't the tea at the Dorchester this afternoon a revelation?

Confidently she made her way towards the lift, carrying three bunches of flowers that she had bought opposite the Cumberland Hotel.

She knocked on the door of Room 609 several times, before a voice replied irritably, 'Who's there?'

'Open the door, if you're not dead already,' she said under her breath, and aloud, 'It's Amira. We met on the plane.'

'Amira?'

The Gulf man opened the door. He was dressed in pyjamas and bedroom slippers. 'Hello! How nice to see you! Come in!'

She handed him the bouquets of wilting flowers and he held them up to his nose and sniffed. 'Lovely! A prayer for the Prophet and his household. They're wonderful!' he exclaimed, although the flowers had no perfume.

Uncertain what to do with them, he eventually put them down on a table, on top of some books about London.

'I'd like to invite you to dinner,' said Amira, 'to welcome you to London.'

'It's late. I've had dinner. Why were you screaming on the plane? Don't you know that our lives are in God's hands?'

'I know. I was confused, that's all. Do you want to come out with me to take your mind off your eye operation? It's tomorrow, isn't it? We could go to a cabaret or walk in Edgware Road.'

'I can't. I have to stay here.'

'I booked a table in a restaurant. I wanted to invite you.'

'Shall I order room service for you?'

Amira declined and sat down next to him. He had not switched off the television.

'The operation is tomorrow, isn't it?'

'I hope so. It's a very simple process with lasers. I'm fed up with the eyedrops. They're making my life a misery, I tell you, especially at night, when my eyes give me a lot of trouble.'

71

'They'll examine your eyes tomorrow first. They'll have to be satisfied with them, otherwise they'll postpone the operation.'

'How do you know? Have you had it yourself?'

'What are these?' Amira pointed to her eyes.

'Eyes.'

'And this?'

'A nose.'

'And this?'

'A mouth.'

'And this?' She pointed at her chest.

He laughed.

'And this?' She pointed below her waist. She lay on the bed and with a gesture invited him to lie beside her.

'I knew you'd be good company. At Dubai Airport I wasn't quite sure whether you were a respectable married woman or a whore!'

As Amira stood up to leave, he asked her to stay another half-hour, until it was time for his drops. After about a quarter of an hour, Amira said briskly, 'Come on, then,' and administered the drops. Before she left the Gulf man gave her even more money than she had hoped for.

She walked along Edgware Road and saw European and Arab women, some in groups and others alone. As she passed the Moonlight Café the street was fragrant with the perfume of narghiles. Inside, she could see that the café was thronging with Arabs smoking, and she quickly realised what was going on: inside there were women like her stalking their prey, while the men didn't dare to glance once in the direction of their pursuers because their fathers- or sons-in-law were sitting beside them.

She stopped off for a shawarma sandwich at Ranoush Juice and saw that it was no longer patronised exclusively by Arabs. It was crammed with English customers, especially young men from the fashion world and the media. She went into the Ladies and sat hunched on a toilet seat, rummaging in her bag for the blonde wig. She put it on, then took out a large silk scarf and draped it over the shoulders of her suit. She adjusted the wig in the mirror and returned to the Cumberland. When she knocked at the door of Room 609 and there was no reply, she said to herself, 'You must have run out of strength. Did Amira wear you out?'

'Who is it?'

'This is Nawal. I'm a relation of Amira's.'

'Amira? Did you forget something?'

'No. I'm Nawal. A relation of Amira's.'

She waited almost five minutes and was about to knock again when the door opened.

'Hello. I was fast asleep.'

'Good morning.'

'Is it morning? Please come in.'

She went in and sat down shyly and hesitantly, keeping her eyes on the ground and rubbing her hands together.

'Amira called and asked me to visit you and say hello. She thanks you very much.' She glanced involuntarily at his expensive slippers.

'What did she really say?'

'That you were extremely elegant and a real gentleman. Imagine, she woke me up! She told me you were going to have an eye operation and would probably move back to your home and then I wouldn't have the chance to meet you because you'd be with your family. She said you were a really good person.'

'She must have said other things.'

'I'm embarrassed to tell you.'

'Don't be.'

'She said it was incredible, but you were better than a boy of eighteen.'

'I don't drink and I don't take any medicines. My conscience is clear, thanks be to God. But your voice is so like hers. It's amazing.'

She put a piece of gum in her mouth, hoping it would distract him from her voice. She helped him off with his pyjama jacket and stroked his chest, and he let out a sigh. She moved her hand down to waist-level and, as she expected, the fish was dead. What had happened earlier in the evening had been a reawakening of life, or a final explosion of life when death was looming on the horizon. She did not try again but moved her hand back to his chest.

'Is what's-her-name, Amira, your sister?'

'No, my cousin.'

'How blonde you are!'

'My mother's Dutch.'

'Praise the Lord! He didn't want to upset Mother or Father, so he gave you blonde hair and dark skin.'

'Amira told me she loved you. She was right about you.'

'She's a good girl, really. She put drops in my eyes. She screamed such a lot in the plane!'

'Shall I put more drops in for you now?'

'I don't know what the time is. I fell asleep.'

'Midnight.' She added on an hour.

'Shall I put the drops in?'

'It's meant to be every six hours,' he yawned.

'I'll wait two hours with you, then put the drops in. You should get into bed and rest.'

'And leave you? I couldn't!'

'The important thing is that you rest.'

They both stood up, but she sat down on the bed and held out her hand to him.

'So Amira said she loved me. What about you?' he asked.

She flopped back, shut her eyes and guided one of his hands to her breast and the other to her stomach. To her surprise he asked her to take her clothes off. She was afraid he would notice that her suit and underclothes were the same. She dismissed the thought when she saw his pupils, tiny and black, like the seeds she used to eat when she was a girl, back at home in Morocco, instead of scattering them for the pigeons. He lost himself in the folds of her flesh, murmuring indistinct words over and over again as if asking her where to begin.

She tried to help him but he was like a turkey-cock's wattle. She

74

writhed and groaned and heard a guffaw. He was laughing, slapping her gently. He turned her over on her back and held her tight, amused and affectionate, and tweaked the mole on her shoulder, shaking his head in disbelief. 'God forgive you! Admit it! You're Amira. Why did you lie? You went to all the trouble of dyeing your hair, changing your voice and your name, everything except that mole on your shoulder. Why didn't you come straight to the point? Admit it, Amira! Be honest. Let me hear you say it. You've fallen in love and can't keep away from me!'

Amira could not sleep. She tried Nahid's mobile phone but it was engaged. She wanted to tell Nahid about the idea that had attached itself to her like a blowfly attracted to the blue light in the butcher's shop.

However much a man such as the one from the Gulf wanted a fling with a foreigner, he was attracted by women of his own kind; it was they who held an aura of distance, of mystery. Or this is what Amira surmised: every time she picked up a copy of *What's On* and read the classifieds the call girls from the Gulf outnumbered those listed as Angie, Stars of Syria, Beauty of Lebanon and the rest. The page was almost full of Gulf names: Flower of the Gulf, Princess and the Angels, A Bedouin Girl in London.

She realised that circumstances altered the nature of men's fantasies. In London, what drew them was the notion of a woman who'd been hidden away in the dark, wrapped in a black veil, like a packet of dates or henna. She assumed that the names in the magazine dissipated the confusion and fear that the visiting men felt when they were faced with London, the big city, and its bewildering array of tightly clad arses; it reassured them that they would get what they wanted, in their own surroundings, and their own language, not in an English that either condescended to them or stole their money.

As a result, Amira had been inspired to reinvent herself as a precious jewel, accessible only to those who knew the secret. She would present herself as a princess, since she deserved to be one anyway. She already lived like one, sleeping until noon, adoring nice clothes and never picking up a dirty plate.

III

The interest that every colleague or acquaintance who bought and sold Islamic art began to show in Nicholas, once he started working on Sayf's collection in Oman, amused and disgusted him at the same time.

David was soon on the phone again. 'Nicholas, will the Arabs buy the gazelle? How high do you think they'll go?'

Sometimes he could not hide his annoyance when, like David, the person made it plain that he or she considered Nicholas an accomplice, a predator, seeking out any opportunity to take advantage of the Arabs. However, it had been Sayf who first approached Nicholas, and asked for his advice and assistance. It was just when Nichoias was starting to feel that life at Sotheby's had become impossible: Liz's gaze was boring into him daily, as if he himself were an artwork that she was trying to dissect in order to put it back together again the way she wanted.

'Do you mean Sayf? No, he won't buy it. He only collects Islamic daggers. Anyway, the gazelle would be out of his range.'

'Do you expect me to believe that there are prices which are beyond their range? Nicholas, please stop being evasive! Are you trying to tell me they know the actual extent of their wealth?'

'No, David. They're too busy trying to count it out on their fingers and toes . . . goodbye.'

After taking his degree in history at Oxford, Nicholas felt no desire to go on with the subject, and he acknowledged to himself that he'd made a huge mistake when he gave up his interest in astronomy, a fascination that dated back to his childhood, when he'd declared that he was going to discover his own star and build a rocket to take him up into the sky, and to a warm summer night on a Hampshire hillside as he lay on his back studying the stars and wondering whether, if his grandmother in London looked at the moon at that precise moment, their eyes would meet.

He had worked in different areas at Sotheby's before eventually settling into the Indian department. At that time London was witnessing a huge inrush of Arab collectors of Islamic art, and Sayf asked Nicholas for guidance over an Omani rifle inlaid with pinkish ivory which he wanted to bid for at a Sotheby's auction. The following day Sayf contacted Nicholas and asked him to accompany him to Spinks, where he'd seen another dagger that he was interested in buying. Nicholas declined but Sayf was insistent. 'I have confidence in you. I don't know why. Perhaps it's the way you look, and my sixth sense. Please!'

'Sorry, Mr Sayf. I can't. They're our competitors.'

However, after Nicholas and Sayf had lunch together and shared a bottle of very good wine, Nicholas did agree to go on his own to Spinks. The dagger had beautiful jade work on the handle, and Nicholas later advised Sayf to buy it.

Instead of thanking him, Sayf asked Nicholas to swear on whatever was dearest to him, his mother, fiancée, wife, that he'd not taken a commission from Spinks.

'Why do you ask, when you said you trusted me?'

'Because you insisted on going on your own to look at the dagger.'

Since this episode they had slowly established a trust between them. They became a team.

Nicholas saw his father's letter on his desk and decided to call his parents.

'Hello, Scott. How are you?'

'Nicholas, when did you get back?'

'A couple of days ago. From India, via Dubai.'

'India? Did you go on holiday?'

'I'm afraid not. I'd tracked down a prince in Madhya Pradesh – central India. He has the most exquisite dagger and, most fortunately, an astonishing rare seventeenth-century gold ball. To show them to me, he had to bring them hidden in his turban and cummerbund.'

'How extraordinary! Did you buy them?'

'Well, as you know, Sayf likes to haggle, especially with Indians. And he does it better than I do.'

'How is Sayf? Did you give him the Bible?'

'To tell you the truth, Scott, I didn't take it with me. I didn't think it would be exactly diplomatic.'

'Perhaps another time would be best. Your mother would like a word.'

'Nicholas. Hello, darling. Don't listen to him. Don't take the Bible next time either. I don't think it's a very good idea. It's a sensitive subject.' He heard her turning away to talk to his father. 'No, no.' Then his mother was on the phone again. 'Listen, Nicholas. The Muslims might think you were in Oman because of religion rather than your job, especially if they knew your father was a vicar.' She broke off again. 'No. I haven't finished what I want to say . . .'

However, Nicholas's father was back on the line. 'Hello, Nicholas. Do you know what your mother did? You know she thinks she's allergic to bee stings? Well, she was stung by one while I was away for the night, attending a funeral in London. She was afraid she was going to die – no, she didn't have an allergic reaction, although the sting hurt – but she thought we'd have to arrange for a post-mortem, so she caught the bee and put it in an envelope with a note to say this was the culprit, then prepared to die, lying there with her arms folded and the envelope on her chest. Let me tell you, I've never laughed so much in my life.'

His mother took the receiver. 'See how thoughtful I am, even when I'm dying.'

'Do you still have the envelope?'

'Of course.' She laughed.

'Helen, listen,' he said to his mother. He almost told her that he'd met someone and fallen in love, but instead he asked her, 'How are the self-defence classes?'

'Excellent. Can we look forward to seeing you soon?'

'Very soon.'

He replaced the receiver. His mother and some of her friends had taken up classes in self-defence after they had started to demonstrate against fox-hunting.

The phone rang and it was his father again.

'Nicholas, I've just remembered. I don't think I told you what happened to Harold when he was serving in the Sudan. One day, as usual, he asked the Sudanese driver, who brought the regular supplies to the church, if he'd like to rest before he set off again, and offered him a cup of tea. The driver noticed the sugar collected in the bottom of his cup. As there wasn't a spoon to hand, Harold stirred the tea with the big cross he wore round his neck. When the driver stood up to go Harold said to him, "Now there's a seminary in your stomach." The man belched suddenly and said, "And there's the first priest coming out of it."'

'That's a wonderful story, Scott, wonderful . . .'

'What I want to say is that there's a willingness for dialogue, whatever the religion, whatever the nationality.'

'Exactly. I know.' Nicholas nearly added that, all the same, it wouldn't be advisable for his father to wear his dog collar when he visited Oman.

'I saw Desmond at a funeral and when I told him you were working in Oman, he was amazed. He said he wouldn't have thought of you as the arrogant, aloof type who'd fall in love with the Arabs and then go off and work with them. I told him you weren't T. E. Lawrence or Doughty or Burton. It was simply that you'd been given this opportunity – God works in mysterious ways – and that now you have a very reasonable income, you even travel Club Class and a large house in Oman has been provided for you.'

'Scott, you forgot to tell him that I'm building the most

important collection of Islamic daggers in the world. Anyway, I must go. I'll see you soon. If you can't come up, I'll drive down.'

'It would do your mother good if we took the train up to London for a visit. Now, son, she's gone to answer the door, so I can say this to you. She's depressed.'

'What's the matter? Is it her health?'

'The usual thing. Don't worry about her health, it's fine.'

Neither of them spoke of what was on both their minds: Nicholas's mother was feeling worn down by continually having to scrimp and save. She had always regarded herself as a middle-class woman but the reality was that she and Nicholas's father lived like paupers. Nicholas decided that he should persuade both of them to visit him – he would take them to Burberry's and buy them new winter coats. At least they'd agreed to let him pay for their trip to Oman, if they ever finally went. He'd find a way to get around their pride.

Having made this decision, he stopped worrying about his parents. He went to his briefcase and took out the Polaroids of the jewelled dagger and the gold orb. They were magnificent. A wave of anxiety swept through him. Had he been wrong not to offer the Prince a down-payment? Should he have insisted that Sayf, whom he'd consulted over the telephone, agree to let him finish the deal once and for all? Could he trust the Prince to keep his promise not to sell the object before Sayf made the trip himself, to see them? But Nicholas thought back to his meeting with the Prince, and felt reassured.

The Indian Prince had locked the door. Then he drew the shutters and flicked on a tape, and the sound of Frank Sinatra, 'New York, New York', filled the room. Furnished with carved wooden tables, chairs and cabinets, the room was stifling hot, despite the fans revolving in the ceiling.

'I don't trust anybody,' the Prince whispered to Nicholas, 'not even my wife and children. I carry my inheritance from my father with me wherever I go, like a cat moving her kittens from place to place, to avoid greedy hands and mouths. My son sold my grand-father's rifle for the price of a dinner and a night out in Bombay.'

The Prince put his ear to the door for a few moments, and Nicholas was reminded of the thief in London who was identified not by his fingerprints, but by his earprint, because he always listened at doors before he forced them open. Having made sure that the room was secure, the Prince lifted his turban and took out a small bundle the size of an orange. He rearranged the turban on his head and loosened the cummerbund that was wound around his waist seven times, and then laid another parcel on the table, which he unwrapped first. Nicholas hid his dazzled reaction under a professional calm as he gazed in awe at the dagger. Its handle was encrusted with gleaming rubies and emeralds formed into flowers, set in a gold inlay of circles and squares. He suppressed another gasp as the Prince opened the round parcel he had taken from his turban and held out a jewelled honeycomb, a replica of a pomegranate with the outer shell removed to reveal the inner gold fibres protecting the ruby seeds. The whole thing was magnificently worked to size, the seeds held concentrically by a craftsman's measurement as precise as that of a butterfly's wing, only a hair's breadth between the rubies and the gold filigree, a perfect sphere.

'Seven centimetres in diameter?' Nicholas asked guardedly.

'No, five.'

'There's an orb like this one in the Persian crown jewels, but it's slightly bigger.'

The Prince nodded in agreement, although he had not previously known of the existence of the other orb. He said solemnly, 'They say my grandfather used to carry this around with him, and squeeze it to ease the pain of his rheumatism, not just with his hands, but between his feet, too.'

The two men laughed, although Nicholas was still slightly breathless. There was a knock at the door, and the sound of voices.

The Prince hid the pieces in Nicholas's bag then hurriedly rewound the sash round his waist and made sure that the turban was sitting properly on his head. He opened the door and a man and a woman carrying trays of food entered, bringing a delicious aroma of spices into the room.

At their arrival Nicholas relaxed, not only because he was hungry and liked Indian food, especially when it was prepared in private houses, but because he realised that the precious objects the Prince had shown him would not be going to a completely different environment. Oman was so much like India in many ways. Even the food smelled the same. Who could tell? Maybe the Indian Prince would be able to retrieve his heirlooms from Sayf in a few years' time, if that was what he wanted. Nicholas curbed his self-doubt and told himself he wasn't joining the ranks of those who plundered the cultural and spiritual heritage of a country. And when, later that day, he headed into Khajuraho with the Prince, through fields of vivid yellow mustard flowers and golden wheat, to tour the famous Nagara temple with its sensuous deities, the business of buying the orb and the dagger became altogether less urgent.

IV

Samir shouted, or was it the monkey? He ran along behind the taxi, his eyes starting out of his head as he watched the couple recede into the distance. He stopped another in the crush of traffic, and fright made his words come out indistinctly. 'Follow that bastard,' he told the taxi driver in Arabic. Then, in English, 'Bastard. He left me with this monkey I just delivered to him.'

The taxi driver's eyes jumped nervously away from the madman back to the steering wheel; he shook his head and roared off.

Samir looked about him, afraid of the street. He went into a shop that sold magazines and newspapers to ask directions to Edgware Road. He confided in the shopkeeper who looked Arab, dark, not English. The man heard Samir out but, at the end of his story, shook his head regretfully. 'I don't understand much Arabic,' he said. 'Take it to the zoo.'

Samir hurried back towards the flat where he'd been held prisoner, but it had spawned hundreds like it. 'Dear God, don't make it difficult for me,' he begged aloud.

He should have noticed something distinctive about the place, but how could he when the buildings were as alike as cloves of garlic? Not like Lebanon, where you could tell them apart from a shirt hanging out to dry, a canary in a cage, a pot of basil. If only he'd memorised the way the paint was peeling round the door. He pressed the bells in a number of buildings, calling, 'Hello. Hello,' and as his despair mounted he began to curse.

After a great deal of effort, he managed to disentangle himself from the monkey and put it on the ground. 'Go on, mama. You're a dog. Do you understand? Can you sniff out the place where we slept last night?'

The monkey froze for a moment and looked at Samir, then jumped into his arms again, wrapping itself around him. Samir thought of the Tabbouleh take-away, and of Amira. He should ask her for help. Where to start? The telephone booth on the pavement scared him. Would he be able to get out if he went in? Of course he would. He picked up the receiver but felt as if he couldn't breathe. He tried pushing open the door of the phone booth again and when it gave way easily he calmed down. He had the piece of paper with the phone number on it and the coins at the ready. The monkey grabbed the paper from him. Samir snatched it back, his heart beating furiously, then he kissed the paper joyfully because it wasn't ripped. Apprehensively he dialled the number. The coins would not stay in and kept falling straight through to the tray at the bottom. He banged the telephone. 'Have you got the runs?' he shouted.

He tried again and the same thing happened. He pushed the door open and asked a woman passer-by in the street to help him. But he did not listen to her explanation, and let the door bang shut because she started asking him about the monkey: was it a capuchin, how old was it, was it legal to keep a capuchin as a pet, where did he get it? Inside the booth Samir was looking at a card that showed a photo of two very beautiful young men, way superior to the cards of women in seductive poses stuck on the walls around the phone. He took the card and looked around as if he were stealing the crown jewels, then stuffed it in his trouser pocket. He had to get rid of the monkey now. He rotated like a spindle in a spinner's hand.

The best thing would be to go to the Tabbouleh take-away, where the Lebanese boys were. He understood them, and they understood him. Once Samir worked out which way to walk and spied the Tabbouleh in the distance, he calmed down. London was not as difficult to get around, or as big, as they said.

'The man called Faruq ran away and left me with the monkey,' announced Samir when he reached the restaurant. 'You've got to help me look for him. He's one of your customers. I want to talk to Amira. You must know her. She knows you. Here's her number.'

'No. We can't make private calls from here. There's a telephone downstairs,' answered one of the waiters.

'Take it to the zoo and get rid of it,' said another.

'I'm scared to do that. They'd start asking questions. I smuggled him from Dubai. I'll have to think of something else.'

The manager was watching and the youths returned to work. Samir went back out into the street and took the fork leading to the half-peeled-garlic-clove buildings. He stood peering up at the windows in the hope of seeing a curtain hanging down, or a broken chandelier. Two boys and their mother clustered round him. The woman asked if it was a capuchin monkey and if her children could stroke it.

'Take it. Take it. He loves children. He's very good-natured. His mother died, poor thing.'

The woman smiled and advised him to take it to a zoo in Dorset, which specialised in all types of monkey, then went on her way, although her children hung back defiantly.

Samir took two walnuts from his pocket and threw them on the ground. 'Run! Run!' he whispered in the monkey's ear. The monkey made a dive for the nuts, scaring the two children, and

Samir accelerated away but the monkey leaped at him and clung on even more tightly than before.

Samir spun round in distraught circles like a dervish, in the hope that the monkey would fall off. Then he murmured, 'Beloved Lord, release me from this monkey and I promise I won't flutter my eyelashes at a single blond.' He paused, then added, 'Not even a dark man, OK?'

As happens in stories or dreams, an immensely long car drew up almost at once, the driver opened the passenger door and an Arab man stepped out. The driver, who was English, greeted Samir politely and asked him where he'd bought the monkey and how much it had cost.

'Have it for nothing. Come on, we're brothers,' replied Samir, ignoring the driver and addressing the passenger directly.

'You're Lebanese? Pleased to meet you. The monkey's beautiful. Is there some reason why you don't want it?' he asked Samir, playing with a long, expensive-looking string of prayer beads.

'Uncle, it's in the best of health but its owner's dying and I'm leaving tomorrow.'

'Does it bite?'

'No. Not so's you'd notice, my friend, and who doesn't bite when he gets angry? My mother, God rest her soul, used to bite raw fish to make sure they were fresh. Please, do take it. There! Congratulations!'

The man laughed, then handed Samir two peach-coloured notes. The monkey tried to take them and Samir didn't stand in its way because the main thing was for the monkey to leave him. Lord, use a screwdriver to get it off me, if you need to.

The monkey leaped across to the other man, trying to pinch the prayer beads he was rattling in his fingers. The man let it play with them for a few moments, then put them away in his pocket. The monkey tried worming its way into his pocket, then changed its mind and fingered the man's moustache, disregarding Samir, who was calling, 'You naughty boy, you know what's best for you, don't you?' Then, turning to the man, 'He knows with an owner

85

like me he'll be homeless and hungry, but with you he'll live a life of luxury. He'll entertain you and be a good cure for stress! You're lucky!'

Samir held out a hand to the man in the car but the monkey shook it instead and took a comb and a brightly coloured handkerchief from Samir's jacket pocket. Samir walked off hugging himself, as if the monkey was still wrapped round him. He shook himself, like a bird trying to dry its feathers.

He would leave the next day. He would save five hundred pounds for his wife and children, and the rest he would spend here, because you should spend money in the country where you earned it – or so said his former neighbour in Beirut, Prosper Luna, originally Abd al-Ghani Qamr, who'd emigrated to Brazil and begun to collect his savings in a reed pipe for the day he returned to Lebanon. When he decided to go back home, he looked in the instrument, only to find that mice had eaten through the notes, layer by layer, so what was left looked like discs of Swiss cheese.

Samir pressed his face against shop windows. Beautiful clothes and even more beautiful shoes. He had to find a cheap hotel to spend the night in. He hurried back in the direction of the Tabbouleh.

'I'm not going there for any bad reason,' he assured himself. 'It's just that it's easy to call from there if the manager's not looking, and one of the boys must know a cheap hotel, and I'll buy a pistachio shirt and a purple tie. In any case, I prefer blond hair and blue eyes.'

But he was thinking of the shy youth behind the counter at the Tabbouleh who'd just smiled at him instead of joining the others gathered round Samir and the monkey. He'd been absorbed in cutting a tomato into a flower shape, and laying it in the middle of a bowl of hummus, then slicing pickles into flower stems and radishes into the flowers' leaves. He'd decorated the dish calmly and skilfully, a sleepy look on his face, his lower lip slack and inviting.

He was wasting his time with me, insisted Samir to himself.

I like blond hair and blue eyes. Just joking, Lord. I won't forget my promise to you.

A car horn blared as he was crossing the street, and he stepped backwards. The car stopped and the monkey's new owner lowered the window and called out to him. He must want to buy ten more monkeys, thought Samir. He bent down to talk to him and felt something climbing up his back as the English driver returned to the car. The monkey hugged Samir affectionately, squeezing him to make him walk on. 'Thanks, brother,' said the man. 'Your monkey's a little devil. It stole my prayer beads and the driver and I spent an hour getting it to open its fingers.'

Samir gave the monkey his sunglasses to distract it while he tried to persuade the man to change his mind.

'Give it a day's trial.'

'It attacked me too. Sorry, but no thanks.'

The car drove off and Samir yelled after it, 'What about your money? Who's the monkey now?'

The monkey bared its teeth in a grimace of happiness, clapped its hands, and curled its lips. It kissed Samir who suddenly felt contented. He kissed the monkey back. 'Just my luck,' he said.

Then he realised why he felt relieved the monkey had come back: he wouldn't have to keep his promise after all.

He carried on back to the Tabbouleh and ordered some food. The waiters raced here and there, busy with their customers. They brought him extra, and stood joking with him and the monkey and one of them suggested he should take up acting. Samir persuaded the biggest and most humorous of them, in a confidential whisper, to bring him the mobile phone, and he called Amira's number.

'Hello. It's Samir. No . . . It went to the toilet in the end, but the man ran off and left it with me . . . Vanished without trace, like a fart in a coppersmith's workshop, pardon my language. Tomorrow I'm leaving it at a church door, or the zoo. Can I come over?'

His arrival contributed to the confusion in Amira's flat. It was all an undifferentiated space; there was no privacy. Warda was playing on the tape machine and two women, Nahid and Bahia, were reading each other's coffee cups. There was a strong smell of Turkish coffee and Amira sat with her mobile on one side and the ordinary phone on the other, fluttering like a butterfly between them.

She asked him if he wanted tea, coffee, orange juice, but he told her he had to feed the monkey. He had bought a bag of food, which he insisted on taking to the kitchen. He breathed a sigh of relief when he found the sink was full of dirty dishes and stained coffee pots of various sizes, soaking, and the remains of leftovers from the night before. He'd been afraid of making a mess in her kitchen, but everything was ready for him to add the finishing touches before he indulged in giving it a thorough clean.

Samir tied the monkey to him like an African woman would a baby. He washed the dishes, then rolled up his trousers and bent down to clean the floor, and the monkey thought he was playing. When it saw him dancing to the music, and singing along with Warda, 'Aah aah aah', it became quite still, and began watching attentively like a man enjoying a show.

Amira insisted that Samir and the monkey should stay with her.

'No, Madame Amira. I'll come back and find you've hung yourself if I leave it here when I go out.'

'You should chain it up,' said Nahid. 'My uncle in Cairo had a monkey like that and he used to tie it up.'

'No, sister,' protested Amira. 'It's got a soul like us.'

'Don't people put leads on dogs? It's the same.'

Nahid's comment solved Samir's problem. He tied the monkey to the sofa and left. He scoured the streets, searching for a blond English boy among the dozens of Arabs. All the English he saw were either drunks or police. He'd imagined that, as soon as the plane set down in London, he'd see rows of English boys undulating like golden ears of wheat, in red jeans or leather trousers, walking hand in hand.

He had to find some nice clothes, but first he'd look for a church where he could leave the monkey the next morning. He would leave it on the doorstep so the vicar would find a monkey chained

in a basket, instead of a baby. Samir burst out laughing, then his
eyes fastened on a shop window and he decided he liked everything there. He was about to go inside when he noticed a beautiful
youth walking to and fro and looking around as if he were waiting
for him. Was it possible, when this street was so lacking in
Englishmen, that it should suddenly produce the flower of their
young manhood? Should he go in quickly and buy the pistachio
shirt of his dreams and come out wearing it? No, for the bird might
have flown.

Samir approached the young man, who was pushing his fair hair
back off his face. Samir imagined it flopping down on to his own
face, imagined those soft hands and lips like strawberries. 'You
look so good, my little duck. I don't know where to start.' He
wanted to sing the song to him in English. He smiled, and the
youth smiled back. Samir felt confused and repeated the sentence
used as an opener by people of all nationalities. 'Do you speak
English?'

'I understand a little.'

'What?'

'A little. I'm from Bosnia. And you?'

'From Lebanon.'

'Lebanon and Bosnia, same same.' He bowed his head sadly, and
put a consoling hand on Samir's shoulder. 'Bosnia, Lebanon, big
tragedies, big tragedies.'

Never mind. Forget about them. The most important thing is to
stay healthy. How was he going to chat him up now he'd made
him feel sad?

'Would you like to have a coffee?'

'Sorry. I'm waiting for a friend.'

'Tonight?'

'What?'

'We could meet tonight. We'll talk about the tragedies in
Lebanon and Bosnia.'

'You're a refugee. Did you buy this jacket from here?'

'Have it. Have it,' said Samir, taking it off.

'I don't want to buy. I was only asking.'

'Not to buy. Just take it.'

Samir did not know how to say 'Try it on' in English, but he didn't want anything to come between him and the beautiful youth. He gestured to him to take off his denim jacket, and he held out his leather jacket to him. When the boy refused it, Samir draped it over his shoulders.

A tall, nice-looking English girl swooped down on the boy and they kissed each other on the cheeks, then on the lips. Their embrace showed no signs of ending and the boy closed his eyes, while Samir stood waiting until finally he could retrieve his jacket.

The two boys from the telephone-booth card had come to life in his pocket, giving off a heat that penetrated through his clothes to his flesh. He hurried along, looking for a café where he could call the number printed on the card. Finally an Asian agreed to let Samir use the phone after he'd put a five-pound note down in front of him and explained, 'It's urgent, and I don't know how to use public phone boxes.'

'Hello.' He tried to speak quietly. 'Hello, I want a man, but a woman. Do you understand? A man who doesn't like women, a man who is a woman. Do you understand? I'm not a woman. I'm a man, but I'm like a woman.'

The receiver was slammed down in his ear.

He heard the man at the cash desk and a waiter sniggering together. The waiter spoke to him in Lebanese, even though he looked foreign. 'Do you need any help?'

'Uncle, if you have trouble speaking English, you're like a blind man pouring oil into a bottle.'

'Tell me what you want, and I'll translate it for you.'

'Thanks. It's all right.'

'Come on. Let me help. I'll tell them what you want, you dirty poof. Get out of here, before I beat your brains in and let your friends hear you crying blood.'

Samir hurried towards the door and the waiter hurried after him, rattling the crockery on his tray. Once he was outside, Samir stuck his head back round the door and called out, 'Did the jinns kidnap you and send you back crazy?'

He stopped a taxi and produced the card showing the two men embracing. 'My son's school is near here.'

The driver opened the door without comment. After a while he began talking on his mobile and Samir was convinced he was reporting him to the police, but he ended the conversation with a 'Bye, darling', and drew up at a building which was nothing like a bar or a club or even a cinema. When Samir showed no signs of moving, the driver called over his shoulder, 'Go on then. This is it.'

Samir entered an office resembling a hospital reception area; not the club, with music, dim lights and beautiful young men that he'd pictured. The receptionist remained seated behind her desk. She said, 'Hello,' and handed him a form to fill in. Samir was surprised to see a photo of a little girl with blonde hair on her desk. He showed her the card and she nodded.

Everything here is done according to laws and protocol, even you-know-what, he thought.

Samir told her he didn't speak English and handed her back the biro and the form.

'I'll help you. What's your name?'

'Samir.'

'How old are you?'

'It doesn't matter how old I am. Do you understand? Please, age isn't important.'

'I don't understand. How old are you?'

'I'm forty. But age doesn't matter. I'll take anyone. Do I pay you?'

'No. That's not necessary.'

'You're generous and we deserve it,' he said in Arabic. He couldn't translate it, so he said simply, 'But where? And when?'

'I don't understand. I'm sorry, I don't understand what you mean. We have to fill in the form.'

'Even the things that people think are going to be difficult are

91

simple in our country . . . There are no contracts or forms to fill in. You can do it in graveyards, garages, at roadblocks.'

'I don't understand you. Anyway, have you caught a sexually transmitted disease as the result of an infection?'

'What?'

'Has the doctor ever prescribed antibiotics for you?'

'Oh yes. Often. These,' he pointed to his neck, 'are always getting swollen . . .'

'But have you had syphilis? After you slept with someone?'

'Why? I don't understand.'

'Sorry, but I have to collect this information before the doctor will see you.'

'The doctor? Why the doctor?'

She looked embarrassed and turned away. Samir stood up abruptly. 'Thank you. I'll go now.'

She came after him, an expression of regret on her face. 'Please. Just a moment. Don't go. Please.' She called an internal number. 'James. Can you help me a second? Thanks.'

'Where are you from?' she asked Samir.

'Lebanon.'

'Sorry, but what language do they speak? Lebanese?'

'Arabic, French, English.'

'Fine. James lived in Egypt and he speaks Arabic.'

Samir relaxed suddenly and congratulated himself. I should have got angry before. If I hadn't got angry, she wouldn't have got a move on.

He tried to picture James. Should he ask if James had blond hair?

'James can't be with you for about an hour,' continued the woman, 'but shall we try together, then if you feel you really want James . . .?'

She wants to try with me, to convince me to give up my habit and start liking women. I understand now, he thought. You put photos of children up so that men will decide they're longing to have a family.

She was like his father's sister who used to hit him and say, 'Walk straight. Like a soldier. Don't swing your hips.' She was the one who'd arranged for him to be married off.

'I'm married. I'll wait for James,' he said quickly, knowing English women were oozing with lust for Arab men.

'Married? Does your wife know about it? Protection. In your situation this is extremely important. Perhaps we can make use of the time until James comes.'

She took several packets of condoms out of a drawer and opened them in front of him, comparing their various merits, then presented him with a packet. 'Try these. Take them. They're free.'

He thought of the sperm that were going to bang their heads against the wall of the sheath and laughed. 'OK. OK. James? Where is he?'

'As I told you, James won't be here for another hour.'

What was he going to do for a whole hour? Perhaps he should call Amira to check on the monkey. He hoped it hadn't pulled over the sofa it was chained to.

He went through his pockets looking for Amira's number, then asked the woman if she could make the call for him, and handed her a pound. She indicated the phone booth in the corridor, but he insisted that he didn't know how to use it. She smiled and led him back to the office. He showed her the card, where the beauties continued to embrace.

'Is that James?'

'No.'

'Is James as handsome as that? I'm happy to pay.'

At last she understood what he wanted. 'I'm sorry. This is an Aids centre. But since you're here, why don't you have a test?'

Samir laughed and the woman joined in, but then Samir remembered seeing a very sick-looking youth in the corridor and assuming he was a drug addict.

He left, thinking divine providence had sent him there to warn him to take precautions. He patted the box of condoms in his pocket, and the publications that the woman had pressed on him.

93

Chapter Three

I

Lamis fetched the material for her language practice – a sheet of exercises and a cassette – but instead of starting with the pronunciation of the first sentence she stood looking at the flat opposite where she'd seen the woman and the child the other day. Heavy curtains were drawn across their window and all she could see was the sink in the kitchen.

'The task of the farm guard-dog was to bark, alarm the yard and calm the last barn dancers.'

Lamis listened to the teacher's voice on the cassette resonate in the emptiness of the flat behind her. 'This sentence should be practised in front of a mirror.' Or a window. She'd imagined that practising would be easy and laughed when the teacher gave her only one sentence to prepare. Now she repeated it, knowing that she wasn't doing it right. She played it back; the echoes of the teacher's voice faded away as her own voice filled the air.

It's the 'r', thought Lamis. I have to stop it jumping on my tongue like a child jumping over a rope. I should make it stay back in the darkness of my mouth, lay it down as if I was preparing it for sleep. But it catches me unawares and runs off like a thief afraid of the barking dog.

'Aha. I know,' the teacher had said. 'Showing the tongue is one of the taboos in your culture. That's why you have difficulty pronouncing "the" properly. An Israeli actor drew my attention to this when I was beginning to despair of his pronunciation.'

Lamis objected. 'But Iraq is an Arab country.'

'Oh, sorry, I got it wrong. Hebrew and Arabic, of course. Israel and Iraq are enemies. I wasn't thinking. It's the same when I confuse the Iranians and the Iraqis.'

'My aunt always used to say "Hello, sweetheart",' Lamis elaborated, 'sticking out her tongue, and we'd say it back to her to make her repeat it, because we thought it was funny. And we chewed gum into little balls, and made it dance on our tongues as if we were dolphins balancing balls on our noses. And if we're enjoying our food, our tongues dart around like lizards in the sun.'

Lamis began her drill again, pausing not just at every word but at every phoneme, but still the treasure in Ali Baba's cave evaded the letter 'r'. She decided to go out and buy something to eat.

The doorman stopped her and handed her a large envelope. She was about to take it, but changed her mind. 'It's all right, thanks. I'll get it when I come back.'

She'd only gone two steps before she turned round, her heart pounding, and took the envelope from him. Had her former husband changed his handwriting? Was he dragging her back to be his wife again, or throwing her out of the flat? Perhaps her son's writing was suddenly more grown-up? Had the men in the investigation offices in Dubai sent her a letter-bomb, or was it the British government trying to take away her British nationality because of the incident in Dubai, to preserve relations between the two countries?

It was a miniature of Majnun Layla at school, accompanied by a postcard on which she read, 'Shall I see you tonight? Nicholas.'

Nicholas, the Englishman she'd pictured in her mind before she found him, in the years when she'd walked over golden fern and wild mushrooms, seen the horse drawn in limestone on the hillside and a waiter pouring tea and milk simultaneously as the train bowled along.

The envelope with its printed label, 'Handle with care', and the miniature of Majnun Layla dominated the empty flat. She was

95

thirty years old and this was the first time she had received a present and words addressed especially to her from a man. She glanced down at the watch her husband had given her, but it had not been a present, more like an addition to the household expenditure, on top of the food, telephone and electricity bills. She wondered if she might be forced to sell it in order to live, like her mother getting rid of one solid-gold bracelet after another when they were refugees in Syria and Lebanon.

She met Nicholas that evening, although they didn't embrace as she'd been sure they would. She didn't offer him her lips and he didn't take her in his arms, and it seemed to Lamis that she might have daydreamed their kiss of two days before. Instead, Nicholas asked if she'd received Majnun Layla, and if she knew of someone who could frame it for her.

She didn't want to go to an Arab film with him or eat couscous in a Moroccan restaurant; she wanted him to hold her and not let her go. She realised he'd chosen a film for her sake, when he leaned towards her in the cinema and said, 'It's amazing to think that the two of us are watching an Arab film together.'

London after the cinema was waiting for a sign from Lamis before it stepped out of its dress and stood naked before her, and Lamis was waiting for a similar sign from Nicholas. The trees and houses and office blocks had suddenly become London. She was with an Englishman and so, like him, she could feel an indulgence bred of familiarity towards her surroundings.

'Where shall we go? Are you hungry?' he asked.

'Whatever you like,' she replied. But in her heart, she said, 'No, no, please. Eating's what I did with my husband and his friends.

'Is that scarf from Iraq?' he asked.

'No. London. I left Iraq when I was twelve and I haven't been back.'

'It's beautiful.' He reached out and felt it. 'But you can go back if you want to.'

'Yes and no . . . who knows . . . I don't know.' She resisted the urge to tell on her husband: he'd once picked the scarf up from the floor in a restaurant and handed it to the waiter, forgetting that it was hers, even though it had been over her shoulders, round her neck, on the back of a chair at home, and hanging in the wardrobe.

At Piccadilly Circus, starlings landed on window ledges, on trees, on the Coca-Cola advertisement, everywhere except the three golden statues erected on top of a building. The traffic noise mounted.

'Shall we go to my flat? I'll show you the Arab dagger I bought in Oman.'

Her limbs relaxed, though she was surprised to realise that even the English used this trick. She released the breath that had been stuck in her throat, but another replaced it and remained suspended until they left the car and went up the stairs and into his flat. At first she stood looking around, then she walked up to the dagger, heaping praise on it.

When he didn't approach her as they sat together, she deliberately summoned up her mother-in-law and sat her down to face her. When she still felt the urge to fidget so that he would move closer, she promptly sat her husband between them, and then their son on his knee. She brought in her mother, everyone who'd intervened to try and persuade her to change her mind about the divorce, until in the end the flat was crammed with people, even their neighbours in Beirut, the customs men on the Syrian-Lebanese border, they all gathered round her, some standing, some sitting, and finally there was Nicholas, who'd contented himself with putting her scarf round his neck for a moment, and bringing the end of it up to his nose. She caught him closing his eyes and he confessed to her that he'd watched her at Dubai Airport.

His English words were flowing into her ears. They broke up into separate letters and slid in, one by one, feeding the little hairs with delicious food so that they demanded more. There was the flirtation with the letter 'r', which Nicholas often left hanging in the air, like his lips, so that she heard 'hia' instead of 'here' and 'lova' instead of 'lover'.

The letter was lost as it tried to settle in her ear, but the word 'firstly' left his lips parted. She squeezed herself in between the last two letters so she would be close to his vocal cords. She saw them like ropes for raising bridges.

Lamis despaired of him ever taking her in his arms, and was becoming convinced that he'd kissed her in Leighton House and brought her to his flat now only in order to sell her something. An English youth had once followed her in the square when she was playing with her son, asking her if the buttons on her sweater were real diamonds. But she didn't want to leave, even though Nicholas was asking her if she was hungry again, and yawning and fidgeting, jiggling his leg up and down. Does he like his own sex? Could that be possible? Why else would he have no wife, no girlfriend, even though he was so attractive, a real catch.

She had not seen a place like his before. It was a single person's flat; everything in it suggested freedom: the capacious sofa that was more like a bed, despite its worn upholstery; books every-where; the tall black lamp and the dining table used for everything but dining; the CD player; the kelim; and then, through the bedroom door, she could see the bed and, keeping it company in its solitude, a round cane table, and a clothes cupboard with some open shelves. There were maps on the walls, maps of the whole world, ancient and modern. She felt well-disposed towards the living room, and at ease in it. She noticed contact lenses on the table and realised she didn't know what colour his eyes were, and smiled at the sight of shoes thrown down on the floor as if he'd been in a rush when he went out.

She asked him if he wanted any help, and he turned from the rice he was washing in a small sieve.

'This is a miracle. What's happening to me is a miracle.'

'A miracle?'

'I can't believe you're here with me in my flat, in my kitchen, and I'm cooking rice for you.' He stopped. 'Rice. That's all there is.'

He laughed and she laughed too and asked him again if he wanted any help.

'Would you have a look for the saffron.' He pointed to a shelf where there were a lot of spices. 'So you live alone in London?'

She forced herself to be casual and answered like a character in a soap opera. 'Yep.' She told him she used to be married.

The aroma of rice and saffron and other spices rising up, the two plates and glasses, and the sight of the bottle of wine in Nicholas's hand all made her happy. They sat down together at the table once Nicholas had pushed everything out of the way, and she ate the delicious rice with him. Even when he asked her if she liked Basmati rice she did not criticise him for being fussy, as she used to criticise her husband and her mother-in-law when they claimed one sort of rice was superior to another.

'How many years were you married?'

'Nearly thirteen. I've got a son, Khalid, at boarding school, who lives with his father.' She paused for breath before she added, 'He is happy to let me see Khalid.'

Nicholas made no comment. He asked her if she'd like to try the salad.

He must think I'm heartless to leave my son with his father. That's what everybody thinks.

'I left my son with his father because I thought I was going to settle in Dubai. I wanted to begin a new life and I didn't want it to affect my son. I didn't want to disrupt his life and school. Besides, he loves London, and his grandmother.'

She hoped Nicholas wouldn't ask whether she would fight for custody now she had decided to live in London.

Her tone of voice, defensive and emotional at the same time, made Nicholas reach out and press her hand.

'It's all right. You misunderstood me. I felt sorry that you were married so young, that's all. I was wandering around the world with no responsibilities the year you got married. I went to India with only a few pounds in my pocket and a rucksack, to try and work out what I was going to do, why I couldn't bear to look for a job, whether it was just laziness, or because I really didn't know what I wanted to be.'

'It seems as if you've discovered . . .'

'Not on my own – because every time I used to think about it, I'd have a sort of panic attack. It was chance that showed me my career.'

Lamis was surprised that this tall man, who reminded her of her father, was opening up to her, revealing his vulnerability.

'I was strolling around like all those tourists at the Gate of India in Bombay, when I found an English child crying. I picked her up and put her on my shoulders, so she could be seen by whoever had lost her. I heard her father calling her name before she did, "Tamsin, Tamsin." He invited me to dinner that night, and he found me a job at Sotheby's. That was in 1987. The year you married your childhood sweetheart.'

'I was forced to marry a man twice my age.'

'Do you mean it was an arranged marriage? I'm sorry, but you don't seem to me to be someone who could be coerced into anything.'

'No. Forced marriage.'

'But why didn't you refuse, or run away? There are a lot of women's refuges here.'

'But I wasn't living here. I was living in Beirut with my father and mother. I tried to refuse the marriage, and I thought my father would stand by me, but he didn't, or couldn't. My mother was so determined that I should marry my husband.'

'I am sorry, so sorry. But why did you live in Beirut during the war? Let me see . . . yes . . . the war was taking place then. Was your father in politics?'

'No, my father's a musician, a lute player, but we left Iraq in 1982. We were about the first Iraqis who fled. The rumours that Saddam Hussein was going to wipe out my city, Najaf, were on everyone's lips. We fled to Syria, but a woman cousin encouraged my father to go to Lebanon, where she lived. Lebanon was enjoying a long lull . . . but the war broke out again. A few months after we arrived there, we found ourselves stranded. But to go back to Iraq was impossible, like returning to death itself.'

Nicholas suddenly embraced Lamis tightly, as if wanting her to forget that period of her life. She forced herself not to cry, not just because she was so moved that he was genuinely concerned, or because what she had been through was devastating, but because she had fallen in love with him, and become as fragile as a paper kite.

'But what about you? What attracted you to the Arab world?'

'Chance too. I met an Omani who collects Islamic daggers. He asked me to help him build his collection, and I accepted. A heaven-sent opportunity. I seem to be having a lot of them lately – it was extraordinary luck that I had to go to Leighton House that afternoon.'

He looked at her as if he were casting his net into her big sea.

'We have a proverb in Arabic which means "a chance meeting is better than a thousand rendezvous".'

'Does that mean that I'm not going to see you tomorrow?'

She nearly told him another proverb, 'Don't postpone today's work until tomorrow', but instead she stood rooted to the spot, hoping he'd look at her, and he did, but not in the way she'd expected. She didn't rush away, not wanting to regret her actions later, but went on standing there like a beggar, too proud or too helpless to hold out her hand.

He stared at her face until she felt embarrassed because he was going to see that she was embarrassed, and when he gathered up the hair falling on her neck and, with his other hand, began following the line of her neck from just beneath her chin to the hollow of her throat, a strange feeling possessed her and she wondered if he wanted to strangle her. He passed his fingers all over her face, almost touching her eyeballs, and when he reached her nose and began mechanically tracing the line dividing her nostrils, she fidgeted uncomfortably in case her nose dribbled, but he began touching it more insistently as if he wanted to stretch it or push it out of sight.

Eventually he responded to her discomfort and left her nose alone. He never took his eyes off her face, but his fingers went to her earlobes. The ears, the fingers, the navel, the man's penis, these are the parts of the body that remind us that human beings are miracles. The faint rustling sensation descended from her ear to her palate, then to her lips. Lamis closed her eyes as if a bright light had suddenly been shone into them.

She felt him touching her lips, his finger moving slowly along them as if he were counting the pink lines from which the lips are formed, line by line. Her mind leaped on again: would her lipstick come off on his finger? Did a man taste the lipstick or the lips? Then he parted her lips and reached her teeth.

Nicholas took off his shirt but kept his piercing eyes on her teeth and to her surprise he began tapping them lightly, like a bird pecking at a biscuit. She was beginning to get impatient and felt confused by what was happening, so she bit his finger and laughed. He laughed too, and clasped her face to his bare chest. She smelled a delicious smell, not his skin, or soap, or a smell left behind by the fabric of his shirt, but a new smell – the smell of a chest without hair, an English smell. She freed her face, her restlessness this time nothing more than a desire that he hold other parts of her close to him. But he did not. He held her face away from him, then brought it close again, then turned his attention to her hair, taking hold of it strand by strand as if he were parting the branches blocking his path. He only rearranged it when he breathed a blessing on it, and sniffed it in ecstasy. His breathing became faster and he finally put a hand to her waist to undo her trousers. She went to help him, but he led her to the sofa.

He dropped her trousers on the floor, then bent over her feet, raising them a little so that he could examine them, as they were far away from the rest of her. He felt the calf of one leg; it was surprisingly muscular. (He was bound to ask her if she rode a bike.) He felt the other leg, pressing the two legs together so one would not be jealous of the other. Then he returned to her waist and started to peel off her tights. He noticed the varnish on her toenails and stroked each nail slowly and gently through the nylon as if he were repainting them. When he reached her thighs he gasped faintly, and closed his eyes for a moment as he continued releasing her from her tights. He was breathing heavily now, almost panting. He took one foot in his hand and bent to kiss it.

He was the Prince's footman, examining the feet of all the adolescent girls before he let them try on Cinderella's slipper, making those around him think that he was doing it to prevent cheating, but actually getting immense pleasure from it.

Lamis felt tired. She was not used to this athletic behaviour. He gave her back her foot. He didn't seem to notice the tops of her legs and what lay between them, and her pants ready and waiting for him like a lighthouse guiding the wavering ship. He touched a black mole on her thigh which Lamis had examined religiously each year by the dermatologist. She began to laugh, trying to move his hand off her waist. She told him she was ticklish there and this seemed to drag him back to reality. Her laughter made him lose his way. 'I like your dimples,' he said.

'If you give me a five-pence piece, I promise you I can make it disappear inside them.'

He let go of her waist and resumed his route, this time to her arm. He raised it above her head and buried his face in her armpit. She began to laugh again. 'I'm ticklish under my arms. Do you want to see some more dimples?'

She turned over on her stomach. There were two dimples in her buttocks. He bent to kiss them, panting as if he had had a hard climb to reach them. She closed her eyes, waiting for another decisive gesture but there was nothing, nothing. Suddenly she shrieked with laughter as he flung himself on her toes, and this seemed to interrupt their journey for good. He asked her if she was hungry.

She said no, she wasn't hungry, and stayed on the sofa, trying unsuccessfully to draw him back into the sequence of the journey. He was like a tourist whose wallet had gone missing: by the time it was found, he'd lost all interest in the place. She tried a different tack, asking him why people were ticklish. Was it something to do with the functioning of the blood and the lymph glands?

'Let me get you something to eat. I'm still hungry, aren't you?'

He was trying to hide his erection when she grabbed him by the foot and smiled at him and leaned towards him and put her mouth on his. There was a pause before he kissed her, letting his tongue search for her imprisoned tongue, pushing against her teeth, which almost melted and fell out one by one with the heat. But he didn't drag her off to the bedroom as she'd anticipated.

She realised she didn't know Nicholas, and became convinced he was odd; otherwise how was it, she asked herself for the hundredth time, that he was still unmarried.

'Why are you sitting far away from me?' she asked him.

'I'm not.'

'What's happened?'

'I'm the happiest person alive.'

'I don't understand you. What's going on? What's scaring you away?'

'Scaring me away? I'm in heaven. I want to look at you, memorise you.'

She did not give him the chance to continue but threw herself on him, kissing him, grabbing hold of his face and drawing his tongue into her mouth, and he kissed her and took her tongue and let his face rest in her hands. Then she took off her pants, but he continued addressing the other parts of her body, as if he was a student trying to find out how these different bits connected to one another, where each began and ended. She saw his erection and was reassured again. The trees rustled outside as if to say, 'We can see you,' and a few light spots of rain knocked on the window, asking permission to come in. He was still enjoying his discoveries, as if he were being confronted with a woman's body for the first time. What could he be seeing that he hadn't seen before? He passed his hand over her armpit and whispered, 'Your skin is so soft.'

When he entered her, she thanked God that she was normal. One year or more – she had thought that her hole might have reverted to flesh, like a pierced ear if you stopped wearing an earring. She drew Nicholas to her spontaneously, she who'd always wondered what sex was. He was on top of her, his face just above hers, his hands out in front of him like the Sphinx, so as not to put his weight on her. His lips only left her mouth to move down to her breasts; he was looking so intently at her that she felt dizzy and had to close her eyes.

She opened them only when her conflicting, incomplete thoughts buzzed a warning note and she saw his face was still buried in hers. Then a clear, unambiguous thought formed itself in her mind: Why's Nicholas still on top of me? What's wrong with him? What do I have to do to make him come? My husband went like a rocket, straight up into the sky, a brief blaze of light, then a rapid descent to earth. I wonder what English women do. Should I move more? Shout or murmur sweet ecstatic nothings? Bite his lips, cling to his back, digging my nails in his flesh, or say 'Give it to me, baby'? Has my body rebelled against me and told him the truth, that it can't feel him?

'Do you pluck these?' Nicholas asked. He passed his finger between her eyebrows. She was not used to talking during sex, nor to her tongue being sucked by another person. Her tongue was only for tasting food. He touched the mole on her neck and said, 'That's beautiful.' He tasted her ears and said, 'Turkish delights.' He held her breasts and then he looked into her navel and said, 'I'm looking for a pearl,' and he left her to kiss her toes and said, 'They smell of mint.'

'What's wrong? Why don't you come?' she whispered to him. It was as if she'd struck him in the heart. He awoke from his reverie and said, 'What? What did you say?'

He thinks he's not supposed to make eye contact with me,

because I'm an Arab woman and I've been stamped with a skull and crossbones, and the words 'Danger, Keep Off', thought Lamis. But all he can see is the desire on my face, then as he plunges inside me, scattering the letters far and wide, he finds himself remaining on the surface, for the inside of me is like shifting sands which subside and sink without trace.

Their movement was co-ordinated, harmonious. They each wanted more, now that their bodies had grown accustomed to the contact and breathed in unison. She knew now that he'd been waiting for her, but she also knew that she wouldn't reach a climax. How could she make herself recall the feel of the wood now? A woman she knew used to keep some of her lover's cologne in a bottle and would make some excuse to go into the bathroom and sniff it, and then hurry back to have sex with her husband before she lost the smell.

Lamis shut her eyes and thought of herself sprawled over the edge of the table. It didn't work. She could hear the voice of her mother-in-law's friend telling her confidentially, 'Take some advice from me. Don't leave your husband for another man. I know. I once met a younger man who showed me what love was. What can I say? He became such a habit with me that thirty years later I still enjoy my memories of being with him. Dream! Don't go ahead with the divorce!'

But there were many men in Lamis's life. She looked for them wherever she went: tables, chairs and other suitable points of contact, and when she didn't find them she was disappointed. They were the men in her life; they looked different and came from different countries. The feel she liked best was the pure ebony wood, dark and warm, of a chair from Goa with a pineapple carved on each arm, which she used to rush to whenever she begged to be left alone at home. Afterwards she would wipe it with a damp cloth, afraid that her son's dog would sniff out where she had been intimate with herself and lick the chair and arouse her husband's curiosity. Her friends had never found out the secret of the muscles in her legs. They stood out like high cheekbones without any of the normal exercises.

Whenever Lamis thought of sex she used to stop what she was doing and hurry to the bathroom, lock the door and put on her lipstick.

'Why do you bother locking it?' her husband would ask, and she answered that it was a habit from childhood.

She would pull the shower curtain to one side to expose the bathroom mirror that took up an entire wall, and part her thighs so that she could press against the maple surface surrounding the basin. She could see the hollow beneath which her backbone lay, reflected in the mirror, and the two dimples and the two mounds of her buttocks sloping down to her thighs as she moved. Her red lipstick was the dominant feature of her reflection in the other mirror facing her over the basin, and reminded her of the riddle: What's red and goes up and down? Answer: A strawberry in a lift.

Lamis lay with her head on Nicholas's chest, and he was quiet with her, stroking her hair and smelling it. She waited and nothing happened. She lifted her head off his chest, trying to reach his lips, but he covered her with kisses and whispered, 'Never mind. Don't pretend. It doesn't matter,' and stayed by her side.

As if he felt that she wanted to confess something, or as if she were a child suffering from a high fever, Nicholas started blowing faint breaths on her forehead. She held him tight and told him about her secret, and that it had started with a chair in her childhood. Not wanting to see his reaction, she stood up and went over to the window after wrapping herself in his shirt. She glanced outside at the buildings, all alike, around the square with its luxuriant trees. A stranger like her might be looking out of one of those windows to observe how the English lived and take her for an Englishwoman pausing for a moment's reflection or to examine the weather.

The brass instruments that wailed from an old soldiers' club every Sunday would never make her feel alienated again, nor would the approach of summer, whose warmth used to bring a chill of loneliness to her.

She looked back into the room.

II

Amira couldn't sleep. Should she ask Nahid to be a partner in her new plan?

Guilt and betrayal had been roaming through her mind ever since the previous night, when she thanked God that she'd not found Nahid – it meant that she could keep her plot a secret – and yet, by thanking God, she was also disentangling herself from the proverb, 'Two arses in one pair of pants', that perfectly characterised her friendship with Nahid, a friendship that had lasted many years, from the first time she and Nahid met, ten years earlier, in a hospital in Richmond, where they were both having abortions: Amira, pregnant this time by a client, and Nahid by the owner of the cabaret where she danced. From then on, they had infused each other with love and tenderness, confiding everything to each other, from the least to the most significant, to such an extent that when Nahid had fallen in love with the Englishman called Stanley, who asked her to marry him after a few weeks, Nahid's first concern had been whether it would threaten her friendship with Amira.

At the beginning of their friendship, Amira ignored Nahid's requests to be introduced to Amira's clients. She advised Nahid to concentrate on her dancing, urged her to brush up on her technique and perform at many different nightclubs: she could enhance her skill by visiting Cairo or, in London, by going to a dance school that taught *raqs sharqi*, belly dancing. Then as soon as her marriage ended Nahid stopped dancing and started to work with Amira.

So this morning Amira hurried over to Nahid's flat, in the parallel street to hers. She'd decided to involve Nahid in her scheme, on condition that Nahid drink less, cease her giggling, her sly winks, her stubborn behaviour, refrain from starting fights with people and, finally, solemnly promise not to tell Bahia.

Nahid was in her nightdress. The sour smell of sleep and whisky engulfed her small flat. Whisky bottles were still out on the table, some of them filled with candles. As usual, Amira asked Nahid to throw the bottles away. 'But why? They are so original, very original.'

'Listen to me, Nahid. You should pay your phone bill.'

'I'm going to ask for a new number.'

'They won't give you one, not unless you pay the existing bill. But why don't you get a reliable mobile phone? Yesterday it was impossible for me to contact you.'

'I've turned it off. I had the blues yesterday. It was the Princess, at the Dorchester. Why God prefers some people to others, I don't know.'

'That's why I'm here now. I'm going to impersonate a princess. In fact, I did, yesterday. After I left you.'

'Why? Did you kill her?'

'I'm not in the mood for jokes. Listen, I'll pretend to be a princess and you'll be one of my companions. We'll get another two, as well. And our profits will be at least five thousand, if not more, for every trick. I'll divide everything fifty-fifty . . .'

'Yeah, I'll be paying that much to bail you out of prison.'

'But listen to me. I've decided. I'm one hundred per cent sure that this will work.'

'It won't. I don't want to be a companion or a princess.'

'At least give it a try.'

'Try without me.'

'Do you want to keep on taking five hundred, three hundred, two hundred, one hundred, then ten pounds?'

'Come on, your highness, let's go to Speedy Gazelle's first.'

They headed for the fabric shop in Duke Street. They hoped

fervently that Bruno – Speedy Gazelle – would be there. Amira spotted him before Nahid. 'There he is! We're in luck.'

They went in and Amira chose some material. Speedy Gazelle made certain that his boss was taken up with another customer, and measured out an extra few metres. Then he offered to show Nahid some fabrics that were not out on display. She followed him downstairs to a passageway piled high with bolts of cloth. Amira dawdled, amusing herself by flicking through fashion magazines laid out on the table. She went to the cash desk to pay and Nahid reappeared, alone, followed shortly afterwards by Speedy Gazelle who carried up rolls of cloth to conceal the after-effects of his intimate encounter with the Egyptian woman. Amira and Nahid glanced at the materials then said goodbye.

Nahid remembered that she was meeting Samir. He had to renew his visa and, since she knew the ropes, she had offered to go with him to Croydon.

Amira left carrying her parcel of material and turned into Bond Street. She was making for a street whose name she did not know, off Hanover Square. As soon as she saw the varnished wooden door, she knew it was the place she was looking for. She'd been there on one other occasion: to fetch a dress for the employer for whom she worked as a maid during her first few months in London.

She was.told she would have to make an appointment. The first was not for ten days.

'Perhaps you can help me,' she said to one of the three young women who were bringing cups of tea to the waiting customers. 'If you take my measurements and I tell you the style I want, then you could explain it to the couturier.'

But the young woman didn't understand what Amira meant. She walked away, her high heel catching in the crack between the floorboards.

Amira wouldn't agree to wait ten days, or even three. She told another of the young women that she was going abroad the next day, she'd been sent by Princess Ferial of Jordan, and she must speak to the couturier for one second. 'Tell him it's a matter of life and death.'

The young woman went away. She came back with the couturier. 'Darling! How are you?' he exclaimed, trying not to look disappointed that Princess Ferial was not with her.

'I want a princess dress.'

His hair was dyed a nice colour, and he had a good skin. Amira would have liked to ask him what cream he used. He examined the material, felt it. He didn't seem impressed.

'Don't you like it?'

'Sorry. It's lovely but it's too thick for a princess-line.'

'I don't want a princess-line. I want a dress a princess would wear.' The princess she'd seen was so ordinarily dressed. But Amira was much younger and prettier. Besides, just as people differ from each other, so do princesses.

'Ah! *Décolleté?* Like Marie Antoinette, and the waist like Lady Hamilton, and a flounced skirt?'

She nodded her head, too embarrassed to say, 'I don't know what you're talking about!' as he cast a surgical eye over her. She felt like a Russian doll trying to swallow all her children inside her buttocks.

'There isn't enough material. In any case, this style will make you look fatter. Are you going to a fancy-dress ball? You can hire a dress from the Strand.'

'No. But . . .'

He turned to address the young women, and a customer who was trying to make a call on her mobile. 'Did I tell you that Mrs Fallaci was trying to find a Little Red Riding Hood dress for her daughter to wear to a Hallowe'en party, and a girl in one of the dress agencies told her to try Ann Summers? The poor woman wrote the name down and phoned one of their branches. The girl said, "Sorry, we don't have what you're looking for, but it's an excellent idea." And Mrs Fallaci only discovered she'd been set up when she walked past an Ann Summers shop one day and looked in the window.'

111

The girls laughed. Amira seethed with annoyance, but pretended to join in.

'OK, I'll leave the choice to you. You choose a style for me,' she suggested to the dressmaker.

'Then you'll have to make an appointment with the secretary.'

'Why? We've agreed what I'm having. You just have to take my measurements. As I said, it was Princess Ferial who told me to come here . . .'

'No, no. You must have an appointment.'

'Don't be so English, please.'

'Excuse me, I'm English and proud of it.'

She cursed to herself as she put the material back in its bag and went off in the direction of Bond Street. She didn't need this tailor. Going to him in the first place was only to prove to herself that now she belonged to another class. Halfway along Bond Street she stopped outside a jewellery shop that she'd once visited with a punter, where he had bought her a ring and she'd managed to swallow one of a pair of small pearl earrings that were on display. She went on her way until she came to the shop owned by Roya, the Italian woman who'd been born in Cairo and who played with the singer Dalida as a child. Her shop was famous with all the women who preferred a bird in the hand to ten in the bush, women who came with men to buy clothes, then a day later, or even a few hours sometimes, returned alone with the dresses. Roya would give them back whatever the men had paid, minus her own inflated commission – but not until she'd personally taken each dress over to the door and examined it closely, wearing her glasses, paying special attention to the collar and under the arms, and wiping her lipstick away with a Kleenex before burying her face in the garment and sniffing it.

Roya was not there, just a salesgirl, who looked like part of the display, sitting at a table with a dark band on her dyed-blonde hair, bright-red lipstick, and an artificial mole painted on the side of her mouth.

'If Roya's here,' Amira said to the girl, 'tell her it's the Princess and she'll know.'

The salesgirl suddenly awoke from her lethargy and jumped eagerly to her feet.

'Please, have a seat, madam. We're at your service.'

The Princess sat down, crossed her legs comfortably, and watched the clothes come and go before her, assuming expressions of indifference or displeasure. Finally she settled on an elaborate outfit, and the salesgirl complimented her on her taste.

'One doesn't know what to wear in the morning,' murmured the Princess.

'You're right, your highness,' cooed back the salesgirl. 'This dress is casual and easy to wear.'

Amira made no attempt to try it on, but said in a bored voice, 'I'll take it to the hotel and try it there, and if I don't like it I'll send it back with the driver.'

The salesgirl did as she was told and began to wrap the dress painstakingly. A flicker of doubt on her face suggested that she wondered how the Princess was going to pay. But the Princess went over to the door and looked through the glass, then picked up her bag, muttering, 'I told the driver to come for me in two hours. I thought Roya would be here and I could take her for a coffee once I'd bought a dress. If he comes, tell him I've gone to Cartier and he should pick me up there. And if my attendant turns up – her name is Iman, remember, Iman – tell her where I've gone too.'

She picked up the bag containing the dress and went off saying, 'Ask Roya to send the bill, please. I'm at the Dorchester.'

The salesgirl, despite her embarrassment at not recognising the Princess and not knowing her name, opened the door and bid the Princess a smiling goodbye.

The fact that the salesgirl believed in her was proof to Amira that she appeared quite authentic. Nobody asked princesses for their identity documents. Everything was possible when you were abroad. You could recreate yourself with a name and parents of your own choosing. She walked for longer than was usual for her, glancing back from time to time, until she had left Roya's shop far behind. If she looked at people at all, it was with disdain rather than curiosity. She went into interior design shops, picture galleries, jewellers and more fabric stores, happy to spend ages looking before she decided on anything. Then she said discreetly that her driver would be back to make the purchase. She asked them to write down the information, the price, and the English respectfully complied. One man offered to open the shop for her after six if she wanted, and she left the shops feeling buoyant and positive.

She flew to her flat, kicked off her shoes, dropped the shopping bag on the bed and lay down beside it. Then she got up and fetched a plastic carrier bag from her wardrobe. She emptied out papers, cards and letters and searched through them for phone numbers. Alongside the numbers were the nicknames she had written down to aid her memory: Tits-like-Pamela Anderson, Who-was-my-father, Arrogant Shit, Cow, Big Mouth, Goldfinger, Bunch-of-grapes, Chewing Gum, False Teeth, Brown Sugar, Fatin Hamama, Eczema.

She chose three names and tried each in turn without success, then called the car-hire company and ordered a Rolls-Royce. 'I want an English driver. Not Indian English, Arab English, African English, Chinese English, Polish English, Scots English or Irish English. English one hundred per cent with a cap and jacket. Yes, yes. I'll pay so much an hour plus tips. OK. Until the day after tomorrow.'

Then she went out in search of the three names she'd chosen – Tits-like-Pamela Anderson, Fatin Hamama, Who-was-my-father. She went to casinos, hotel lobbies, cabarets, and when she caught up with each woman she took her aside and told her, 'Right, Cinderella. I'm not promising to help you marry Prince Charming, but I'll show you the way to his fat wallet, on condition that you listen to what I say, do as I tell you, and keep it a secret.'

So Amira the fairy godmother, who was also Amira the Princess, hired an English driver instead of the dog-coachman, a Rolls-Royce in place of the pumpkin, and three companions as her retinue rather than coach horses.

III

The casino was in one of those old buildings with venerable pasts, which often still housed cultural institutions and organisations dedicated to reconciliation between peoples.

Gazing at the lights trained on the tables and at the young men and women dealing the cards, Samir realised why the word 'casino' had always entranced him.

All eyes were on the tables. The air was filled with cigarette smoke, and with the deep sighs and mute dialogues of people continuously fighting with themselves. They all needed courage, whether they were miserly, rational, heavily in debt, or merely skilful gamblers who had promised themselves to stop gambling. A single question hung unsteadily in the air, 'Should I play this time or not?'

Instead of lusting after the women dressed in their best and showing off their curves, the men pleaded with the numbers that were everywhere: in their bank accounts and their pockets, as well as on the gaming tables. The money bled away, slipping through the players' fingers, and their faces turned gloomy as their mood changed.

'It's like a wake!' said Samir. 'Let's go, Amira.'

She smiled and took him into another room where there were slot machines round the walls, making sounds like popcorn-makers. Tables and chairs were dotted about, and waiters brought drinks and sandwiches. The monkey, which Samir had named Cappuccino, was there too, under Samir's coat and scarf.

It was only when an acquaintance told Amira of Umm Ibrahim's death that Amira found an empty place and sat down with the other women.

Umm Ibrahim had taken up going to the casino when her son died young; she had found it an appropriate solution to her sorrow and loneliness: open all night, it was the only place that she could enter without any obligation to entertain others or be entertained by them. 'The casino is the only thing that makes me feel alive,' she used to say. 'I sweat with fear and joy there, and it's the one place where I can climb the stairs without using my stick.' Then one night she had stayed away from the casino, and died as she lay in bed watching the hail falling from the London sky and thudding on the windowpanes.

The conversation moved on to Mr Kubani from Nigeria. Rumour had it that he was going to visit the casino as soon as he arrived from Miami, where he had been given the sobriquet Goldfinger. Or so they'd been told by a relative of his, who'd been losing heavily for a week now. Goldfinger was in the habit of giving tips of thousands of dollars to everyone he encountered: masseuses, flight attendants, entire bands of musicians.

Amira stood up and circulated between the slot machines and gambling tables, shaking a hand here, ignoring an acquaintance there, asking about such-and-such a person. She left Samir sitting near the old women who were resting from playing the machines, the wives waiting for their husbands, looking sullen and bored, and the beautiful Arab and foreign girls, who gathered there when they were not strolling about, drinking and eating, keeping an eye on what was happening at the tables so that they could come back and report.

The monkey, which had been quietly settled in the warmth of Samir's coat, began to get restless. The waiting wives and the women who were spying on the winners and losers gathered round the moment they saw the monkey; it was a welcome diversion, even if all it did was turn its head from side to side, and examine its tail, or blow kisses in the air. One of the women was daring enough to want to hold it. She knew it was a capuchin, assuring Samir she'd been brought up in India where she'd had dozens of monkeys as pets.

When the monkey refused to let her hold it, Samir joked, 'It's a female. It likes men.'

The waiter noticed the monkey and asked Samir anxiously how he'd got past the door. 'Monkey? What monkey? This is a dog that looks like a monkey,' teased Samir.

Amira called the waiter over and pressed something into his hand, whispering that Samir and the monkey were part of a prince's household – a very generous prince – who would be joining them shortly.

Amira looked at her watch. There was not a single clock in the casino. She hadn't found anyone to prey on so far that night and Nahid hadn't shown up as she'd promised. Amira loved the casino's clientele, whether they were miserable or ecstatic when the roulette wheel stopped turning, and she often took one of the casualties home in a taxi, cursing aloud because she didn't know what time it was, so he would give her his wristwatch, pleased to discover that he was still capable of giving.

In the casino a cancan was playing. Behind the bar a tapestry depicted monkeys: one pulled a peacock's tail, one cast a fishing line into the water, others aimed rifles at birds in the trees.

Samir's monkey, with its black-and-white markings and its fur shining in the casino lights, looked itself as if it were dressed in a white shirt and a black shantung jacket. However, Cappuccino remained a skinny and puny creature, even with its marvellously agile tail, curled like a lock of Louis XV's hair. Samir smoothed down the fur on the monkey's head, trying to cover the slight bald patches that were creeping over either side of its forehead. He could tell that the monkey loved this warm place, and that it loved him, especially tonight, when Samir himself was acting more like the monkey than ever, with his rapid gestures and inquisitive eyes, making the women laugh with the sounds he produced, as he regaled them with fictitious tales about Cappuccino.

*   *   *

The cancan was still blaring out. Amira enticed Cappuccino to stay with her by offering the monkey some food but the music and the noise and the women clustered around made the animal want to break free. Amira did her best to hold on to it, for fear the monkey would run away altogether. However, the monkey had no thought of escaping and it stood where it was, on the table, and bowed low as if to royalty. When it was sure all eyes were upon it, it picked up its tail like the hem of a dress, and made the rounds of the astonished women. It held out a hand with an imploring look in its eyes. It singled out one woman and began opening and closing its nostrils in front of her. She offered the monkey some food, which it promptly ate, but it didn't move away. The woman didn't know what to do when the monkey continued to look at her pleadingly, then intently. She gave it a gambling chip she had in her hand. The monkey held it close to his face, then threw it on the floor and held out a hand again. She searched through her bag but the monkey finally lost patience and moved on. When the next woman had her donation of a paper handkerchief rejected, she reached back into her bag and gave the monkey a pound. The monkey held it up to its face, then nodded gratefully, so another woman gave it a fiver and it beamed and grasped her arm, while everyone waited expectantly. The monkey turned its head from side to side, uttering little noises, and made as if to go towards Amira, then changed its mind and turned back to the women to go through the same routine all over again. Finally it bounded back to Amira and clung on to her, and they all laughed.

'Amira!' said one in mock reproach. 'You've even taught a monkey your love of money!'

'I swear to God, I didn't know he was such a devil. When Samir was teaching the monkey these tricks, I thought he was mad!'

Amira covered up the monkey in Samir's scarf and coat, afraid of the two security guards who were looking suspicious. The monkey kicked out inside Samir's coat. Amira cursed and gave it a shake, and the monkey let out a shriek that stopped everyone in their tracks, even the players who were on the point of losing.

118

At the sound of the monkey's cry, Samir rushed over. The moment Cappuccino heard Samir's voice, it broke free of the coat with a jubilant expression, opened its clenched fists, and released the money into its master's palms.

'So there really is a God,' said Samir humbly, embracing the monkey. He wanted to weep, but could not, as his astonishment was so profound it overpowered the emotion he felt at the love the monkey was showering upon him. The monkey must have known that Samir had lost ten pounds on the slot machines: a twin always knew what the other twin was thinking.

Chapter Four

I

The sun coming into the car was the same sun that had dried the windows of Westminster Abbey that morning. The light it cast over everything seemed more vigorous because people had missed it so much and complained about its absence. Lamis saw the tourists staring up at Big Ben as if they were keeping an eye on it, while the inattentive ones looked enviously at the cars rushing past, not guessing where Nicholas was taking her.

Lamis's heart went out to the Iraqis who were gathering in Trafalgar Square, men, women, children, holding banners protesting against Saddam Hussein, and demanding that he should be tried for crimes against humanity, and she tried to choke back her tears. She was a spectator, looking at the Iraqis just as the English did, and the tourists, before their attention went elsewhere – as if she were not like them, as if she'd never been scared, or looked into the darkness of the night wondering, 'Where shall I sleep tomorrow?' and 'Where shall I wake up?'

She was a tiny bird that found itself in its nest every morning, but with creatures other than its own kind.

Her feelings, as always, fluctuated between sadness, guilt and great relief – that actually she was not one of the protesters, not one of the Iraqi refugees who appeared in the news in a suburban church in London. Her mother used to sigh, homesick for Najaf, 'I even miss its dust,' but every time her mother heard of an attack or more trouble in Iraq, she felt secure, at peace, and even happy, because she'd left.

'But, darling, if you're that sad, why don't you show solidarity. Join the Iraqi demonstrations. My feeling is that you don't care that much; your sadness doesn't last. It's how you respond when you hear the news, or read the papers, or see a demonstration,' Nicholas said.

'I don't know. I never felt I wanted to be in a demonstration.'

'It's very easy. You should make a decision. You go, or you don't. But perhaps there's another reason. Perhaps you don't want to bump into your ex-husband or mother-in-law?'

'Him and his mother? There are different classes of Iraqis . . . even of refugees. They don't do that kind of thing.

When Lamis was married, the sitting room in her flat used to become a reception centre for the men: every morning fifty different brands of cigarettes circulated while the rattle of prayer beads sounded like the men's ripples of laughter as they recalled what the papers had said about Iraq, Saddam Hussein and the opposition groups.

Her husband would appear in his best suit and tie, and sink comfortably into the sofa, his watch twinkling like the visitors' gold teeth. They all used to sit there, silently sizing up their fellows: he's a millionaire; he used to be a millionaire; he's the son of an ex-minister; that family are all ambassadors; they're from the real old families; they're new money. All of them wanted to take Iraq away from Saddam Hussein.

Lamis's relationship to these gatherings had been mainly confined to observing them from a distance and complaining about the smell of cigars. Sometimes she had not been able to stand her home being occupied for hours on end, and had marched into the room and flung open the windows in protest. The moment the last of them left she attacked, emptying the ashtrays and plumping up the velvet cushions, as she compared her husband's gatherings with the groups of newly arrived Iraqi refugees whose anti-regime publications she read and admired.

121

'I don't understand what you're telling me. This is all very contradictory. Are you telling me that your husband's family would stay aloof from the refugees because they looked down on them, and yet that this same family didn't care that you were from a different class? Oh, don't misunderstand me, I haven't forgotten that for your husband you were a trophy wife but, according to what you're saying, they would've rejected you if they'd thought you were a poor refugee stranded in Lebanon.'

Lamis could not understand why Nicholas bothered. Why did he take these things to heart? Why was he so serious about it?

'Well, my ex-mother-in-law concocted a story about me, and then she believed in it herself: she decided that my family was very well known for being wealthy and scholarly in the Marshes and Najaf, but when we fled, we left everything behind. In private, though, she never ceased putting me down, even though I bore her a grandson. If I ever showed any sign of independence, she sang '"Oh window, give me a piece of bread" – it's a well-known song about a poor girl, who married a prince who fell in love with her beauty. But she couldn't forget where she came from, and whenever she heard a vendor selling bread, she used to leave the table, which was crammed with the most extravagant dishes, caviar, peacock's liver, and hurry to the window to stretch out her hand singing "Oh window, give me a piece of bread".'

They entered a building and she read its sign, 'Oriental and India Office Collections – British Library'.

Nicholas asked for a book, reference OP5323, reading the number out of his little notebook.

The woman behind the desk looked it up in the catalogue. As soon as she raised her eyes. Nicholas said quickly, 'I know it's not available to the public. Is Miss Porter upstairs?'

'She's moved to the British Museum. Do you know Dr Baker? If he'll sign the form, I can get you the book.'

The place was filled with long tables. Hunched over them were academic types who looked as if they'd not left the building in a lifetime. Nicholas put his and Lamis's coats on a chair at the back and then led her to a locker for her to leave her bag. They went into the canteen.

'You've changed the tablecloths.'

The woman at the till smiled at him and nodded without speaking. The tablecloths were garish plastic.

They returned to the first room and Nicholas bestowed a relieved smile on Lamis when he saw Dr Baker enter carrying a dark-red box aloft, holding it as a mother does when she wants to keep a plate of cakes out of the children's reach. Dr Baker asked them politely to take great care of the manuscript. He made sure that they had no pens with them, and wished them an interesting time. Like an obstetrician lifting a child out of the mother's stomach, Nicholas drew out the manuscript. It had a thick cover, the red of watermelon flesh.

He propped it up on the bookrest in front of him and glanced down the first page. Lamis peered at it. Nicholas was expecting a reaction from her, but she didn't know what to say and felt awkward. The rules of Arabic grammar were a mystery to her. She'd never really concentrated at school in Damascus and Beirut; she'd passed the time hoping that the teacher wouldn't write her name on the blackboard, mortified by her Iraqi accent, which the children mocked, and by her American second-hand clothes.

Too bad. I'll read it without the proper endings if he asks me. He can't read Arabic anyhow, she thought defensively.

The letters and words were delineated clearly and were as decorative as the pictures next to them, painted in black, gold and red, but Nicholas flicked quickly through the pages, only giving her time to read the titles and to glance at the accompanying drawings: Triangulum, Pegasus, Canis Major, Argo Navis flashed past her; Canis Major, the Dog, looked out at her and she read the headings, 'What is visible from earth' and 'What is visible from the sky'.

Nicholas pushed the bookrest along so that Lamis found herself forced to look at the manuscript properly. Nicholas's hand stopped at the constellation of 'The Woman with the Chair,

Cassiopoeia'. Lamis read, 'She is sitting on the back of the camel where she nestles amongst the brilliant stars . . .' and Nicholas's hand moved down to her thigh. As Lamis went on reading, 'which make up her face, her neck, the side of her breast, her hand . . .' his hand moved on very slowly, until it rested between her legs, 'and her other hand resting on the sceptre, or on the edge of the seat, and the crook of her arm, the end of her plait of hair, and finally the tips of her toes,' and Nicholas's hand found where it wanted to be, only to withdraw when Lamis became engrossed in the manuscript.

According to the text, Cassiopoeia was a woman sitting on a camel litter, although there was no image of a woman shown in the picture alongside, which depicted the constellation 'as she looks from earth' and, on the facing page, to illustrate the position of her stars in relation to the surrounding constellations, 'as she looks in the sky'.

The manuscript, *Suwar al-Kawakib*, *Pictures of the Stars*, by Abu'l-Husayn Abd al-Rahman Ibn Ummihi al-Sufi, dated from the thirteenth or fourteenth century. Lamis marvelled at the fact that the Arabic language was still the same as when she'd left it thirteen years before – clear and familiar to the eye, and in her mind. The letter *sin* – 's' – was like a wave of the sea, a carnation flower, a bird's wings. This book must have been passed from hand to hand, from crate to crate, from camelback to horse's saddlebag, from little boats to big ships, until it came to rest on a bit of land by the Atlantic Ocean, or the 'sea of darkness', as she was taught in school, the terrifying sea where Arab ships dared not set sail, for fear that they would be lost amid its huge waves, overcast skies, lashing rain and bitter cold, and never see land again.

Lamis felt as if she could smell jasmine: in the past they said that the smell of jasmine made people more aware, quick-witted, edgy. Her mind was alert and teeming with thoughts. She had never seen an ancient manuscript like this before, with its pages the colour of brown sugar and yellow lemonade, even though her grandfather's attic in Najaf had been full of old books – serving as teapot stands, close to the brazier, making the letters on the pages leak out and spread because of the heat from the tea. Although the manuscript was so old, reading the Arabic, she saw that the language was still as it had been hundreds of years ago: she read the sentences with the greatest of ease; her heart pounded with affection for her language. So it was true, then, the picture that they'd painted at school, of the way Arab civilisation flourished in the past – here was a proof of its long history. She thought about the hands that had turned these pages, and felt a sharp pang of regret that, when she'd been in Dubai, she'd thought that being Arab was an obstacle in her life.

She saw her grandfather squatting on the floor, bent over a short-legged table, penning words. Hidden away from the brightness of the day in his room, he would stop from time to time to drink an infusion of herbs and rub his eyes, and explain to Lamis the meaning of the saying, written in a calligraphy that looked like drawing, 'My hand has written so many books; my hand will wither but the books remain.' And when she asked him, as she pointed at the books, 'You've written all of these?' he smiled.

Lamis used to visit her grandfather in the afternoons, in order to hold out her palm and receive a few drops of the perfume that he kept in a drawer. She would sniff it and repeat after him the refrain for inhaling a beautiful fragrance, 'May God pray for the Prophet and his family.'

Her grandfather would untie her hair ribbon, comb her hair and then braid it. He would take the ribbon, which he'd folded around his finger, let it unwind, and steam out the creases over the vapour rising from the samovar.

When Lamis was nine years old, she began to be aware of her grandfather's criticisms of her parents, especially of her father, who often hid in the basement when her grandfather visited their house. He would scold his daughter: 'I know you're covering for him. He's in the basement, amusing himself with his lute and drinking alcohol, interfering with God's creation. Look at all these birds,' he would exclaim, striking the birdcages with his stick, surprised by the loud commotion made by the birds' flapping wings relative to their small size. 'If the Almighty had wanted bloody sparrows to sing like nightingales, he would have given them different larynxes. Your husband's a degenerate.'

By her side Nicholas twitched and Lamis realised that her reading had tailed off.

'I'm thinking of my grandfather.'

'Your grandfather?'

'Yes. This manuscript makes me think of him. Would he ever have imagined that his little Lamis would be in England, falling in love with an Englishman.'

'Living in Londris, Ingelterra, falling in love with a Franji . . .'

'I wonder if my parents ever thought when they pushed me into getting married that I'd be living in London and that they were imposing a new culture and language on me. And on their grand-children, too.'

'But darling, I'm grateful they thought nothing of the sort. I can't imagine life without you now.' And he returned his hand where it belonged.

They were lovers.

Lovers' breath is hot, their eyes lock in a permanent, fiery dialogue, their saliva runs, they breathe loudly through their noses, their chests are as fragile as glass and threaten to shatter when they inhale and exhale, and their spines bend like cucumbers.

All this was harmful to the manuscript, which had been kept in the museum storage room at a constant, even temperature, much like Lamis herself who, up until then, had been preserved from the heat of the passion that the Franji's eyelashes, lowered in longing for her, had now engendered, and from the damp caused by his sighs, that seemed to rise from his entrails.

The Cassiopoeia of stars relaxed the tightness in Lamis's brain cells, where she'd hidden her masturbation secrets. She felt that each part of her was stretching into life in front of what she used to fear the most, men. 'Oh, there is nothing to hide, nothing.' And, as if for the first time since she'd been wrapped in a blanket as a newborn infant, she found herself standing completely naked in front of the mirror of reality – Nicholas – and feeling like a child who, upon seeing herself for the first time, becomes aware only by degrees, with a few moments of doubt and fear, that the image in the mirror is really her.

People who saw Lamis and her husband together thought that she was his secretary or an interior designer. He was like a eunuch who felt no sexual desire, or at least no urge for physical contact with her, and if their hands happened to touch when he was taking a cup of tea from her, he might as well have been touching the saucer, while she only felt the money that he gave her in English pounds. All the same, the eunuch and his secretary shared the same bed. And his seduction routine had all been concentrated in one question, 'Are you asleep?'

Later that day, in his flat, Nicholas bent over her as her father used to bend over his lute when he noticed the tone was degenerating. Lamis embraced Nicholas; she clasped her hands round his neck, then his chest, so that he would not see her face. His fingers on her, trying to rouse her, were like the little cupids in the painting of Venus and Mars, fluttering over the sleeping god to try and bring him back to life.

Nicholas touched her strings one by one, his touch varying, depending on the tune he wanted to hear. Like a teacher who had not yet despaired of his pupil, he tried again and again, with infinite patience, until she fidgeted and said into his stomach, 'It doesn't matter. I'm happy as I am. It doesn't bother me.'

'It bothers me.'

He was like a mother weaning her child off the breast; as a child who screams and only wants milk, Lamis only wanted the touch of wood. And as the mother offers affection, so did Nicholas. Nicholas stopped and lifted himself off her the moment Lamis felt her body had become a thick barrier, resistant to the pounding waters. He moved aside and lay along the wall and she looked furtively at him, her eyes travelling all over him, taking in his neck, shoulders, stomach, thighs. She'd never once lain naked side by side with her husband in all their thirteen years together, and he'd never got out of bed without curling up into a ball and pulling on his pyjama top, and sometimes the bottoms too.

She felt as if her eyes had left her body and were hovering above her, watching them as man and woman – Adam and Eve. From such intimacy, a hand on a breast, a hand on a thigh, hands and eyes tranquil, from a feeling of closeness like this, life had begun.

Then he made her kneel and spread her thighs so she was crouching over him and finally Lamis lost her centre. She did not know whether to respond to her nipples and her beating heart or to what was there between her thighs. The feel of him made her cry from her long orgasm, and forget the feel of wood for ever, even lignum vitae, famous for its oily resin.

II

Lamis's ex-husband was waiting for her with their son at the door of the Trocadero. She'd been hoping that some minor illness would keep her away: she was afraid of meeting her son, afraid she would cry and cling on to him and ask him to forgive her. Her husband was without his customary thick cigar, and he was wearing a new cashmere jacket. As soon as he saw her approaching he said to his son, 'Right. Don't be late. You've got a lot of studying to do.'

Lamis caught her ex-husband's eye as he was going and asked how he was. He mumbled a few words and kept walking, but Khalid stopped him. He wanted money. Lamis said quickly that she would give Khalid any money he needed, but his father put his hand in his trouser pocket and handed the boy a ten-pound note.

Lamis had prepared herself for an ultimatum in case her husband took her aside and tried with all his might to convince her to go back to him.

His pride and his lack of ability held him back as usual. Before she'd gathered the courage to ask for a divorce, he'd witnessed her bouts of nausea, her insomnia, her habit of leaving the bed to swallow sleeping pills and tranquillisers, and shutting the bathroom or the bedroom door in his face. Why don't you go to the doctor? he would often suggest. His admiration for her youth, beauty and apparent serenity was one thing but to let that beauty disrupt his life was something else.

Is it possible that he used to touch me with that hand once upon a time? thought Lamis, that I shared his life, and that if it wasn't for him I would never have set foot in this country and got to know Nicholas? And I was the one who insisted that Khalid would always be my son, whatever anyone said.

But now she was replaced by Khalid's grandmother, who had taken him in her arms when he was first born, weeping with love for him, while Lamis had wept because she was suffering from urine retention and was scared the nurse would come back and stick a rubber tube between her legs, and because she was afraid to hold her baby in her arms.

She could see now that Khalid and his father had unintentionally joined forces against her. It was as if they were singing the Egyptian song she used to sing with Khalid, pointing to the passers-by, 'We're together, together, while the dog's alone, gnawing at his flesh.'

Except now they were both pointing at her. Then she glanced at her ex-husband and changed her mind: he couldn't sing, and he didn't make jokes. She was just feeling guilty.

She took Khalid in her arms and when she smelled him she had to pull away and break the moment by laughing and pretending that she had got a fright after momentarily losing him in the crowd.

'Darling, you've grown up so much. Have you really got taller in one month? You hair's the latest fashion! I love the kiss curl! And that black leather jacket?'

'Oh, shit, I forgot to tell you to make Dad let me go back on the tube alone.'

'Next time . . . and no swearing, please.'

'This time. He'll never know. I'll tell him you brought me right to the door. Please.'

'No, no, no.'

'You're both such scaredy-cats all the time. Nothing'll happen to me. I'm not a child. I'm nearly thirteen, remember.' And he smoothed his hair down.

She wanted to laugh. He always smoothed his hair down as if it was the clue to understanding what he was saying. She took his arm and said, 'I've really missed you. And your grandparents in Dubai and your auntie and cousin all miss you too. I'm so happy that I've left Dubai, and that I'm back here for good.'

'Me too, but . . . I was looking forward to visiting you in Dubai. Did you get me the things I asked for?'

'We'll get them here, today!'

'Does that mean you didn't bring me anything from Dubai? Everybody goes to Dubai to get all the computer games and you were there and didn't buy anything. Mum!'

'Things were difficult.'

'I don't believe it. I don't believe you were in Dubai and didn't buy anything.'

'I decided to come back to London a few hours before the plane took off. It's amazing I got a seat at all.'

'What about the airport? They have all the computer games for less than five pounds.'

She had a sudden memory of watching Samir at Dubai Airport, then visualised Nicholas holding her and drew her breath in sharply.

'But I thought your father and grandmother told you what happened. Do you know what happened to me?'

'I know they're totally stupid there.'

Khalid doesn't love me any more, Lamis panicked. How could he after she'd abandoned him, even though she'd promised him that she would come back to London to see him every two months, and that his father would send him to visit her in Dubai between times. But of course he loves me, she chided herself. He's so young. It doesn't occur to him that I'd like to be shown proof.

She waited for a hint, a gesture. She wished that there were a thermometer that she could place on his forehead to gauge his reactions – I-love-you's or I-don't-love you's – like the one she'd used for taking his temperature when he was ill.

When she had shouted at her husband and his mother that she wanted a divorce, Khalid had been at the computer having a conversation with his friend Timothy. He had looked up from the screen and asked her if she were really going to divorce his father because this time he really felt it in her voice. She hurried over and flung her arms round him saying, 'I love you. I don't know, but I love you,' whereupon he returned to his e-mail and typed, 'I don't think they'll get divorced. They quarrel but they'll never divorce.'

Lamis and Khalid went into Planet Hollywood. She could not attract Khalid's attention or draw him into conversation: his eyes and ears were riveted to the screens that were showing clips from different films, while his mouth was busy masticating food. She wanted to be put on trial now, and for Khalid either to pronounce her guilty, in which case she'd attempt to justify what she'd done, or to clear her, and then she could rejoice and relax. But he was absorbed in trying to guess which films the clips were from, and hinting that she should buy him a red leather jacket with the restaurant's name on it. Would he become friends with Bruce Willis or Schweizhof if he wore it? she asked.

'Schwarzenegger,' he said sarcastically. 'Schweizhof's the name of a hotel in Switzerland, Mum.' Then, 'Mum, I don't like it here any more. It makes me feel sick, it's so noisy. Please can you take me to the aquarium?'

'At the zoo?'

'No, near Big Ben. Past Westminster Bridge. The taxi knows.'

'An aquarium with fish in it?'

'No. Elephants.'

She smiled at him. She would rather he was cheeky like this than miserable because she had left home.

He stopped a taxi with a wave of his hand and told the driver they wanted to go to County Hall.

It turned out that the aquarium was in an old building facing Big Ben and the river. Its calm atmosphere made her think it would be the ideal place to talk to him and make him understand how much she loved him. She sensed that her son was developing some independence. If he had access to money, he wouldn't need her to take him on outings. The days when she'd been his guide in the outside world, the tongue that spoke for him so that he could look and learn and try things out, were gone. She didn't now know that he was interested in fish, or in anything apart from the latest technology. But he wasn't making for the aquarium; the fish and the sea creatures didn't receive more than a passing glance from Khalid.

When Lamis's own mother was a little girl, she used to say to her father, the cleric, whenever she liked a song that was playing on the radio while he was twisting the knobs, trying to find the Qur'an, 'It's on the right station, Dad. Straight after this song, they'll recite the Qur'an.'

Her son dragged her to the Namco arcade, next to the aquarium. Lights shone in her eyes and bounced off the stairs and walls and ceiling, and there were machines with knobs, flashing colours and music blaring. It was like walking into Las Vegas. Khalid dived into a red sports car, pressed the accelerator, and went racing through the streets, the cold wind blowing in his face and ruffling his hair.

'Look, I'm driving, Mum. I want to learn how to drive.'

He went from one machine to another. He was a pilot, a soldier, a professional racing driver. He had to destroy tanks that were blowing up everything in their path. He was a giant who chained

132

up a woman, beat her, then licked the chain clean. He did not listen to his mother, he urged her to play the games with him, implored her desperately for a moment, then forgot all about her, shrieking enthusiastically as he became absorbed again. Lamis grew used to the flashing lights and the din, and to being a mobile bank feeding the pounds into these machines, and to watching her son grind his teeth in his efforts to concentrate, as if he were sharpening them to attack the one-handed giant.

'Fifty-three video games, Mum! I want to try Choker. Timothy told me it was cool.'

'No, don't. No means no. It's an electric chair.'

'No, Mum. It's not real.'

'I know, but I don't like the idea of it.'

'Mum, read what it says. Read it. Please.'

She read, 'Try the electric chair. Test your strength. Can you bear it? Simulates lethal voltage with intense vibrations. Totally safe.'

'See? Did you read it? They say it's not dangerous.'

A man was sitting on the chair, gripping levers on either side of it, lights flashing at his face, then he grimaced and began shaking. 'Cool,' he said to his girlfriend as he got off. 'You feel as if you're touching a lethal current.'

Lamis moved away, aware that she had gone back to being a mother, dragging her son along by the hand as if she were still at home.

Khalid could not believe his mother didn't know how to play the games. He set about teaching her, still eating chips and KitKats between shots. The lights, the noise, the flashing colours, her son's adrenalin, finally conspired to make her feel that she was the same age as he was, in a city of electronic marvels. This gave her a feeling of familiarity and warmth. Her divorce seemed inevitable. She thought Nicholas had been wise to advise her to let her son suggest their first outing. She rode the red car, the Ridge Rider, at the entrance, the cold wind flying in her face, and found herself putting her foot down harder and harder.

They waited for a taxi. Big Ben was in front of them, and the river and the bridge. Dusk was the best time in London, when the weather was good: it rarely seemed to rain at this time of day. The twilight sky was like a field of red anemones. People said that this was the colour of pollution, but she thought that London wanted to see itself clearly, and it chased away the clouds of daytime long enough for the sun to wink an eye before the grey calm returned.

They boarded a taxi and she asked the driver to take them to Regent's Park. She put her arm round her son because she felt a lump in her throat.

'Do you want me to come back, darling? Do you miss me?'

'Yes, I miss you, but you were always unhappy. I used to see you crying.'

She cried now, holding him tight, and he hugged her back.

'I love you, Mum.'

She hugged him again and choked back a sob. They were getting close now, and the taxi was passing in front of the statue that had always made her feel anxious. It was of a woman shading her eyes from the sun or the rain so she could see better. The woman was watching people approaching from a distance, and on her bad days Lamis used to imagine her mother-in-law had ordered this bronze woman to spy on her.

She asked the taxi to wait until she saw her son hitting the electronic numbers to open the door. If only she could go after him and hug him again. Her heart lurched when she saw the wrought-iron gate with its gold curlicues bang shut behind him, then immediately she breathed more easily because she was outside it. As the taxi drove off with her she wiped away her tears.

She'd thought this flat would make her happy – as she had every time they had moved in the past – and stood looking out of its windows on to Regent's Park, beneath the neo-classical stone figures and blue mouldings that, reminiscent of the Greeks and Romans, seemed out of keeping with the damp misty air and English buildings. But she came to recognise more with each passing day that the flat was her prison. From it she was able to see the trees in the park and the lovers looking across at the resplendent houses under the majestically sculpted figures, and wishing they were inside them, never imagining that in one of them stood a woman envying them.

As soon as she said the name Eccleston Square to the taxi driver, she felt warmth take over her whole body.

'Your husband should see the bed each time he looks at you,' her mother had counselled her.

And here she was thinking of Nicholas, and thinking that he was waiting for her in bed.

III

Amira prepared herself in every possible way for taking on the title of Princess, not forgetting any detail that would help her bring the role to life. She asked and enquired, made telephone calls – international and local – and she taped conversations with clients from the Gulf and Saudi Arabia, from embassies and offices. She asked trivial questions in order to hear one word or another, or to note a particular phrasing: 'I don't want that', 'Come here', 'I want to go', 'Come, take me to', 'What is this?', 'For sure.'

She found it difficult. What type of personality should she adopt? Should she be a princess who loves poetry and reads literature, or one who loves films and songs . . . should she be involved in charity work and schools, or be a fashionably modern princess who wants to know all the latest restaurants, shops, clubs . . . or what about a princess who loves massages, who devotes herself to the art of well-being, to make-up, even plastic surgery?

With Wasim's help she was engaged as an interpreter to accompany a genuine princess for a few days. The Princess had to go to hospital for a simple operation and Amira acted as go-between for her and the hospital staff. Amira ordered the tea, coffee and food from the restaurant for the Princess's entourage; she arranged for a bigger television, and films for the video. And she paid close attention to the Princess's every gesture, big or small, to her demeanour and her manner of speaking. Amira quickly learned when to show affection and when to be aloof; when to use a low- or a high-pitched tone of voice; how to move her hands; when to throw a smile, or to frown, or laugh; when to speak and when to stay silent; and, of course, when to be very generous, generous or less generous; as well as how to relate to another member of the family, a mother, aunt, father, uncle.

And when the time finally arrived, Amira left her building wearing a modest suit – a jacket covering her hips over a long skirt – and her jet-black hair not quite touching the abaya around her shoulders. The only glitter to be seen came from her ring, her wristwatch and the buckle of her Loewe black crocodile-leather handbag. So as to avoid the inquisitive eye of the porter, and any possibile trouble from Samir and his monkey, she did not ask the Rolls-Royce to fetch her from the flat, but from Wasim's salon. There, she made sure that the three young women accompanying her looked modestly sexy, while at the same time very timid, and that they did not rush to open the car doors or joke with the driver, but waited for him to open the doors for them. Although Amira observed that her non-stop instructions over the preceding few days had been effective, the luxurious car and the awareness that their deceit might be detected made the attendants very nervous, and she put them at ease by making them laugh: 'Don't let's be like snakes chewing their own tails . . .'

She chose to carry out her first trick at a bank for two reasons. Firstly, it was not possible to con a bank: there were rules governing the exchange of money, cheque books, transfers, etc. And secondly, because there her victim would be so close to his money.

The driver parked the car by the corner of the Arab Bank on Park Lane. Amira handed him a sheet of blue paper that she had bought from an expensive stationery shop, with her name written 'al-Inud, bint . . . ibn . . . ibn . . . ('al-Inud, daughter of . . . the son of . . . the son of . . .') exactly the way a prince or a princess would have written it.

'Would you please ask the bank if any transfers in my name have arrived from the Kingdom?'

'But . . . do you think they'll trust me with it, your highness?'

'Just ask them if it's arrived. I'll go in for the money myself.'

'Of course.'

Amira had rented the Rolls-Royce and its driver for three days from a specialist car-hire, paying on behalf of Princess al-Inud, signing her own name, as 'attendant and interpreter'. They had insisted on the full amount, in advance. These days they did not trust anyone who came in asking to rent a car on behalf of a prince or a princess – unless it was for royalty known to them personally – because he or she might just disappear without paying.

As if she really was waiting for a bank transfer from her uncle, Amira began to tell her worry beads. One of her attendants asked her whether Nahid was unwell.

'Not as far I know Why? Did someone say she was?'

'I must have made a mistake.'

Amira hurriedly dialled the number of Nahid's mobile phone.

'Nid, Nid, where are you? . . . Oh . . . You aren't sick or anything? . . . Good . . . Yes . . . At seven, for sure.' She switched off her mobile and said to the young women, 'Whenever her sister comes to London, Nahid gets ill.'

The driver came out of the bank and, leaning down to the car window, spoke to the Princess. 'I'm sorry. The transfer hasn't come through yet. They suggest you try at,' he read out from a piece of paper in his hand, 'Bank al-Riyadh or the Bank of Kuwait.'

'Let me think about what to do now.'

'Your highness, I don't think we can park here . . . but perhaps I could explain if a traffic warden turns up . . .'

They drove around the block a few times; stopped for a few minutes, and then drove on again, following Amira's instructions, until she saw a man in his sixties who was approaching the bank.

Amira asked the driver to stop. She stepped out of the car followed by her attendants, who stopped chewing their gum and competing over who could blow the biggest bubbles. Amira speeded up slightly, so that she and the man arrived on the bank's doorstep at the same time. When he noticed Amira and her attendants, he stepped back, so that they could enter before him. Amira did not thank him; nor did she deign to look in his direction. As far as the Princess was concerned, this man was of no more interest than a security guard. Once inside she sat down to wait with her attendants and when her turn came, she approached the teller's window with studied, slow steps. She let one of her attendants ask, in her most modest voice, about the bank transfer. The teller couldn't quite understand and Amira stepped in, speaking in broken, confused English. The teller asked them to wait, saying that he'd fetch a colleague who spoke Arabic. Speaking in Arabic, Amira then gave the bank clerk the name that was festooned over the wall of the bank. Just as Amira had foreseen, it also rang in the ears of the client. He was standing, watching, eyeing each of her women attendants in turn, while they stood trying to look their best, holding their abayas or leaving them draped over their shoulders.

The Arabic-speaking clerk excused himself for a moment, and checked the computer. Amira then told him the name of her uncle. At this, the bank clerk asked if she would like to wait in the VIP reception. Amira declined, looking at her watch. The teller told her that she'd have to wait for a while. She went back to her seat but when she saw that the client had finished his business at the bank and was preparing to leave, she walked over towards the door with one of her attendants, asking the others to wait, and started to talk on her mobile.

'I don't know what to do. I really don't. The cheque hasn't arrived. I'm outside the bank now and the man with the furnished flat won't wait. The embassy? I'd rather die. They'll send messages back home to check, and then the Ministry will contact my family, then they'll get back to the embassy, and so on and so on. It's a mess.'

Naturally the Arab man was listening to her conversation. For his benefit, Amira added, 'I'm by myself outside the bank. I'm fed up, really fed up.'

She switched off her mobile and put her hand to her forehead, murmuring to her attendant, 'My head.'

The attendant supported her, as if the Princess were about to collapse; then Amira met the man's eyes, regained her composure and said, 'I get so fed up with banks sometimes.'

'I'm sorry. Can I help?'

'No thank you.'

'Excuse me, but please consider me as a bank. When your cheque arrives, you can pay me back.'

'No thank you. May God protect your children and loved ones.'

The deputy manager came over to Amira and introduced himself. He told Amira that the bank was prepared to help her out and give her whatever she needed. She thanked him but refused his offer. He apologised to her before he left. She turned to the other man, and thanked him again.

'We're both strangers here, far from our homes and families.'

'No thank you, I couldn't.'

The attendant chimed in with, 'But, madam . . .', as if she were trying to persuade her otherwise.

Amira went silent, looking at the ground bashfully, like a child who has just wet herself in public, and her silence was her consent.

'Is ten thousand enough?'

'I'll give you my watch then.'

'There's no need.'

'Thank you.'

'Will you wait? I'll just be a few minutes.'

Amira walked over to the car, her footsteps weighed down by tiredness and by disappointment with the bank and its associates. The attendant brought out the others, who waited beside her.

Amira sat in the car, took out her prayer beads and began passing them through her fingers while the English driver stood to one side of the Rolls and the attendant said under her breath,

'God, please . . . please, God.' The man came hurrying over. Amira lowered the window and held out her hand, saying, 'Give me your name and address.'

'It's not important,' he said. When she insisted, he said politely, 'My name's Haris, and I'm staying at the Dorchester.'

'Write it down, dear,' she said to her attendant. 'The Dorchester, Mr Haris.'

'God willing, tomorrow we'll be in touch with you and return your kindness.'

He handed her ten envelopes and, quite unperturbed, she took them, smiled at him, and said goodbye.

Amira asked the driver to take them to a Lebanese restaurant in Shepherd's Bush. Although no one in the restaurant uttered a word, it was known immediately that a princess had just walked in with her entourage. Without having to ask for what they wanted, they were brought more than twenty plates in quick succession, and four waiters hovered, and the way that Amira and her companions ate showed how nervous they had been at the bank. The young women asked for toothpicks, which Amira forbade them to use. All of a sudden they remembered the driver. A waiter asked one of the companions whether he should take the plates of untouched food out to him. 'No,' she answered, 'the Princess wouldn't like that. Give him a menu and let him choose.'

Amira knew that the young women were impatient to have their money the minute the meal was over. Where could they go? She was afraid to let the porter of her building know what she was up to. They could go to Nahid's – but no one answered Nahid's phone. She found herself digging into the envelopes in her handbag, counting out five hundred pounds for each of the women. Two accepted happily. The third was not satisfied. 'But Amira, you have ten thousand pounds.'

'I'm the Princess,' Amira snapped, 'but here, each of you take one hundred pounds extra, and now pay the bill, and the waiters.' She handed over two hundred pounds, which the attendant divided between the waiters who were standing around drooling like dogs.

Amira stood up, knowing that everyone's eyes were on her table, including those of a client who thought he'd seen her before but couldn't tell for sure – Amira appeared a changed woman. It was not the shorter black hair, nor the face devoid of make-up, or the tailored, unrevealing jacket. It was the eyes that looked different: their hungry, scheming expression, as if a fox stalked inside each of them, had been replaced by a look of contentment, almost of lethargy.

As the car drove towards Bond Street, Amira made her three companions swear again on the Qur'an that they would never utter a word to anyone. She promised that she would increase their share next time. 'Anyway,' she added, 'now I'm going to buy each of you a small gift from Cartier.' Inside the jewellery shop, the manager went without question to fetch rare pieces from the vault, and Amira believed that she was a princess, a determined princess who knew what she didn't like. Afterwards, Amira the Princess scolded her attendants for not having chosen anything. 'But everything we saw cost much less than our large budget,' they retorted sarcastically.

'Well, I promise you that all of us will have something from Cartier in a few weeks' time.'

Amira dropped the three women at Wasim's salon and directed the driver to take her to Nahid's. On the way she fantasised about declaiming to her brothers, both of whom had stopped talking to her when they heard what she was really doing in London, 'I told you I'd be very rich. Look what I have in my purse. The water seller's daughter is now a princess with a British passport.'

She and her entourage were working at full stretch; Amira the organiser, the brain behind everything, tailoring her schemes to suit the encounter. She always varied her reasons for needing money, adapting her story to fit different faces and personalities.

141

She never gave the same rationale twice, and discovered through experience that the simple explanations worked the best.

Sometimes she had to come up with inventive excuses for not paying back the men who'd given her money. The money order had been lost, and the bank was looking into it. She took pleasure in accusing a bank – it had taken her money and ploughed it into its profits – and telling amusing stories about how her mother sent back her allowance from Saudi Arabia when she saw the travellers' cheques instead of English pounds, insisting that they were just pieces of paper. 'Where's the Queen's head? I don't want paper, I want real money.'

Sometimes Amira would claim to be afraid of annoying her 'uncle', or her 'brother'. 'He's always busy,' she would say, 'if I bother them I'm afraid they'll say come back home. Or they'll never allow the women in our family to go abroad again.'

She would add that it was hard for her because she was a princess, and people were looking at her one hundred per cent of the time.

However, there came a day when Amira found herself paying off her debt in another way, and one that suited her best, leaving her with a clear conscience. She was at Claridge's for afternoon tea. It was full of American and English women, the latter wearing hats like tea cosies.

Amira's three attendants, having helped her out of her jacket, poured and distributed the tea, whispering to one another, covering their mouths in embarrassment, and sinking their teeth into their palms when they laughed. Amira sat calmly maintaining her poise despite her growing fears that there was no one to con at the hotel that afternoon. But she was a princess, wasn't she? Real princesses didn't suffer anxiety or nervousness, for everything was within their reach – people and their immaterial souls, as well as all the material goods they wanted. Among themselves Amira and her companions began to debate whether or not they should gather up their courage and try the Dorchester, taking a risk on whether the real Princess was there, when a visiting Arab, whom

Nahid had recently mentioned to Amira, arrived in the company of three Iranian men. The men looked around and chose a nearby table – Tits-like-Pamela Anderson's abaya had slipped off her shoulders by then.

Amira took out her mobile phone and tried to use it. She indicated to an attendant that it wasn't working. Whereupon her attendant managed to manoeuvre the loan of a mobile from the Arab sitting at the nearby table, explaining to him that the battery on the Princess's phone had run down, and assuring him that they were calling London, not Saudi Arabia.

'What are the children having for tea?' Amira asked down the borrowed phone. 'Good. I'm really grateful to uncle for sending that sack of flour in the private plane. Can you call my aunt in the Kingdom and tell her there isn't a size 44? But I do feel embarrassed: it was my mother who told the girls to ask him to send the flour – the stuff here makes the dough stick to the pan. I'm waiting in the hotel. I've sent a driver and a car. Don't be too long.'

Amira handed the phone to Tits-like-Pamela Anderson to return to its owner, thanking him with a nod of her head. But the Arab stood and fetched it himself, then went back to his table. Amira cleared her throat and went off with an attendant to the bathroom, walking like a princess, her back a slab of marble, her steps slow and measured. When she re-entered the room, she saw from a distance that the two other attendants were talking to the man, assuring him that they'd be there the next day as the Princess loved Claridge's, and had actually been born in one of its suites.

The following day the Princess reappeared, wearing additional jewellery. Amira took off her jacket to reveal a red blouse straining over her prominent breasts. The visiting Arab changed his mind and decided that the Princess was younger and prettier than he'd thought. The Princess did not look at him, although one of her attendants surreptitiously indicated to her that he was there. She ate a quarter of a slice of gâteau with great care and concentration and sipped her tea calmly, then asked the waiter to bring more sandwiches and cake for the girls. The Princess's mobile was working again and when it rang she shrieked down it, 'God forbid! Where? A hospital in London? Oh God! It doesn't matter about the driver. I'll take a taxi. No, really. It's strange. I don't know. Did you tell them she's related to the Princess, daughter of . . . Did you tell them who my uncle is? It's strange they're insisting on being paid in advance. Let me do what I can.'

Amira clutched her head and one of the girls brought her a glass of water. They stood around her, as if wanting to hear what had happened and full of concern for her at the same time.

'Kauthar got her hand stuck in the lift. She's in hospital. Pay the bill,' Amira told them.

She opened her bag and one of the attendants took a note from her and waved it at the waiter.

'I don't know how much money they're going to want from me until I get there,' exclaimed Amira emotionally. 'London is so hard to understand sometimes.'

She held up a hand and the waiter came over. Looking at her watch, she asked the waiter when the banks closed.

'Half-four, madam.'

One of the girls handed him two fifty-pound notes. He hesitated, and realising what was on his mind, she said, 'We're paying the bill.'

He flushed. He'd thought that they were tipping him for telling them when the banks closed; in fact the sum did include a fifty-pound tip.

Amira tried beaming her thoughts across to the rich Arab: Why don't you give me the three thousand in your pocket? I know that's what you withdraw each day for the casino. I'm waiting, waiting, waiting.

She looked around helplessly, while the attendants did their best to appear pathetic. And then the man got to his feet, approached her and very respectfully asked the Princess if he could help.

'Is it true that the hospitals only take American Express cards or cheques? I don't have either. I get a bag of cash every Friday from the Kingdom, and today's only Wednesday.'

'Please, if you don't mind, let me give you what you need.'

'No thank you. I'm afraid my brother would be furious with me.'

'He'll never know. When the bag comes, you can pay me back.'

'But the banks are shut.'

'I've got cash on me. Is two thousand five hundred enough? I can get more.'

He kept the cash distributed between the pockets of his jacket and trousers, and there was even some in his overcoat. Her attendant took the money graciously.

'Thank you,' he said humbly, as he handed the last lot over. 'Do you need me to come with you . . . I'm like your brother.'

Amira asked one of her attendants to take his telephone number so that they could let him know that everything was fine, 'and put your mind at rest'.

The next day she managed to see him alone and to insinuate herself into his room at the hotel. She asked if she could hide there for two hours, she was afraid that somebody would see her. She'd tricked her mother, her aunts, everybody, even her driver, to be at the hotel that afternoon to see him. The Arab, put on the spot, agreed. When the Princess saw that he had a room, not a suite, she apologised. Nevertheless, she didn't try to leave. She sat on a chair. 'Never mind, you're like a brother. You were so chivalrous yesterday, real, old-fashioned courtesy. I bet you recite poetry,' and Amira began to recite the only poem she knew:

> Is it your saliva, rainwater or wine?
> In my mouth it's so cool, and in my heart it's like fire.

She let a tear fall. She asked him to turn on the television. They sat and watched, then she wept and expressed her greedy desires; she was a wronged, repressed princess. She screamed that she didn't want her jewellery and she began to undo her necklace and take off her bracelet and hurl her jewellery into the middle of the bedroom; she tore off her jacket and blouse to reveal her large breasts and her coloured lace bra. 'Since I first saw the light of day, I've been starved of romance and affection,' she said, closing her eyes and rolling around on the bed. She flung herself on to the floor, then pretended to think that she might have broken a limb and began to wail, pushing up her skirt and exposing her thighs.

'Is my arm broken?' She rested her arm along her thigh fearfully, and the man, on his knees beside her but hesitant about touching her, heard her whisper in his ear that she was dying for a kind word, a gentle touch, and then she took hold of his hand and said dramatically, 'This throat of mine is dry from swallowing so many tears, for it is my name . . . like a curse on me . . . al-Inud . . . al-Inud . . . the cloud full of rain.'

Then she seemed to be positioning the man above her so that he could examine her arm, but her fidgeting and constant mindless chattering made her move with a certain rhythm that aroused him and he fell on her, not caring about her origins, or whether what he was doing would land him in trouble. With the routine cadences of sex, she forgot that she was a princess and resumed her trade, letting slip a word or a gesture that fired the man's enthusiasm in spite of his surprise. Then she realised her awful mistake and said something in tones closer to those she'd used at first, while she recovered herself and reverted to being withdrawn and shy, as if her shameless behaviour had been an aberration. Her eyes were closed throughout, even when she stepped out of her skirt, and they appeared still to be closed as she gathered up her jewellery, fastened her blouse buttons, picked up her bag and left the man in a state of blissful happiness, as if he had just slept with one of the houris of Paradise. Had he really fucked royalty, a distressed, unfulfilled princess? He'd thought that by helping her royal highness he would have acquired a certain status, and her family would be beholden to him. The hotel had been transformed, in spite of its luxurious drapes and comfortable bed, into a course of obstacles and terrors that he had overcome. He was Clever

Hassan, hero of thousands of folk tales, who had reached the jewel in the dragon's mouth and snatched it from the flames.

Amira left the hotel full of self-confidence, without having given the man so much as a conspiratorial backward glance to acknowledge what had happened between them.

IV

Samir was in Amira's flat with John the Policeman, hardly able to believe that this was not one of his daydreams. John took off his uniform, including his policeman's helmet, then pulled his vest over his head to reveal taut muscles and a smooth stomach. Samir barely stopped himself from exclaiming aloud.

John went up to Samir and took hold of his nipple and Samir went into ecstasies and felt as if he were going to faint. When he came back to reality, he shouted, 'See, John, I'm a virgin. A virgin, not a prostitute.'

John did not understand most of what Samir said, but Samir made him laugh. At the same time Samir felt cheated. He'd paid eighty pounds for John the Policeman to touch his nipple for a few seconds.

John had been investigating a traffic hold-up in Edgware Road when he had seen an apparition in red boots and a purple boa weaving her way, laughing, between the cars, as she tried to cross the road.

'Bloody hell,' he said to the other policemen with him. 'Did that witch just fall out of the sky?'

'Witch? Me?' Samir had turned round reproachfully, envisaging an old hag flying through the air on a broomstick. 'Don't say that, mama. But you're a very beautiful policeman. I'd go to prison for you!'

Samir tried everything he could think of to make John the

Policeman stay longer in the flat; he said he wanted to introduce him to one of his friends, an Egyptian musician, who'd never tasted the English; he tried tempting him with a glass of whisky, or a meal, but only the monkey succeeded in keeping him a few minutes longer.

'But John the Policeman, you were so quick with me.'

'Listen, mama, we agreed on eighty pounds. Besides, if your friend Amira comes back and finds me here with you – that is, with another man, in her flat – she'll hit the roof.'

'Why should she mind? Are you a thief or a leper? You're an English policeman, a beauty. She'd be honoured.'

'Maybe she'd be jealous. I'm sure she fancies you or she wouldn't let you stay here for nothing.'

'Firstly, she and I are soulmates. Secondly, didn't I tell you that I help her? I'm her right hand, her both hands. Look at how clean the flat is. I cook, I iron and wash everything. Open a cupboard and see how organised everything is. I pray to God for Amira day and night, and He listens to me. "Oh God, may the sand Amira touches turn to gold," and she knows by now that my prayers are all answered.'

'I can't see any gold. Only broken furniture.'

Samir nearly told John the Policeman just how generous Amira was. All the time.

'Johnny Guitar! Nahid couldn't help me extend my visa. The man she wanted to contact has left the Home Office. Can you help me, please?'

'I'll try, but you've already told me you have five kids and a wife, back at home. Were you fibbing?'

'What do you mean, fibbing?'

'Were you telling me a bunch of lies?'

'Never. They are there, all of them, in Sharjah . . . the Emirates. Why did you remind me of them?'

'Jesus! Do you need people to remind you?'

'No, I mean right now. I remember them always, but I'm so happy on my own here. But I'm going to go back and visit them soon.'

Samir had been in London two months. It was strange, he felt he belonged there and nowhere else, and he missed nobody. If he dared to tell the truth, he would say that he didn't even miss his children. He opened his eyes every morning to see the monkey and his face lit up. He felt as if he were in a hotel, on holiday; everything around him was new, and had nothing to do with him. A great contrast to his life in Sharjah, where everything depended on him, from the oven – seeing if it needed gas – to the fridge – seeing that it was full of food. Furthermore, he hated the sound of the air-conditioning there, where it was endemic, a must. Here, he and Amira had so many things in common. They shared the same taste in songs, films, jokes. She made him enjoy the company of women: 'They hug you, wipe away your tears and tell you their secrets.' He had a new family now: Amira, the monkey – and Nahid, even though she sometimes fumed for no good reason, as she did a week ago when Cappuccino stole her lipstick. But the most important reason for loving it here was that he was doing what he always wanted to do: make people laugh, and he was being paid for it, rather than doing it for nothing as he had for so many years. There was a respect here for everything, even for laughter; it was his job, a career, like any other, just like being an engineer, a doctor or a bus driver.

Back home people thought that London was walking in the mist wrapped in a heavy coat and a furry pair of boots (as indeed he had when he arrived) and that London was Piccadilly Circus, Oxford Street, Big Ben and Buckingham Palace.

London was freedom. It was your right to do anything, any time. You didn't need to undergo a devastating war in order to be freed to do what you wanted, and when you did do what you wanted, you didn't have to feel guilty or embarrassed, and start leading a double life and ultimately end up frustrated.

God must have started up the war in Lebanon so that people would leave him in peace, Samir had thought, so that they would stop watching him and to enable him to give up his job in the hotel peeling potatoes. God had given everybody life and death to play with, and, in that war, Samir wore what he wanted, telling his wife that if he disguised himself as a woman he could avoid trouble at checkpoints and buy bread more quickly. He wore brightly coloured trousers and a long coloured shirt, and glasses with red frames. Sometimes he dressed as a dancer in a club and performed for the soldiers when they were high on drink and drugs and loneliness. He moved about between the various factions of fighters wherever he could, in trenches, in beautiful villas that they'd appropriated when the owners fled. He bought and sold bottles of gas, and he filled up containers with water in one part of the city and took them to other parts, where the water was cut off. His mother was the first to praise his brilliant subterfuge, as he presented her with additional sacks of foodstuffs that he'd been given by a militiaman – even though she'd been the one to have him admitted to a mental hospital when she first saw her son wearing a dress.

Samir's mother had caught him singing and dancing on the roof terrace wearing her blue nylon nightie, her lipstick and high heels, when he was eleven years old. She called her husband who was having a siesta and edged away from her son, scared that he would throw himself off the roof if she went closer. Her crazy relative had jumped off a roof. Mad people hated anyone touching them when they were having one of their fits.

In the psychiatric hospital the doctor advised them to show Samir plenty of affection and to take an interest in him – his father, especially – and said that children of that age fantasised a lot. But three years later they took Samir back to the same hospital, after he had attempted suicide.

Chapter Five

I

Lamis glanced over the flowers she had arranged in vases and distributed over the fireplace, on the hall table, even in the cloakroom. Just as if I was still living with my husband, she thought, as she filled glass ashtrays with water and scattered rose petals in them, and lined dishes with coloured paper to receive the pistachio nuts. There were two things she had not done before: burned Omani incense in the incense-burner next to the dishes that Nicholas had prepared, and bought ready-made hummus and stuffed vine leaves from Marks and Spencer's to supplement them.

Ever since the previous day, Lamis had been restlessly anticipating this evening, when Nicholas was going to introduce her to his friends and acquaintances, so that she would have a 'family'. 'So you don't go on being alone,' he said to her.

'But I'm happy as I am. I'm satisfied with you. Unless you're fed up with me?'

The friends began to arrive and she felt as if she were crawling instead of walking. Babyish sounds came out of her mouth.

She tried to brush her mind like a shoe so it shone bright and sharp, to regain her composure, but failed miserably. Their conversation moved quickly in a sphere of which she had no knowledge, total Englishness, in which she was incapable of being polite, hypocritical or inventive. The talk revolved around local politics and rules and regulations. She decided she would have to learn the newspaper by heart in future, but then realised this wouldn't work, because their conversations were like artefacts inlaid with the whims and preoccupations of the individual. Even when talking about food they constantly slipped in phrases she did not understand, like 'gastronomical delights'.

She found herself blaming Nicholas. Like a silkworm, she had been spinning her cocoon slowly and, deeply content, she had been preparing herself for flight. But Nicholas had taken her out before she was ready.

Surely she could break into the guests' closed circle in a single step if she spoke a sentence. Why didn't she chat with them as she did with him? After all, she could tell that he found her interesting, amusing. One sentence. She should let it out now.

She had to be quick. Her chance had come. There was a breeder of falcons at the table who had lost his job because a sheikh in the Emirates had declared himself bankrupt and sold his birds. She was about to intervene and say that her father used to train birds to sing, but she stopped herself, because she would have to link this story to the falcons, and then one of the guests was asking the breeder if a blue-beaked falcon was in the sheikh's collection, a strain said to cost between eighty and a hundred thousand pounds.

'Oh yes. They smuggle them from the south of Siberia with the hawks. The Russian authorities are starting to uncover vast smuggling operations on a daily basis.'

'Maybe the Russians want to sell them to the Mafia!'

'Do you think they're a protected species?'

OK, she had an idea now. There was something she could say. She was going to come out on top here. They liked joking. If only she could make them smile, she would become worthy of their notice.

She wondered how they would react if she told them about her aunt who had rushed out of their house in Najaf, slamming the door behind her, running across the stony ground shrieking and wailing, 'God help us! They're all at it in there. The child's fucking the chair, the birds are fucking their perches, and the parrot shouts, "Hello! God is great!" all the time and mounts the other male.'

She continued to smile and agree, trying to pitch her voice in anticipation of speaking her first words. She did not want them to come out in a series of short squeaky sentences because she was unused to talking in a large group of English people.

At last one of them, who must have sensed her growing unease, turned and addressed her. 'You're Iraqi. So you must have come to London to escape from Saddam's repression?'

Lamis answered confidently, 'Actually I came to marry an Iraqi man who was living here.'

With one sentence she had extinguished the expectation in the man's eyes. Nodding his head, he said, 'Aah,' then turned to talk to the person on the other side of him about British politics and their boycott of the Iraqis. So he'd decided that because she'd come to London in what he deemed normal circumstances, she wasn't worth spending time on.

She tried to recapture his interest, and interrupted him. 'We fled from Iraq to Syria and Lebanon before coming here, also my father was an artist – a musician – and he couldn't bear the way religious fanaticism dominated his life, and my grandfather . . .'

'Religious fanaticism? But Iraq isn't Iran, or Algeria! I didn't know there were Muslim extremists in Iraq.'

'I mean Najaf. My father . . .' Then she fell silent. It was a long story and would require many digressions. She made do with saying, 'It's a long story,' waiting to see if he asked her what it was before she continued, but he excused himself and turned away to pour more wine into his glass.

She blamed herself for not telling him that they fled because they were frightened of Saddam Hussein, and felt guilty she couldn't bring herself to tell her story.

'Nicholas tells me that you're from Iraq. From Baghdad?' Another guest was addressing her in very correct Arabic; he'd obviously decided that he had to have bulging eyes and protruding lips in order to be able to pronounce it.

'No. From Najaf.'

'Najaf, the holy city! I've never been there, although I visited

Baghdad in the late sixties and stayed in a small hotel owned by a Sabaean family. They were certainly persecuted. I remember they said their prayers in the cellar. What attracted me about their religion was their belief that there was a link between the stars and music. You should tell Nicholas about them. You know he's interested in astronomy?'

Then the guest moved on to discuss the civilisation of ancient Mesopotamia, and Lamis felt like a geography book and history book rolled into one. A thought crept into her mind and nudged her increasingly low self-esteem into the abyss: Nicholas thinks of me in the way these people do.

'I believe there are about forty thousand Iraqis in England. Am I wrong?'

Lamis nodded her head. 'Going by the official statistics there are forty-five thousand, or fifty. I think fifty would be closer,' she lied. 'In Germany they found fifty-four Iraqis hidden in sealed crates. They had just enough food to keep them alive and they'd been smuggled out of Istanbul on a mystery tour. The smugglers sent them to Germany and charged them three and a half thousand dollars a head. The funny thing was that the German police asked them how they'd got into the country!'

When he did not react, she repeated the story, then smiled fixedly until he finally registered some kind of amusement. She found herself switching into her mother-in-law's voice and re-counting her tale as if she had metamorphosed as suddenly as the woman in the television series *Bewitched*. She told him about the pretender to the Iraqi throne and that some of the Iraqis in England hung around him because he reminded them of the young King Faisal, who was murdered; about one of her mother-in-law's relatives who hid in a rubbish bin in Iraq because she was afraid of Saddam's son, Uday; how the Iraqis kept up the custom of trilling for joy at weddings, even in London's grandest hotels, and having traditional mourners at funerals, to convince infiltrators from home who might be present at these gatherings that they were genuine, and dissuade them from interpreting them as anti-Saddam demonstrations.

Then, to raise the tone of the conversation, she brought in the UN, Amnesty International, the Committee for Lifting Sanctions. But it was as if a television screen had been installed between her and the other guests: they were the viewers and she was the correspondent from Iraq, not there to be talked to or argued with, but to deliver information.

She busied herself with hospitable tasks, asking them if they wanted more to eat, going round with the red wine, but again she forced herself to try and construct a bridge between herself and them. She would see some of these people on a continuing basis. Nicholas was introducing her to one person after another, and she was trying – against the barrage of difficult words, the insistent beat of their rapid pronunciation, the sparring between them to prove who was the most knowledgeable, the most serious, the most witty – to interact with them. When, despite her desperate, breathless attempts, she didn't succeed, she became almost certain that there was a conspiracy. She switched her attention to the plates and glasses again and took them out to the kitchen. In the same way she knew these English words, she knew the structure of the language, yet found it hard to talk, because the language was like a private club, barred to any individual who hadn't had it planted in his mind like a tiny seed, so that it sprang from his lips automatically and was always correct. These English were born to it as they uttered their first cries in an English hospital. How could she ever hope to have the history, literature, politics all mingling in her head, so that when she heard 'the Scottish play', instead of asking what it was, she knew automatically it was *Macbeth*? What images would words like 'fiver' and 'cuppa' evoke, if she hadn't learned the hard way that they meant a five-pound note and a cup of tea? When David Copperfield sits with Peggotty 'by the parlour fire', she would never feel the fire's blaze or smell its smell in the same way they did.

She soon realised that it was only her presence that made their conversations deviate, albeit slightly, from their normal course. They were set in moulds according to their jobs: politics, the antiques trade, the international business community. She found herself on the edge of a conversation.

'I didn't see you at Anthony's this afternoon?'

'Poor old Anthony. I couldn't face it. How are his children?'

'Bearing up. They're being remarkably brave about his death.'

Lamis gasped in dismay.

'Oh, did you know him?' One of the speakers turned to look at her. 'I thought it was only Nicholas who did.'

She coughed to cover her confusion and said, 'No,' in a voice nobody heard, but did not say, 'We don't sit there in silence when we hear someone has died.'

'I chose some of Anthony's books and records, and a wooden hand from his collection. One of the records was in the wrong sleeve. Instead of Ravel, I found I had Hutch.'

'Never mind. I like Hutch,' somebody said, and Lamis wished that she had been the one to say it.

It was a simple remark, but it would have shown she was following the conversation, even though she didn't know if Hutch was a singer or composer, and if it were not for *Boléro*, she wouldn't have known who Ravel was.

'I was flicking through Mrs Beeton and the pages fell open at the letter "c", and there was a little stash of coke powder next to roast cod!'

'Great filing system he had!'

Everyone laughed, including Lamis.

How did you get to know Nicholas? When did you get to know Nicholas? Do you work with Nicholas? They were circling round one another asking questions, as if they had some strange gauge on which they could measure Nicholas's personal and social standing by seeing what number he registered.

Towards the end of the party, a blonde woman appeared from nowhere. When she walked in the guests stopped talking and eating and drinking. Anita the blonde, in red shiny pants that ended at the knee and showed off the tight triangle of her hips and bottom, spindly stilettos that threatened to snap at every step, a child's jersey that flattened her breasts and emphasised her rib cage, and a pretty face; she was carrying an artist's portfolio with a fake-fur cover.

'I was passing in a taxi and I guessed Nicholas was having a party and hadn't invited me.' She said this with great coyness as she embraced Nicholas. Lamis watched the blonde stare into Nicholas's face and felt her tummy clench, and not waiting for the inevitable introduction she rushed to the bathroom even though, ultimately, she knew she'd have to meet this tall beautiful blonde lady.

Lamis was pretending to be busy offering her guests more drinks, until Anita cornered her and introduced herself.

Anita's accent was worse than Lamis's, her pronunciation variable. She left out letters or changed them, and pronounced the letter 'j' as a 'y', saying 'enyoy' for 'enjoy'. Yet all the same she raced ahead, conversing without restraint, even though nobody asked her about Denmark. She understood and made herself understood, engaged in equal dialogues; the conversation between her and them floated along, and went deeper sometimes, spontaneously and with no forced effort. Because she's from Denmark, thought Lamis. Because she's European.

'Oh, you're from Arabia?' Anita asked Lamis.

Nicholas corrected her, seeming irritated. 'From Iraq.'

'Yes, yes, from Arabia,' said Lamis not wanting to complicate things for Anita.

'By the way, Nicholas, I have answered your message and left you several in return . . . do you think you would be able to get a special price for a Pierre Loti? The one where he's dressed up as Nefertiti! Sorry, I've forgotten your name.'

'Lamis.'

'Lamis, do you know Loti? Pierre Loti. It was him who made me love Arabia. He talks about its smell. He says it's like the smell of musk, invigorating and delightful. He makes me really want to go there. Oh, those photos of him in Arab dress are beautiful! You must see them. They're really inspiring.'

She looked at Lamis and smiled. Lamis mumbled something as if praising Loti, whom she'd never heard of, and thought: Why hasn't Nicholas fallen in love with her? Or has he been in love with her in the past? Lamis found herself suddenly wanting very much to be confident and European.

'Listen, Nicholas, OK, listen, Lisam. Sorry. Ah, Lamis. I like your name. I've been thinking about Arabia all this week, and then I meet you! Did you know the harem is a sadomasochistic institution? Nobody realised that before me, not even the Orientalists. The women in the harem used to help each other bathing, beautifying, massaging, getting dressed and made up, preparing themselves for one man. Then they sat there waiting for him to choose one of them. Just like that. Can you imagine the jealousy, the torture, when he chose one rather than another! I want to take some photos portraying the harem. I don't know how to do it but I've got an idea about how the Sultan should look.' Lamis and Nicholas finally caught one another's eye and the tension evaporated as they burst out laughing – Anita joined in without understanding why.

Nicholas left them to say goodbye to the last guests. Anita congratulated Lamis on the beautiful flower arrangements, and moments later, Lamis opened herself up, confiding in Anita and telling her everything as if she were a little girl eager to be accepted by the most popular girl in her class.

'Is it difficult getting divorced? You're an Arab woman.'

'It wasn't difficult in practical terms. Psychologically, yes.'

'Why did you do it?'

'I had depression for months. Every time my husband and I had sex, I threw up.'

Anita looked completely taken aback by Lamis's unexpected openness, while Lamis didn't notice a thing, only happy to be making a new friend.

'Sometimes I couldn't help laughing when Nicholas was screwing me.'

Lamis's heart sank. Does she know about us?

'He was so romantic and gentle! Anyhow, I don't like normal sex any more. It's boring. When I know you better, I'll tell you what I mean!' Lamis swallowed the thorn but asked casually, 'How did you get to know Nicholas?'

'At some party. He asked a friend of mine who's in the theatre why she was wearing orthopaedic shoes. They were boots she'd paid a hundred and fifty pounds for! When I asked him where he got his nice shirt, he ripped the collar off and handed it to me!'

Lamis's heart sank further and she wondered if she really knew Nicholas, but Anita went on. 'I was so happy when he invited me back to his flat, and then he opened the Bible and started looking for a particular bit, while I was almost panting with lust for him. Can you imagine a man inviting you back to his flat, giving you a really sexy kiss on the lips, then opening the Bible and reading something about daughters of Zion and their anklets?'

Lamis saw herself with Nicholas at Leighton House and the British Library; she also saw him with Anita, even heard the anklets of the daughters of Zion and felt somehow betrayed.

Once Anita had finally left they both cleared the glasses and dishes, before they prepared themselves to go to bed. Lamis felt as if they were married and she was the jealous wife.

'But, Lamis, there was nothing, nothing between us. We played games, that's all! It was thoughtless of her to tell you.'

'And you called her on your arrival, though you told me that you'd fallen in love with me in the taxi . . .'

'Stop it. Just remember that we didn't know each other then. Besides, did you expect me to be a virgin?'

Lamis calmed down because she remembered wondering the first time they were making love how any woman who had slept with him could bear to be away from him, and in her imagination there were many.

In bed, Lamis and Nicholas talked about the evening. Lamis turned over.

'Thank you, Lamis, you were an amazing hostess. Now tell me, did you have a good time, apart from Anita? I couldn't believe that every single bloody person came. I saw you talking to David and Matthew. As soon as David set eyes on you, he asked me if you had a sister. He envies me.'

'Why? He told me he has a girlfriend, but she's abroad.'

'Oh, so Lamis is fishing for compliments now! In their opinion you're an exotic bird. Despite how familiar they are with other cultures, and how much they've travelled.'

'What about you? Because, actually, I found myself wondering during the party whether the fact that I'm an Arab attracted you. It never occurred to me before . . . only when everybody talked to me as an Arab – Iraqi – rather than as a person. It made me wonder about you and me.'

'I thought about it too, when I found myself so attracted to you. Was I drawn to you because I was involved in the Arab world? I agree, it happens sometimes . . . but only at the beginning . . . It's like having a beautiful Arab dagger in your hand. After a while, you cease to think about where it came from. You marvel at the wonderful craftsmanhip but otherwise its origin is neither here nor there. You appreciate it and love its beauty for itself . . . but tell me, did David flirt with you?'

'I didn't like him. He asked me whether I was the one who'd introduced you to Sayf, where I was living in London before, if I'd met you at Sotheby's, *and* if I knew the pretender to the Iraqi throne! Apparently he's met his father-in-law who's extremely rich.'

'That's David. You should have just gone along with it. But did the women ask you what you did, and when you said nothing, dismiss you?'

'I lied. I said I was a volunteer Arabic teacher at the Saturday school for the Iraqi community.'

'My beautiful liar.'

'Well, Nicholas, you know I'm looking for a job, but not just any job . . . and tell me, who was the young woman with grey hair? When she found out that I was an Iraqi, she was so hostile to me, because Iraqis are fleeing Iraq. Then I told her something that shut her up. I told her about my grandfather and my uncles, and my auntie's family, who were wiped out by an Iraqi bombardment when they were waiting with thousands of others for help from the Americans.'

Nicholas looked at her again. 'The more contact I have with other cultures, the more I find us naive. We really don't understand the political situation in your country. And the more I travel, the more I discover ways in which we English are odd. In my childhood, I thought we were quite normal; yet now I think of the English as being introverted, shy, clumsy. We lack self-assurance. We have so many taboos – over money, wealth, religion and especially sex . . . That's quite a list.'

They laughed, and Lamis agreed. 'It explains why the English start their conversations with the cliché, "I am afraid that . . ." even if they're telling you that they are about to go on holiday!'

Nicholas laughed and held her nestled in his lap so they were like two spoons in a drawer.

'Oh, your mother called, Nicholas. I forgot to tell you,' Lamis said, feeling comfort in their closeness.

'Did you chat with her?'

'Yeah. I think she liked me. You didn't tell me that you'd sent her my picture!'

'Well, since you were refusing to meet them . . .'

'I'm postponing it, not refusing. She's very amusing. She told me she'd got rid of your father's old gloves and the dog took them out of the rubbish, all muddy and dirty.'

'Did she tell you whether they're still coming the day after tomorrow? I'm having lunch with them, before I take them both shopping.'

'Yes, she told me. I said I was sorry that I couldn't be there . . . my son, et cetera . . .'

161

'You mean you lied to her! I'm in heaven, Lamis. Are you tired? We shouldn't have stayed up with Anita.'

Lamis thought of asking him now about Anita but instead she kept Anita's image hidden behind her eyelids, talking, moving and laughing. She pulled his hand up to her mouth, kissed it, and returned it to him. He knew she was going to sleep. She turned her back to him, disengaging herself, preferring to sleep at the edge of the bed. He could not persuade her to sleep close to him all night, as close as two spoons – the expression was his mother's.

II

Amira had rented a room in a five-star hotel and when she was settled in, she had a bath and used the body lotion provided by the hotel. The amount in the miniature jar was insufficient. After tonight, God willing, I'll lose weight, even if I have to go into hospital, she said to herself, although, since she'd started to put on weight, she frequently told herself that the pots didn't contain enough lotion to smooth over the whole of her body simply because she was tall.

She dressed again hurriedly, still smelling good. Being fatter made her sweat more profusely. She composed herself before phoning the switchboard.

'Could you put me through to the Prince's suite?'

She swallowed, and a voice from the suite answered.

'Yes please?'

'Good evening. Is May-He-Live-Long there, please?'

'Who's calling, please?'

'He knows who it is.'

Silence. Silence.

'Hello?'

'What's your name, please?'

'He knows. If you could get him for me.'

'Where are you calling from?'

'From London. Is he there, please?'

'Just a moment.'

She swallowed again and heard the sound of footsteps down the receiver.

'Would you mind giving me your name?'

There was a knock on her door. 'Police! Police! Open the door.'

Amira put the receiver down and picked up her bag, then was not sure what to do next.

'Police! Police! If you don't open the door, we'll have to force it.'

She opened it, shouting at them in terror, 'I'm alone. I've only just taken this room. Ask the hotel management. Search the room. Search my handbag. You won't find anything.'

Three plain-clothes detectives entered, and an Arab, who looked Lebanese. One of the three closed the door while the other two took it in turns to look in the bathroom. She heard the shower curtain being drawn back and drawn to again, cupboards opening and closing, then they transferred their search to the bedroom. She felt reassured suddenly. There was some mistake. They were looking for a criminal. One of them bent down to look under the bed, then he pulled back the curtains, opened the window and stuck his head out briefly, closed it again and closed the curtains, arranging them as if he were helping his wife get ready for guests.

Very politely, another of them said, indicating the chair, 'Please have a seat. Just a few quick questions. Have you used the bath?'

'Yes.'

'What's your name?'

'Amira.'

'You just phoned his royal highness.'

'No, I didn't.'

'Do us a favour.'

'I didn't.'

'We know you did. The telephones here are computerised. You

called the switchboard operator and asked for his suite. Could you tell us how you knew his royal highness was in this hotel, and what you wanted from him?'

'I didn't call him.'

'What did you want from him? He doesn't know you.'

'Who told you he doesn't know me?'

'What about your passport. It says . . .'

'What's my passport got to do with it? The Prince could have been lying to you when he said he didn't know me.'

'We'd better take her to Savile Row,' said another.

'Sorry. What are you proposing? I didn't catch it,' said the Arab.

'We'll take her to Savile Row Police Station.'

'Where the tailors are?'

'Exactly. Savile Row Police Station.'

'I want to go to the bathroom,' said Amira.

She put her hand in her jacket pocket, touching the little mobile phone as if it was Aladdin's magic lamp.

'You can wait.'

'How do you know? Are you inside me?'

She went into the bathroom, flushed the toilet, called Samir, then flushed it again and came out.

The Arab asked the Special Branch men if he could speak to her in Arabic. 'Look, madam. The Prince is on a secret visit. Don't make matters worse for yourself. These men are English, not Arabs. They want you to give them the pure milk.'

'What?'

'I mean tell the truth. The more you lie, the deeper in you get. They think there's a plot against the Prince and they're treating it as a serious case. Did you come to make some money?'

'And who are you, sir?'

'The Prince's secretary.'

Feeling as if a weight had been taken off her shoulders she asked him if he knew Maureen.

He smiled. 'So she was the one who told you. Look. Keep this a secret, or I'll lose my job.'

He smiled again.

'OK, OK, I did call the Prince,' she told the policemen.

'Why?'

'I wanted to talk to him.'

'Why?'

'I wanted to borrow money from him. I'm ill. I need treatment.'

'How did you know he was here?'

'I came, as I always do, to buy an Arabic newspaper in the hotel and I saw a lot of cars and people who looked like minders and bodyguards at the entrance, and one of them was saying, "Prince, Prince."'

'Who told you his name?'

'I don't know his name. I said to myself, I've arrived at just the right moment, and I took a room because I knew that the hotel wouldn't let me talk to him.'

'Are you certain you just wanted to ask for financial help?'

'Yes, I swear on the Qur'an!'

'Did anyone else know about it?'

'As I told you, I acted on the spur of the moment.'

'Why do you need money if you've got enough to pay for this room?'

'I thought I'd be able to pay with the money he was going to give me.'

'So you were confident he'd give you what you wanted?'

'Definitely. Princes are extremely generous, especially if someone's really in need. A colleague of mine had to have an operation and a princess she didn't know at all paid for the whole thing. And there was Prince – I've forgotten his name – who gave money for the child on TV who needed a liver transplant. On *That's Life*.'

'What are you doing in London?'

The secretary intervened. 'I'll ask the Prince if he's ready to pay for her room. And perhaps he'll take pity on her and give her what he can.'

'Do you mean you're going to drop the charges?'

'I think so. I'll go and explain things to His Highness and come back and tell you.'

The Lebanese left the room with one of the detectives, while Amira collapsed in relief, saying, 'Thank you, my brother.'

'Oh, so you think the Prince will take pity on you like his secretary said?'

'I don't know. It seems I scared him. His wife must be with him. Or his wives.'

The two men laughed.

'Come on, let's put money on how much he's going to give me,' said Amira.

'Don't involve us, young lady. And we're policemen, not a betting office.'

'Thank you. Thank you.'

'Don't thank me. Thank his secretary when he comes back and signs something to say he waives his rights.'

'I'm thanking you because you called me young lady. Anyway, what happens to me if he doesn't drop the charges?'

'We take you in for questioning, then who knows.'

She wasn't worried. She had the secretary eating out of her hand. He came back; he was extremely elegant.

'The Prince has agreed to everything, and we'll take care of the room.'

He handed her an envelope.

'If only I'd asked for champagne and caviar!'

The secretary laughed, and the others joined in.

'So. Can we consider the case closed?' the Scotland Yard officer said, astonished, convinced that the Arab mentality was a puzzle. The Prince had made a complaint, then forgiven the woman. It was as if she'd broken into a shop and the owner not only dropped the charges but invited her to take what she wanted.

'Yes. I hope the lady stops playing with fire.'

'I'm at your service, if you need anything,' she said to the secretary.

'Take care. Goodbye.'

Amira picked up her bag, looked at the bed and said to the secretary, 'You shouldn't pay for the room. I didn't even use the bed.'

As a result of her brush with the law, Amira started to feel like a suspect as she went over the evening's events again and again in her mind. One new factor in particular made her worry. She'd given the hotel the details of her credit card in order to book the room – Scotland Yard could use that information to find her again. Why, when Maureen told her that the Prince's secretary was arriving to have his chest and back hairs removed, had she jumped at the opportunity, instead of remaining with her companions in the harmonious surroundings of the hotel lobbies, the bedrooms, the Rolls-Royce? But she needed more money, and she needed it fast.

In order to be a princess she had to keep cash moving in a steady flow, into the Rolls-Royce, her attendants, restaurants, the afternoon teas, the tips for her informants who worked in the hotels, casinos, airline companies, banks, cabarets, and the stylists in the hotel hair salons, all of whom gave her the names of their regular clients. Amira also followed the doings of the princesses and sheikhs in the Arab newspapers and weekly magazines that were published in London.

Her mother had always believed that the poor spent money on the rich, not vice versa – she had once used up all her savings organising a huge lunch for a relative who worked as a nurse in the Gulf. She had been anticipating a length of silk, or a gold watch, but the relative brought along nothing but her fat bottom, which had gained an additional kilo by the time she finished licking the plates clean.

London evaporated from Amira's mind. She could think of only two things: she must find a taxi, and see Nahid. She did not open her bag to check the money, as she usually did; she was afraid that her newly earned cash, which she was aware of with every beat of her heart, would burst out of her bag like air bubbles and disappear.

Nahid was not home, and her mobile phone was asking Amira to leave a message. Amira looked for Nahid at Bahia's, and at a few coffee shops. Only when she asked Samir did she remember that Nahid's sister must have arrived. 'But why's Nahid hiding from me? Her sister likes me.' She went back to Nahid's and decided she'd wait for her outside her door, for hours if necessary. But this time Nahid was there. She opened the door and kissed Amira on both cheeks and joked with her as if nothing had happened.

'So are you punishing me because I've turned into a princess? I don't see you any more. Where's your sister, anyway?'

'I made her cancel her trip. I told her that I'd moved to your place because the roof of my flat was leaking. I've been generally feeling a bit under the weather, as the English say. For no particular reason.'

'I know why. It's the whisky.'

'I swear by my eyesight that I had only one drink yesterday, and that was in great secrecy because Bahia invited Katkouta over.'

Amira was jealous. But what did she expect her friend to do now that Amira was a princess, a lonely lioness out hunting for prey on her own, instead of in a team, as she and Nahid had been in the past?

She told Nahid what had happened to her in the hotel.

'Thank God! But now the young Lebanese man is going to kill Maureen, and then she'll kill you.'

'Everything in life has a price. I've paid Maureen already. But tell me what's going on. Why are you upset with me, Nahid? Why are you avoiding me? Please tell me. I want to know what pillow I'm supposed to be sleeping on . . . please open up, tell me what's wrong.'

'Do you remember when you came back from Dubai, and you wanted to take stock of your life and think about your future? Well, it was contagious. I have started to consider my future.'

'Good, then be my partner for a year. That's all it would take. Then we can retire, happy and secure.'

'And start to have baby boys and girls, you mean? We should have kept our babies.'

'Don't think of the past. Let's go to the casino and have fun.'

'You're so right. But don't you think that God might be at work here, making me so irritable day and night, and sending you that visit from the police?'

'Thank you, God. But where were you before, God? Why didn't you visit us before?'

The memory of making this choice of career flashed through Amira's mind. The same thought fleetingly made itself visible on Nahid's face. Both women pushed the memories away immediately.

Amira could remember when she decided to become a prostitute. It was when the cook and the driver at the restaurant where she'd worked tried to jump her, or maybe even before that, when her uncle pulled her hand and forced it against his crotch, insisting that she was his wife now – he'd agreed to a registry office wedding with Amira, after the Moroccan government stopped issuing passports to single women because they were rushing off to Europe in hordes like locusts; and there were the men who made the shawarmas in the Syrian restaurant, and the gardener at the mosque, they'd all tried to jump her, just as if she were a pigeon in the park, and she'd begun to make the connection, and to think seriously about her body and men and wealth.

Revulsion and surprise struck her when the Syrian woman for whom she worked as a cleaner told her she must be pregnant. Her employer had noticed Amira run to throw up in the toilet at the sight of wax dripping down the side of a candle, and taken her to a doctor who'd confirmed that she was pregnant, although Amira persisted in saying that she was a virgin – how could she be pregnant from a few minutes squashed in the van with the Pakistani driver she used to see every day when he brought the home deliveries? He'd torn her pants and promised to marry her as soon as he got his law degree.

How could she lose, she'd thought, if sex was over that fast, and was that ordinary, like a seed popping in your face, a private act performed by the man, at which she felt merely a spectator, as uninvolved as the van seat.

If only I'd just arrived in London, she thought. Eighteen years and I still haven't bought a house by the sea in Morocco or a flat in a new building, or even a little sandwich shop. If only my name was still Habiba and I was walking down the narrow alleys in my home town . . .

When she ran angrily away from her mother and her pail of dirty water, an English tourist stopped her, and asked her in French if she could tell her the whereabouts of the famous old wall. Habiba waved a hand then said in French, 'Follow me. I'm going there. I'm going to . . .' She did not know how to say 'commit suicide' in French. She walked along with the tourist and felt as if London were walking beside her to the high outcrop of rocks beyond the old town wall, a place much frequented by local people. Everyone in the town, government employees newly awakened from their siestas, housewives, old people, adolescents and children flocked to the spot where the waters of the Atlantic pound against the wall, to watch the sunset.

'London' stopped briefly, looked out at the wall and the sea and back at the houses of the old town clustered behind her, then thanked Habiba and said goodbye. Habiba thought how nice 'London' was, and how well mannered, and she no longer wanted to take her own life.

She wished she could have asked the tourist a lot of things about London, and went on an urgent mission to find her uncle, seeking him out in the streets and shop doorways and, when she could not find him, she went looking in the Divine Refuge Café, built into the rocks, where an assortment of tourists and local hash smokers sat round the tables smoking joints. Boys hung around the doorway, afraid to go in, and parents hurried their children past as if the place was contaminated, and they could not believe it when they saw Habiba stride in just like a man. As soon as she was sure her uncle had seen her, Habiba turned and walked out again without a word. Habiba, wailing and swearing and striking her face, ran towards the sea and climbed the rock beyond the wall. Standing at the place where single women always stood – if seven waves touched their feet, it meant God would answer their prayers and send them husbands – she threatened to throw herself off the wall. Her uncle did not ask her why. He did not seem to care, until all of a sudden he screamed at her, 'You foolish girl, have you lost your virginity?' But the only thing wrong, as he later discovered, was that Habiba wanted to go to London, and find a job there.

'Look, Nahid. How beautiful London is.'

They were in a taxi on their way to the Mayfair Hotel casino. They passed South Audley Street, and checked to see if the two huge elephants were still in the window of Goodge and Sons.

'Listen, Nahid, don't feel guilty and low because of what we do. It's not just you, or me. Have a look at all those buildings. They're there because of sex. Hospitals for delivering children, for making people better to make more children, and schools to educate them, and shops to feed them and clothes to keep them warm, and casinos for people to win or lose so they'll have more money and sleep with more women. What's all that for? It's for what you and I do. Everything. Even airports, planes, telephones, computers – everything comes from what you and I do . . . manhood proves itself, and women get pregnant; like a male peacock spreading its feathers, a man spreads his millions . . . his virility. Believe me, this is what it's all about.'

'You forget those two elephants in the window, Amira. Do they exist because of what you and I do?'

'Of course. The man who buys them will feel strong and mighty and powerful when he brings them home to his wife or his mistress, who'll then jump into his bed even before he does.'

'But the elephants aren't for sale.'

'Even so, I mean, because they're not for sale. That only goes to prove my point. When Mr Goodge told his wife how much he was offered for the elephants, and that was for just one of them, so double it, and that he'd declined to sell, she fainted out of admiration and lust – his power was such an aphrodisiac it was as if she had sniffed the powder made from rhinoceros horn.'

III

Samir started to look for Mrs Cunningham after the art student and his friend smiled at him at the bus stop. They were smiling at his scarf. Samir pulled it off and handed it to the boy, who began inspecting it like Cappuccino inspecting his tail for lice. Samir insisted he take it, and the boy refused: he couldn't afford it.

'You won't pay anything. Believe me, it's not a problem,' Samir assured him.

Then Samir backed down suddenly, afraid that the boy would disappear into the great unknown of London, and he did not let him go until he had taken down the boy's phone number, promising to tell him where he could get a scarf like it.

Samir wanted to be close to the boy, and would have been content just to walk in the park with him. A glance from him satisfied his craving and made life longer. He was like Boy George, especially his pencilled eyebrows.

' "Karma karma karma karma karma chameleon, Red, green and gold, Red, green and go-o-o-old," ' he sang.

His oldest son used to love that song.

Amira did not know how the scarf had landed up in her house. 'It's definitely not from Morocco.'

Samir dialled the boy's number several times but all he ever got was the answering machine, and he repeated the same message. 'There's no problem. Take the scarf today for seven pounds, please. Call me on this number. Don't forget to call me. If seven pounds is too much for you, I know you're a student, give me five, OK. OK? Don't forget to call me. I'm waiting.'

He called again one more time, then went to sleep full of bitterness. He had a dream in which he saw the Englishwoman, Mrs Cunningham, cutting the scarf into pieces and distributing it among the patients in the hospital in Lebanon. Samir saw his hospital bed and remembered the feel of the sheets, and heard the squeak of the bed's metal feet on the tiles. He began to toss and turn until he woke up, his heart beating. Mrs Cunningham. How was it he'd not thought of her before? Would she remember him, an adolescent in Lebanon for whom nobody else had any sympathy? Mrs Cunningham had sent him with her driver to the dentist and undertaken to pay for his treatment, and bought some shoes for him when she saw him slopping along with his feet spread out flat, because the shoes he'd inherited from his father were too big, even with three pairs of socks.

The English student would go out of his mind when he saw the fabric Mrs Cunningham had woven, and she would make Samir look good in front of him too. He had always had it in the back of his mind that he'd known one English person before he came here, and was overjoyed he'd remembered her. He began his quest by contacting all the Cunninghams in the phone book.

'Please, I'm looking for Mrs Margaret Cunningham, a lady who lived in Beirut, in the British Embassy. I have to find her. It's very important.'

Then somebody suggested he should contact the Foreign Office and a week later an answer arrived from her son, a little card with his mother's address, saying that she'd be happy to see him.

He took the two students with him and in the flood of happiness that came over him he could only congratulate himself for being so clever. The world had begun to teach him some lessons, or was it London? London didn't like different types mixing together. John the Policeman, an admirer of Amira's, would not like Mrs Cunningham, while these two would be fascinated by her, and not give Amira a second glance.

'Her picture was in all the magazines, I swear to God,' he told them.

The two did not understand much that Samir said, but they were grateful for his interest in their art. He had bought them a lot of fabric and scarves from Edgware Road, which were not to their taste. The scarf that they had seen on Samir at the bus stop remained their favourite piece, and the first boy had begun to wear it as a sign of gratitude to Samir. Whenever he met them near their college, Central St Martin's, and invited them to lunch or afternoon tea, Samir would take care to wear the most beautiful clothes he could find, for he sensed that his clothes were a point of contact between himself and the boy. Or rather the two boys, as they were always together, which irritated Samir. They admired the way Samir mixed clashing colours and unwittingly wore seventies fashions that were, according to him, expensive originals that people had heaped upon him in Lebanon and Dubai.

Samir was glad when the taxi dropped them outside De Vere House in Queensgate and he saw the luxurious building where Mrs Cunningham lived; then for a moment he was worried. What would happen to Amira and the monkey if she invited him to come and live with her here? When Samir saw a woman sitting at an enquiry desk he assumed that this must be where Mrs Cunningham worked rather than her home. The two students exchanged glances. And when an employee came to show them to Mrs Cunningham's room, one of them asked Samir when he'd last visited his friend. Before Samir had finished his calculations, they were being shown into the room.

'It's not possible. There must be some mistake. This isn't Mrs Cunningham,' he said to himself.

He tried to explain this to the two youths, but was unable to catch their eyes as they were looking eagerly round the room.

Mrs Cunningham had been a frequent visitor to the psychiatric hospital in Lebanon when Samir was there as a patient. He first met her when she tried to interest the patients in fabric. One morning Mrs Cunningham asked them to start unravelling some pieces of material: 'Pull until you reach the black dot, then stop.'

The nun moved among the patients fearfully, warning and

watching those she felt were incapable of following instructions. One patient unravelled half the material, and when she stopped him, he tried to weave the threads back in, and pulled his hair and wept in frustration. Samir was delighted by the beautiful, bright, slippery cloth. He had not felt silk before; he was used to thick cotton and muslin. He began to play with it, winding it round him, then draping it round his shoulders like a shawl. When the nurse tried to stop him he ran away from her and the material trailed after him. Rather than telling him off, Mrs Cunningham liked what she saw and took photos of him, recounting to the nun how activity of this nature restored 'their' vitality and mental energy. When Samir stopped running, he went up to Mrs Cunningham, lifting the train of material clear off the ground, like a bride.

'How nice this material is!' he said boldly to her. 'It slips through your hands like a fish. You should make it into a dress and put a sky-blue *tabaq* on the front, or orange-red like the sunset. It'd look fantastic.'

'Do you mean by *tabaq* the dish we eat from?' asked Mrs Cunningham, who knew a few words of Arabic.

'No.' Samir tried to correct her, while everybody laughed at the way he described the dress. '*Tabaq* means a big open flower, you can say, one that's as big as a dish.'

Mrs Cunningham touched the pullover that Samir's mother made him wear all through the winter, and asked him where he got it, complimenting him on the wool and the beauty of the knitting.

'My mother knitted it. Please take it, Mrs Cunningham.'

She found her way to their house, and asked Samir's mother to knit ten pullovers in the various colours she'd chosen. She paid his mother handsomely and even thanked her again in a postcard from London, which Samir had preserved for ages.

'Remind her who you are.' The nurse pushed him forward now.

Samir was sure that this wasn't Mrs Cunningham in spite of the furniture inlaid with mother-of-pearl and the Lebanese hall-stand.

Obeying the nurse, he bent towards her. 'I'm Samir, from

175

Beirut. Samir from the Asfouriyeh Hospital. A-s-f-o-u-r-i-y-e-h.'
He spelled out the hospital's name very slowly. 'Samir. You let
your dentist Mazmanian put my teeth right. When you gave me an
apple I screamed in pain. I'm living here now. These are my
friends. They make material like you. See what they make.' Samir
indicated one of the students, who had brought her a piece of
cloth he had woven himself, but he cleared his throat awkwardly
and said to Samir, 'Never mind. Don't upset her.'

But Samir snatched the packet from him and opened it and
showed her the material. Mrs Cunningham tried to talk, but only
her eyes said anything. She handled the material lovingly, then
looked at Samir and the two youths and nodded, trying again to
articulate dumbly. She stood up and the material fell to the floor.
She went over to the wardrobe and tried to open it. One of the
students got up to help her and she took out a thick book, almost
dropping it, but holding on to it doggedly and turning its pages,
pointing to photos of paintings and costumes. It was one of the
loveliest books the two had seen and they stood on either side of
Mrs Cunningham, turning the pages for her, to her obvious joy. A
certain photo caught her eye and she tried to talk, 'A-a-a,' pointing
to it.

Samir was uncertain what to do. He couldn't help looking at the
Arab furniture, which gave him the fleeting sense of being in
Beirut; then the happiness that he felt because the two boys liked
Mrs Cunningham and hadn't been disappointed by the visit began
to change into annoyance as they ignored him completely and
lavished all their attention on the book and Mrs Cunningham. One
seized her hand and kissed it and the other fetched her silver brush
and comb and did her hair for her. When she was tired of them
they left her alone and examined the furnishings in her room,
especially the glass vase in the shape of a mermaid. Each of them
handled it at length before standing back to make space for the
other, both repeating, 'Divine, divine.'

Then one of them seized the dead flowers and yanked them out
of the vase and, not finding a rubbish bin, headed for the door and

disappeared outside. He came back with a nurse who picked up the vase, poured the water into the toilet and returned the empty vase to the table. Samir noticed the trail left by the stale water but did not roll up his sleeves as he usually did when he saw something needed cleaning. He was besotted with the first youth, and wished Mrs Cunningham would doze off. The regular movement of his hand as he brushed Mrs Cunningham's hair had aroused Samir, and she did seem to be taking a catnap now, but the youth pushed Samir away. 'Shh,' he said, then asked him again, 'Didn't you know she was in a home?'

Chapter Six

I

Lamis caught sight of Nicholas and asked the taxi driver to stop a short distance from the theatre in the Strand, afraid that she'd be embarrassed if Nicholas watched her getting out. She still felt awkward when she was with him; she never drank water fast in front of him in case she made a noise when she swallowed. She walked slowly towards the theatre, observing Nicholas, and a little shiver of excitement went through her. Every time she had gone to the theatre with Belquis she had dreamed that one day she would wait for a man at the entrance to the foyer and he would come through the rain to her, closing his wet umbrella, and plant a kiss on her cheek as he greeted her. Later they would stand sipping wine together, talking about the play.

'Hello, darling.'

'Am I late?'

'It gave me a chance to watch you. You looked as though you'd come out of the sea, with those colours, and the way you do your hair, and I have an erection . . . can you tell me what to do about it?'

'Oh Nicholas.' She blushed awkwardly.

'Give me a kiss.'

She went up to him and looked around before pecking him on the cheek.

'Who's going to see you? Didn't you say you hardly ever saw another Arab at the theatre or opera? Hang on, have I gone mad

178

too? See how you've affected me? Fuck them! See? I'm English again.'

'It's a great idea to go out in the evenings. I feel so happy!'

But she did not tell him she felt liberated because she had bought a mobile phone so her son could reach her at any time.

An old man grinned conspiratorially at Nicholas when they both happened to glance at their watches simultaneously.

'I think only old people here are like Arabs,' Lamis said.

She and Nicholas looked about inquisitively. Another elderly person stood with a quizzical expression watching a dog trotting along behind its owner, apparently resisting the urge to run behind it and pull its tail. An older woman directed a female tourist to Trafalgar Square and peered down the street after her to ascertain whether she was going the right way.

Lamis felt confident because she was with someone who knew the rituals of going to the theatre: how to inspect the ticket, when to rush and when to dawdle. He whispered in her ear, 'I want to be inside you now,' and she listened intently like a thirsty lizard that had already absorbed a little moisture through its skin.

She saw two plays, one on the stage, and the other acted out in her mind – The Setback, which convinced her that she could never belong to the old England she was seeing on the stage. Although she consoled herself with the thought that even Nicholas didn't belong there, one look at him and at the rest of the audience with their eyes fastened on the actors was enough to make her change her mind again. She observed the way the features of those in the audience responded to the words, forming a frown or a smile. They were bringing themselves to the situations and dialogues on the stage, and however much those differed from their own reality, the seeds of them were buried deep in their consciousness.

Her frustration had been building up in the English classes, although the teacher still maintained that she was optimistic. 'Five words out of seven, Lamis. That's not bad. All that concerns me is that when you leave here you don't think one sentence in Arabic, or everything we've achieved will be wasted. But that's asking a lot. God help you!'

Every time Lamis imagined a type of food – bread, olives – she subconsciously said its name in Arabic; whenever she spoke her own name or that of her son, she was talking Arabic. She found herself climbing back up the attic stairs and saying tearfully to the teacher at the next lesson, 'My memory's all in Arabic. As if I'm a parrot. Don't parrots ever lose their memories?'

Nicholas took her hand and brought it up to his lips, then put a paper ring on her finger, a bit of the theatre programme that he had been painstakingly twisting into a circle.

He was not satisfied with her smiling at him. He wanted an answer, or was she answering him by keeping the ring on her finger, and smiling when he put on a paper ring too? She took his hand and squeezed it. Did that mean 'Let's get married'?

They sat in a restaurant wearing their paper rings.

'Let's order champagne to celebrate.'

She laughed.

'Yes or no?'

'Nicholas!'

'Yes or no? I want you to marry me. And don't tell me that we've only known each other two months.'

'I can't.'

'Why? Because you don't want to spend a few months in Oman? But you nearly lived in Dubai.'

'Because . . . because I can't just now!'

'Thank you for that word "now". You won't believe this but sometimes I forget you were married and that you have a child. Let's order champagne anyway because you're beautiful and I love you.'

Nicholas ordered champagne and as they raised their glasses, he noticed the awkward expression on her face.

'Lamis, you don't look happy. Is there something bothering you?'

'I want to go to the Ladies.'

He stood up and moved the table out for her.

She examined her face as she dabbed it with pink powder, and said to her reflection as if it was to him, 'I love you. I love you. I want us to go home now, but maybe waiting will make me want you more.'

'So, did you think it over in the Ladies? Do you want me to help you bring your things over here tomorrow?'

'And live in your flat?'

'No, in a tree, what do you think? Lamis, I don't believe you. Look at your face. After all I've said to you. Why don't you move in with me? Come on, now. Let's go together to the flat that I'm not allowed to see, and get whatever you need.'

'They'll say I got divorced because of you.'

'You'll explain to your son that it isn't true.'

She did not tell him that she was not sure that she wanted to introduce him to her son so soon, or for the three of them to be together under one roof. 'What about the rest?'

'Didn't you get divorced because you realised you felt unconnected to your husband, to the whole lot of them? Yes or no? It's something you attach a great amount of importance to.'

'I know. I can't help it.'

'But you spend most of your time at my place, apart from a couple of hours or so at your flat during the day. You're like a scared husband, who feels he has to establish his presence in his own house, but you're doing it for the sake of the doors and walls. Or perhaps it's for the porter and his wife, so they can keep checking up on you. Or would you like to own that flat despite your ex-husband and his mother? I'm still not convinced you've completely let go.'

He was right; when she went out of her flat in the afternoons she used to wait until the porter and his wife were busy having tea. She had always been able to change the course of a conversation with Nicholas, but not tonight. He didn't respond to her trying to excite him, nor to the stories she related to him.

'OK then, don't move in with me right now. I know, my place is so small. Let's go to Oman together. Just for a month or two.'

'Oman? I couldn't possibly go with you to Oman.'

'I promise you, you'd see one thousand five hundred stars instead of five hundred in London.'

'I can imagine them!'

'I can't postpone my trip any longer. I have to go in a few days.'

'Anyhow, we couldn't stay together.'

'Why? You've got a British passport. Oh, I've just thought, Omani law says unmarried British women under the age of thirty-five or forty can't enter Oman, unless they're married to Omanis.'

She felt relieved. Sultan Qabus had come to the rescue.

'I'm joking, Lamis.'

'But we're not married.'

'It doesn't matter. You're British.'

'But my name's written in my passport, and my place of birth – Najaf, Iraq.'

'OK, we'll stay in a hotel and take two rooms. You'll be my guest. I don't care if I spend everything I've got on you.'

He exuded happiness and confidence because she no longer had an excuse.

'Nicholas. Don't smile like that, please. I'm the one who knows the system, not you. I know this Jordanian Muslim woman married to a Lebanese Christian. They moved to one of the Gulf states and the authorities said their marriage wasn't recognised, even though the husband lied and said he had converted to Islam and had a forged document from Lebanon to prove it. But they insisted on testing him and gave him some books on Islam and obliged him to take lessons for several months.'

'But that doesn't happen in Oman, I promise you. Anyway, I'll make some enquiries and if there's any obstacle you won't go. It's quite simple.'

'I was told that Dubai was the Oriental Monte Carlo. It seems you've forgotten what happened to me there.'

'No, I haven't forgotten. But you have to put that incident behind you.'

'It wasn't only an incident. It was a terrifying experience. And to be honest with you, my fear extends even to the Iraqi opposition. Any of those groups might lapse into the violence they're meant to be opposing. I remember only too well the way I started avoiding my grandfather, who I adored, after I watched him hitting the birdcages and heard him furiously criticising my father and mother.'

Nicholas took her hand and kissed it.

'Darling, let me help you not to fear anything.'

II

London was like the palm of a human hand intricately criss-crossed by deep and superficial lines, along which Lamis and Nicholas were trying to drive in Nicholas's tiny car. He took Hyde Park Corner then Park Lane on the way to Mount Street, where they were going to view a flat belonging to one of Nicholas's acquaintances. They passed the Dorchester Hotel, where Lamis had been married. She nearly told Nicholas, laughing, that, as soon as she and her ex-husband were in their hotel room, he'd been preoccupied with finding somewhere to hide her diamond ear-rings, panic-stricken at the idea that she might have lost one of the diamonds during the wedding. Her heart skipped a beat. She remembered that she'd given her sister's address in Dubai to Selfridges, when she stored her jewellery in one of the store's safe-deposit boxes. Now she should give them Nicholas's address. Of course it shouldn't be the address of the flat still belonging to her husband; she was afraid that her mother-in-law could go into the flat, look through her things any time she felt like it. She might find the key in the tiny envelope, go to the Selfridges basement and take everything from the tin box that lay hidden along with hundreds of other boxes, in a quiet, dim place, where there was a faint echo of music, far below the shoppers' footsteps.

'There's something I don't understand about this flat. As Mayfair prices go, what he's asking for isn't at all bad – maybe because it's no longer residential, with all these offices and antique shops – yet Mount Street is still considered one of the prettiest streets in London; it reminds me of Petra – in its colouring, I mean. Don't you think?'

'I haven't been to Petra, but I hear it's magical.'

'I'll take you soon.'

She did not dare say again that she was afraid to travel with him, even as a tourist, to any Arab country, even if they took separate rooms.

'This area of London was the one we adored as children, my brother and I . . .'

Lamis played with his hair, wishing she could have seen Nicholas as a child. But she didn't wish that he could have seen her. Najaf's sun used to dry her hair and make it hard to manage and in her only two childhood photos she looked unkempt, as if a comb wouldn't go through her hair; her brown dress with red circles looked like an old woman's dress, she wore worn-out shoes, without socks.

'Did you come up to London very often?'

'Not really. Our visits up to town were like a trip to a foreign country. My brother and I would look forward to them for months. My favourite place was the Planetarium, where the darkness lit up with stars and you could see the planets. I would sit mesmerised; I believed it when my mother told us to prepare ourselves because they were going to fly us in our seats to the ceiling, to touch the stars.

'Even getting into a black cab was a treat then. Also the Tate gallery, where we could buy lots of cards. Oh, and the tube. That was the best treat of all, and seeing other children travelling on the tube on their own, independent, and not looking at the map

184

the way we had to. Now I've talked too much. It's your turn. What were your special childhood treats?' But before she said anything, he said to her in Arabic, 'Chewing gum, sweets and a big doll.'

'You still remember the Arabic? My genius! And now, tell me, do you feel you're a Londoner?'

'I wish. Anyone who looks in an *A to Z* isn't a true Londoner. I think the newspaper-sellers are. That's why you hear the cliché from people like me repeated so often, "I want to leave, I want to leave London." '

The flat in Mount Street was like two tiny sardine-tins on tall, pinkish sticks, like the other pinkish-coloured buildings in the street.

'Our first disappointment. Never mind. We still have Fulham to check – we're like two birds trying to find the perfect nest that has nothing to do with our past. I'm sure we'll be able to find a spacious flat – and when I say spacious, I mean the British idea of spacious. Sayf and the other Omanis laugh at our architecture. They say how can the English live when the dining room is on one floor, the bedroom on another, the sitting room on another, and the kitchen in the dungeon.'

Lamis smiled but said nothing, relieved about that Mount Street fiasco and hoping that the Fulham flat would be worse.

'What's wrong, sweetheart?'

'Nothing.'

'I hope you're not disappointed because I vetoed Little Venice? But believe me, it is so dead. It's like a suburb. You have to go all the way to Oxford Street if you want to buy a book.'

'OK. OK.'

' "OK, OK" – as if you want to shut me up. This is what I have to put up with while I'm in Oman or in any Arab country, "OK, OK", amazingly understood by nearly every inhabitant of the globe. Do you know that "OK" was invented unwittingly by the seventh American president, Andrew Jackson? He was semi-literate and he ratified the documents placed in front of him by

185

writing "Oll Korrect" using the "o" and "k" instead of "a" and "c".'

Lamis laughed, wondering how he could love her when she was so boring, with no stories to tell, and wondering why she couldn't be candid with him. What was the point of their relationship if she was not open and truthful with him? Why had she agreed to go with him, and let him think that she was looking for a flat or a house for both of them, when the truth was that she'd already gone with the woman from the estate agent's to see two places, and both made her feel that she was a sheep on the way to slaughter. As soon as the woman had turned the key to open the door, she wanted to leave: each step she took inside was against her will, and almost physically painful.

On both her visits to view places on the estate agent's books, whether or not people were living there, the word 'family' had flickered up, neon-lit, increasing her sense of alienation, her feeling that she was not ready to build a new home yet. She preferred to be in-between, his flat and hers.

Should she confide in Nicholas now, or would he think that she didn't trust him?

She recalled how surprised he was that she received no alimony from her husband; she hadn't asked for it. Nicholas asked her if that meant that she and her ex-husband had not sat down and discussed a divorce settlement, and she felt then as if Nicholas were acting like her parents, handing out one insult after another – as if, like them, he didn't understand that she needed nothing except her freedom. She was neither homeless nor penniless.

Lamis put her hand on his neck and caressed it. How could she love him so much and yet leave him in the dark about the reality of her life? Her father had rung from Dubai the day before, and told her that he and her mother were still on medication, due to her divorce.

'Listen, sweetheart,' said her father. 'Now you've tasted freedom, is it the paradise you expected? Of course it's not! How can it be when you left your son, a jewel bestowed on you by the

Almighty, to treasure? You're living in your ex-husband's flat and you haven't organised a job for yourself, and money goes as it comes. Why don't you go back to your husband? A friend of his called me. I think he was trying to act as a go-between.'

Fear seized Lamis, and she shouted at the top of her voice, 'No, no, no. I don't want to go back to him.' She began to sob uncontrollably.

As if her father had issued an edict declaring that she should not fall in love and lead a new life, as if Nicholas might be banished. As if the helicopter, which she used to see circling London's sky, could land, kidnap him and take off.

Lamis looked at Nicholas now, not believing that she nearly owned this human being, his body, mind, everything was hers. She was going to live with him under one roof. He was a gift, as 'The Nile was a gift to Egypt' – that was the first sentence in her school geography book.

But as soon as she saw the man from the estate agent's waiting for them on the steps of a building in Fulham, her previous feelings of alienation and distress rushed back, partly because the man was an Arab. She could tell from his accent. He proceeded to show them the flat on the third floor. It was magnificent. From the kitchen window Nicholas and Lamis saw gardens, high trees and the sky.

'It's beautiful, *habibti*.'

Hearing the Arabic for 'darling' from an Englishman's lips, the estate agent told them he was from Lebanon.

As the estate agent and Nicholas compared notes, checked the available light, where the sun would enter the flat, that there was no damp on the walls or the ceiling, Lamis became annoyed at being unable to imagine herself living with this man, although she knew very well that living without him would be like having an arm amputated.

187

Amira put the headphones of her Walkman over her ears. Umm Kulthum sang inside her, 'Your eyes take me back to times that have passed,' but this musical craving for love gave her a craving for chocolate and she switched it off and hurried to open the capsule and sniff. The smell of chocolate wafted up her nostrils. She had done this dozens of times already, and still her craving had not gone away, as Peter the specialist had assured her it would. He did not believe in diets, only in the use of scent to halt the cravings. Whenever she had a craving she opened the inhaler – like a tube of Vick's – and sniffed. If she had a craving for chocolate she inhaled from a chocolate tube, or for chicken, from a chicken tube.

'What about Lebanese falafel, or Moroccan *bistilla* and couscous and *harira*?' she'd asked him.

He promised he'd suggest the idea of catering for the foods of other nationalities to the American scientists who were always creating new tubes.

She stood up and started to look for the chocolate she had hidden in one of the suitcases on the highest shelf in her cupboard. There was a noise at the door. She ignored it for at least ten minutes, until curiosity got the better of her, and she looked through the spy hole and tried to decipher the excited hubbub on her doorstep, the horde of children, the clothes, the big suitcases and numerous carrier bags, but she could not relate their faces to anybody she knew. Only when she heard the name Samir did she open the door. She stood before the clamour of Arab voices, wearing her pink nightdress and sunglasses, so that the commotion appeared to be taking place in semi-darkness.

'Where's Samir?'

'Isaaf and the children? Come in, come in,' said Amira.

'You know our names?'

'Please. Come in.'

Samir's wife was wearing a very expensive coat two sizes too big, its sleeves nearly covering her fingers; she pushed her children and all their things into Amira's flat.

'So . . . he went without for so long, then broke his fast on an Egyptian woman of all things,' Samir's wife snapped, misled by Amira's rapidly shifting accent. 'He told me he was living with a Lebanese man.'

She couldn't help remarking on Amira's nightdress and gold-rimmed spectacles and pink slippers trimmed with feathers. 'Well, there was never the money for me to dress like that! I always had a kid in my arms, another on the way and a third round my feet. Where is he? Go on, take the baby from your sister's arms,' she instructed her eldest son, seeing that her daughter, who was only five years older than her baby brother, was nearly collapsing from the weight. 'So . . .' she shouted at the top of her voice, 'he left us just like that, to give the monkey to its owner. It's been three months since he disappeared. I suppose he thinks he's done his duty. A few phone calls, a bit of cash, and that's it.'

'Listen. Samir's gone out with the monkey,' interrupted Amira placatingly.

'Thank the Lord I decided to come and see for myself! Otherwise Samir might have got away with it and left me with his kids. We're going to make your lives a misery!'

At this, Amira could no longer contain herself and snatched the sunglasses off her face to reveal bruises around her eyes from her cosmetic surgery. Staring at Isaaf's widening pupils, Amira screamed, 'Listen to me! Me and Samir . . .'

'What? Did he give you a beating? Was he jealous? He's never been jealous about me. He never hit me once.'

Amira stamped her foot in a fury and went into her room and locked it from the inside. The children looked at their mother, who was holding her head, and the baby began to cry and tried to wriggle out of his older brother's arms, insisting on going to his sister, then making her fall over with him on top of her.

Samir's wife rushed over and knocked on Amira's door, shouting loudly, but Amira ignored her. She was trying to contact Samir on the mobile and wondering where this fit of jealousy would lead. Would Samir's wife be just as jealous if she knew her rivals were young men? Young men whose names Samir didn't even know how to pronounce, and whom he knew only a specific part of, who disappeared before even his head had stopped spinning with pleasure. She'd begun to be afraid for Samir as his obsession with finding a man seemed to have become chronic, and she'd bought him dozens of packets of condoms, for she was familiar with the English and their meanness: Maureen used to reclaim the cost of condoms from her punters.

Samir had told Amira that his wife never suspected that he liked his own kind; on the contrary, she was sure he had many mistresses. Once in Sharjah she even thought she'd nearly caught him with one of them, when she descended on him unexpectedly at the cabins where he worked as a cleaner. On hearing his wife knocking on the doors calling for him, Samir immediately took off his dress and scarf and hid them in a drawer. He lowered the radio and put on a pair of shorts and a T-shirt before he opened the cabin door. Because it took Samir so long, she suspected something and started looking for a woman but found only the scarf and the dress, with its fresh stains of sweat mingled with Giorgio perfume. And when she nearly went out of her mind looking for the woman, Samir found himself confessing that he liked to wear women's clothes. 'Don't you remember what I used to wear during the war? I don't believe you've never heard the stories about me wearing my mother's clothes when I was young . . . but you must remember the women's panties you found in my pocket?'

She'd become obsessed with the blue lace panties with satin ribbons and left them on the side of the sink, the dining table, the sofa. Whenever he told her to stop, she'd say, 'I can do what I want. I like them. I'm waiting for the children to ask about them.'

But she did not believe a word of what Samir was telling her. On the contrary, his explanation made her all the more convinced that Samir was a liar who invented weird and unthinkable excuses.

Amira told him that his wife probably couldn't comprehend the fact that there were gays and drag queens, especially as, in his case, they'd produced five children together. She told him about her own aunt, who lived in the Rif area of Morocco: this aunt's daughter asked her mother not to accept gifts from Amira because they were bought with contaminated money. The aunt answered that Amira would never steal. The daughter lost patience and told her mother bluntly that men paid her niece to sleep with her, but the aunt only shook her head saying, 'What's wrong with that? At least they pay, they are nice people . . . generous.'

One of Samir's children ventured into the first bedroom; he called his mother to come and see his father's coat lying on the bed. She fell on it, sniffing it for the scent of possible lovers, then threw it down and picked up a heavy chain, like a dog's, and coloured pencils and a small child's scribbles. He'd had a child. No, he'd adopted the woman in pink's child, and they must have put that basket on top of the wardrobe to keep it out of harm's way. It contained toys, packets of biscuits, and there was an old pillow that the child had dribbled on. She swooped on the wardrobe and flung it open and saw lots of gaily coloured shirts, two with frills, one purple, one white, and shiny leather shoes with gold buckles.

'They're like what the singer Prince wears!' exclaimed her eldest son in delight.

She examined the grey leather trousers and red jeans and picked up a striped cap and a purple feather boa and considered each of them in turn, while the children played with the basket and its contents. The girl seized hold of a brightly coloured embroidered shoe. 'Look!' she said to her big brother. 'It's like the picture of the boat in your book!'

He was desperate to try on the magnificent shirts and ignored her. But when his mother gave a yell and held out a pair of nylon leopard-skin patterned panties and a matching sleeveless top, the son decided they had made a mistake and this must be the woman's wardrobe, not his father's.

He said so to his mother, but instead of calming down she shrieked, 'Even their clothes are all mixed together.'

Amira didn't open the door until Umm Kulthum's voice on the Walkman was interrupted by Samir's as he knocked, begging Amira to back him up and let his wife apologise.

'Please, Amira. Swear to her on the Qur'an that you're like a sister to me.'

'I won't swear anything if she comes to my house and insults me. Your wife's mad, Samir. But right now the important thing is, where are you all going to live, now there are seven of you?'

Samir turned to his wife. 'Where are you all going to sleep? Why did you come? How did you get here? Who bought your tickets? Who bought this coat for you?'

'Some women from the ruling family took pity on me and the children. Remember you have five children? Did you think what you sent us was enough? That's why.'

'Don't change the subject. Who bought you the tickets? Women or men? Amira will tell you how I work day and night so you can hold your heads up in public, while you've been dragging my name through the mud. How am I going to go back to Dubai now, if my wife's turned into a brown Natasha?'

'The women bought the tickets for me, and gave me this coat. I told you how Mahasin took me with her one day, and I read their coffee cups for them, and everything in my fortune-telling turned out to be true, so they began sending a car to fetch me twice a day.'

Samir kept up the pretence of jealousy; it was the only way he could control his wife. 'These women thought you were manna from heaven, I'm sure!' he said sarcastically to her. 'You must think I'm stupid. I swear if I hear a single word from Dubai I'm going to throttle you.'

Samir's wife calmed down. He was jealous about her. She was his property. He'd threatened to hit her, even strangle her. Did she need any further proof that he loved her? Look at him now, exhausted. He still didn't believe her. She saw how he glanced furtively at her coat, trying to find out the truth. But when she showed him the return tickets, Dubai–London, London–Dubai, and the one-year visa stamped on her passport, his eyes flickered distractedly, and he found himself shouting, 'I'm finished, no work, no fun, only six chains around my neck – you and your children.'

Amira had to intervene, even though she knew she would lose Samir. 'Thank God a hundred times that you have such beautiful children, Samir, so disciplined, so . . . Go, go and hug them.'

He hurried to hug his children, looking at them as if he were seeing them for the first time, while the jealous Cappuccino let out a series of shrieks that gave them all a fright, except for Isaaf, who stared at his jacket, wishing she'd pretended to hold him close so she could have dug into his pockets. Then she snatched his bag from around his wrist, certain it must contain some of his secrets.

IV

Lamis woke up in the middle of the night, called Nicholas in Oman and told him that she wanted to live with him. As usual, she didn't go into any details, not even mentioning the friendship she'd struck up with Anita whom she called often and tried to see nearly every day. After all, who had she met who knew Nicholas better? And she really wanted to know Nicholas.

He wouldn't have understood her need to do so anyway, especially after that night at Anita's just before he went to Oman, where the three of them had intertwined like three ribbons on a maypole. Anita flirting with Nicholas openly and laughing at his rejection, encouraged by Lamis, whispering in Lamis's ears, asking her the simplest questions, and by the end of the evening, the three of them laughing – everything between them defined.

Later that night in bed, Nicholas asked Lamis very gently, 'Why were you teasing me? Just tell me. I'm confused. Is it because I had a relationship with her and you're punishing me? Do you want to show me you're daring? What is it? Tell me, please?

Lamis enjoyed her friendship with Anita – with her, she was seeing the other London, the one wrapped in a big scarf, tucked away from the tourists and the isolated people like her. Anita took her to have tea at a graveyard, to walk among butterflies in a butterfly house. With Anita, Lamis became almost uninhibited, she even found herself posing for Anita's camera lens and enjoying what it demanded of her, fascinated by this revealing of her body in its natural state, not wanting to arouse or be aroused, but alive, moving, sitting, uncovered. She was like a child undressed for the beach, drumming happily on her bare stomach before rushing to embrace the sand and the sea. Of course, her ex-husband, or her son, or her own mother and father, never saw her body. All they knew was her face. If her mother had known her daughter's body, or thought about it, she wouldn't have been capable of marrying her off as she did.

Lamis decided to live with Nicholas after visiting Edgware Road with Anita, who was looking for a particular shop that she had heard sold women's shoes in off-the-wall styles. Anita chose a pair with red hearts that lit up and flashed on and off, as if the hearts were beating, and another pair in the shape of lips.

That night when Lamis closed her eyes the smell of the cigars that her husband and his friends used to smoke filled her nostrils. She dreamed she was a cigar and each time her husband took a puff, her head began to burn. Her visit that afternoon convinced her that she had gone over to the other side; she'd grown away from the society of Arab men she had seen there, confident that they belonged, despite the fact that they were as ignorant of life here as it was of them.

The next day she wrote on a sheet of paper:

1. My son √
2. Love √
3. Learning English ?
4. Work: I still can't decide whether to do flower-arranging or learn to make silver jewellery ?

She plucked up the courage to open one of the boxes in the hall but was distracted by the sight of the buildings outside the window. Even the BT tower had changed its nature over the years. This notion inspired her finally to attack one of the boxes.

She pounced on the clothes putting them in suitcases and black bin liners. Every time she closed a bag, she sealed off a phase of her life, and as she forgot what she had put in the previous bag, she rejoiced. She left the flat quickly, before she could change her mind, and took a taxi to a charity shop. The assistant was an elderly woman who was reluctant to take charge of all the bags; she asked Lamis to wait, or come back when she had more help. Lamis stopped another taxi to take her and her bags to a place behind Harrods, where her mother-in-law used to buy second-hand clothes with famous labels to send as presents to her relatives in Iraq and Beirut, and even Germany.

Lamis let the woman there open one of the cases. There was a rustle of cellophane, yards of lace, then finally a wedding dress emerged. The woman froze in shock: How could you? You people are sometimes so tremendously selfish and greedy. What about the memories? Your daughters? But she said only, with consummate hypocrisy, 'Oh, that's wonderful! You must have looked like a princess in it! I understand completely. The cupboards in our houses can't accommodate dresses like these. Oh, it's marvellous! A friend of mine took the train off hers and turned it into a perfect evening dress. This embroidery, you're right . . . You want another bride to enjoy it. There's a shop that specialises in selling wedding outfits. Anyhow, I'll buy it from you. I won't put you to the trouble of going there. I'll do that for you.'

Lamis shot across the shop like an arrow, scared of bumping into her mother-in-law, and heard someone calling to her. She ignored the voice, but it pursued her. It was Amira, who fell on her, kissing her.

'This is incredible! Madame Lamis, you're not going to believe it. We were talking about you, Samir and me, yesterday. Your ears must be burning. I called Nicholas the other day and he told me you were friends, well, lovers, and that he was off to Oman for a while.'

'Yes, Nicholas is in Oman and he's coming home tomorrow. But how are you? You've changed your hair. How's Samir, and his monkey?'

'Yes, yes . . . Samir and the monkey. That's a real story. They were living with me, until his family arrived. Listen, come with me now for a few moments, then we'll go to Harrods or Richoux. Like a fool, I bought four bags all the same, in different colours. I need to sell three and just keep one. What about you, what did you sell?'

'Nothing. Actually I have to go home now.'

'Actually, you'll have a cup of tea with me, and I won't take any excuse. Shall I keep the black or the maroon, what do you think?'

'The maroon.'

Lamis agreed to wait for Amira, who was back in no time, her carrier bag still in her hand.

'They're robbers! I'll give them away or throw them away rather than sell them for nothing. I had a fight with her. Imagine! She examined the buckle to see if it was real! Then she came up with an excuse worse than the offence – she said a lot of women cut real buttons and buckles off the genuine articles in the shops and put them on their imitations at home. I told her, I'm an Arab, not an American. I only want the real thing. On the whole I don't like giving or receiving second-hand clothes, because the diseases and troubles and bad luck contained in a person's body heat must be transferred to them. Look, I get goose pimples just thinking about it!'

Lamis wondered for a split second whether whoever bought her clothes would be happier than she had been in them. She tried to sit as near to the back of the café as possible; her mother-in-law had always insisted on sitting by the glass door to observe the Arab women coming in, as if to mark them out of ten for their appearance.

Amira objected to the position of the table. 'Are we being punished? Come and let's watch people.'

'It's quiet here,' said Lamis.

'Who wants quiet?'

She pulled Lamis to a table near the entrance, but the minute they sat down, she stood up again. 'You're quite right to be afraid when you're with me,' she said, 'but I promise you round here I'm a respectable woman just like the rest!'

Lamis tugged on her arm, trying to make her sit down again. 'God forbid! I swear the thought hadn't crossed my mind for a second. I just don't want my mother-in-law to see me.'

'But you're divorced! Your ex-mother-in-law must be a terror if you're still scared of her. Lamis, don't you think it's strange that we bumped into each other today?'

'To tell you the truth, I feel bad for not phoning you and apologising about dinner, that day we arrived from Dubai and you kindly gave us a ride in your taxi.'

'Apology accepted. Don't you know the saying, "Older by a month, wiser by a lifetime"? And I've got a bigger bottom than you as well as more experience.' Amira laughed. 'Meeting you like this today makes me shiver. I told Samir that I'd phoned you when I hadn't, and that we were going to meet today. Honestly.' She put her hand on her heart. 'And so we shouldn't waste the opportunity. I mean, I shouldn't. Have you got half an hour to come with me to the casino?' she begged. 'Please. Your face brings me luck.'

'The casino? Now? In the daytime?'

'Please. You'll be doing me a favour. I won't forget it. Stand beside me while I place the numbers. That's all.'

'But I've got to . . . I can't. Sorry.'

'Five minutes. Please.'

Amira called the waiter and opened her bag and, despite Lamis's attempts to pay, held out a ten-pound note. Lamis found herself following Amira. I must be a weak character, she thought. But she smiled at Amira's bottom, a world unto itself as it bobbed happily along. The men enjoyed watching it and Lamis felt secure when she looked at its huge expanse, and then remembered her mother-in-law saying to her, 'What happened to you? Did you leave your bum behind when you got up off the couch?'

Amira took a pen out of her bag to write the letter 'k' in Arabic on her right ring finger, then stopped and laughed. 'I forgot you were with me!'

Lamis laughed back. 'Verses from the Qur'an to bring you luck in the casino!'

She'd heard of the new fashion among the women of the Arab community: they wrote initials from Qur'anic verses on their fingertips to bring them luck, and spread out their fingers in the face of difficulties. An Egyptian woman had been responsible for popularising the heresy. Her daughter failed her driving test several times until she agreed to go along with her mother's beliefs, and did her test with her fingers spread out so that the letters transmitted their magic to the steering wheel.

Lamis was astonished by what she saw in the casino. It was obvious from the hairstyles and faces that most of the women gathered around the tables were Arab and Iranian, and a fair number of them divorcees.

The air was thick with greedy pleasure and tobacco smoke, a pall that prevented the players' eyes from meeting and made them disbelieve the losing numbers. The older women's hands were spattered with freckles and their fingers bulged with protruding veins that stopped their rings from sliding off. Amira pulled Lamis along with her and stopped by a table.

'Give me five numbers. Single or double figures, as you wish.'

'Five, eight, nineteen, twenty-four, thirty-one.'

'You play them. Go on.'

Lamis hesitated. She had nearly been imprisoned in Dubai for drug trafficking, then become a tart, so why not a gambler? The notion made her reach her hand out recklessly as if a weight had fallen from her shoulders: five, eight, nineteen, twenty-four, thirty-one.

Then she drew back her hand and Amira grabbed it, closing her eyes and muttering prayers, then opened them to see five, eight, nineteen, twenty-four, thirty-one.

*   *   *

Later, as Lamis soaked in the bath, the phone rang. She was afraid that Nicholas might have postponed his return, but he was about to board the plane back to London, and reproached her for not answering his calls. She was embarrassed, afflicted by a sudden stammer, unable to tell him that she'd been thinking about him all day, even while with Amira, and getting his flat ready, with flowers, bread, wine, chocolate and fruit. She had hesitated when buying the cheese, but bought it anyway and promised herself she wouldn't eat it, so her breath wouldn't smell. She had derived great pleasure from choosing all these things by herself and hurried back to Nicholas's flat to put everything away in its place before she began preparing herself for him.

She tossed and turned all that night expecting that when the bell rang in the early morning she could jump out of bed quickly, gargle with peppermint mouthwash and put a bit of red on her cheeks before she ran to open the door. In the event she found that even her famous insomnia slept sometimes. Nicholas came in when she was fast asleep. She sat up suddenly when she sensed he was in the room, but he undressed and slipped into bed beside her and she waited, like an open goal or a basketball hoop, to see which way he was going to approach her. Later that morning he unpacked the presents he had bought her, including a cheap doll in a wedding dress with a wedding crown on her head.

'She's someone very important in my life,' he said.

Lamis laughed and picked up the doll and its leg fell off.

Chapter Seven

I

Her meeting with Nicholas after his second trip to Oman was not like the first – not even the kiss, which the first time had been like a distillation of yearning, such was the love and longing it expressed. So she had been expecting more than a brief embrace, but now he was breathing regularly, and she felt herself deflating as she realised he'd fallen asleep like barrels of whisky in a distillery, sleeping for years and years.

She got up and tiptoed about like a ballet dancer, restraining herself from rolling around on the floor in an anguish of disappointment. Her eye fell on the letter, or rather the collage he had put together and sent her from Oman. She opened it at the sketches he had drawn, of coconut palms and Arab men reading women's magazines, and of bathers jumping up and down as the burning sands scorched the soles of their feet, and ugly-looking frankincense trees, and he had pasted in an advertisement – an expanse of blue sea and a woman spraying herself with cologne – next to a photo of Sultan Qabus in a blue abaya. Eagerly she studied these images in case she could read anything between the lines.

She tried to remind herself that making love sometimes had nothing to do with love. There were men who made love to prostitutes, 'sellers of passion' as they were called. But that thought plunged Lamis into even deeper depression, and she thought: If men can have sex with women like that, then why doesn't he do it with me, unless he's stopped wanting me?

She remembered him talking to her from Oman about how much he missed her, and urging her to visit him. 'It's ridiculous for you to be alone in London while I'm alone here.'

She had changed the subject, sure that telephone operators in Oman listened in on calls, and must have heard him asking, 'Do you only want a sexual relationship?' That must be it: the way she had cut him off without an explanation. Or was it because she brushed aside the subject of the flat in Fulham every time he asked if she'd checked on whether it was still available? Or had the happy times that she'd imagined were piling up waiting for her, now that she was divorced, already slipped away?

Nicholas got out of bed and kissed her and hugged her and took her earlobe into the warm oven of his mouth. He counted three tiny warts, the size of pinheads, on her neck. One had come in his absence. He kissed them all, but in spite of this he didn't make love to her. Instead he asked her what she wanted to do that day. She decided she wouldn't hold back. She wanted to understand. So she asked him what had changed.

'Sometimes I like to love you like this, and save you up,' he replied. 'Like a child saving chocolate for later.'

'I didn't know I was a lucky penny you were keeping for a rainy day.'

He did not argue with this notion. He laughed and held her face like a determined mother who, tired of giving her daughter the same advice so many times, had decided to make her listen. 'I want us to live together, as you promised. Please, please. Think about it and give me your answer.'

'Yes, I want to, I want to.' Lamis found herself pacifying him. They made love after all, but not as in the past. As she watched him going into the bathroom she was terrified by the thought that he'd stop loving her one day, and felt again as if her hand or foot had been cut off.

She began to tell him that she was still looking for a flat and that he shouldn't be disappointed about losing the Fulham one. If it had been meant for them, it wouldn't have been sold to someone else so quickly.

The next day she fetched one small suitcase and moved in with him. No one would ever know about her change of address and the mobile phone was the solution to all her problems and of course her son could reach her any second he wanted. In the morning, however, she found herself going back to her own flat as usual for a few hours.

She did not ask what was wrong with him the third time he returned from Oman, even though he got out of bed on his first morning back after giving her a quick hug, saying he wasn't tired, and went into the kitchen to switch the kettle on.

She ignored him and went to get herself some orange juice, without putting any clothes on. When she saw him dressing she asked, 'Are you cold?'

She sat on his knee as he pulled on his socks. He dropped a little kiss on her shoulder as if he was shooing her away. She lifted herself up from him and began to dress.

In the evening, however, when he stood up, avoiding her caresses and attempts at seduction, she was reminded of some of the excuses she had used with her husband: 'I've got a headache' or 'My throat hurts' or 'I've got a period' so that her husband had suggested innocently that she should visit the gynaecologist as she'd had a period for more than two months.

'Have you got a period, Nicholas?' she asked him.

He hugged her and kissed her, and she sighed with relief, responding, rising above the sofa like a yogi in her ecstasy. Just as she began thinking how happy she was that everything was back to normal between them, he seemed to read her thoughts and stopped suddenly. She left him for a little, then asked what was wrong.

'Nothing. Reaching a climax shouldn't be the be-all and end-all.'

'I've decided not to hide anything. I don't want to go back to being the person I used to be. I don't care about my pride. You have to tell me why you stopped.'

'I've told you. It isn't the most important thing to come each time.'

'Perhaps you don't want to, but I do.'

'Sorry.'

Her feeling of humiliation was as great as her sorrow. Was nature having its revenge because she had gone against the course of her life and said no to motherhood, and to a husband and family and roots? How could she have been given a sense of taste after all these years, only to have her tongue ripped out? When she heard him whistling in the kitchen she found herself feeling her wetness with her eyes closed. She had not touched herself since being with him. She was unsure whether she wanted to come because it meant she wouldn't need him any more, or because she wanted to provoke him. She tried to keep going even when she heard him walking back into the room and shouting, 'Jesus Christ!' She opened her eyes, and it was her faint smile that made him completely lose his temper. 'You're like an animal,' he yelled in a fury. 'Stop it! Stop it!'

She stopped, put her clothes on and left. She felt like a different person. Her legs were trembling. It was as if she were walking along the street for the first time, and she did not look round although she knew he was up there on the second floor. Her eyes did not even stray to the window of the room where she had fallen asleep and woken up so many times. She looked at the junction box at the corner, and wondered if her voice would ever run along the phone wires again.

Nicholas put out a hand to Lamis who had just stopped a taxi. He bent to apologise to the driver.

Lamis walked along beside him in silence. On the bed he began removing her clothes very gently, bending down to pull off her tights, and she yielded to him without helping him. She did not even turn over on her back, but held whatever position he put her

203

in, just like a rag doll. Calmly at first, then in an incredible frenzy, he undressed and threw his clothes on the floor. 'What do you want' he whispered. 'Ask for anything you want.'

II

'Bahia had more than twenty slaughtered sheep delivered to Regent's Park Mosque this morning for the Big Eid. The mosque has promised to distribute them to the poor and needy,' Samir told Amira. 'Last month Bahia gave the mosque one thousand pounds, in cash, and when the Imam wanted to give her a receipt, Bahia wouldn't tell him her name, she said, "An anonymous donor who loves charity." '

Amira realised that Samir admired Bahia for having stayed anonymous. 'Bahia was afraid that if the Imam knew what she did for a living, he would refuse her donation,' she said sarcastically. 'But tell me, Samir, did Nahid go to the mosque with Bahia?'

Samir ignored her question. He was trying to find room in Amira's freezer for the lamb that he had taken to the butcher to be jointed after Nahid arranged for it to be sent to him from the mosque.

In return for a promise that Amira would find his brother a job in Saudi Arabia, a Moroccan who worked in an Arab estate agent's allowed Samir and his family to stay in a flat rent-free. Nevertheless, Samir still spent most of the day and part of the evening at Amira's – which pleased her – leaving only after she came home at night, when he headed out to a club, before returning to his family at dawn.

Amira had left so many messages on Nahid's mobile phone, even singing her a voice mail: 'Visit me once a year . . . don't completely forget me', and 'Make up with me today, we can be enemies tomorrow', that she was beginning to lose hope. Nahid did not return her calls.

Apparently she wasn't going to budge; she was still upset with Amira since their fight at Claridge's.

The days when the two of them had been like sisters, quarrelling one minute, friends again the next, were gone. Nahid was getting on Amira's nerves and Amira was losing patience. 'My patience went for a walk the other day, and hasn't come back.'

A man Amira met at Claridge's and whom she saw a second time, welcomed her suggestion that the Princess should spend a week with him at the hotel, giving her family the excuse that she'd gone to a health farm in the country, and he welcomed the idea that she bring Nahid, her indoors attendant, with her. The two women planned that Nahid would seduce the man when Amira left the hotel to go shopping. However, as soon as Nahid saw the spacious, beautiful, expensive hotel room, she found herself taking off her clothes, putting on her pyjamas, and luxuriating in the warmth of the hotel bed. She felt as if now she was really in the heart of London. Around her were the clean, glamorous streets and shops full of everything she could ever desire. She asked for and devoured everything room service could offer, especially the most expensive malt whisky. She sat on the bed and talked on the phone to Cairo for hours. She stayed in the hotel until the following evening, when Amira forced her out of the bed, helped her to dress and instructed Samir to call a black cab, ask for the room where the Princess was staying, and come and take Nahid home. They hadn't spoken since. Amira was waiting for her friend to make the first move. Nahid was the one who behaved badly, disgraced her and nearly exposed her, but the news of Bahia and the mosque made her eager to talk to her friend – besides, she missed her, and the punishment had taken its toll.

Outside Nahid's flat Amira knocked several times, although she was sure that even if Nahid was there, she wouldn't open the door. All of a sudden she had an idea: she would buy return tickets for both of them, to Cairo. They would go on a short trip. Nahid could spend a few days with her family, and Amira a few days at the Mena House Hotel; she would ask for a room with a view of the pyramids, where the tiny birds came and ate from your palm. As Amira turned to leave and walked to the stairs, the door opened and a woman with her head muffled, wearing a long djellabah, stood in the doorway. For a moment Amira thought she must be looking at Nahid's mother or sister, but it was Nahid herself. While Amira continued to stand there in astonishment, Nahid spoke out in her usual cheerful way.

'What's wrong with you? Have you seen a snake? Come in, come in.'

'I thought you were still angry with me. What about you? Have you got earache? Are you ill, and you haven't told me? I've been trying to get you on the phone for God knows how long.'

'No, I've decided to become a proper Muslim, thanks be to God. Tea or coffee? Did the cat get your tongue?'

'What happened, Nahid?'

'Nothing. The Prophet came and woke me from my sleep. To tell the truth, I was dead drunk and wanting to be more drunk. The pig I'd been with wouldn't pay. He said I was always in too much of a hurry. Anyway, when I went back to the flat, I walked into the bathroom, thinking it was the bedroom.'

'Did he pay? Did the bastard pay?'

'Is that all that bothers you? You don't change, Amira! I was banging the empty bottle against the bathroom wall, and then I felt the Prophet's hand (peace be upon him) leading me into the bedroom, helping me into bed, and protecting me till morning.'

Nahid burst into tears.

She must have been trying to tell Amira something, getting drunk like that in the hotel, and being so short-tempered, yet Amira had not stretched out her hand to her friend. Instead, she'd been annoyed with her. Amira had screamed at her in Claridge's, nearly hit her, made her stand for about half an hour with her head over the toilet so that she wouldn't be sick over the beautiful carpet. Then, when she'd asked Samir to take Nahid away, Nahid had clutched at Amira as if she were drowning in her own dangerous ocean, pleading, 'Amira, don't leave me, please. Please. I have nobody except you.'

'Does covering your head mean you can't speak on the phone? Or aren't you allowed to talk to sinners like me?'

'My situation's changed. Anyway you'd be bored with me now. I go to the mosque and a woman comes to teach me about the Qur'an. Why don't you try it?'

'God and I have an understanding. But tell me, Nahid, what are you going to do with your fur coat?'

'Wear it, of course. See what stupid ideas people have! What's a fur coat got to do with belief and repentance?'

'Nothing. I was just asking.'

Amira regretted her nastiness, her attempt to prove that her friend only cared for material things, and felt an overwhelming affection for Nahid, and yet she felt she couldn't reach out to help her or have a heart-to-heart talk with her, or try to understand her. She shifted around uneasily, uncertain whether to stay or go. Suddenly the doorbell rang. Nahid glanced at her watch and opened the door to several women wearing headscarves. For a moment she seemed unsure of how to introduce Amira, then, without a flicker of a smile, she gestured towards Amira, 'My sister in the days of my *jahiliyya,* my ignorance.' Then, indicating the other women to Amira, 'My sisters in Islam.'

Amira left the flat confident that Nahid would ring her that evening, and make her laugh, telling her all about her adventures with her sisters in Islam. One week went by, and there was no news from her – not even a telephone call to Samir. Nevertheless, Amira could not believe that she'd lost a friend; she decided that Nahid had finally found a wealthy punter who kept her very busy.

When another week went by and there was still no sign of Nahid – she had not been seen by Bahia or by her friends at the casino or by her former colleagues from the nightclub – Amira was determined to make contact. She went to Nahid's flat with a bouquet of beautiful flowers, a box of caviar, and two return tickets for them both, London–Cairo, along with some travellers' cheques for Nahid.

Nahid opened the door without delay. Seeing Amira with the flowers, she threw herself on her friend, wailing, 'Your heart has guided you. I'm dying. I'm saying goodbye to the world.'

Seeing the shock on Amira's face, Nahid pulled herself together and tried to be funny.

'The one that you and I fear the most came to me and said, since you are so scared of me, I've come – here I am – and now you don't have to be scared of me any more.'

Amira hit herself on the face; she pulled her own hair, beat her chest, bit her fingers. All she could see was herself, pushing Nahid's head over the toilet bowl so that she wouldn't throw up on the floor of the Claridge's bathroom.

The next day the two friends embraced and held each other for a long time. Amira had spent the night with Nahid, listening to her talk about her cancer. Who knew, the disease might sense the depth of their friendship, and bid Nahid farewell. Or maybe the Prophet, who gave Nahid peace of mind, would intervene with the Lord on her behalf. Amira held Nahid close to her, to show her how much she loved her, and to reassure her that she wasn't scared of the cancer transferring itself to her. She wanted to be near it. To face it. She wanted to punish herself for not being sensitive enough to realise that there had been something the matter with her friend for months, even before she went on that trip to Dubai.

'Why didn't you tell me, Nahid? Why?'

'I didn't want to scare you.'

Amira assured Nahid that she was going to call by and see her that evening. Nahid asked her to come tomorrow, 'And if you're busy tomorrow, never mind, you're always with me.' At the door Nahid joked with Amira, 'Now I know why you want to come this evening – so you can eat the caviar you brought for me.'

Amira laughed, but descending the stairs she cried and cried and cried.

III

When Lamis let herself into Nicholas's flat one afternoon and noticed the flowers were not in their vases, her heart missed a beat. She made herself calm down. Julia the cleaner must have thrown them away. Julia didn't like beauty; she complained about the yellow drizzle left by the stems of mimosa, was scared of the orange powder dropping out of lilies, which dyed the sofa and Nicholas's shirts, and tossed out the twisted branches Lamis used to put in with the flowers. But Julia didn't come on Wednesday.

Lamis went into the kitchen and realised that Nicholas must have thrown away the fresh flowers and left them to die a lingering death in a plastic rubbish bag. She hurried to examine them to see if there was some good reason, a lurking scorpion or a snake maybe, as sometimes happened in Najaf, and was shocked to see her jar of honey and her packet of tea in the rubbish too. She understood that this was a declaration of war, but then the sight of squeezed oranges, an empty tin of tuna and cut tomato ends comforted her slightly, surely someone who was about to go to war wouldn't have had such a leisurely lunch? She hurried into the bedroom and there on the bed were her small suitcase and carrier bags standing upright like the three pyramids.

She opened them and saw all her things: her nightdress, slippers, toothbrush, perfume, even her nail file; the shirt she'd given him, a drawing, a vest. She collapsed on the bed in a state of shock, then walked round distractedly, unable to believe that he'd cast her out of his life just like that. She wondered if her mother-in-law had had a hand in it, but put the thought out of her mind, as she could imagine Nicholas's scorn at her continuing obsession with the woman.

She did not know how much time passed before she hurried to the phone to try and contact him; then it was just like her nightmares, in which she tried to call and forgot Nicholas's number, or the telephone had a hole in it and her voice dropped through and bounced on to the floor.

She tried his mobile and a recorded voice answered: 'I'm sorry. It's been impossible to connect you. Please try later.'

She checked the messages on her own mobile in case Nicholas had left her a message, then she rang the number of his mobile again, without success, three, four, five, twenty-five times, and she let the voice of the operator go on and on until the phone shrieked like a fire engine. She tried to calm herself down. This was a black cloud that would pass. She had seen it with her mother and father who quarrelled a thousand times in one day.

She got up and took the packet of tea and the jar of honey out of the rubbish, made herself a cup of tea and forced herself to sip it, then took one of Nicholas's vitamin pills as if it were a capsule of blood she was squirting into her veins. She returned her things to their proper places, humming a tune, then noticed a sketch in the rubbish bag. It was a drawing done by Nicholas of a woman's face in profile, a cone-shaped cactus ending in a strange, almost terrifying, green flower with its mouth open greedily: a Venus flytrap.

She picked out the drawing and looked at it with a shock of recognition. It was her face. She froze; the woman stared back with a hard expression in her eyes. A man's penis extended from her head round into her mouth and the face had swallowed most of it. Lamis threw the drawing down and ran out of the room, but it pursued her.

She collected the whole lot and returned them to the rubbish. She did not rip the drawing up. Instead she placed it in the middle of the bed, but the feeling of anger which had enveloped her quickly evaporated and she wondered if Nicholas had left her a message in her own flat. She hurried back there and when she saw the answering machine flashing her heart leaped and she rushed over to rewind it.

'Lamis, my love. Call me. It's important.' (Amira imitating an Iraqi accent.)

'Mrs Lamis. It's the estate agent. I think I've found what you want. Please give me a call.'

'Mummy. Hi. Mummy, when the teacher found out that grandfather was from the Marshes, he asked me to write an essay about him. Do you think grandfather would write about his childhood, in Arabic of course, and you could translate it for me?'

Her son's voice lingered on in the room. She dialled Amira's number. As soon as Amira heard Lamis, she said, again in a mock Iraqi accent, 'Sweetheart. Will you come with me to Cambridge tomorrow?'

'Nicholas. He's disappeared. He's left me,' said Lamis breathlessly.

'Perhaps he got drunk! Or he's been taken ill. He couldn't leave you. He told me once he was the happiest man on the face of the earth.'

'Did he really, Amira?'

'I swear, but do you think it's possible he'd leave you just like that, for no reason? You know best, I suppose. Why do you think he would?'

'It's to do with us living together.'

'Because he loves you, and when an Englishman's in love, he wants to get married, but when an Arab's in love he marries someone else!'

'Why do I have to go through this?'

'Lamis, I'll come and see you. Where are you?'

Lamis collected herself. 'No. Thanks, Amira. I'll call you this evening.'

She called Nicholas's mobile again, and then his flat, Anita's, and left messages, Christie's, Sotheby's, Spinks, even India House. She called Oman. She thought of Nicholas's mother, whose number was in her little phone book. She dialled and put the receiver down at the last digit. She ought to have looked to see whether the suitcase Nicholas usually took away with him was still in the flat. She really would find a flat for the two of them the next day. Also, she would tell Khalid at the weekend. That's all it would take.

She climbed the stairs to Nicholas's flat slowly. She wanted to take him by surprise. She would have to control herself, so she could say calmly to him, 'I was waiting for you. Why are you so late? I love you.'

She waited there for five days and the flat seemed to be waiting with her. Only after a week did she feel the crushing weight on her chest shifting slightly, but it left her diminished and yet fiercer, like a newly sharpened pencil.

She finally ventured out and went to visit Amira, who had decided to stop being a princess for a day, and was wearing her tight clothes that emphasised her breasts and stomach and bottom, and kept joking: 'You'll always be able to find him, Lamis. He's so lovely and tall! He'll never be able to vanish into thin air!'

Lamis passed the time at Amira's talking to Samir and trying to phone Nicholas again. Umm Kulthum was playing on the tape, and the monkey was hobbled in the corner with a nutcracker, where it was shelling hazelnuts and almonds, squeezing them with the nutcracker, breaking them, digging out the nuts and finally eating them, and scattering the shells on the floor. The sight of Amira and her broad smile as she weighed things up, clearly and realistically, inspired confidence in Lamis. Whenever she blamed herself for not having read a situation right, not bringing a certain logic to bear which, in retrospect, seemed so obvious, Amira interrupted her. 'Live a lot and you'll see a lot. I've had the cares of the world on my shoulders since I was a child!'

'But why's he done this? I wasn't unfaithful to him. All I did was love him.'

'You didn't want to live with him.'

'But we spent every night together.'

'Do you think by taking a small suitcase over to his place, you were moving in with him? You were supposed to announce to everybody that you were living together, go abroad with him for a bit, then marry and have kids.'

'But why did he disappear like this? We were so close, like a nail and its varnish . . . how could he disappear in this way? Why didn't he talk to me, argue with me?'

'Each one of us has a different way of showing anger, and showing love too. Your ex-husband must have wondered why, all of a sudden, after thirteen years of marriage, you refused him. He must have said to people, "But what did I do wrong? How did I drive her away?" '

Lamis went back to her own flat and it, too, was unchanged and waiting for her return. There was another phone message from her son. She dialled the school's number and promised Khalid that she would fetch him the day after tomorrow, and that this time he could stay overnight with her. As she put down the receiver she thought it was lucky that he wasn't living with her. She called Oman, Nicholas's flat in London, Oman again, his flat, and finally Anita, and left her an urgent message about what had happened. She looked out at the BT tower before drawing the curtains and closing her eyes in bed, thinking that the reason Nicholas had left couldn't have been because she didn't want to move in with him, nor because she hadn't told her son about them since, although now she had left messages, lying and saying that she was sorting everything out, Nicholas still hadn't responded.

As soon as they stepped off the train, her son's attention was fully occupied by London. He wanted to go to Namco again – 'There's one in Piccadilly Circus, Mum' – but she insisted on taking him to Hyde Park, once they had had something to eat in the Hard Rock Café.

She led him towards the tearoom with the weeping willow in Hyde Park. Should she ask him if he remembered what he'd said about that tree? No, she mustn't be sentimental. He'd thought the twigs under the tree were its tears, and one day he'd walked in among the branches on his little legs and pulled them down so that they touched the ground, saying, 'Look, it's dried its tears now.'

Was it possible that this boy trailing along behind her sulking, because she didn't want to buy him rollerblades so he could join the dozens of rollerbladers in the park, had once said such sweet things about a tree?

'We're not going shopping. I want to talk to you.'

'What about?'

She suddenly wished that she could share with him her devastation about Nicholas.

'About your school. Your friends. How's William?'

'Do you know what my grandmother did to him? She made him eat Iraqi *kibbeh*. His stomach was really sore and his mum phoned my gran to ask her what was in it. And my gran was furious.'

'Never mind. We'll ask him to come with us to Namco next week, if you like.'

'His mother wouldn't let him. She phoned and said we spend too much money on him when Dad takes us out, and she can't do the same, and my gran got fed up with her and said that it was a tiny amount and Arabs are generous.'

She was frustrated and saddened by their conversation; she realised how young her son was and how much he was in need of her to pull him away from the life she had run away from.

'If your father agrees, you could live with me! Shall I try to persuade him?'

'I don't want to have a different room. Anyway my father won't let me, I know.'

She glanced at him. He was watching the boats gliding over the lake among the ducks and gulls. He had taken a rowing boat out with his father once.

'I want to row. Let's hire a boat,' he said suddenly.

'But I don't know how to.'

'I do. I do.'

I ought to be happy he's taking it this way, she thought. From tonight I'll sleep with my eyes shut, not like a ghoul. A deep sleep.

His self-confidence gave him the upper hand, and she acquiesced and sat in the boat, thinking fearfully: Why do you always go backwards when you row? How can people see behind them?'

'Khalid, let's go back,' she said aloud.

'You're scared. Swear you're not. Swear you're not.'

She was worried her son wouldn't be able to get them back.

They were far away from dry land, and he was rowing more laboriously.

'Let's rest for a bit.'

'You're scared. You're not like a mother. I know you're scared of water, snow, horses, riding a bike, insects, the dark, dogs. But I taught you to like dogs.' He reeled the list off triumphantly.

'But I got you a teacher to give you swimming lessons when you didn't want to, and your father and grandmother were against it too.'

'I remember peeing on the teacher's feet.'

'Let me row with you.'

'You don't know how to. You're scared.'

'Teach me. I want you to teach me.'

She let go of the oar and her heart jumped after it in a panic, but she retrieved it. She felt more confident as she followed Khalid's instructions. Unusually for her, she concentrated and listened to him and they were soon heading for the shore.

They crossed Hyde Park to Park Lane and hailed a taxi. Khalid was so pleased that he'd taught her how to row, but as they entered the flat his disappointment was obvious.

'Mum, I don't believe you live like a poor person. Everything here's ancient, and the TV . . .'

'I'm going to change it all. But not for a bit. I want to make a room for you, like your room at home, because you're going to come every week and stay with me. Did you have a nice time today?'

'I love you, Mum.' He hugged her. 'Why don't we go to the cinema and Planet Hollywood?'

IV

As the sun intervened in the lives of the English, so it did in the lives of Amira and her entourage. When the first signs of the real summer appeared and the roses opened in pots and tubs, in squares and parks, like women in beautiful hats bending their heads to see who was passing, the English streets and stores filled up with black abayas and veils trailing perfumes that lingered but never blended with the stale London air.

Amira and her attendants entered Hyde Park, an oasis for Arab families, where there was water, and trees and grass, ducks and geese, horses and rollerbladers. Unlike the park's elderly English patrons, the Arab promenaders enjoyed watching the young rollerbladers, who each had his or her own way of turning, dancing and jumping.

What upset them were the dogs, especially the ones that ran free, sometimes far from their owners. They felt a prickle of fear and disgust at the thought of having contact with them. So the Filipina servant girls hurried to gather the chairs scattered here and there on the grass, searching out and cleaning up the traces left by the dogs in the spot where the family had chosen to sit. The daughters of the family asked the adults' permission to walk by the lake. They pushed the black abayas back off their heads on to their shoulders, and looked like coloured butterflies with dark eyes, stealing swift glances at the young men from their countries, who had come to Hyde Park to meet their future wives, even if only at a distance. For this was the age of getting acquainted and exchanging a few words before making an offer of marriage, and London was the ideal place, far away from society's prying eyes and whispered remarks, and Hyde Park offered plenty of chances, in poetic surroundings. Edgware Road and Whiteley's had become too much like home.

The bridegrooms-to-be, although often close enough to see each other's facial expressions, walked around chatting to one another on mobile phones, which often carried pictures of their countries' leaders or national flags, a speciality of a shop next to the Park Lane Hilton. They swaggered about wearing flamboyantly designed Italian suits, drenched in cologne so pungent that it drove the ducks and swans back into the water.

Mingling with the crowds, Amira knew what was going on in the minds of these men: Here we are at last, a paradise that has all the elements of the old adage – water, greenery – now all we need is a beautiful face.

She and her retinue crossed Hyde Park, stopping at Speakers' Corner to listen to the laughter and noise around an Arab orator who was haranguing the crowd in English.

Amira felt as if a queue of words was forming in her heart, tumbling up her throat, then stopping before it reached her lips. Words with which she would have liked to push the speaker off his two Pepsi crates, so that she could announce, 'It is so simple – in this world there are the rich and the poor. The occupation of the poor is to milk the rich, to save the rich from being bewildered and confused about how to spend their fortunes.'

Having found no nectar in the park, she thought of taking her retinue along to the Lanesborough Hotel at Hyde Park Corner.

Amira sat sipping tea with two of her attendants in the tearoom which she had been told resembled the Royal Pavilion in Brighton. To her disappointment there was not a single Arab there, although she had heard that Arabs liked it, and that one wealthy customer had left without paying a bill of several thousand pounds. She wondered why the hotel still welcomed Arab guests after such an incident.

She sent an attendant off to reconnoitre, another bee seeking out the sweetest flowers. The young woman wore bright-orange lipstick and Amira saw it flashing like a beacon at her as she returned to let her know she'd found an Arab man. Amira got to her feet and went over to the telephone. Because she had filled her stomach with two pots of tea and several slices of gâteau, she found she was unable to think up a new story and she repeated the old one about the flour she needed to bake special loaves, making sure that the Arab her attendant had pinpointed was listening, and adding for good measure, 'London's nice, but life here can be complicated. You get tired of it . . . From the phone in the hotel.

They say the mobile can give you a blood clot in the brain and my uncle . . . told me not to use it.'

The name she gave her imaginary uncle was the musk on the seal, the gilt on the gingerbread, the crowning touch, that made the man's pocket handkerchief tremble in surprise, and the buttons on his jacket and his gold watch begin to rattle. Amira returned to her table and waited for him to finish the cake he had ordered. She shouted, 'Oh Lord!' so that all the tables turned to look at her. She tipped her bag upside down, emptying its contents on to the table and into her lap.

'I've been robbed,' she announced loudly to her attendant. 'Cheque book, credit cards, and seven or eight thousand pounds, I'm not sure exactly how much, in an envelope. Perhaps it was in Harvey Nichols, when I put my bag down for a moment to try on that nightdress.'

She sent for the driver so she could tell him to go to Harvey Nichols and the police, but from that first cry, the man had been hers, with his Arab decency and chivalry, and she stayed with him in the hotel until the following day, having sent her companion back home to look after the 'children'.

'Don't smoke in front of them,' she'd warned her. 'Order Lebanese take-away from Maroush. I'm embarrassed, but never mind, tell them to make a note of how much I owe.'

Naturally this had prompted the man to hold out a wad of notes to the companion.

Amira was ecstatically happy with him. She was the rebellious princess, the adventurer, who'd at last found the right man after being loved by Omar Sharif and Izzat Alaili. 'They were crazy about me,' she told him, almost convincing herself of her star-studded past.

She did not leave him until noon, with money for her shopping and the rent. They arranged to meet back in the room around four.

Amira hurried home, afraid her young woman attendant might have disappeared with the money, but when she arrived she found a message on her answering machine from Bahia, saying that

Nahid wanted to see her. She called Nahid's number and an unfamiliar voice said, 'Come quickly. Nahid's very ill.'

Amira held her heart and felt the end had arrived. A few days before, when Nahid had not been able to tolerate Amira's perfume and Bahia's handbag, she had sensed that her friend was half gone.

Nahid's flat was bursting with people and smelled strongly of fish. Amira pushed her way through to where she was lying in bed and hailed her, laughing and fighting back the tears.

Nahid smiled and reached out a hand to Amira.

'What's wrong?' Amira said. 'Come along, let's go out and enjoy ourselves.'

'Tell me a joke,' Nahid said. 'Cheer me up. And don't eat the fish. It smells awful.'

If Nahid had not been on her last legs, the two women would have laughed uncontrollably at Nahid's friend, the drummer, who had gone to the trouble of bringing her fish from Egypt, fully confident that if she only ate it her health would be restored. One of the women Nahid had met recently at the mosque, who was standing guard at the bedroom door, kept repeating to Nahid's English ex-husband, Stanley, 'No, no, no. You can't.' Then she raised her voice: 'Please, can someone explain to the foreigner what's going on? Help me, please.'

Another woman spoke up, her mouth full of fishbones. 'It's forbidden in our religion, Stanley. You're not allowed to go in and see her. You don't have the right, now you're divorced.'

'I want to see her,' yelled Stanley. 'I want to talk to her, say goodbye, and give her this bunch of flowers.'

'Give them to me, and I'll take them in to her.'

'No. I want to see her myself. Have you said to her that Stanley wants to see her? I bet you haven't.'

Amira stood up when she heard Stanley sobbing like a child. She whispered in Nahid's ear, then rushed out to confront the woman who would not allow him in. Controlling herself so that she did not slap the woman in the face, she screamed, 'Are you saying that quack faith healer who took the Dupont lighter and said he'd have her back on her feet in a couple of days has more right to be in her room than the man she lived with? What kind of nonsense is that?'

But when the fish-eating women grew more determined, the musicians and dancers from the cabaret massed outside Nahid's door and began pushing away the woman with the headscarf, so that in the end Stanley got in.

Amira found herself sitting near the fish-eaters and, to tease them, she asked one of the musicians, 'Do you remember when Stanley fell in love with Nahid – he tried to warm her up with his coat as soon as she'd finished dancing. After that night they ended up getting married, and she took him to Egypt. It was love at first sight! How happy they were . . .' Amira did not continue with the story of how they were divorced a few months later, straight after their return from Cairo. They had gone there on a visit, so that Nahid could crow to her family that she had found a husband even though she was a dancer, and for Stanley to see the pyramids, the Sphinx, to ride a camel and smoke hashish. But he began slinging insults at her and her compatriots, prompted by the sight of the emaciated, overworked donkeys. 'Look, look! See their ribs sticking out. You're savages.'

As a result Nahid threw his clothes over her parents' balcony one morning. The neighbours gathered them up and brought them back, and her mother, who'd been getting on well with her son-in-law until then, shouted incredulously at the couple, 'Are you really quarrelling like this about donkeys you don't even know?'

As soon as Stanley left her room, Nahid said, 'Pray for me, Amira. I'm dying. I can't breathe. The phlegm's stuck in my throat.'

Amira tried to find Nahid's doctor, then called the hospital who promised to send an ambulance, despite the objections of the women wearing headscarves. Then there was Bahia, whom Amira hadn't noticed before, coming up to embrace her and the two of them started crying, then Bahia composed herself and said, 'We must collect money for the funeral expenses, the coffin, the grave in the Muslim cemetery and the clerics from the Regent's Park Mosque to recite the Qur'an for her.'

None of this had occurred to Amira, but she tried to make up for her oversight. 'We must contact her family,' she said. 'I'll call them. We should take her back to Egypt.'

'But it would be very expensive for us.'

'It doesn't matter. I'll pay for everything, even if it costs a million pounds.'

'Amira, you're such a loyal friend. Lucky Nahid, I want to die with a friend like you beside me.'

Amira and Bahia went in the ambulance with Nahid and, when they saw that she was settled, they left the hospital feeling their breasts for lumps. 'Shall we go to Whiteley's?' asked Bahia, but Amira demurred, so Bahia went back into the hospital, not knowing where else to go.

Since Nahid had been confined to bed, Bahia had visited her daily and felt for the first time that she had a routine that filled the void in her life, much to the relief of the rich man who had bought her flat for her.

Amira went back home and when Samir was not there, she began to feel annoyed with him. She hid the five thousand pounds under her mattress. She would have to send Samir to the Moroccan joiner in Ealing where the coffins were half the price of the normal ones.

When, over the phone, the joiner tried to discuss the dos and don'ts regarding Muslim coffins, Amira begged him to stop, as she was wary of letting religion intrude in her life.

She had a bath, but although she was absorbed in beautifying herself, Nahid's face kept appearing before her. She left a note for Samir, asking him to call her on the mobile as soon as he got in, and took a taxi to the hotel. As she went up in the lift to the man's room she said to herself, 'Five thousand more, and I'll go back to Nahid.'

The man was waiting for her. He bent to kiss her hand and she wished she could tell him the truth, and weep for Nahid in front of him. She wanted an explanation. How was it that Nahid was all right the day before yesterday, and now she was dying. The man asked her where her shopping was. 'In the car,' she lied.

Then he began questioning her about her children and her uncle and whether the police had contacted her. He noticed her expression change suddenly at the mention of the police and he reminded her slyly of her lost money. Her mobile rang just in time to save her from further embarrassment. She rummaged urgently through her bag for it and heard Samir's voice at the other end. 'Come to the hotel at six,' she told him. 'Bring the girls and the car. Awatif knows it. It's by the Pizza on the Park.'

Out of the blue, the man cut in, 'Tell him I'm waiting for the girls too, so that I can line them up on the bed and fuck them one after the other.'

These shocking words hit her like a jet of scalding water, or a sudden cold sweat. Shaken, she ignored him, gearing herself up to escape, pretending she was still listening to the voice on the other end of the line, but the man went on, 'Tell him that I'll do things he wouldn't be able to imagine to you as well, even if you are a princess.'

She swung round to him and screamed, 'You slept with me, didn't you? What difference would it have made to you who I was or where I came from? Do you screw a woman, or is it her title or nationality?'

Her sudden outburst terrified him, and she took advantage of this to pick up a glass of water and throw it at him, then run out, her determination fired by fury. Once she found herself in the open air she made for the Pizza on the Park and sat there, her heart still pumping, and called Samir to tell him to come and pick her up, and to leave the monkey at home.

She put her head in her hands, and jumped whenever she heard a noise. The waitress asked her what she wanted to drink, and she let out a faint shriek and tried to calm herself. She thought about

222

Nahid, and how they'd laughed together and what they'd been through. Perhaps what had happened with the man in the hotel had been a sign telling her to go back to Nahid.

Why didn't he just laugh, she wondered, and tell me I was a fraud and demand his money back? I would have given it to him, once I'd deducted my fee. Anyway, why should I care? It's true I'm a prostitute, not a princess.

When she heard Samir's voice at her side she again yelped in fright and told him that she'd been found out.

'Did he follow you here?'

'No. I threw a glass of water and swore at him and ran away.'

'So what are you afraid of? He's never going to find you, and what can he do to you anyway? We were together the whole day. I can vouch for it.'

As they devoured a pizza Amira knew she was herself again, and as if the pizza had endowed her with strength, she ordered another. Samir called a taxi and she hurried to get in, glancing back at the hotel and finding it exactly as she had left it, with a porter standing on the steps, and not dozens of her clients pointing her out to the police as she'd imagined.

Chapter Eight

I

'Sweetheart, dear child, Lamis, write that they're draining the Marshes, depriving them of water. O water of the Marshes, which was my milk, and land of the Marshes, which fed me the dates from your great lofty palm trees. O River Euphrates, they're drying out your heart, and yours, oh Tigris. Your fish cease to breathe, and die. O birds in your skies, big and small . . .'

'Dad, that's beautiful, but Khalid wants information about the Marshes. I know the draining is important, but what he wants is information about life there, in the past, when you were a small boy. Did you go to school? What sort of games did you play? Was there a doctor where you lived? A shop? What did you eat? What were the different seasons like? Briefly, how do people live when they're surrounded by water?'

'I know what you mean. Write, my dear. Write this down. My great-grandfather and great-great-grandfather . . .'

'You talk about yourself and I'll put it into shape later.'

'My father, God rest him, forbade me to play or listen to music. Everything I saw around me I perceived first by hearing it. How could he ban music when everything around me was music, bestowed on the Marshes by the Almighty?

'I would hear the river swell and know that its water had turned red with mud and would flood any day now. I heard the squawking of the ducks and the croaking of thousands of frogs, the call of the kite, the wailing of children, the barking of dogs, the rustle of palm leaves as the trees bent their tall frames towards the water, and the sounds of the buffalo. And I liked the splatter of my little brother's pee hitting the water.'

Lamis heard her mother's voice in the background. 'Why don't you tell her about the spring?'

'Dear child, in spring there were hundreds of *burhan*, the waterfowl . . .'

'No, no. I meant the fleas in spring. They were everywhere, even jumping into your nose and mouth,' called her mother.

'Are you with me, dear? Your mother is interfering as usual. She saps one's resolve and destroys one's imagination. Where was I? Ah . . . hundreds of waterfowl rising up off the water, preparing to migrate, beating their wings, bringing a darkness over everything, which disperses when they're gone. When the water lilies open, the mosquitoes suck their nectar and their humming is like the taste of sugar in the mouth, and the music they make is yellow, purple, silent white, and it makes the buffalo race as if they're running from slaughter, when they come close and listen to the music.'

'Dad, what's wrong? Please don't cry. What you're saying is so beautiful and soulful.'

'What are you telling her, you selfish man? Why are you crying in front of your daughter, and scaring her? Let me smell your breath. You must have been drinking.'

'Shall I tell Lamis how lucky I was to go to Najaf and meet you?'

'No, tell her the truth. Tell her what an ill-fated day it was.'

'I'll tell her that, if my father hadn't forbidden me to play the lute or the tambourine, I would have stayed in the Marshes and never got to know you, and we wouldn't have had our sweet little Lamis. I'll tell her how we met, and how you loved my lute even before you met me, and how you hate it now, how you've smashed three instruments so far . . .'

'Hello? Dad?'

But her mother's voice ripped along the wires again, and made the receiver quiver in Lamis's hand.

225

'Write to her, or send her a cassette, or what will young Madame Lamis think, that she's still paying for her victory and having to spend money left and right? Remind your daughter that at least she should be paying her own phone bills and electricity bills – unless she doesn't care that her in-laws think of her as a parasite, living off them – and remind her that she doesn't own the flat. She's just living there temporarily because the father of her child feels sorry for her. Above all, let her engrave in her mind the saying "Out of sight, out of mind" – her son will eventually forget she exists.'

Lamis slammed down the receiver, wanting to feel angry, but the beauty of her father's voice remained with her, its reverberations attuned to the beat of her heart, untainted by her mother's shrill complaints. Her father's sensitivity made her think of Nicholas – how might Nicholas have talked about the Marshes? Always, she returned involuntarily to Nicholas, although she had finally stopped going to his flat and was avoiding anywhere linked to him, even the supermarket where they used to shop. She had collected up everything that reminded her of him and put it away: the miniature of Majnum Layla, the little bride-doll, the silver bracelets, even the matches he used to light her single cigarette after dinner. She had started to keep the bedside light on all night because, when she put it off, Nicholas had taken it as a sign that he should come to bed with her; then he'd become like a piece of quicksilver between the sheets. In her desperate efforts not to have any communication with him, she had even wondered feverishly how she could block out the BT tower, as she had hidden the telephone on occasions so that she wasn't tempted to contact him.

The fleeing lover takes his face away with him, so the other will no longer claim him back, or pursue him and catch him unawares.

Yet Lamis smiled at the thought of Nicholas, then checked herself, as the pain returned. She still loved him, but she was also becoming more certain of his selfishness with each passing day, more aware of his lack of patience. Nicholas had declared war against her and vanished – although she understood, or Amira made her understand, that we all have different ways of ending relationships. After all, she'd not wanted any give or take with her husband, but had just wanted to escape without offering any reasons, hadn't she?

'But I didn't love my husband and I love Nicholas.'

'So why don't you go to Oman?' Amira asked slyly.

'Without being sure he's there?'

'He'll know that you tried.'

She called her father again and agreed with him that he should write a letter or send his memories on a tape.

'My dear, write this one sentence before it slips my mind, because sometimes I note things down so fast that I can't read my writing, or don't understand what my signs mean:

' "A child of the Marshes can hear before he can see, so that our hearing was like a dog's." No, no. Put that it was like another heart. "My ear was so sensitive that I couldn't sleep whenever I could hear my own breathing not keeping time with my ear's pulse beating on my straw pillow . . ." There. Goodbye . . .'

A week later, Lamis found an express package from her father in the post, containing tapes, accompanied by a long affectionate letter:

My dear, I can't help but relate to you all my conflicting feelings. Take out whatever you want to and be sure that your father will understand and won't hold it against you. But I must stress that you should encourage Khalid to be English. There are Englishmen with Arab names.

I begin my journey with these words: *The alphabet seemed to me like a homeless child with no place to live, even though it was kept cased in a museum, and I began to follow it in its wanderings, so I could take it in my arms.*

Lamis read this and thought what a poet her father was until she read on. 'I borrowed these lines from the poet Adonis.'

She put the tape on. 'Hello. Hello.' Her father's voice echoed in the flat as he addressed his grandson.

227

'Khalid, you should explain to the teacher that the lute was what brought your mother to London. If it hadn't been for the lute you wouldn't have been born in London. The lute took me from the Marshes to Najaf, and led me to marry your grandmother, Neeran – her name means fire – it carried me away from my world, my family and my childhood companions. And you, my dear child Lamis, forgive this lute, which you were always trying to look inside; it was what made you grow up without roots, without a proper education, and even without a bed of your own. One, two, three. We've begun.

'The lute was the young man's passion when he arrived in Najaf from his birthplace, the Marshes. Neeran saw the lute on the table, when she was peering from behind the washing hung out to dry, trying to see into the room of the student who'd recently moved in. Her heart leaped. The sight of the lute made her think of a film with Shadia and Abd al-Halim Hafiz singing beautiful love songs, which she'd seen in Basra when she was visiting her aunt.

'The lute turned her thoughts to love, a sentiment far removed from this city, where there were no cinemas and where music was more or less forbidden, and the radio disapproved of, unless it was playing recitations of the Holy Qur'an and the Traditions of the Prophet. But Neeran knew about love from the songs she listened to with the volume turned down to a whisper, and from stories about the poets of Najaf and their secret lovers whose identities were known only to the pages of letters, and also from Egyptian films which only a few saw, but whose stories were told and retold.

'Neeran stole a glance at the young man who'd come from the Marshes as he played the lute in the room. His eyes were closed and she couldn't hear any notes. He was playing in his heart, while his fingers moved up and down the strings. Nevertheless he drew her to him, like a male bird drawing in a female. He was respecting the atmosphere of that city where sleeping and waking were regulated by the calls to prayer. Only the crowing of cocks and the call of migrating birds claimed the right to be heard, while an old woman was disregarded when she tried to silence the chirping of one happy sparrow. "How can you allow yourself to sing here?" she scolded.

'But it was music that brought me, that young man, to Najaf. My father's worst fear was that I would become an entertainer at weddings and circumcisions, or a professional mourner, and this made him listen to the UN adviser to the Marshes; he was urging people to send their children to school and then to the big cities to continue their education and, as a result, my father sent me, not to Baghdad or Basra or even Mosul, but to the holy city of Najaf to do religious studies.'

Then suddenly her father's voice was raised in irritation, and Lamis started in fright.

'What's happened? Why are you cutting me off?' he asked.

For a moment Lamis, whose thoughts were far away from London, didn't understand. She wound the tape back and heard her father ask irritably, again, 'What's happened? Why are you cutting me off?' Then there was a pause, then again, 'Why are you sitting looking at me? Didn't I say I don't want you here?'

'I'm not interfering. I'm just sitting here to cut my nails.' Lamis heard her mother's voice on the tape.

'Do you think I don't find that expression on your face intrusive? That unpleasant, self-righteous, sarcastic smirk?'

'Stop the tape if you want to ask me why I'm smiling.'

'I've stopped it.'

But it seemed that her father had not succeeded in stopping it, in his agitation at her mother. Her mother's voice came on the tape again.

'I can't help laughing at you when you take yourself so seriously, and describe yourself as a musician, as if you were of the calibre of a player like Sharif Muhi al-Din Haydar.'

'Ah, if I'd realised my hopes, you'd be talking in a different tone now. You'd pick up that lute as if it was your child.'

'But who stopped you doing what you wanted?'

'Your city stopped me. Your family.'

'So why did you stay?'

'Love dulled my senses. My passion for you deluded me into

229

thinking I could delay confronting the uncertainty I felt in every pore of my body, and be content with you.'

'Love is supposed to feed art, whether you're happy or unhappy.'

'Not when your beloved wakes up scowling and says, "My sister's fridge is bigger, my cousin's bracelet is better," and when she turns her back on you in bed and you try to please her and win her round, and she gives in, but says, "So will you buy me anything I want?" '

'I was putting pressure on you so you'd stir yourself and find a job.'

'Of course, everyone who didn't go to the Gulf wasn't really working, you're right. What about my job in the post office?'

'You yourself said that that job was for a half-wit . . . Oh, I'm sorry, I'd forgotten that you were the head of the music academy,' she said sarcastically.

'Go on, make fun of my birds, but if it hadn't been for the lute, would we have got over the Iranian border? If it hadn't been for the lute, would the British customs official have treated us with such respect?'

The tape stopped here.

Lamis double-checked that it was finished, then went to fetch the other tape. Before sitting down to listen she went to the kitchen to make a cup of tea. She thought back to their home in Najaf, and to the birdcages that became the most important feature of the house for her, with their anonymous little sparrows with drab feathers. Lamis's father had set himself the task of brainwashing the sparrows so that they would forget the limited songs they had been born with and load up the spirals and convolutions of their brains with songs that were mellow and rhythmic. Day and night he played them a tape of nightingales singing until they learned to copy the sounds perfectly. Their powers of imitation were so exact that he caught them trying to copy the click of the tape, and thanked God he noticed before their vocal cords popped like so many bubbles. He would take hold of them one by one and kiss them and give them their graduation speech, 'Go out into the big wide world and spread your sweet song among the tombs and mosques.'

Then Lamis thought of their arrival at Heathrow for her wedding, when he'd talked to the customs official who began inspecting his lute so that the customs official would know that he was not from Najaf but from the Marshes, and of how her father explained that Lady Drawer had distributed toys and warm hats to them when he was a small boy, and 'Wilfred' had taken a photo of him, and that this was proof that his family was not against the English.

Lamis suddenly could not bear to listen to the other tapes, could not take another dose of sorrow over her father's failure and her mother's resentment. Her father, the beautiful dolphin who'd lost his sense of time and place, yet still led his family out, in the belief that they would otherwise be embroiled in daily harassment, only to find himself in a swamp trying desperately to breathe. Her father blamed her mother and love, because both had made him turn aside from following his great hope.

She saw her father now as a man, as an individual with limitations – not as a machine called 'father' who has to manufacture solutions, hope, happiness and wisdom. She found herself watching a hand peeling away a thin mask that had forbidden her to breathe or to laugh for so long, a mask similar to one that she saw in her childhood, being peeled off the face of a young woman who wanted to remove her freckles. Taking with it the wailing, sobbing, sighing and whispering that made her heart beat faster and faster to free itself from the lungs and find a safer place to hide. Away from her childhood home, her father's drunkenness and his smell of alcohol. The troubles and rumours in Najaf, the terror that engulfed her town expecting Saddam Hussein to come in person and wipe them all out. Away from the mountains and valleys where they were waiting for smugglers to take her family and others to safety, while adults wept out loud and her mother coated Lamis's and Lamis's sister's bodies in sand mixed with water to disguise the smell of fresh flesh from the hyenas. Then the safety that was squatting in run-down places in Damascus and Beirut, seeing everything and saying nothing, and finally came the marriage, a frozen oasis, and still she was seeing everything and saying nothing!

She had to find Nicholas. She didn't want Khalid to have to sit there one day listening to the crackle of her voice as she blamed herself and her parents and him because she'd fallen in love, and been afraid to live with the one she loved.

Her father's voice took her back to their house in Najaf. She wondered what Khalid would think if he ever had to listen to a tape made by her: would she talk about the willow tree in Hyde Park or the whine of video games, or her lying in bed reading and crying? Or would she write a letter telling her son how her father had decided to get his family out of Iraq the day his dead mother visited him in the basement where he was hiding – drinking and playing the lute.

'My right eye and my left eye,' he had said to his daughters, 'I promise you I'm taking you on the wings of a bird to a lovely place with big dolls and chewing gum and sweets, where all the people spend their days eating ice-cream and dancing and singing.'

She dialled her father's number in Dubai and, when he answered, she told him that he was not only a musician, but a poet and a psychiatrist. She stopped for a second to gather her strength, willing herself not to cry, while she told him that she missed him and also she missed her mother.

'Your sister told me about the Englishman.'

'Ah, Nicholas. You'd like him, but . . .'

'It doesn't bother me, my dear. An Englishman would be very good. Between you and me, it would be your best chance of happiness. What does he do?'

'But I'm not seeing him any more.'

'He didn't want to marry? He wanted an open relationship? You were right. You were always so wise!'

'He wanted to get married and I said no.'

'If you had the same outlook on life and you loved each other and there was no interfering matchmaker or Snake-in-the-Grass, why didn't you let fate take its course?'

Lamis laughed at Snake-in-the-Grass, her mother-in-law's nickname.

'In a while, Dad. Let me wait and see. Not yet.'

'They say that Snake-in-the-Grass is searching high and low to find your husband a wife.'

'I wish him well.'

'And the boy?'

'What about him?'

'He'll get a wicked stepmother.'

'There's more to Khalid than meets the eye. Anyhow, that's all a long way off.'

'You're right. But I don't understand what you mean. Not yet? You want to wait? Do you want this Englishman, and do you understand each other or not? That's the important thing.'

'I don't know. I'm scared.'

'Scared of him?'

'No. I'm scared but I don't know why. Of my mother-in-law, of people – Khalid, Khalid's father, my mother . . .'

'Don't be afraid any more. I know everyone criticised you for leaving the boy. But he's fine.'

'Does that mean you don't blame me for what happened?'

'I blame myself, day and night. And I blame your mother . . . listen to me, my daughter . . .'

Lamis quickly changed the subject. 'I've got a surprise for you.'

'Shall I close my eyes?'

'I know somebody who could introduce you to the anchor of that music programme at the Arabic radio station in Dubai.'

'Let your mother and me live quietly in Dubai next to your sister, and let's not have any more problems. Snake-in-the-Grass must have contacted the authorities about your shipment of dried flowers, may God bar her from His Paradise! To this day your mother and I are taking medication.'

233

'Dad, she didn't know that I sent dried flowers.'

'Don't be naive, dear. That woman would even spy on herself.'

'I love you, Dad.'

To her consternation he suddenly broke into dry sobs. 'I love you too, Lamis,' he hiccuped. 'I'm sorry. I've made you and your mother suffer so. If only we were at home in Najaf, it would be heaven. I miss the birds, and the smell of the earth mixed with the smell of the brazier. And I'd even rather have the muezzins any day than those Russian women singing Umm Kulthum.'

'You're just feeling nostalgic. If you were there now, you'd be trying to get out all the time. You were tremendously happy when you fled with us. You promised us a country where people spend their days eating ice-cream, chewing gum, and dancing and singing.'

'It's fine to escape in your mind.' His voice broke again.

'But Dad, you probably saved us from being killed. Look what's happened since we left.'

'Forgive me, I treated you badly because I was afraid of your mother. I should have stood up to her and stopped her forcing you to marry.'

'It doesn't matter, Dad. I'm divorced. That's the main thing.'

'I'm afraid you've got a complex about men.'

'Don't worry.'

But she too began to sob: they had married her to a man who never hummed a tune, or called her darling, or listened to a song, and who was never seized by any powerful emotion without suffering from severe flatulence. Plans for taking her revenge on her mother and father used to circulate endlessly in her mind during the early years of her marriage, especially when she was told the details of her parents' own love story for the first time: how her father had cut his head and beaten his chest with heavy chains at the memorial feast of Ashoura, so that Neeran would see his bare chest and, according to tradition, reach out her hand to rub it in the blood, so that she could smear it on the faces of her younger brothers and sisters; how he'd threatened to kidnap her if her father wouldn't agree to let them marry because of his lute.

II

Was it possible that they were still in London, Samir wondered, as he tried to find the joiner's workshop in Ealing. The streets and faded shopfronts straggled on endlessly, and the sky here seemed duller, and mist brushed against the windows and hung around the street lights. Among the blackened buildings were a bingo hall and a bowling alley, the most significant landmarks these streets had managed to produce. Samir could count the other people in the street on his fingers. He wished he hadn't left the Tabbouleh and longed for the noisy welcome of the boys behind the counter.

But soon enough the joiner's shop took him back to Beirut with its smell of wood shavings and glue and the sound of nails being hammered in. He felt at home as he sat there waiting for the truck driver and a tape of one of his favourite songs played in the heart of Ealing.

The driver returned with bags of food and groceries. Commenting that Ealing was definitely cheaper than London, he loaded the coffin into the truck, helped by a young lad who worked for the joiner, who kept asking Samir if he knew the boxer Prince Naseem, because he wanted to be like him. Samir went into the toilet and put on hairspray and checked his clothes while the truck driver, an Egyptian, accepted the joiner's offer of a cup of tea.

'I hope we'll see you again soon,' said the joiner, shaking Samir's hand.

'No, please God, I won't see you and you won't see me. I've got five children.'

The joiner and the Egyptian driver laughed at the way Samir

expressed himself. Samir opened the passenger door and found the seat occupied, not by one passenger but many: packets and packets of toilet paper, vegetables, blankets, bottles of fruit juice and huge cartons of Persil.

'Where shall I sit?'

'On the back of the truck, to watch the coffin.'

'Don't scare me, mama. Who'd want to steal a worm-eaten coffin? Did they tell you it was for a Pharaoh?'

'No, no. Don't worry, I was joking. Nobody steals round here, but I wouldn't fancy eating the food if it had been next to the coffin.'

'But it doesn't matter about me?'

Samir climbed reluctantly on to the back of the truck and sat facing away from the coffin. He soon forgot about it, in spite of its rattling. He began to feel happy. Sitting in the back of an open truck, like the joiner's shop, made him nostalgic for Lebanon. He thought of the market porters travelling around in trucks like this, carrying ropes slung over their shoulders, and remembered a soldier who'd thrown a tablet of soap from the back of an army truck, making Samir wonder for days whether the soldier was making a generous gesture, or didn't like bathing.

He felt cold, and curled up with his hands under his head, enjoying the jolting of the truck. He thought of the shy boy behind the counter in the Tabbouleh. This was the first time he'd allowed himself to fall in love since his teacher, Salah.

He had thrown stones at Salah's windows on his wedding day and one had hit the bride's mother in the chest. He called the teacher's name repeatedly, 'Salah, Salah,' and rolled around on the ground and banged his head as if he were heading a football.

In the hospital far from Beirut, among the pine trees and singing nightingales, a nun took a liking to him and asked him to water the garden every afternoon. When she and the doctors agreed that he was cured, and should leave, he bent to kiss her hand. She told him to forget Salah because Salah was a young man like himself.

'No, *ma soeur*, he's much older than me. I'm only fifteen.'

'I know. I meant he's like you, he's a male. While your mother, for example, and your sister and I are all females.'

'But you've got a moustache, *ma soeur*.'

'That's true! You're so funny! I meant you and Salah are the same sex. It's not right for you to love each other and get married, and you'll never be able to have children together.' She fetched a picture and explained to him in detail what distinguished a woman from a man, then tested him to make sure he understood. When she had finished, he asked if he could pick a bunch of flowers from the garden, to take with him when he left the next day.

'Who's the bouquet for, Samir? Your mother or your sister?'

'My teacher, Salah.'

'But as we've already agreed, Salah is a man and it's not right for you to love a man and you know the reason why.'

'I'm too young to be thinking about having children. I'm not going to have children. My father tears his hair and beats himself on the face and says, "Having children was the stupidest thing I ever did." Anyway Salah found out that I've got a hole too, like a girl. And I feel like a girl since I wore my sister's red dress and stood on the roof dancing and singing. Look, *ma soeur*, I was singing, "Katkouta, katkouta, my sweet little chick . . ."'

'Stop! Stop! I don't want to hear it.'

Samir recalled the sweet downcast look of the boy in the Tabbouleh as he cut tomatoes into flower shapes that unfolded at his touch, the same colour as his cheeks. This was true love, not blond hair or blue eyes.

They seemed to have reached their destination quickly, as the truck was drawing to a halt. Samir stood up, ready to get out, but realised the truck hadn't stopped altogether. A creaking sound made him look around and he saw the coffin lid rise and a figure emerge.

'Are we there?' asked the figure.

Samir threw himself off the truck just as it started gathering speed again. He cried out in pain. The speeding cars swerved round him as he wept and pleaded in Arabic and English. One car drew up, followed by several more, and the driver of a blue Volvo called an ambulance on his mobile. Samir lost consciousness and regained it as he was being lifted into the back of an ambulance, swathed in blankets, with the Egyptian truck driver at his side, repeating, 'Thank God you're not hurt. It's nothing. You just had a fright. It was the kid that works for the joiner. He wanted a free trip to the centre of town and I was afraid his boss would think I was helping him skip work.'

His words revolved in Samir's head and he fell asleep, then woke to hear the paramedic saying on the car phone, 'Middlesex Hospital.'

'No!' shouted Samir. 'I've mended my ways. Take me to a normal hospital.'

III

Amira and large numbers of other women lined up in the main hall of the mosque, clothed in black, but decorative black: transparent headscarves, some with lace and black sequins, and jewellery round their necks and wrists. One woman apologised to her neighbour, as she tried to hide her rings: 'I was afraid my flat would be broken into.'

'Look,' responded the neighbour, opening up her handbag and showing the first woman all the jewellery she owned, wrapped in chamois leather.

Nahid was in the coffin and two clerics were praying over her. Amira was fuming: she'd clashed with the doorman on her way into the mosque because he'd made a remark about the length of her skirt which came to just below her knee, despite the fact that she was wearing a black headscarf and no make-up.

The cortège prepared to move off to the Muslim graves in Walthamstow Cemetery. It was not a normal funeral procession, as it contained in its ranks the owner of the cabaret, the musician, and the cleaner from the same club, as well as Nahid's close friends who had brought along their own close friends, for death in exile was one of the hardest things faced by the friends and relations of the deceased. Nahid's mother had advised her daughter, in the period when she was pleased with her because she'd given up her dancing career, 'Whenever somebody Egyptian dies, Nahid, even if you don't know them, you should go with them to the grave-yard.'

The drummers, the champagne waiter, the revue-bar compère, all those who never rose before three o'clock in the afternoon, had got up at ten that morning. It was raining, as the English say, cats and dogs, and as the Arabs say, hard enough to split the sky in two. The gravedigger had to go down into the grave with a bucket to scoop out the rain and mud. As fast as he emptied out the water, the heavens replaced it. Those carrying Nahid in her shroud grew impatient as the rain began to seep through. They tried to push the covering more securely round her body and the longer they delayed putting her in the grave, the more mud and water the grave discharged. A collective gasp went up as part of Nahid's naked corpse appeared. Amira and a veiled woman pounced, demanding that the gravedigger provide plastic bags and trying to shield Nahid with their umbrellas. The gravedigger came running back with black dustbin liners, and again the assembled company gasped, but the two women were unconcerned and tried to cover Nahid with the bags, to hide the body that had worked for her all her life.

The cleric bent over Nahid, speaking his final words of warning, 'Beware of the Devil, Nahid. Drive him away. Say to him, "Get out of here! I'm a Muslim, Islam is my religion, the Prophet Muhammad is my prophet and the Qur'an is my book.'

The rain began beating down on the cellophane wrapped around the bouquets of flowers, berating them, and the card Stanley had written to Nahid turned to a navy-blue pulp.

The English put cards with their bunches of flowers, as if fully expecting that the dead would rise up and read them, or else that the spirit of the words would reach them, even though they were dead. And why were the flowers wrapped in cellophane, instead of being scattered on the ground around the grave?

Along with the huge bouquet that she carried, panting under its weight, Bahia had brought a toy cat. The cat annoyed Amira, and she criticised Bahia to herself for the way she blindly copied the English.

Nahid's death and this burial were a space where Amira could come to a stop and reflect. Those who had come in answer to death's summons were the ones Nahid had withdrawn from in the last days of her life, but she remained one of them in life and in death. Even her family in Egypt had said to Amira in sickly-sweet tones of flattery, when she suggested bringing Nahid's body to Cairo, 'Don't go to all that trouble, sweetheart. Bury her near her friends. All of you are her family now.'

Did Amira believe what people said as the grave filled up with water, and the earth turned to mud and silt, 'It's as if God doesn't want to take Nahid back.' Did she cover her head and become a good Muslim before she knew she had cancer?

I wonder who'll be at my funeral, she thought.

Funerals were like weddings, a superficial display of a person, a snapshot of a place taken from an aircraft. This is what the dead person was like; a character study in a couple of words, like the quick competitions in the press that show the eyes of a well-known personality. And she would be Amira, the whore, and perhaps they'd say she was a good laugh too.

Amira was full of aches and pains and was forced to stay in bed after the day of the funeral. Most people assured her that it was the shock of grief for Nahid, or perhaps she'd used muscles she'd never used before as she walked through the cemetery, extricating her feet from the mud at every step. She wanted to include these among the reasons why she wasn't having sex as before.

Samir, who had come out of Middlesex Hospital that evening, brought her food she did not want, repeating prayers for her

240

speedy recovery loud enough for her to hear. He had trained his monkey to sit beside her, and to turn a page of her magazine each time she fed it with a peanut, while she kept asking Samir, 'Why didn't I talk to Nahid more? Why didn't I stop everything to be with her?'

IV

Lamis was convinced that the heart could think, it projected its own logic – she felt she had to visit Nicholas's flat in Pimlico. She felt her mind had been cleared of hostile thoughts that had grown up like weeds around her image of Nicholas and this encouraged her to enter his life all over again, as if she were the one who'd walked out of it.

She passed the Chocolate Society shop; aside from being a chocolate addict she wanted to be in the place where she had been with Nicholas, where she'd listened as he asked for the chocolates in his delicious English. She'd gazed at the ones he liked – chocolate-coated strawberries, brandy truffles – and feeling their names inside her was like eating chocolate: it made her mouth go warm and her heart beat faster. Whoever said chocolate and sex were connected spoke the truth.

Nicholas's flat was on the corner.

She hurried to the building, devouring chocolates tirelessly. She rang the bell to his flat several times, keeping her ear to the entryphone. There was no answer. She pressed the other bells, and when nobody responded Lamis took out a bunch of keys and unlocked the main door. The sight of an envelope sticking out of Nicholas's letter box convinced her that he wasn't there. Lamis turned the key in the lock.

His things were as before, waiting, everything covered with a mournful layer of dust – or was it her imagination? Nicholas could not have returned to the flat at all during the past four months. Lamis's card to him still lay on the table.

She read what she had written: 'If you miss me, get in touch. I miss you.'

Even Julia the cleaner did not want to be co-operative: she merely said, whenever Lamis asked about him, that Nicholas wasn't there.

There were no traces of another woman in the flat, the black rubbish bag on the bed was gone, so was the drawing of an insect-eating plant. Lamis played the taped phone messages: she heard her own unsteady voice with its Arabic accent, an English-woman's voice, his father, his mother. She replayed the woman's voice, and listened closely, to check whether there was excitement in the voice, or whether it was just a business call. She opened the box of chocolates she'd bought for Nicholas and began eating again.

On the table Lamis saw the Arabic Bible. Some coloured pins of hers were still in the Japanese dish. She read the envelopes of his mail – advertisements, invitations – in case some woman had written to him, in case he now loved someone else, and suddenly saw her own name on an envelope. She was about to stamp on her nervous optimism, telling herself it was the particulars of flats and houses, sent by the estate agent, but recognising the Omani stamp she let out an excited cry.

It contained a single sheet of paper, a watercolour of a tulip, its stem bent. Its delicate head was turned towards the onlooker, and pollen was scattered on a peach-coloured petal that was partly unfurled.

Lamis did not know what to make of the watercolour. She tried in vain to gather clues, looking under the stack of books and the mail. She spotted drawing paper in a pile at the end of the table. At first she did not realise that they were sketches of the Devedasis, but was only vaguely reminded of the female luminaries of the temple, kneeling, standing, erect, moving, smiling or frowning; the sketched figures came to life only in the play of the shadows drawn in black charcoal. Then she saw that he'd drawn them all with her face.

Had Nicholas drawn those sketches while he was in Oman, and brought them back with him? Did he do them in London? There was a mixture of smaller and larger sheets; some of the drawings were complete, some nearly so. Lamis's heart throbbed with love and then uneasiness and finally anger. Nicholas must have returned to London and not contacted her. He must have sat at his table and made these sketches. There were sticks of charcoal on the table. She was sure that Nicholas must have used that charcoal to draw the sketches. He drew me when I was less than a mile away, Lamis thought. A sentence came to her aid: 'Isn't it a miracle that we've met in a country with so many millions of inhabitants,' Nicholas had once said to her.

The sentence provoked more pain, then anger. She took her head in her hands and cried, and she only stopped when she murmured to herself, 'He's a very complicated man, Lamis.'

Hearing this, Lamis made up her mind and decided to leave. She put her keys on top of the drawings, closed the door behind her, and did not look back.

Chapter Nine

I

'That?' replied Samir, when his wife challenged him with a red lipstick, 'That's one of the tools of my job. I wear lipstick to make people laugh at me. I swear it's mine. But why were you looking in my pocket?'

'You bastard,' she replied. 'Do you think I'm stupid enough to think you need lipstick for your job, and panties and bras?'

'If you don't like it, you can go back to Beirut.'

He knew she took fright whenever he appeared to have misgivings about her being there. Where could she go? Even if she went back to Lebanon, how could she live with the four older children and the youngest, born disabled because of the bombardment in progress when Samir was on top of her. He remembered how she shook him and shuddered, and tried to make him withdraw, but he'd not managed to, until she'd slapped him on the face a few times, and then it had been too late.

She became unbearable when he started spending most nights at Amira's after Nahid died. She went to check on him there and, when nobody opened the door, she assumed that he'd married, and she made Amira swear on the Qur'an he'd not married her or any other woman, but she didn't believe Amira either. His son told him that she'd begun visiting churches, starting with the local church near Nahid's old flat, where they were living for the time being. She asked to see the priest, and when he came forward with his hand extended to shake hers, she declined, and put her hand on her chest, mumbling indistinctly. He assured her quickly that the church was for all faiths, for refugees from anywhere, and that there was a free meal for everyone once a week, whether they were from Iraq or Albania.

She turned away from the priest to take a piece of paper out of the front of her dress, which she'd folded into a small square, just like a child's fortune-teller game. She pointed at it, 'Jean, Jean,' and gave it to him. 'Did my husband Samir and Jean get married in this church?' she managed to ask the priest haltingly.

Samir was thus forewarned when his wife chose the time he was at his least sharp, just after he had woken up, to ask him if his jacket needed ironing. She gave it a good shake in front of him and the piece of paper, which she'd replaced, dropped out of one of the pockets. She bent to pick it up, opened it out and read, 'Jean. Jean.'

'Are you trying to learn English, Isaaf? Not bad!'

'I have to, so that I know how to talk to your wife and can get along with her. I'm right, you have married again, haven't you?'

'Poor Amira! How can you think such things about her with all she's doing for us!'

'If only it was Amira. Mrs Jean, you liar . . .' She handed him the bit of paper.

'That's Jason. A man's name.'

'How did you think up that name?'

'Do you want to talk to him? Come on. Bring the telephone here. Set your mind at rest.'

'Let me dial the number.'

That afternoon Samir felt obliged to take his eldest son and the monkey with him when he went out. He had stopped trusting his wife with the monkey after his eldest son saw her sprinkle cleaning powder into the monkey's food. He told his wife he was taking the boy to the dentist. Each time the boy opened his mouth he screamed in pain at the inrush of cold air, which made his teeth tingle.

'It's wicked to pour money down the drain,' shouted his wife.

'Come here, son, and gargle with salt and water.'

But Samir, who still leaned heavily on Amira, had paid attention when she swore that she wouldn't speak another word to him unless he took his son to the dentist.

'Stop eating sweets, son,' said Samir. 'Then your teeth won't sting. Just give me five minutes. I've got an appointment in this hotel. Then I'll take you to the dentist. Wait for me here at the news-stand.'

He gave Cappuccino a piece of toffee and his son three pieces. 'These are for Cappuccino, in case there's any problem . . .' and then he gave his son a severe warning. 'Monkeys are forbidden, son. Here even the dogs have identity documents and medical certificates, and all their names are entered on a computer. Watch out. Even if it bites you, just grin and bear it, but don't let go. You know, the monkey is our main source of income.'

The boy nodded. 'OK, Dad, don't worry. But don't be long.'

Samir looked back at his son while he was waiting for the lift. Nobody would guess that he was carrying a monkey. As usual, Cappuccino had wrapped itself round the boy, just as it did with Samir. He saw the curled end of Cappuccino's tail in his son's overcoat pocket, under the big scarf, and felt reassured. The toffee would keep the monkey quiet, sticking to its teeth and the roof of its mouth.

He entered the lift, looked at himself in the mirror and combed his hair and couldn't help thinking that he'd become an addict, never content unless he was alone with another man, except that it was no longer a question of being content, more of surviving, or of regaining his equilibrium. He was so desperate that he even took young men to Mrs Cunningham's bathroom, a safe place away from the prying eyes of Amira's porter, or the smell of the public baths. Mrs Cunningham's bathroom was extremely clean, with a vase of flowers on a side table and coloured soaps in a beautiful dish, and all of these bolstered his importance with the Englishmen. Except for the art student who preferred to comb Mrs Cunningham's few strands of hair than to give Samir another glance.

In the hotel room that he had taken especially on account of the art student, having guessed from the time he first went with him to Mrs Cunningham's that he would only get this youth into bed in aesthetically pleasing surroundings, Samir had finally settled on his story. He was from a family that was extremely rich. However, they couldn't get used to his passion for the wrong sex, nor to his taste in clothes, and when they realised that they couldn't change him, they forced him to leave Lebanon. He'd then come to London where he'd been faced with another problem: his wealth attracted the wrong type of person; this made him lose his faith in friendship and he'd begun preferring the monkey to human company.

'I've got property,' he told the young Englishman. 'I'm a very rich woman. I'll buy you a lizard, I mean a genuine lizard jacket from Gucci, and you'll live a life of luxury.'

'Am I the boy in *Death in Venice* and you dirty old Dirk Bogarde? Or are you Keith Richards, or a sheikh from Arabia, who'll be my patron, and support my talent after I graduate?'

'What are you saying? I don't understand.'

'You look like Keith Richards.'

'Is he beautiful?'

'Yeah.'

'OK . . . no time . . . you . . . please, you smoke me first, you understand?'

The art student laughed so hard he could barely think straight. 'I knew this hour wouldn't be wasted.'

Instead of giving Samir what he wanted he started to ring his friends, one after the other, to recount the joke to them, until Samir was driven to distraction.

God is punishing me again, Samir thought. Even the man I hired this room for has turned out not to be worth it. All of this because I couldn't find the right words. I said, 'Smoke me like a cigarette,' and now he's laughing as if he's lost his mind. Each time he goes quiet, he rolls over on his back and starts up again, and then calls another of his damn friends.

247

'You'd think we had all the time in the world,' Samir shouted at him finally.

Samir emerged from a corridor and came down the stairs, waving to his son, who shouted at the top of his voice, 'Dad. The monkey ran away and went into the wedding,' and raced towards him, crying.

'What wedding? What did I do to deserve you?' groaned Samir. 'How did you let it escape?'

He did not wait to hear what his boy had to tell him, but hurried towards the noise and the music and the big flower arrangements in the ballroom, and began rehearsing what he would say: 'I work at the zoo. I know how to get hold of it. Mind out of the way.'

His words were swallowed up in the noise and excitement of the wedding reception, which rose in volume as Cappucino leaped from table to table, and clung to the flowers and branches intertwined decoratively round the pillars. The shouting and laughter grew louder. The bride wept. The men chased after the monkey, which had climbed up on to the brass curtain rail. Samir and his son watched, dizzy with horror. One of the hotel employees, who were crowding into the room, had brought in a tall wooden stepladder.

'Let me go up. I understand monkey language,' Samir shouted.

Nobody heard. All eyes were fastened on the monkey, and on the man who had reached the top of the ladder, close to where Cappuccino was clinging to the curtain. As soon as the man put his hand out the monkey leaped down from the curtain on to the table that held the multi-layered wedding cake. It grabbed hold of a layer of the cake and began gnawing on it as if it were a stone, then hurled pieces of it at the onlookers and licked its fingers.

Samir froze, and in desperation seized his son's hand and whispered to him, 'What are we waiting for, son? Come on, your mother's expecting us. We don't know this monkey. Understand? It's nothing to do with us.'

He moved back out of the ballroom, dragging his son with him, and marched him out of the hotel; then the two of them began running until they reached the bus shelter, where Samir sat down, took his head in his hands and began to cry big gulping sobs. He had left Cappuccino to be a sideshow at a funfair, and run away. The monkey would search for Samir among the crowd to show off to him. It would have expected Samir to have heard the laughter as it jumped on to the whitewashed edifice of the cake, attacked it with relish, then pelted people with the remains. Eventually the monkey would be captured by the hotel employees and, at the thought of this, Samir spoke pleadingly to his son. 'Son, I can't live without him. Any time now they'll catch him and lock him up and maybe kill him. They'll probably think he's rabid. Shall we go back and rescue him? But the families of the bride and groom might take me to court. No, he's had it. If I try and get him back, it'll be the end of me, and you and your mother and brothers and sisters.' He started lamenting for his monkey exactly as the women did back home. 'Poor Cappuccino, whose piss was enough to flood the neighbourhood! I'll die without him! If he knew how to talk he'd tell them my name, so thank God he doesn't.'

Samir could not stop crying, even though his son moved close to him and said, 'Dad, people are staring at you.'

Samir's eyes had grown arms in the ballroom in his eagerness to bring the monkey back to him, and he had hardened himself and stood watching, alongside the people who were furious with the monkey for spoiling the wedding. He'd abandoned it like a father who comes across his son begging in the street and passes by on the other side.

'Dad, Dad, stand up. Come on, people are watching. They might send for the police.'

It's my child, thought Samir tearfully. Not you, or your brothers and sisters. I don't know where you all came from. It was because I was scared everyone would talk about me and say I liked men. Every time the spiderwoman got pregnant, a weight was lifted off my shoulders and I could stop feeling guilty for a year.

'Dad, stand up. People are staring at us.'

It should have been the monkey who talked and called me Dad.

Cappuccino never got bored or fed up. Every night we went to three cabarets and restaurants. Cappuccino assembled the electric train, pretended to be a nurse, begged for cash. Even when we just walked about between the tables everyone gave us money. And what do all of you do besides eating and shitting and saying, 'Give us some money, Dad. Give us some money'? Every time I turn round I see a dozen hands reaching out. Before you all turned up in London it was the first time I'd been happy in my life.

Samir and his son did not take a bus until Samir had convinced himself that Cappuccino would be in the zoo. Tomorrow he would go there and look for him. Should he go to the place the Englishwoman had told him about, outside London, that specialised in apes and monkeys?

'Son, listen to me. The people in the zoo can't be that hard-hearted. If I go and tell them the story, they won't report me. They'll understand why I'm attached to the monkey. They might let me play with him sometimes, and who knows, maybe I'll be able to go back and buy him off them one day.'

The boy put his arm round his father's shoulder and pulled him close, then asked him, 'But how can we survive without it, Dad?'

'God will provide. My father, God rest him, used to say, "When you've got a penny you're worth a penny." And I'd started to say, "When you've got a monkey, you're worth a penny." God will provide.'

Then to himself Samir added, 'I make everybody laugh, but who's going to make *me* laugh now?'

II

Routine had not played a part in Amira's life for twenty years. She would find herself standing for ages in front of the wardrobe choosing clothes then change her mind and choose different ones.

She would take a bath, rub herself with perfumed lotions, outline her eyes with black kohl and, since she had become a princess, burn incense in a burner on the floor and raise her dress, so that the incense would penetrate her underclothes and the pores of her skin. The sound of a voice when she talked into an entryphone sent the adrenalin coursing through her body, alerting every part of her as if she had drunk fifty cups of coffee one after another, and the fear of not finding a punter made her see flashing lights until she recited her mantra, 'Men always want sex.'

If only she'd been content to stand on the shore catching little fish with her rod, since those innocents gobbled up her bait greedily. But ambition had made her venture on to the high seas where there were fish of all types, and whales, and big sophisticated sharks grown to maturity by eating the bait and pissing on the rod. She reminded herself that she was brilliantly intelligent and cunning. She'd beaten Scotland Yard once, made a fool of the Prince and had his private secretary eating out of her hand.

The prince Amira was setting her sights on this time was not like the minor royalty who did not know all the names of their relatives because their families were so large. He was the exact opposite, someone who went into the tiniest of details, especially where his brothers and sisters and close relatives were concerned. He believed in honour, and the importance of a good name, and did not hesitate to discipline his young relatives if he heard scandalous tales about them.

When he heard stories of the Arab prostitute who was passing herself off as a princess and as a member of his family, he did not laugh as the others did, nor did he fly into a rage then forget all about it. He had made up his mind to find her and he did this in such a cunning way that he outsmarted Amira, who thought she was the one who was out looking for him.

She knocked once, twice, and, under her breath, told God she loved Him as He'd always taken care of her.

Amira stood looking down at the floor, arranging the fine black scarf half over her face so that her mouth and brown skin showed and one eye told half the tale. She smelled of incense, and her feminine modesty was designed to arouse, saying, 'I'm at your mercy. Even a drop of water will be enough.' And yet at the same time she presented herself as an impregnable fortress, living as she did surrounded by women and children.

'London can be frightening sometimes,' she murmured to the Prince, averting her eyes shyly and not explaining why. If the conversation were limited to a few words, that would count as the height of respectability between a male and female relative. She told him that she was weak and defenceless because she'd had so little experience outside the security of her family and country. She hoped he would get excited right away so that his mind would stop turning. When a man got an erection, his brains buried themselves in the earth.

She stole a glance at him and he appeared to be frozen to the spot. Everything about her made the situation more confusing for him: her clothes, behaviour, voice, accent, manner, smell, but he had her registration documents in front of him and her real name was Habiba Mustanaimi and she was Moroccan.

In order to make him flustered, to convince him, and to give herself the courage to continue with her charade – since he looked as fierce as a hawk – Amira asked him if she could use the phone.

'Please do.'

She had obliged him, the Prince, to respect her as a princess. Thank God! She dialled a number.

'Awatif, what did you have to eat? Tell the driver to go to Maroush to get food, and then pick me up at the hotel in an hour. And turn off the television.'

'Please. Have a seat.'

The Prince sat her down on the sofa and asked her what she'd have to drink. This was the first time she'd met somebody of his social standing and she wished she wasn't only playing the role of a princess; he had gentle manners, a beautiful voice and was impeccably dressed. When he asked her what the problem was, she decided on a different scenario: she wasn't going to tell this man she needed urgent medical treatment and was still waiting for the money to arrive from home; some people didn't like to go near a sick woman. She told him her flat had been burgled and, certain that he would forget the whole affair as soon as she left, she added that naturally her brother would reimburse him in full.

'Who? Muhammad?'

She nodded her head shamefacedly.

'Don't worry,' he said. Then he called another room. 'Can you come here for a minute, please.'

The rapidity of her thoughts distracted her and she could not decide how much to ask for. Any sum seemed either too big or too small, as she wondered uncertainly whether to thank him graciously or merely mutter that it was his duty to help a member of his family, especially a woman.

Should she cry, or tell him the story of her husband leaving? But they all married more than once. She could give him the one about not being able to have children, or tell him she liked composing poetry.

No, not tonight. Another time. He didn't seem to be in the mood for stories. He looked extremely serious, and so did the man who knocked at the door and came straight in without being required to identify himself.

One word had given her away: television.

She looked at the man's empty hands and they balled into fists and he began aiming blows at her face, her head, her chest and her arms. When she cried out in pain, he hit her harder, on the legs and thighs, and she did not know where to put her hands. The blows came harder and faster as if she were being hit by more than one person.

She put her hands up to protect her face, like a boxer who's lost all ability to defend himself in the ring, who forces his opponent to aim his punches at specific places. She opened her eyes to see if the man was wearing a ring. That was what made scars. When she couldn't see one she sighed with relief. He was her father, brothers, cousins, any number of men from home beating her up. This was what she'd feared each time she went back to Morocco on a visit. If the Prince himself had hit her, she would not have felt so humiliated. She couldn't bear the thought that this sidekick felt superior to her.

The Prince must have humiliated him, so now he's getting his own back. The harder he hits me, the freer he feels, she moaned to herself, and then she wondered if she'd spoken out loud and not heard her own voice. The Prince didn't seem to hear her either, even though she could see his expensive slippers. Only when he cleared his throat and began to speak did the beating stop.

'It's very wrong for an Arab woman to play such tricks. Very wrong. At least next time, say you're a princess from your own country. Don't involve our country in your degrading behaviour.'

She was sure she couldn't stand up, but the Prince picked up some papers from the table and read out 'Habiba Mustanaimi' and, as if she was at school, the minute she heard her name she rose laboriously to her feet.

'You see, everything about you is down here in black and white. What happened tonight is a warning. But watch out! If I find there's been another occurrence, I'll . . . There's no need for me to threaten you. You know what will happen.'

She said words without any meaning, perhaps because her mouth was now closer to one ear than the other, but she was afraid she'd be forced to leave London. She could no longer breathe through her nose. She went down in the lift holding on to anything she could for support, her movement further impeded by the fact that the black veil had fallen down over her face. It was in order to be able to walk into hotels like this with her head held high that she'd become a princess. Now the dim lights pierced her eyes like skewers and she put up a hand to shade them. Her leg hurt. She must have bumped into the table, or else the man thought he was fighting Rocky Marciano. She started to cry. She'd tasted the violence of pimps and the resentment of malicious men towards people like her for the first time. All the men she'd done business with up until then had left their authority at the door, and succumbed to her affection and her willing ear. For this reason she'd never understood why foreign prostitutes were subjected to violence and relied on an English pimp instead of selling direct to Arab punters.

But the pain of knowing she hadn't defended herself was fast overtaking the physical pain. Why had she let him hit her if she didn't feel she deserved it? He'd not even hit her in that vicious way because she'd impersonated a princess and extorted money and slept with her victims: he'd done it because she was a prostitute, a whore.

As a favour to one of her clients she'd once agreed to talk to an Arab student who was doing a dissertation on the wholesale transfer of Arab society, including prostitution, from Beirut to London. At the end, when he finished his interview, she asked him what he would do if he found out his sister was on the game.

'Impossible,' he repeated, then finally, when she kept goading him, 'I'd put a knife through her heart.'

Now, since she'd been unable to defend her pride, it seemed that she'd joined the ranks of the other foreigners and the English. Her expensive clothes and diamond watch hadn't helped her, nor had her affiliations – she refused to sleep with Iraqis after they invaded Kuwait, then stopped sleeping with Kuwaitis because they drove other Arab nationals out of Kuwait. But she'd stopped getting involved in politics – prostitutes, whores were not a part of society. They weren't born of a mother's womb: they grew on trees, without fathers or brothers or sisters or relatives of any sort. One punter was shocked when she told him she was an experienced chef, as if she wasn't entitled to any other job.

She'd often escaped from dangerous situations before, so what had gone wrong tonight? Had she lost sight of her own fallibility, as she became convinced that all men were carbon copies of one another, like trucks discharging their loads in a single uniform manoeuvre? She remembered a punter screaming at her, pulling her hair, 'I want to . . . I want to . . . will you let me or not?'

'Of course I'll let you,' she'd answered. 'You've paid me and it's my job. You're hurting me. Please stop it.'

She let the dark, thin scarf cover her face, as if not wanting her mother to see her in that state, even though her mother was far away in Morocco. On one of her visits, her mother had shaken her in the middle of the night. 'Get up! Get up! Don't sleep here, it's not right. Your sisters are pure. You must make up a separate bed.'

So Amira had got out of bed, still warmed by the breath of her little sisters, each of whom wore around her neck a gold chain brought by Amira on a previous visit, from which dangled miniature Qur'ans or the words 'Ma sha' Allah' (What God wills) written in decorative calligraphy, or blue beads to ward off the evil eye. She pulled her mattress away from her sisters, wishing she were only as old as they were. Her sisters' breathing rocked her to sleep, but she woke up the next morning to her mother cursing as the milk boiled over, then her sister banging on the door to hurry her up as she squatted in the privy, and she was glad to be going back to London to live in comfort with hot water, taxis, foreign perfume, restaurants, entertainment, health-care, all in easy reach.

Amira loved her mother and understood why she could not accept the money she brought her and would not let any of her sisters touch it. Her mother left it on the table, waiting for Amira to go out so she could call her pious old neighbour, who would climb the stairs and sit down with her prayer beads twined around her fingers, drinking tea and asking for another spoon of honey, before she started on the cleansing of the polluted money, not with water but with her prayers and incantations. Then she blessed it by leaving it on top of a closed Qur'an for a few moments before Amira's mother began drawing a blue eye on each note and stowing it away in a secret place.

What would she do if she gave up her job? Even her mother had stopped asking her to repent and come home and get married. Who was she without it? How could she back out now when she'd given it all her youth and energy and intelligence? For its sake she hadn't become a wife, a mother, or even a mistress. She knew the men who slept with her were, on balance, more interested in owning a fast car or an expensive coat. Still, she reminded herself of her good fortune; she'd come a long way since her first few months in London when she used to walk around in the freezing cold without tights or women friends or a permanent roof over her head, going from one maid's job to another. In a few hours her strength would return to her and the violent pain subside. In any case, she was lucky: she was free; she wasn't an Englishwoman on her way to the police station, after being caught in a squad-car's lights trying to pick up a john, nor was she from the provinces, bussed in with others like sheep to spend a few days in London, opening their legs in cockroach-infested hotels. And she'd never been sexually abused when she was a child, or cheated by a punter.

She stopped a taxi and asked the driver to take her to Regent's Park Mosque. When they arrived she asked him to wait while she went in to find out if her mother's body had arrived from the undertaker's. She believed her own lie and started crying, and the kindly driver assured her that he would switch off the meter. 'Take as long as you like. I'll be here.' She took a few steps, then on an impulse went back and paid the driver off and gave him a pound tip. She entered the mosque. Nahid was a poor thing. 'I used to think of myself as worthless. That's why I did what I did,' Nahid had told Amira one day. Amira didn't know whether she was crying for Nahid or herself. She thought of herself as highly intelligent, as possessing an instinctive calculator for assessing time and money – just five minutes with a man . . .

The warden at the desk asked if he could help her, and she enquired whether her mother's body had arrived. After establishing her mother's name, and the time the corpse was supposed to be delivered, he went away, then came back and asked her if she was quite sure.

'That my mother's dead?' She began to cry.

'I didn't mean that. Please. Just wait there. Do have a seat. If you could wait a moment. Shall I make you a cup of tea?'

Her tension disappeared. She felt secure and sipped the tea as if she were tasting its sweetness for the first time in her life. She raised the veil from her face to take a sip, then put it back.

She thanked the man and got up to leave, saying perhaps she'd got the date wrong after all. As usual on such occasions she took a ten-pound note from her bag and pressed it into his hand and he thanked her, murmuring that he hadn't done anything.

She came out into the biting cold and looked around her. If anyone had followed her they would have decided she'd gone into the mosque to repent. She couldn't see a soul, but she had to be on her guard. She waited some time before getting into a black taxi. Was it because she covered her face that the other taxis didn't want to stop for her? One of the drivers even spat at her, and another asked her, before he knew where she was heading, how big a tip she was going to give him.

'Fuck you,' she said in English. He looked thunderstruck for a moment then gave her the finger and drove off.

If only she were in the Rolls-Royce with her attendants, waiting for the drama to begin, and anticipating the success that would leave her heart beating like a drum with excitement and happiness. The memory of it made her able to move her stiff leg more easily. No, she didn't want that way of life to disappear, or to exchange it for the pre-princess mode, the life of ordinary people. She was so secure and dignified, even those closest to her felt her power and had become respectful, including Wasim and Samir. People had stopped calling her anything except Princess – even a relative who came over from Morocco and stayed with her until he found a job. She'd heard him asking Samir if the Princess was there. And she behaved like a princess with everyone she met. She would sit in her flat listening to stories, being entertained by the people who'd begun to flock around her in the hope of benefiting. from her connections with generous Gulf Arabs.

'Your highness,' one of the English drivers had said to her, 'can you help me get cheap petrol, since you're from one of the oil states?'

'I'll try,' she said, looking at him solemnly. 'You're a good man.'

She didn't want to go back to chasing men in casinos and cafés, who, as they grew older, wanted younger and younger women; and London was packed with young girls. She was no longer the actor she used to be, someone who knew all her roles and adapted to the other actors who'd forgotten theirs. Going on like that she might have become a madam, or a 'mother', like the woman with a headscarf she had seen working Edgware Road.

She couldn't, and indeed didn't want to, induce others to follow her way of life: she wanted to be responsible only for herself. What others did was no concern of hers.

She allowed Samir to wail at the sight of her, then cut him short and told him she'd slipped and fallen on her face. He brought cold compresses of crushed ice wrapped in a towel, and laid them on her face. She burst into tears and, like a child who hasn't learned how to talk, she pointed at her face and moaned, and when he pleaded with her to tell him what had really happened she said she'd walked into a lamp-post. Then she laughed and said she'd finally met a super-jealous prince who'd had her beaten. He was very sexy, she went on, especially the smell of his robe, and the way he spoke.

'You're hallucinating, Amira. Hallucinating. God preserve you! A lot of people have it in for you.'

He led her over to her bed and laid her down on it.

'Don't worry, Amira. I've always said if you touch sand, it turns to gold.'

Unimpressed by his faith in her on this occasion, she closed her eyes and whispered to herself, 'What shall I do? What shall I do?'

III

The fog transformed the dimly lit BT tower into a rocket that was slowly starting to burn. It drew Lamis in along the streets and through the different neighbourhoods like a lighthouse guiding a ship. She reached it finally, happy because she'd not resorted to a taxi or worried about getting lost.

She stopped at the foot, where the tower began, her gaze travelling upwards until it reached the top. Everything starts from a single point. The engineers had stood where she was standing now and said, 'Here.' It was as if, by looking at its base in daylight, she was divesting the tower of the fanciful attributes she'd projected upon it. From now on, if she looked at the tower again from her window at night, she'd be able to picture the ground floor, where employees went to and fro, as in any other building.

She stepped inside and asked, 'Is it possible to go up the tower?'

'It's not open to the public.'

'But it's really important!'

'Call the BT information office. Here's the number.'

She noticed that she'd used her non-English accent, whereas a short time before she used her proper English accent to reply to an American tourist who asked for directions to Oxford Street. She'd swallowed the 'r' and 'e' in the word 'here'; she said 'I dare say', and added an 'actually'. She was exercising the power that came from living here, and from being here: she knew what lay beyond a certain street, what you could buy in a particular shop. When the buses drew up in early December and regurgitated passengers from outside London coming to shop beneath the decorations of Regent and Oxford Streets, she knew how they felt and walked ahead of them with a superior air when she saw them clutching street maps. Poor things, they were strangers in London.

It was only in the month of December that she saw the British not singly as usual, but out in families or with their friends and neighbours, carrying bags of shopping. She saw them alone again in summer, women in Laura Ashley dresses and flat sandals getting on the bus as if they were climbing the steps of a temple.

She pictured the face of the language teacher, Alison, and her cat. The teacher was chuckling as she told a new student, 'I had an

Iraqi woman who almost choked on the piece of wood I put on her tongue to hold it down when she said the letter "r".'

Lamis arrived at the Montessori nursery opposite Selfridges, the polling station for the local election. She looked at the statue of the woman holding the clock at the entrance to Selfridges. Whenever the clock struck while Lamis and her son were hurrying to the nursery, they used to stop, raise their linked hands and bring them down with each chime. She went into the school now, looking at the wall on her right in the hall, where the coat hooks used to be, and the names of the children, including that of her son Khalid, next to a photo of his dog. She went into the classroom, a smallish room with white walls covered in children's paintings. She did not see the bronze statue of St Mark or the piano or the dark-brown chairs and tables, only new, brightly coloured chairs and tables piled up at the side to make room for the polling booths.

When he first joined the nursery she stayed with him for ten days. She did not like to see him cry when she got up to go, and had welcomed Mrs Lubbock's suggestion that she should stay till he got used to the school. Any place away from the house had been paradise then, even among twenty children coughing, swallowing their phlegm and wetting their pants.

She used to share in all their activities, listening to stories, singing songs, being taught how to hold scissors. If she had not always drifted far away in her thoughts, she might have improved her English pronunciation a lot then, as she was only eighteen years old at the time. When Mrs Lubbock complimented her on her patience, Lamis nearly told her that she was happier there than at home, but thought better of it. How things had changed; she used to have a strong affinity for this place, as if she believed that her son was going to remain that age for ever, like the size of Chinese women's feet in tiny shoes.

She made her mark next to the candidate's name, and dropped it in the box, and found herself saying to the young woman in charge, 'My son went to school here.'

The young woman merely looked at her sleepily and forced a

smile. On her way out a woman handed her a pamphlet from a local residents' association. Lamis recognised her as being the mother of a girl who had been at the school with Khalid, known as Plum because she was fat, round and red in the cheeks. Lamis spoke to Plum's mother, who pretended she remembered Khalid and asked where he was at school now, then tried to find out which way she'd voted. What concerned Lamis was the feeling that she belonged in England; the politics of the candidate she was voting for were secondary.

Lamis walked along reading the pamphlet; it was urging the authorities to agree to give priority parking to local people, Sundays too, now that Oxford Street shops had Sunday opening. St Mark's Church needed a financial miracle. There was still a blazing row going on over the bar that disturbed local residents' sleep. The publication regretted the closure of the post office – it had been replaced by a shop selling cotton T-shirts – and feared the street would begin to lose its charm.

Finally Lamis read about Rose Dunn, aged one hundred and three, who lived in a council flat above the very room where she'd first seen the light of day. Rose Dunn was born as Tchaikovsky's *Pathétique* had its première, grew up in the period when Wilbur Wright made his first flight and Oscar Wilde died, had lived through two World Wars and the reigns of six kings and queens. She had outlasted the muffin man and dancing bears in the streets, and now heard revving engines instead of the clatter of horses' hooves.

Where do I stand in all this? Lamis wondered as she walked around and came to a halt in front of the buildings where Rose Dunn lived. What do I contribute, apart from my confusion, the sound of my footsteps and my vote in the elections? How can I reach the heart of the place and make it see me?

What she was reading did not concern her, and yet it lay on her chest like a heavy weight. A pigeon flew into a rubbish bin and she was afraid it would get trapped, but it flew out again. Here, where I'm looking now, Rose Dunn is sitting with her stooped back, and

I'm allowed to look: because I'm not from here. I can swagger about wherever I please. Like an eagle circling I can alight on any spot I choose and declare that this is where I'm going to settle down. Not like Rose Dunn who lives directly over the place where she was born.

She went back to the flat and called the BT information office.

'Why do you want to go up it?' asked the impatient English voice.

'Because I want to see London from above.'

'Sorry. It's not possible.'

'Just a minute, please. The writer Jonathan Raban in his book . . .'

'Sorry, no. Goodbye.'

Jonathan Raban had climbed to the top of a building in Sanaa in Yemen. Whoever took him up had felt proud that a foreigner wanted to see his city from above. However, it was impossible for an Englishman in an official position to think: This woman's not from here, and she's called dozens of times. I'll let her go up the tower.

She knew there were foreigners who developed fixations about certain features of their adopted cities. There was that Asian woman who'd sneaked into an office at Scotland Yard and come out undetected, in full riot gear, or Samir who thought his monkey could climb up to the clock on Fortnum and Mason's and get him either Mr Fortnum or Mr Mason.

'The tower guides me like a lighthouse, as if I'm a lost ship.' The comparison must have appealed to the BT office because one of their staff eventually rang her back. 'We've sorted it all out. Please bring some proof of identity with you.'

So the British were like the Arabs after all: they found loopholes in the regulations when necessary.

The waiting area in the BT tower was like a bar in broad daylight. An isolated patch of yellow on the carpet nestled against the blues and greys, not wanting to be on its own.

The lift attendant taking Lamis up to the thirty-fourth floor told her that he didn't feel dizzy with the speed and his ears didn't pop. When the woman assigned to accompany her showed Lamis out and she stood in front of the thick aquamarine glass, face to face with the sky, she knew the reason for the lift attendant's pride. She looked out at the rays of sunshine distributed equably over the whole of London: if scientists were to attempt to measure them, they would not find an iota of difference between one and another.

Now she realised how the sun lit London, and that the sky was a protective skin. At any moment she expected to see God in human form, as he appeared in religious paintings, the light descending from his fingers like rods of water which had gradually become frozen over hundreds of years.

Buildings stretched to the horizon and rose up like cacti in cowboy-film deserts. She looked down on buildings that were unremarkable except for their windows, which were like kohl-rimmed eyes; a touch of mascara opened them up and coloured eye-shadow lent them a magical allure and whisked them out of the bedroom into a carnival atmosphere. Blue and orange neon lights were locks of hair falling on their foreheads. The tallest skyscraper, Canary Wharf, appeared lit up with happiness because it was not alone. There were turquoise domes greenish with rust, the Tower of London holding its brother's hand, afraid it might fall, the green of the grass pushing against buildings, then being pushed aside in turn by ponds and lakes. But she couldn't see the ducks and the geese.

In her mind's eye she saw her son Khalid, like a young shrub in a garden, in a house that carried no trace of her. It was crowded with his father's friends. Each of them sat on his inflamed prostate, which was swollen up like a giant prayer bead. Khalid was surrounded by electric wires, computer games, and by money – coins dropped here and there, and notes – each time the boy touched something, money dropped into his hand and he filled his pockets. His grandmother defending her grandson regardless. In that flat, Iraq turned into a mere word tossed against the walls, not a country, a country that was so far from her, in distance and in memory.

Her eyes returned to the buildings, which breathed from their tops, while New York buildings breathed from their feet. She saw Nicholas gazing at his sketches of the Devedasis, concentrating on their eyes, as if trying to interrogate them about Lamis's reaction when she realised that the drawings were also her, and to quiz them about what she meant when she covered the sketches with the bunch of keys.

Where do I have to look to spot Anita's neighbourhood? Anita hadn't been able to deal with Lamis's pleading telephone messages – she left them hanging in the air without answers. When finally Lamis caught her on the telephone, Anita had lied 'that she had been away' and interrupted Lamis's repetitive saga saying that all stories of lovers leaving each other were utterly boring.

She picked out the main features on the wall map and let her eyes run over them: the Roundhouse, London Zoo, Baker Street. She looked out at the designated spot and saw the square and the buildings, a flag on an embassy, and her eyes moved rapidly to the back of her building. She could make out the colour of the roof tiles, the two little lips: her bedroom window.

She saw herself in her bedroom, looking out at the tower, and looking back from the tower to the bedroom. There she was, a pebble stuck in midstream, no longer carried along by the current. Nobody stared out of the window like that so earnestly, except a lonely stranger willing herself to fly out and alight in those places that she observed so often, places that gave her the feeling that their inhabitants would welcome visitors coming to sit on their sofas, and at the end of the visit would wave them off; she saw herself without a roof over her head, and with no income, and she imagined herself summoning her courage and entering the flower shop she had always admired and asking for a job in it.

As Lamis left the tower she received a packet of chocolate and a folder with her name on it from the reception desk. She opened the chocolate as soon as she stepped outside and munched on a light-brown telephone, followed by a dark brown. She opened the folder and there was a certificate stating that Lamis . . . had climbed 158 metres above London on 14 November 1999. She bumped into a man, knocking against the paper cup he was carrying, and coffee spilled on the ground, spraying his shoes.

'I was in another world,' she apologised. 'I've been up the tower.'

'Never mind. The view must have been fantastic.'

'It really was.'

'I didn't know the restaurant was open to the public again.'

'No, it's not. I just wanted to see London from above.'

As she walked she continued thinking: I wanted to see London like an outstretched palm, like something lying in front of me without a past or a present, or like the past holding the present in its grasp: the Tower of London, the river and the South Bank – all on view, without foreigners, accents, languages, the Queen, homeless people, traffic wardens; and to see the whole place disappear when I put my hands over my eyes, and when I took them away again, to see a spot of colour – children playing basketball in a school playground, dots of colour, their skin and clothes all mixed up.

She hurried to the flat as if she needed to remove a stone from her shoe and relax, but found many hindrances awaiting her, the first of which were the remaining boxes that blocked the hall. She opened the box closest to her and immersed herself in her past life briefly, and then it died. She opened one after another until all of the past contained in the boxes had died. She went back to the English-language exercises and read them again, but discovered that after all her efforts she still hadn't managed to change the way she spoke to her satisfaction. How could she exchange the English word 'dishwasher' with the Arabic word '*washwasha*'?

'Lamis, give me an Arabic word – any word without an "r" in it, and with a "sh" sound and a "w".'

'*Washwasha*.'

'That's a nice word. What does it mean?'

'Whisper.'

'Great. It's a word without an "r" and it's going to be a big help to us because as you know the letter "r" is the stumbling block and if it's not there you can relax. Every time you want to say "dishwasher", think of the word *"washwasha"*. *Washwasha.* Dishwasher.'

Washwasha. It evoked the voice of the speaker sliding into the listener's ear, a discreet bearer of secrets. Was the teacher turning it into a machine to wash plates?

She had a British passport, and despite this she felt that the country was remote from her, that she was still on the margins. She was certain that Dalal, Samira, Fatima, Zaynab, Suad and another Lamis, schoolfriends with whom she used to share milk and biscuits and cod-liver oil capsules in Najaf, were going around now shaking trees and digging in the sand to feed their children. She would be like them now if she'd stayed, sweating and crying, trying to nourish her sick children with kisses. She used to want to be a nurse, and had stolen white gauze dressings from school until her father promised she could study medicine. Of course he forgot his promise after they left their home in Najaf, when she was twelve years old, and went looking for another, which they never found, in the valleys and on mountain tops and arid plains.

When they first stopped to rest on a rocky hillside, Lamis complained to her mother that she wanted to keep going until they got there, with the doggedness of a child who sensed that nobody knew where 'there' was.

Lamis felt now as if she had been asleep all the years since, that she was just waking from her sleep in London, as if she herself were twelve years old, with a son almost the same age, who asked her where Patagonia and Queensland were, which she'd always thought were countries out of *Peter Pan*, and whether Somalia was an Arab country. She used to hide her embarrassment at her ignorance and blame leaving Iraq, bad schools, marrying too young.

'I want to begin where I left off. I want to study again,' she told the woman at the local college.

'Do you have a school-leaving certificate, anything from Iraq or Lebanon that we might be able to use?'

'Nothing.'

'Then do a couple of A levels and when you pass them you can get into a university.'

'Study with people much younger than me?'

'There are places for mature students. But you haven't said what areas you want to specialise in.'

Lamis kept silent. How could she know, since she felt as if she were only twelve, the age she'd been when she left her home and school in Iraq, sporadically attending schools in Syria and then Lebanon, insignificant schools because she was a refugee with no money, depending on aid from governments and political parties. The woman sensed Lamis's confusion and smiled, and said, 'Of course, it's early days for you, and very difficult for you to decide what you want to specialise in. But I think there is something on the bulletin board . . . try to have a look at it before you go.'

Lamis thanked her and on her way out she read the clipping pinned up on the noticeboard:

The *Independent*, Monday 29 November 1999

A medical secretary, aged 37, has beaten off competition from 18-year-olds throughout England to score top marks in this year's A-level English exam. Frances Hill, who left school at 16 to work in a factory, will receive a silver medal tomorrow from the examination board, the Assessment and Qualifications Alliance. To gain it, she beat more than 62,000 other candidates.

Epilogue

The Arabic phrase 'my tongue's warm', meaning 'I won't tell your secret', translates into English as 'I want to be kissed'. At least, that was how Samir translated it when he reassured John the Policeman that he would be completely discreet if he called the station asking for him.

'Do you see, Samir,' said John, 'how you flirt with me constantly, wherever we are? I don't want anybody to know, especially about the money I took from you, otherwise I'm finished!'

'Of course everybody knows,' replied Samir in Arabic. 'When I first saw Rock Hudson in *Pillow Talk* I said to him, "Who are you kidding!"'

But in English Samir said, 'You beautiful girl, Johnny Guitar, you wicked thing!'

Amira was managing to deflate the ball that rested in her stomach and making some headway with the other two that constituted her buttocks. She had succeeded in losing weight by eating buttermilk mixed with a substance that tricked the stomach into thinking it was full. She had even gone back to work, not as a princess in a fix, after all, but as a witness to what had befallen the Princess. Her clients laughed and were much entertained, and asked her to repeat a phrase or a tale as she recounted how she'd outwitted the British intelligence services, this sheikh, that prince, and how they'd all believed that she was a princess. Word got around, and people queued up to listen to her stories and descriptions of men in high office, how she'd ridiculed them, how she'd said to one, 'Are you sleeping with a woman, or is it her title or nationality that turns you on?' Or, 'I've done you a service by posing as your relative. Imagine if you'd really taken advantage of a woman like that being down on her luck, where would you hide your face when you went back home?'

As she took on the role of jester, Amira reflected that she'd lost her innocence. She should have believed in love, the love of her fiancé whom she left because she was humiliated by and angry about his mother's spiteful treatment of her when her own mother failed to provide the promised dowry of a lounge suite. It was after this that Amira had decided either to take her own life, or to disappear and return only when she was rich beyond belief. The fiancé went on writing to her for years in his tears and saliva, as he put it. If she'd believed in his love she wouldn't be afraid of life now. Samir came in with a tray on which were several lettuce hearts. 'These'll make you sleep like a dead man.'

He bent down and unplugged the phone and then switched off the light.

'The light, fine, but why unplug the phone?'

'So that you and I both sleep. I'm tired. Very tired.'

On Nahid's death, Amira insisted that she wanted to call Samir Nahid, and his answer was 'On one condition – that I call you Cappuccino.' Cappuccino had been adopted by Monkey World in Dorset, and Amira and Samir both knew that they could not go on with their lives unless they felt attached to somebody day and night.

Samir, with whom Amira was as close as a comb is to hair now that his family had left for Lebanon (and he had moved in to live with her full-time again), worked all hours. He went round the streets looking for cars parked in spaces where the meters were about to run out; he fed the meters with coins, then waited for the car owners to appear so he could inform them that the heavens had sent him in the nick of time, and if it hadn't been for him, they would have had their wheels clamped and been fined hundreds of pounds. The vehicle owners were happy at their lucky escape and gave Samir ten pounds, or sometimes twenty. At night he went around the Arab haunts entertaining customers with tales of

Cappuccino, playing Cappuccino and himself in turn: acting out what Cappuccino had done at the wedding and how he, Samir, had responded.

Amira tossed and turned in bed. She wasn't sleepy. The truth was, she felt like eating another lettuce heart. She got out of bed and heard Samir talking in a whisper to an escort agency.

'Do you have a man like the athletes on TV? Did you see them this evening? The big strong one doing the – what is it – high jump?'

Laughing, Amira switched the hall light on. Samir was crouching on the floor and he jumped and mumbled into his mobile, 'I'll speak to you in five minutes.'

Weeks had passed since Lamis had gone into Nicholas's flat. She tried to encourage herself with blind hope, and she indulged herself in chocolate-eating, and making telephone calls to her son. She worked on her homework for college, and at the flower shop, where she had found a job the day after her trip to the BT tower among the flowers, the buds and pots exactly the way she would have wanted it in Dubai. With one difference – that here she was surrounded by some flowers and colours she was seeing and smelling for the first time in her life, while in Dubai she would have worked with dead dry branches and flowers that had no veins, no oxygen, no vigour . . . At the end of the day she took the tube back to her flat, exhausted, in order to sleep.

But a certain letter that arrived, bearing unfamiliar writing and an English stamp, stormed her heart one morning and turned her life upside down.

Darling Lamis,
I have discovered that the Venus flytrap is a shy plant that likes a sweet taste, and not the evil carnivore it is reputed to be! But what reminds me of you is the tulip. Anyway, I want to explain, or rather excuse myself for my behaviour. I'm paying the price for it and have been far too ashamed to get in touch with you.

A lover is convinced that his beloved has entered his feelings and even his past life – indeed was present at his birth – which is ridiculous when I've never even seen you with wet hair and the curls that you've talked about.

I never thought I wanted to be in a relationship with a woman and stay in it. I used to think that I was still at an age that made it impossible for me to contemplate sharing my life with one woman. I was always aware of my eyes having a life of their own, eager to be stimulated. I've told you about Liz and others. Instead of repeating the old phrase, 'I don't know what happened to me when I met you,' I want to tell you that I know exactly what happened. All of a sudden I became a thirty-five-year-old man, someone made only for sharing his life with one woman – you. My eye turned into a compass directing me towards you.

I felt for the first time that, if I sat confronting space through the telescope and observing the stars and constellations, I wouldn't be filled with that dreadful terror that paralysed my limbs and prevented me from leaving the chair, as had happened sometimes in the past when the question of existence aroused a deep sense of loss, and those clichés about a person being a drop in the ocean or a mustard seed in the forest took hold of me.

It got so that we were only half there when we made love to each other: the contentment, the communication, the opening up was replaced by a sense of your absence and my lack of trust.

I began to see you as a tourist who'd come to London on holiday and decided in advance to enjoy herself while she was there, and have the adventures she'd only dreamed of, that had no connection with life in her own country. So she'd got to know an Englishman out of the blue, behaving just like an English-woman who goes on a package tour to a hot sunny beach, and has a sense of complete freedom, which prompts her to have a fling with a local man. I convinced myself I was just another English-man to you, someone you identified with London, and that as soon as your holiday ended, I'd become a ghost, or someone in a photo standing by Big Ben, or perhaps I should say by the Queen Mother's Gate, the one you like – which, by the way, is dreadful, though I couldn't say that to you before.

I felt that our relationship was a burden to you and that I was putting pressure on you, to the extent that you felt you had to lie to me. You had to pretend that you wanted to move in with me, to a place of our own, where we could start a new life together. Two drops in the ocean, or two mustard seeds in the forest. But I found myself assaulting you, when all I wanted was to get closer to you. I didn't have any desire to be parked in a drawer and brought out at specific places and times, then stuffed back in the drawer again because the circumstances weren't right – the ex-husband, the ex-husband's mother, the Arab community *en masse*. I won't go on about Khalid, since I promised I wouldn't come between you and him but I would at least have liked to have met him.

I felt there were matters you needed to sort out and think about, but my existence was making this more difficult for you, perhaps taking you in the opposite direction from where you wanted to go. In short, I was complicating things, muddying the waters. You could accuse me now of not being direct with you, and say that I should have talked to you about whether we should live together or separate. But how can I force you into a situation? How can I urge you to have certain feelings towards me, knowing that I took the initiative, not you?

I didn't answer your messages because I was scared they were the result of other emotions masquerading as love: a sense of loss, the attachment to a habit, a feeling of waste, pride, not wanting to turn your back on a challenge, even mere curiosity. Am I right? You still live in your husband's flat and who knows maybe deep down you want to go back to him; there was no path we'd taken together – no leap. I confess that I was greedy, impatient, but people in love always are. I know I was in a hurry, but if I hadn't been, would I have been a proper lover?

Nicholas

PS. I am in Oman. I asked someone to post this for me in London – the envelope and English stamp were to trick you into reading this.

Nicholas was so close to her that she felt he must be in her bedroom, in the kitchen; she would hear his key turning in the lock at any moment. The long-awaited Mahdi was returning. When, in religious studies class at school, Lamis heard how the Mahdi disappeared in the cave of the great mosque at Samarra, she asked her grandfather whether, if the Mahdi turned up, his mother would punish him because he'd vanished without telling her where he was going – or would she rush to kiss him, glad he'd come back?

London went to bed without undressing or bathing. Only at seven in the morning, after it had yawned through the mist, did the workers begin cleaning the city, collecting the rubbish, removing the empty beer barrels left on the pavement outside pubs and making the place ready for the day. And so the city prepared to be narcissistic again, circling its reflection reflected in its shop windows, with its flowers and green grass. It looked at the trees and the trees looked at the clouds, and the statues and the figures on the façades of buildings exchanged greetings with one another.

Lamis called Sotheby's and double-checked with them that he was out there at the moment. She was afraid she wouldn't find him, that he might even be coming back in the same aircraft, taking the same seat as hers, on the return flight to London. Should she leave him a note? – but would he look in the pocket in front of him? She began to be certain she wouldn't find him in Oman. He'd probably gone to the beach with some members of the diving club, or else she'd see him in the distance sitting with an Englishwoman under the coconut palms.

She picked up the little packets of airline pepper and salt and the tinfoil sachet containing the scented tissue, and read the names in Arabic. She held them affectionately, fingering the words. Had she really once considered substituting these for others and doing away with her heritage, no longer seeing, hearing or speaking, and consequently ceasing to breathe?

In the last lesson with Alison in Primrose Hill, Lamis had confided, 'If there is really a Queen of Words, please help me, for I seem to have forgotten my Arabic too.'

But the teacher always loved the way Lamis bewailed her plight. 'Don't lose that,' she implored her. 'It's what distinguishes you from us.'

Lamis asked the teacher, when a big fly came into the attic room through a half-open window and its buzzing took Lamis back to Najaf, 'If flies sound the same in both places, why don't people all speak the same language?'

The plane flew over the mountains of Muscat and Lamis did not hear the Beethoven that had blared out of Nicholas's car earlier in the evening and rolled down the mountains or been blown back inside the car by the breeze, although he had not been alone. His clothes were impregnated with frankincense from the Bustan Hotel, where it burned day and night, and a Tunisian woman with a pretty face and radiant smile was at his side. Her English was excellent, and she talked vivaciously, gossiping about the British employees, or discussing local and foreign politics, on the strength of her job as a journalist with the English-language weekly.

Although the beauty of the place often accentuated the loneliness felt by the single men and women there, and made them draw close to one another, Nicholas had avoided flirting with her, so when he heard the sound of her car brakes followed by a knock on his door, long after he had dropped her off at her place, he turned out all the lights and sat in the darkness until she drove away again.

The aircraft was approaching the Gulf of Oman. Lamis promised herself she wouldn't bother trying to make her accent fit her conversation; she would translate on the spot from Arabic to

English, even if her logic appeared convoluted; she wouldn't put off talking about a subject for fear that explaining it would involve a lot of terms whose English equivalent she couldn't find. She would copy Samir, who could carry on a discussion, even when instead of 'et cetera, et cetera' he said 'in cetera, in cetera' and added 'innit?' after every sentence.

In the days before he disappeared Nicholas tried to discuss their relationship with her, to hear her view of the future. He was painfully sincere: 'I don't want an affair. I want a commitment, a framework for my life.'

And she'd sat looking at the lines on the carpet, trying to work out if each colour had a border and how the colours were combined. She'd not been able to find an answer because she'd not dared to think about the question.

She gathered up her history and English exercise books to put them back in her hand luggage, and read the first sentence of the essay she had written for her new English class: 'I have to sit and write now to record what I feel, because London is a vacuum cleaner that sucks up everything, even the air.'

Lamis looked down and saw the rugged mountains, the blue expanse of sea, the white houses and the sand.

She noticed a red plus next to the Grade A that the teacher had given her: her son must have added it when he wrote a list on the facing page of the things he wanted her to get him from Oman or, even better, Dubai, if she could summon the courage to make a stop there on her way back to London. Then she checked her passport that the English passenger, Nicholas, had found.

The man who had brought her back came from the green Atlantic, the sea of shadows.

A Note on the Author

One of the contemporary Arab world's most acclaimed
writers, Hanan al-Shaykh grew up in Beirut. Her novels
include *The Story of Zahra*, *Women of Sand and Myrrh* and
Beirut Blues. She lives in London with her husband
and two children.

A Note on the Type

The text of this book is set in Berling roman. A modern face designed by K. E. Forsberg between 1951–58. In spite of its youth it does carry the characteristics of an old face. The serifs are inclined and blunt, and the g has a straight ear.